THE FAR SIDE
OF THE STREET

THE FAR SIDE
OF THE STREET

Fifteen Short Stories
Selected and with an Introduction by

Alan Sillitoe

W H ALLEN · LONDON
1988

Set by Input Typesetting Ltd, London
Printed and bound in Great Britain by
Mackays of Chatham Ltd, Chatham, Kent
for the publishers, W.H. Allen & Co. Plc
44 Hill Street, London W1X 8LB

ISBN 0 491 03256 0

M 82284
F

CONTENTS

INTRODUCTION

Writing an introduction to this selection from my total of forty or so stories is a task which should not, I realise, be treated with levity or leniency. After agreeing in an unguarded moment to write one, I told myself that such an Introduction ought to make the stories more readable by showing the writer to be as interesting as one of his characters. Therein lies the difficulty, however, since I have no obvious connection with any of them.

The earliest story, The Match, was first drafted in 1952 (and was first published in French, though I never saw a copy!), and the last, The Sniper, was written in 1980. Most are set in the geographical locality of Nottingham, though they were written in places as far apart as London and Tangier, Majorca and Israel, as if Nottingham had more power over me the further I was away from it, or at least as if I saw the area with greater clarity when writing in a plausibly different landscape.

Few of the events in the stories actually happened (as far as I know) but people who took part entered my mind with such self-assurance that I wondered afterwards whether I had actually met them at some time. They were so much part of the streets and houses I had known, of the smells, different faces, and the unforgettable lingo, that they were even more familiar than people I had really met.

Perhaps those people with whom I was directly acquainted did not have a story, and were only useful in forming a backdrop to the fictitious characters. A writer is nothing if not ruthless in this respect. My imagination could not supply the fuel which would launch them into a story, though every person has a story of some sort, perhaps more than one, suggesting that it is not so much the tale which is important but the soul behind the face. One comes up at last against the old adage that it is not so much the story as the way you tell it.

A story presents a person who, unknown on first appearance, is absolutely familiar by the end. The less known the person, in fact, the more force there is behind the narrative invented for him, so that after the story is finished, and during the rest of my life, I occasionally wonder what he (or she) is doing now. Real people would fade from my consciousness much sooner.

Perhaps those characters who come so frantic and unbidden into the mind indicate some psychic power in the writer's ability to create those he has never known, though the person demanding that his story be told has appeared for his own purpose. He exists, and you give him a name, so that you get to know everything about him as the narrative proceeds. There is little temptation to kill him off. He has become so human that it would be close to murder. Such an end would be too final, rather like cheating, because you want your characters to go on living exactly as you left them.

It is as if that person came to you out of the void because he is already dead. The spirit pushes before you so forcefully because he or she does not want to go into the ultimate void without some memorial to their having lived. When you have told their story they may be content to vanish forever.

Speculation is immaterial, unimportant, and inconclusive, the only test being whether, in spite of the reality with which this imaginary character takes you over, you are able to convey that same experience in words and action.

I have no difficulty in understanding people from the kind of life I knew in Nottingham, who come into my mind with their stories. Appearing from the void, perhaps they know with temperamental precision who to attach themselves to when they have a story to be told. Characters choose an author who will suit their purpose. Author and character between them create a reality where nothing previously existed, like that indefinable matter separating the negative and positive plates of a Leyden Jar, which seems to generate power out of the half submerged forces of nature.

The common denominator which they share has nothing to do with the sociological and political definition of 'class'. A writer is formed by heredity rather than the environment in which he was by chance brought up, and there is little in common between Tony in The Ragman's Daughter, for example, and the philosophical postman in The Fishing-Boat Picture; or between Margaret and the forlorn woman in Before Snow Comes. The stage is crowded with their faces, but their souls are diverse.

Each story is a separate world, in spite of similar scenery. The half formed story is tenuous, like an invalid child, and has to be nurtured into a series of positive events, drawn into the open air by the reality of language. The mortality rate is high, in that many stories succumb to neglect or weakness. The subject may change his or her mind, and the beginning of a story is often like an orphan who refuses to be rescued from the fury of a storm.

As in a poem, the inspiration prompts me to begin writing, but when for no discernible reason it stops there is no point going on like a penny-a-liner to force a conclusion. A decade may elapse before the resurgence of inspiration which will allow me to finish. Some stories come relatively complete in the first draft, but most need to be re-written many times.

I generally use Nottingham as a stage but, far from it being easy to operate in such a tight topographical boundary, that fact imposes an added discipline. Complicated people may be easier to present, but the problems of the simple are the problems of the gods, and the art of writing is to explain the complications of the human soul with a simplicity that can be universally understood. The storyteller must resist the temptation to resort to gothic verbiage in order to make his tale appear more profound. Writing is a matter of making the right choices, and refining the language.

If a certain person announces himself, one has to select those details which will unforgettably define him. A story may deal with one or two people, one basic incident, one state of mind to which fate is about to give an almost intolerable twist, but the possibilities of extension within these limits can be wide enough, and the people of the story should not be in the same state of mind at the end as at the beginning, sure proof that a tale has been told.

People do sometimes triumph over malign fate. Otherwise there are only two alternatives – madness or death. Death is a door that can be broken down only in fantasy. Madness can be used, as in Mimic, provided the stricken person remains recognisable. Tony, in The Ragman's Daughter is less mentally disturbed, which gives him a surfeit of energy, though eventually, as with everyone else, life takes its price.

These stories are about individuals, not themes or incidents, or messages of any kind except perhaps to say that people who live and suffer make up the sum of anything worth writing about. People threatened by adverse or desperate circumstances have the same sufferings as kings and queens. Their daily problems are more fundamental and tormenting, and their soul is of the same depth, and as finally unreachable. As the great poet King David said: 'Let them be ashamed and confounded that seek after my soul: let them be turned backward, and put to confusion, that desire my hurt.' These are the assumptions on which all my stories have been written. One treats with a soul, but takes care neither to demean nor destroy it.

Such people are with me until death do us part. Their court is a street-corner, or a slum, or a housing estate. It is only by this attitude that I can hope to show the dignity that is intrinsic to them, and get anywhere close to their problems. How far I succeed in joining the authenticity of their tales to my own ability can finally be judged only by them – which means everybody.

Alan Sillitoe
Wittersham, Kent, 1987

THE SNIPER

Just before closing time in The Radford Arms an old man leapt up on a table and started to dance. The other drinkers were so preoccupied that his clearing of pint jars with such speed went unnoticed, though some of them saw how his polished shoes in which their faces shone tapped with a clever sort of energy on the wooden top.

The landlord was trying to decide when to put the towels on (for in Nottingham the clocks seem notoriously unsynchronised in this respect), and for a few minutes his fingers ferried a hand along his watch chain as if he wouldn't get out his timepiece till everyone saw him and ran in panic to the bar for their final pint – which some of those who considered themselves more deprived than the rest had already stood up to do.

The old man sat as much by himself as was possible on a Saturday night, by the door from where he had a good view of the saloon and could judge when to act. He waited till near closing because at turned-eighty his energy was limited. Everyone later agreed on his cunning, for he caught the land-lord at a time when he was unable to imagine such an occur-rence, which allowed the old man to get in some minutes of tap-dance and sing-song before the night was brought to an end.

As he waited by the dregs of a second pint, his free hand began to shake, and his slate-grey eyes took on such a glitter that it seemed unlikely they provided him with much visibility. He drew his sleeve across his mouth to wipe the beer away, but also to erase any tremble that might betray his intention, suggesting a strength of character from former days that had not yet totally vanished. He blinked nervously and, when his arm came down, his tongue darted twice across his lips. He wore a knotted tie over a white collar that turned up at the ends, and it could be seen that his dark grey jacket and trousers didn't quite match.

In the general astonishment at the clattering dance everyone looked at his shoes rather than his face, sensing that if a collapse were to come it would begin with them, and they would see the full drama from the start. Yet the face was more interesting if only because it was difficult to fix on, and hard to accept what it was saying to those who thought only to observe the feet. Anyone who did look at his lips might realise he was trying to tell them something. His hands were held flat in front as if to push off his audience should they try and drag him down – as he expected and dared them to. They hardly heard the tapping of his feet, and few made out the tune he was singing, for the pub was far from quiet.

His mouth moved to a definite song but the words were hard to catch. He relived the murder, but no one listened to his gospel-truth. His sneer was like spit in their eyes though they did no more than grin, or call to get his knees up, or ask him to remember his age and not be such a loon. Or they ignored him while supping their final jars.

He would dance while he could, and tell again what he'd whispered in that shell-hole near Gommecourt fifty years ago. He shouted names and phrases, and sometimes made them rhyme, till a few listened, though heard little that made sense. He tapped the rhythm and told it clear, and wondered when they'd pull him down and ask why he'd never been taken to the cop-shop and relieved of his money, belt, braces, shoes and false teeth, and got thrown into a stone cell, and brought into court (where he'd have said nothing from start to finish), and finally taken into the hangman's yard as a proper end to a wickedness he hadn't repeated to a soul till an age when the edge of his younger days came back and time had no meaning because there wasn't much of it left.

Every stone had beetles underneath. They lay still and quiet, because of all creatures on earth they were good at knowing how, but in the last few months they'd been growing bigger, till he felt the boulder ready to surge into the air and crush him to even less than a beetle when it came down. The crime had kept him loving and industrious ever after, and even now God hadn't paid him out.

Nevill passed the house of a blacksmith's noisy family. The up-and-down stretch of common known as the Cherry Orchard was blocked from the west by Robins Wood. The sun glowed on a bed of clouds, and the surrounding grass appeared so green from his place of hiding that it seemed as if a secret kingdom shone from under the ground.

Too far off to be noticeable, Nevill saw the man walking towards the wood – having been daft enough to think that secrets could be kept. Silence increased the quality of the glow. The stark side of the trees stood out as if they would melt, part of the most perfect summer since the fourteen year old century had turned.

Nevill watched Amy follow her fancyman from the lane, by which time he was already waiting in the wood. He plucked a juicy grass stem and, now that they were out of sight, moved along a depression – in case they should be looking from the bushes – towards the spot a hundred yards above where they had entered.

A breeze which carried the smell of grass made him hungry. He had come out before his tea, tracking to where he thought she had gone. There had to be a day when he came home early. The farmer he worked for lent him a gun so that he could stalk hares and be sure of hitting them. He moved like a tree that seemed always in the same place to the delicate senses of a rabbit. Then he took five minutes to lift his gun so that they didn't stand a chance. Even so, one sometimes escaped in a last-minute zig-zag too quick to be sighted on. Because the farmer gave only one cartridge at a time he could afford no waste. A big rabbit lasted two meals, and made a smell for any man to come home to.

The last of the sun flushed white and pink against his eyes. A raven circling over the wood told him they were still there, and hadn't gone out the other side towards the west. Its black gloss turned purple in the evening light.

Kneeling, he wondered whether or not to go back to the house and leave them alone. Now that he knew for certain, there seemed no point in pursuing them, for he could call the tune any time he liked. But his legs wouldn't stop his slow encroachment on that part of the wood they had gone into. A cloud of gnats pestered him. If he had been walking at a normal pace he could have reached home and forgotten all about it, but the deliberate putting forward on to the grass of one foot after another was as if he advanced on a magnetised track impossible to side-step.

Shadows aggrandised each tree and solitary bush. Two rabbits ran from the wood. One stared at him, then sat up and rubbed its paws, while the other turned away with its white tail shivering in the breeze. He heard a hooter from Wollaton colliery, and the blink of his left eyelid wasn't sufficient to warn the rabbits, one of which was big enough for the pot.

Fingers itched for the safety catch, the shotgun lifting inch by inch. One would be dead for sure, but he fought his instinct, staying the gun while in the grip of something firmer. Rabbits swarmed so much this summer that a week ago he caught two with one bullet.

The long dusk began. A platoon of starlings scoured back and forth on a patch of grass to leave no worm's hiding place unturned. He wanted to light his pipe and smoke off the gnats, but any movement might reveal his place, so he became a flesh statue with head bowed, green jacket blending into green.

The crack of twigs sounded and she walked, without turning

left or right, straight across the Cherry Orchard and back towards the lane. It wasn't the nearest way home but, when close to the house, she'd expect him to see her coming from the Woodhouse direction in which her mother lived. He smiled at such barefaced cunning, in which they'd talked up their little plot together, he deciding to stay another ten minutes in the wood after she had got clear of it.

Nevill needed only a few paces to reach the trees. Dodging the brambles, he walked from the thigh, toes and balls of the feet descending so as to avoid the heel on unseen twigs. He heard the stream that ran down the middle of the narrow wood. Blackberries were big and ripe. A pigeon rattled up, and he made towards its noise, advancing at the crouch, knowing every patch because his cottage was on the northern tip. When a match scraped along a box he stiffened.

The odour of fungus and running water on clean pebbles was sharpened by the cool of the evening. It wasn't quite dusk, but Nevill had to peer so as not to mistake him for the shadow of a bush. Looking for the first star, he lowered his head before finding one. The sky was still pale blue.

He saw him by the stream smoking a cigarette. A loosened tie hung around his neck, and he irritatedly brushed leaves from the legs of his dark suit. He whistled the bars of a tune, but suddenly stopped, as if not wanting to hear anything that would take him so far from what had just passed between him and Amy.

Nevill lifted the gun, butt-first. When a frog plopped into a side arm of the stream he saw the rings, and the man turned sharply at the noise as he decided it was time to get out of the wood. After two paces a shadow came at his head which had the force of the world concealed in it. An electric light went on for a second and revealed the trees roundabout. Often when a rabbit wouldn't die he battered the neck, and his rage was so great that it was no more difficult to smash the man's temple while he lay on the ground. There was a smell of hard drink when he knelt to make sure he was dead.

At the edge of the wood dusk was coming across the Cherry

Orchard like a scarf. When Nevill fired, a rabbit spun on the ground. Then he fastened its two back legs together and walked towards the darker part of the common.

Standing at the door to look for him Amy heard the shot softened like a thunderclap in the distance, and shivered at the evening chill. Nevill passed by the blacksmith's house and went down the lane, under the long railway bridge to Lottie Weightman's beer-off in the village. He sold his rabbit for sixpence, then drank a pint. They were talking about the war, of how everybody was going, some saying what damned fools they were, while others thought it the only thing to do. He sat observing them with his slate-grey eyes, smiling at their expressions that did not seem to know what life was about.

Next day he went back into the wood and, hanging his jacket from the spike of a dead branch, hauled the body from its hiding place. He scraped off the turf and hacked at the roots. The soil was dry, but moistened lower down. With Amy last night he had lain back to back, thinking he'd never touch her again. Each press of the spade, pull at the handle and lift, reinforced his feelings about her. From the clear land of the Cherry Orchard he heard children, so put his jacket on and went swiftly to the edge of the wood.

'You can't come in 'ere.'

They were three ragged-arsed kids from Radford. 'We on'y want blackberries.'

'It's private.'

They grumbled.

'Gerroff – or you'll get a good-hiding.'

He looked as if he'd do it, so they went, though one of them called from a distance and before fleeing 'Fuckin' owd bastard!'

He worked more quickly and, when the neat oblong hole was deep enough, heard the body thump to the bottom. The smashed head vanished under a first curtain of soil. Dead twigs and leaf-mould disguised the grave. He leaned against a tree to smoke his pipe, till sweat subsided and his breath came back, then he walked through the deepest grass to get the soil off his boots, for it wouldn't do to be untidy if you were going into town.

Walking up the hill towards Canning Circus he met others on the same errand. He spat on both hands for luck and rubbed his palms on hearing the clash of a band outside the drill hall, thinking that the army would be as good a place to hide as any.

The smell from his skin went as quickly as the spit dried. After passing the medical and getting his shilling he drank a pint in the canteen. Two hours later and still in their own clothes they were marched back down Derby Road to tents on Wollaton Park – only a mile from the wood where the fresh body lay buried.

Farmer Taylor could keep his job at fifteen bob a week. With two hours off the next day, he called to say he had packed it in, and expected to be turned out of his cottage, but the farmer smiled: 'I knew you would. I told you he'd be the first to go. Didn't I tell you, Martha? You wait, I said, he'll go, Nevill will! I'll lose a good man, but I know he'll go. Wish I could be in the old regiment myself. I know of no finer thing than going to fight for your country.'

There wasn't much need to talk. He was invited into the parlour and given a mug of ale.

'You'll mek a fine sowjer,' Taylor went on. 'I expected no less. Come and see us when you've got your khaki on.' He gave him a florin above his wages: 'Your wife can stay in the cottage. I'll see nowt happens to her.'

'I expect she'll be able to look after herself,' Nevill said cheerfully.

The farmer gave him a hard look: 'Ay, you'll mek a fine sowjer. Your sort allus do.'

He went home: 'I've gone and enlisted. You can carry on all you like now, because I won't be coming back.'

She gave him some bread and cheese. 'God will pay you out, leaving me like this.'

He wanted to laugh. When she went on the prowl for her man it wouldn't do her much good. He went upstairs to change into his best suit. The small room with its chest of drawers and flowered paper was part of them, as was the bed with its pillows and counterpane. She kept the house like a new pin, he had to admit, but it made no difference. He tied his working clothes and spare boots into a parcel, and pushed it under the bed with his toe-cap. He wouldn't be back for any of them. Most other men in camp wore their oldest clothes, some nearly in rags, but he wanted to look smart even before the khaki came. If they took him away to be hanged he didn't want to take the drop looking like a scarecrow.

He stood in the doorway for a last look at the kitchen. 'Everybody's rushing to the colours.'

'More fool them. It doesn't mean you've got to join up as well. You're nearly thirty: let the young mad'eads go.'

He didn't know what she had to cry for. She should be glad to get shut of him. He put two sovereigns between the pot cats on the shelf: 'Don't lose 'em.'

When she took off her pinafore and began to fold it he was frightened at having taken the King's shilling. One thing led to another when you killed somebody. Birds were whistling outside the open window. She'd hung the mats on the line. In his weakness he wanted to sit down, but knew he mustn't.

She rushed across to him. He lost his stiffness after a few moments, and held her. They had been married in Wollaton church five years ago, but when they went upstairs he felt that he hadn't known her till now.

He forgot her grey eyes and her auburn hair when walking back by the dark side of the wood. If God paid him out it would be because God was a German bullet. As for the bloke whose brains he had knocked in, it served him right. He was tempted to dig by the bush and look at the body, to make sure everything wasn't happening in the middle of a dream, but he didn't have a spade.

The day was rotting. He breathed dusk through his nostrils, a smell that was enough to turn you as balmy as a hayfork, especially in such silence before rain. Happiness made him walk upright across the Cherry Orchard without looking back.

'You'll dig yourselves ten feet under,' the sergeant shouted, 'when the first shell bursts.'

On parade he was ordered to tie a white tape on his arm, the mark of a lance-corporal, till uniforms came and he could sew on the proper stripe. He was a more promising soldier than the rest, for he did not live from day to day like most of the platoon, nor even from hour to hour as some of them cared to. He existed by the minute because every one contained the possibility of him being taken off and hanged. The grave was a deep one, and the man not known in the district – he reasoned hopefully while lying in the bell tent with eleven others and listening to raindrops hitting the canvas. It was also a time when scores of thousands were going to other towns to get into their favourite regiments, so maybe no one would even look for him.

During every package of sixty seconds he gave absolute attention to the least detail of military routine, and became the keenest man in the platoon. When rifles were issued he was careful that each round reached a bull's eye. The sling was firm around his arm and shoulder, body relaxed, feet splayed, and eye clear at the sights.

Every battalion had its snipers. 'On a dark night a lighted match can be seen nine hundred yards away,' they were told, 'and that's as far as from the Guildhall to the bloody Castle!'

It was also the distance from here to where *he* was buried, Nevil thought.

'Pay attention, or I'll knock your damned 'ead off!'

The sergeant savvied any mind that wandered, and Nevill knew he mustn't be caught out again.

He slid into the loop-holed sniper's post built by the sappers in darkness. Sacking was around his head, and mud-coloured tape swathed his rifle. He looked slowly from left to right, towards wire and sandbags across ground he had been over in darkness and seen in daylight through a periscope. He knew each grass-clump and crater. A faint haze hovered. Smells of cooking and tobacco drifted on the wind. He savoured the difference between a Woodbine and a Berlin cigar, till a whine and a windrush eruption of chalk and soil caused his elbow to tremble at a shell dropping somewhere to the left. The camouflage net shivered. He heard talking in the trenches behind. An aeroplane flew high.

Amy worked on filling shells at Chilwell factory, earning three times the amount he got as a corporal marksman, but he sent half his pay for her to put in a bank, though he didn't expect ever to get home and claim it because either a bullet or a rope (or a shell) was sure to pay him out. I always loved *you*, and always shall, she wrote. Aye, I know, same here, he answered – but not telling what he knew, and cutting her from his mind in case he got careless and was shot. He smiled at the justice of it.

In the space between one minute and the next he expected to see a party of men coming to get him for the hangman's yard whose walls would smell like cold pumice and rotting planks. He was ready for it to happen from any direction he could name, so that even in the débris of the trenches there was no one smarter at spotting misdemeanours in his own men, or fatal miscalculations on the enemy parapet.

A machine gun half a mile away stitched thoughts back into his brain, eyes turning, head in a motion that scanned the faint humps of the broken line. He didn't want to give up his perfected system of counting the minutes which kept him going in a job that held little prospect of a long life. All snipers went west sooner or later. He was glad that whole days passed without thinking of Amy, because she took his mind off things.

A smudge of grey by a sandbag, and then a face, and he lined up the sights instantly and pressed the trigger. The crack travelled left and right as he reloaded almost without movement, the bolt sliding comfortably in. The bullet took half a second to reach the face that had sprung back. He heard the word for stretcher bearer – *krankentrager* – and wanted to laugh because, as in a game of darts or cribbage, he had *scored*. The more he killed, the less chance there'd be of getting called to account. He didn't want to know more than that. It was dangerous to think. You're not here to think but to do as you're effing-well told – and never you forget it or by God I'll have your guts for garters and strangle you to death with 'em. But they didn't need to roar such rules at him.

A retaliating machine gun opened from three hundred yards left. He saw the gunner. Chalk that jumped along was nowhere close enough. An itching started on his cheek, and an impulse to scratch was fought down. When it came back he turned his body cold. It was an almost pleasurable irritation that couldn't be ignored, but he resisted it, minute by minute. You had only to be at the Front for an hour and you were as lousy as if you'd been there ten years.

Last week he'd had a fever, and hadn't been able to do his work. No sniper was allowed out with a fever or a cold. With a fever you shook, and with a cold you dozed – though a true sniper would forget such things in his moment of action. Yet an experienced sniper was too valuable to waste. He sensed as much when he moved along the communication trenches at dawn or dusk, and observed how the officers looked at him – after their first curiosity at seeing such an unusual specimen – as if he were a man singled out for a life even worse than death, cooped up like a rat that only waited its turn to kill without fair fight. He knew quite plainly that many didn't like him because sniping was a dirty weapon like poison gas or liquid fire.

The trench was disturbed. Every eye fixed his stretch of land. They looked but did not see. He let his body into complete repose so as to make no move. The range card was etched on to his brain, and his eyes caught all activity, had even sharper vision because of the body's helplessness. The whole view was exposed to his basic cunning. His itching leg was forgotten when he pressed the trigger and killed the machine gunner.

Out of the opposite trench, a few fingers to the right, came a man who stood on the sandbags and beckoned. He wore a dark suit. A tie was unfastened around his neck. He bent down to brush chalk-grit from his trousers. When he straightened himself, he smiled.

Nevill lay in the water of his sweat, his teeth grinding as if to take a bite out of his own mouth. His body wasn't dead, after all. The man was afraid to come closer. Grey clouds formed behind his head, till he became part of them, when Nevill took a long shot almost in enfilade, and brought down a man who looked up from the second line of trenches.

If the man had still been alive Nevill would have shouted at him for his foolishness. Mistakes were as common as Woodbines. Even the old hands made them occasionally, as if tired of a caution which wouldn't let them be themselves. Something inside decided, against their will, that they'd had enough. In an unguarded moment their previous carefree nature took over – and they died. He smiled at the thought that no such fecklessness could kill him, no matter how deep down it lay.

He couldn't get out of his place till darkness. Danger time was near. If he chanced one more round they'd get a bearing and smother his place with shot shell and shit. Papier mâché heads painted to look real were put up so that when the sniper's bullet went clean through back and front, a pinpoint bearing could be made between the two holes which would lead with fatal accuracy to him. So when he saw a head tilted slightly forward and wearing no helmet he didn't shoot. If he kept as still as dead they would never see him, and he'd known all his life how to do that. When he played dead he was most alive. He felt like laughing but, knowing how not to, was hard to kill. As if in agreement the earth rumbled for half a minute under another nearby burst of shell. It grew in intensity till it sounded like a train going through Lenton station. He wanted to piss, but would have to keep it in.

Tomorrow he would be in a different position and, corked face invisible, could start all over again. He lay by the minute, sun burning through clouds as if intent on illuminating only him. A shot at dusk might succeed, when the setting sun behind sharpened their line of trenches, but only one, because they would be waiting, and he was too old a hand to get killed just before knocking off time.

Raindrops pestered a tin can, and caused an itch at his wrist.

There was better visibility after a shower, though gas from his rifle in the dampened atmosphere might give him away if he fired. Their eyes were as good as his when they decided to look. He felt like a rabbit watching from its burrow, and counted the minutes more carefully. If they found him, he'd die. He craved to smoke his pipe. No sniper was taken prisoner. Nor their machine gunners. He felt cramp in his right foot, but tightened himself till it went.

The minute he woke in the morning, either at rest or on the march, or in the line, his first thought was not to decipher where he was but to realise that he hadn't yet been taken up for the man he had killed. He kissed his own wrist for luck. Other soldiers roundabout wondered why he smiled, while they only scowled or cursed.

Lying in his cramped hole sometimes brought on a faintness from which the only way out was to spread arms and legs as far as they would go, then get into the open and run. He would certainly be killed, so when blood packed at the extremities of hands and feet, thereby thinning at the heart, he called the minutes through and counted them. Sixty minutes made a platoon called an hour. Twenty-four hours formed as near as dammit two battalions of a day. He deployed his platoons and battalions of time and sent them into the soil. A shell once burst too near and he pissed into his rags – but kept his place and his life. When a machine gun peppered around no-man's-land in the hope of catching him, a man from his own trenches stopped the racket with a burst from a Lewis gun.

The minutes he hewed out of life, from the air or his own backbone, or plucked even from the din of the guns, saved him time and time again. In pushing aside the image of the hangman coming to get him across no-man's-land (or waiting in the form of a Provost Marshal's red cap when he went back through the communication trench and up towards the broad light of the day that was to be his last) he had only to punctuate his counting of the minutes by a careful shot at some flicker on the opposite sandbags. Away from the trenches, he could not wait to get back, even if on frontline duty as one of a back-breaking carrying party, or as an enfilading sharp-shooter during a trench raid. But mostly he belonged in a sniper's position that needed only eyes, brain and a steady finger at the trigger while he lay there all day and counted the minutes.

A week in the trenches was as long as a month or a year. He counted the minutes while others marked off the days. But all of them were finally without time and covered in mud, one in ten lost through shellfire, raids, frostbite and bullets.

They drudged to the rear and one night, wet from head to foot, Nevill joined his company in a rush across the churned turf of a field towards the bath-house. Everyone stripped to let the sanitary men get their underclothes. Lice were everywhere. Scabies was common, and spread like chalkdust on a windy day. Some scratched themselves till bloody all over, and were treated with lavish doses of sulphur – which might give them dermatitis if they got too much of it. Nevill endured the terrible itching, even in his sniper's post, but on normal duty he woke himself after a few hours' sleep by a wild clawing at his clothes.

Water gushed from the taps only one point off freezing. They had expected it to be hot, so sounded as if a pack of ravening lions had got loose. The captain, transfixed by their mutinous swearing, hoped the sergeant-major would be along to get them moving into the water no matter how cold it was. Hard to understand their rage when they endured so much agony of life and limb on duty in the trenches. One man slipped on the slatted planks, and cursed the army.

'This is the last straw!' he shouted.

No one laughed, even when he was advised: 'Well, eat it, then.'

Nevill, the icy chute spraying at him, let out a cry that stopped everyone's riotous catcalls: 'Fucking hell, it's too hot! It's scalding me to death. Turn it off! I'm broiled alive. Put some cold in, for Christ's sake!'

They began laughing at the tall thin chap fooling around with knees and knackers jumping up and down, a look of mock terror in the fiery stillness of his eyes and the falling line of his lips.

Once fastened into the separate world of his own outlandish shouts, Nevill went on calling loud and clear: 'My back's on fire! I'm broiling in *hell!* Turn that effing water off, or put some cold in, *please!* This steam's blinding my eyes. Turn it off!'

Others joined in and shouted the magic phrases like a chorus line at the music hall. They no longer hung back, but took to the water without further complaint.

Nevill stopped, and gripped the soap to wash. The muddy grime swilled off, and his face turned red as if steam had really worked the colour-change, not shame. Then he laughed again with the others while they blundered around fighting for the soap.

They collected warm and fumigated underwear. After break-fast came pay parade and later, with francs in their pockets and a few hours' kip behind their eyes, they were away to the estaminet for omelette, chips and wine, where they went on singing Nevill's catch-line: 'Turn that effing water off, or put some cold in please!'

What made him shout those words he didn't know, but the captain marked him for his sergeant's stripe, seeing a priceless N.C.O. who could control his men by firmness – and displays of wit, however crude. Apart from which, there was no better off-hand shot in the battalion, though as a sergeant his sniping days were over.

After a hard week's training for 'the battalion in attack' they went back to the line with buckles, boots and buttons shining. The noise of guns took up every square inch of air around the face, kept a trembling under the feet for days. They said that gunfire brought rain. Cordite gathered full-bellied clouds that emptied on trenches to make all lives a misery. At the best of times a trench was muddy. The common enemy was rain, and the guns that shook soil down.

The few shells from the other side blew the earth walls in, no matter how well-revetted. When Nevill was buried he thought the hangman had come and gone already. He smelled quick-lime. In his tomb, yet knowing where he was, made him wonder if the man had been alive when he had buried him in Robins Wood. But he hadn't gone back till next day, and he'd been dead by then right enough.

Nevill was earthed-in with bullet pouches, water bottle and rifle. In other words – as Private Clifford said, who found him more alive than two others whose names he couldn't remember as soon as they were dead – he was buried with full military honours, and you couldn't want more than that, now could you, sarge?

The pattacake soil-smell was everywhere, and the only thing that saved Nevill was his tin hat which, being strapped firmly on, had enough all-round rim to trap sufficient air for him to breathe till he was pulled free.

Every fibre of skin bone and gristle vibrated to the pounding. Could anything live under it? He drew himself into his private world and remembered how Amy had answered that she had nothing to forgive him for. She was never to realise he'd known about her love affair, though no doubt she wondered still where the chap had hopped it to. Maybe to the Western Front, like the rest of us. And if he hadn't sent a letter, what was funny in that? Nevill felt almost sorry she'd been ditched by two instead of one, though perhaps it wasn't all that rare when so many men had gone away at once.

Yet he needn't have worried about her wellbeing, for she sent him a parcel of tinned jam and biscuits and salmon, and a note saying she was working at Chilwell Depot till as close as she could get to her confinement which, he surmised, couldn't by any stretch of counted minutes be his kid. By earning her own money she could do as she liked, and in any case he had bigger things on his plate than to care what she got up to. 'I expect my missis is having a little bit on the side while I'm away,' he heard Private Jackson say. 'Suppose I would if I was her, damn her eyes!'

Being in a webbing harness of cross-straps and belt, with all appurtenances hanging therefrom, made him feel he no longer belonged to himself, since a devil's hook in any part of his garb could swing him from here to eternity without a by-your-leave. He had a date with some kind of hangman, and that was a fact. The unavoidable settled his gloom, and was only lifted when his duties as platoon sergeant made him forget.

Under the hangings of equipment he was almost skeletal. The other sergeants – when he shared Amy's food parcel – chaffed that a bullet wouldn't find him. But he ate like a wolf, and no flesh grew. He worried, they said. He worked too hard. He was never still. You needn't let a third stripe kill you. The men didn't like him, yet under his eternal fussing felt that he would never let them down.

Drumfire crumbled the walls between compartments of the minutes. A shake entered his limbs that he had seen in others, and which he thought would never afflict him. As a sniper he had gone over after the first rush of infantry, but now there would be no distinction. He'd be in the open without his hideaway. It wasn't the first time, but they'd been trench raids, and not the big attack. He held his hand down, and counted till the trembling stopped.

The guns were finishing off every living thing, and all they had to do was walk across on the day and take over what was left. 'Only, don't scratch your lily-white ankles on the rusty barbed wire, lads. And don't fall into an 'orrible shell-hole. And if you see a hot shell sizzling towards you, just push it to one side with your little finger and tell it to piss off' – he'd heard Robinson diverting his mates the other day. Nobody else thought it would be a walkover, though he supposed a few of the brass hats hoped against hope.

He walked along the trench, lifting his boots through the foot-depth of mud.

'Had yer rum?'

They read his lips in the noise. 'Yes, sergeant.'

'Had yer rum, then?'

'I'm tiddly already, sarge!'

'Answer properly when yer're spoken to.'

There was no doubt about the next one: 'Had yer rum?'

'Yes, sergeant.'

'Wake up then, or you'll be on a charge.'

'Bollocks.'

He swung back. 'If yo' don't have less chelp, Clifford, I'll put yer bollocks where yer fucking 'ead should be.'

The man laughed. 'Sorry, sergeant.'

Live and let live. He moved on. 'Had yer rum?'

'It makes me sleepy, sergeant.'

'You'll wake up in a bit, never bloody fear. Had yer rum?' – and on till he had made sure of everyone.

He stood by a ladder and drank his own, except for a drop in the bottom which he threw into the mud for luck. They called it the velvet claw because it warmed yet ripped your guts. Some couldn't take it, but those who could always drank any that went buckshee.

He saw that the stars had turned pale. The guns made a noise that two years ago would have torn him apart had it been sprung on him. He pressed his feet together so that his knees wouldn't dance. There'd never been such a week of it. Every minute was hard to drag out. Darkness was full of soil and flashes. The counting melted on his tongue. For a moment he closed his eyes against the roaring light, then snapped them open.

One dread stamped on another. Explosions from guns and Stokes mortars dulled the feel of a greased rope at the neck. His cheeks shook from the blast of a near-miss. With bayonet fixed and day fully light the only way out was over the bags and at the Gerries. The shuddering of his insides threatened to send him into a standing sleep, so he moved up and down the trench to cut himself free of it – and to check every man's equipment. Nothing bore thinking about any more. Under the feet and through the mud a tremor which rocked his temples was connected to a roar in the sky travelling from the south. Another explosion came, and more until the final whistles began. They were letting off the mines before Zero.

Faces to either side were dull and shocked. One or two smiled stupidly. A youth muttered his prayers (or maybe they were curses) and Nevill knew that if he stopped he wouldn't be able to stand up. They were trapped, no matter what they had done. The straight and cobblestoned gas-lit streets of Radford replaced everything with carbide-light clarity. It was a last comforting feel of home, and when it vanished the trap was so final that it seemed impossible ever to get out, though he never lost hope.

Some leaned, or tried to fold themselves, wanting soil for safety. One man was eating it, but blood and flesh and scraps of khaki were up the side of the trench, and his arm was gone. Nevill shouted at them to stand up. He was thrown to one side as pebbles and slabs of chalk spattered his helmet, but he still called hoarsely at them to stand up to it. Screams came from the next bay, and another call for stretcher bearers. Lieutenant Ball examined his luminous watch, and Nevill wondered how much longer they'd be.

Over the parapet he saw flashes in the smoke and mist, an uneven row of bursts where trenches should have been. His watch said seven twenty-five. Amy's letters showed more tenderness than either had felt when they were together. There was more than there would ever be for him should he get back, because it wasn't his baby she was carrying. He won his struggle against her memory by counting each blank minute, knowing there weren't many left before they ascended the swaying ladders.

It was a hard pat at the shoulder that made him turn:

'Yes, sir?'

A company runner stood by. The pale-faced lieutenant of nineteen looked forlorn under his helmet, but regained sufficient competence to tell him: 'You're to go back to Battalion Head-quarters, Sergeant Nevill.'

'Now, sir?'

Lieutenant Ball smiled, as if to indicate that such a lunatic signal had nothing to do with him. 'Seems so. You're to go out of the line.'

Nevill gripped his rifle, a vision of himself raising it to the

'on guard' position and bayoneting his officer. The horror of it
broke his habit of obedience.

'What for, sir?'

The barrage would lift any second. Lieutenant Ball looked
at his watch again, and didn't turn from it till the guns stopped.
'How do I know?'

The hangman would be there, for sure. 'Let me go over, sir.
I've waited a long while to have a proper go at them. I can
see what they want at Brigade as soon as I come back this
afternoon!'

Nevill had fathered the platoon, so it would be vile not to let
him take part in the big attack. Silence was filled by the noise
of the birds. They were always busy, even when the guns were
at it. He stuffed the message into his pocket and said:

'See that you do.'

'Thank you, sir.'

Whistles cut along the crowded slit in the earth, and Nevill
shouted them into the open.

Full daylight met them as soon as they were up the ladders.
Many clawed their way by planks or soil to gain freedom from
the stink, shadows and uncertainty of the trench. Men on either
side were falling under loads they could hardly support. High-
stepping through their own wire, they went on under the mist
as if that too weighed more than they could carry.

Shells of shrapnel balls exploded above their heads. They
stopped silently, or rolled against the soil as if thrown by an
invisible hand. Or they were hidden in a wreath of smoke and
never seen again. The wire was like a wall. The guns had cut
only one gap so they were like a football crowd trying to get
off the field through a narrow gate on which machine guns
were trained.

He sang to himself, wanting to get on. The men walked
slowly because they couldn't go back. The biggest paper bags
in the world were bursting above their heads. Minutes were
unimportant. Every second was a king. He had to see his men
through the wire. Lieutenant Ball disappeared as if he'd never

existed. When they lagged, Nevill cursed from behind. He wanted to run but didn't know whether front or back would be any good so got ahead to coax them through bullets and shrapnel:

'Come on, move. Keep your dressing there. Keep your dressing. Keep moving, lads.'

They couldn't hear, but read his lips if they saw them, and came on as if they too had been counting the minutes, and were terrified of some hangman or other. He wanted them to know that safety lay in doing as they were told and in getting forward. A few of his platoon were in advance of the company. He didn't know where the others had gone. While still in the German wire more shellbursts caught them. He was anxiously looking for a way through. You couldn't hear the birds any more. Machine guns never stop.

He knelt, and fired towards the parapet, loading and reloading till he felt a bang at his helmet, and was pulled as if he were a piece of rope in a tug-o'-war. If it went on he would snap. In the darkness someone screamed in one ear when he was drawn icily apart, and he wondered why there was no light, thinking maybe they were going to bury him in Robins Wood, except that he was in France near a stink-hole called Fonky-bleeding-Villas.

He didn't know who was trying to yank him clear, but there was a smell of steel that burned so fiercely it turned blue. He rolled over and over. He opened his eyes, and took off his waterbottle to drink. The shrapnel had stunned him but he was unhurt except for a graze on the scalp.

The man by his side said: 'Not too much, sergeant. We'll need it for later.'

The stream in Robins Wood ran through his mouth. He counted the minutes to stop himself drinking to the bottom. 'Who are yer, anyway?'

'I'm Jack Clifford, sergeant. You know *me!*'

'I was bleddy stunned.' He looked around. 'Where's your rifle?'

'I lost it, sergeant. I don't know.'

'Oh, did yer? You'll be bleddy for-it, then.'

He began to cry.

'Where are yer from?'

'Salisbury Street, sergeant.'

'Got any Mills bombs?'

They were too far off to be any use, but he had.

Pulling off his burden of equipment, and without his helmet, Nevill edged to the rim of the crater. A leg with a boot on it hung over the other lip. He beckoned Clifford to follow, but indicated not too quickly. After a full minute, raising his head, and positioning himself, he fired a whole clip at men on the German parapet. Clifford got higher and threw a grenade, shouting: 'Split this between yer!'

Machine gun bullets swept across. Clifford screamed and rolled back.

Something had struck Nevill's shoulder, and his arm felt as if gripped by an agonising cramp, but with shaking hand he bound both field dressings across Clifford's white and splintered ribs: 'That'll see yer right till we get back. The fuckers are picking us off like rabbits. We don't stand a chance, so we'd better stay where we are.'

'The red caps'll 'ave me. I've lost me rifle,' Clifford said.

Nevill wanted to tell him that it didn't look as if anybody would have him any more, though you couldn't say as much to a young lad. 'Them boggers wain't come for you,' he comforted him. 'It's me they're after. They sent a signal for me.'

'They don't come over the top,' Clifford said, 'do they?' He tried to spit, then seemed to think that if he did he'd die. 'Not them, they don't. If the Gerries didn't shoot 'em, *we* would, wouldn't we, sergeant?'

'Happen we might. Just keep still, and don't worry.'

Blood was pumping like a spring in autumn, but he knew no tourniquet would hold it. 'Let me tell you summat,' Nevill said, thinking to take his mind off it.

Clifford tried to laugh. 'What, me owd cock?'

'In September, I murdered somebody. Lay still, I said, and don't talk.'

His white face grimaced in agony. 'You're having me on!'

'Before I enlisted, I mean.'

'Got to save our strength. The Gerries'll get us.'

Nevill fought to stop himself fainting. 'No time. I'll tell you about it if you'll listen.' He looked around as if someone else might hear, then pulled Clifford towards him with a desperate grip, shouting into his ear when shells exploded close, and telling his story so that Clifford, behind eyes that stared wildly one minute and were closed the next, couldn't doubt his confession.

A greater truth was choking him, but he forgot to be afraid of machine guns and searching shrapnel while Nevill spoke his deadly tale in which he embroidered the homely Nottingham names to divert Clifford from the agony that would not let him live. He brought in the sound of Woodhouse and Radford, Robins Wood and Wollaton, Lenton and the Cherry Orchard and all the streets he could think of, as many times as possible to divert him and make his account so real that even a dying man would see its truth – though hoping that by a miracle the talismanic words would save his life.

'It's on'y one you killed, sarge,' he whispered. 'Don't much matter.'

After dark Nevill dragged him a few feet at a time. 'Find somebody else,' Clifford said. 'I'm finished. I'll never be old.'

Nevill had to get someone back to safety. 'Don't talk so bleddy daft.'

He carried him a yard or two, thinking that as long as he hung on to him he need never consider the hangman again. He sweated grit and spat blood and pissed sulphur – as the saying went – and knew he was always close to conking out.

'Why are we in a tunnel, sergeant?' Clifford's eyes filled with soil and tears. 'Yer off yer sodding nut. Yer pulling your guts out for nowt.'

Occasional rifle shots sounded, but the machine guns and artillery had ceased. 'They'll hang me,' he said. 'Shut up.'

Clifford pulled both legs into his chest, choking on his blood. 'They'll shoot me, without me rifle. I don't like this tunnel, though. We went over the top, didn't we, not in a tunnel. Must a bin a mistake.'

He knelt close and saw his face in the light of a flare. 'Yes, we did go over the top, and you're wounded, you fool, so shut your mouth.' He whispered into his ear as he lay down beside him: 'A real Blighty one yer've got. You'll be out of it for *good* soon.'

English voices called low in the darkness, and stretcher-bearers found them. When they pulled at Nevill's arm to part him from Jack Clifford he screamed in agony.

The adjutant went through the rolls at Battalion Head-quarters and said: 'Sergeant Nevill? Wasn't he the one we sent the signal for? Don't suppose he got it in time. All they wanted was for him to come back and explain why he had indented for too many ration replacements last week. We'd have put him down for a medal, bringing in a wounded man like that while he was wounded himself, if only the chap hadn't died.'

When Nevill was demobbed in the spring of 1919 he went back to Nottingham and found Amy. She had her own small house, and took him in as if he'd just come back from shooting rabbits in Robins Wood. Three months later she was pregnant again, and he was already at work on a mechanic's job that was to last thirty years. He looked after Amy and her first son, and then she had two by him, but he was never brave enough to tell her what he told Jack Clifford near Gommecourt. He was on the point of it often, but sensed that if he let it out they wouldn't stay together any more.

Those good souls who helped old Nevill from the table in The Radford Arms averred he was no more than a bag of skin and bone. He trembled as they sat him down, and the landlord nodded at one of his bar-keepers to bring a dash of whisky and water. It had already passed closing time, and two more men who were also good enough to order him something were forced to drink it themselves.

'Funny bloody story he was trying to spin us,' one of them said, 'about killing somebody in Robins Wood.'

'Couldn't make head nor tail of it. I've known him years, and he wouldn't hurt a fly. A bit senile, I suppose. Come on, get that turps down your throat, then we'll drive him back to his missis in Beaconsfield Terrace.'

Nevill thought he would have a word or two if ever he met Jack Clifford again about the secret he'd foisted on him but which nobody else had taken notice of when he let it out in the boozer. Not that he had much of a wait before discovering whether or not he'd see old Jack. Nobody was surprised when old Amy found him dead one morning, sitting fully dressed by the fireplace. Having heard about his dancing on the table in the pub, the neighbours had supposed – as they said at the funeral – that it couldn't be long after that.

BEFORE SNOW COMES

The lights below glowed red like lines of strawberries. Snow had been forecast, and when it fell he thought they would be buried. The smell of frost and smoke had softened, and he could taste snow on his lips even before the first flake drifted down on to his hair.

The only thing was to drink, drink, drink, and try not to forget. With glass after glass her face came back with much greater clarity than when he was sober. In dull ordinary everyday light she stayed dim and far away, out of sight and all possibility of mind. But in memory she never stood so close that he could touch her.

He recognised the garden because of the rosebush growing in it. The palings leaned as if they would never get up again. They had not been thumped by a good-natured drunk, for then they could have been willingly straightened, but sagged as if someone had deliberately kicked them in passing because he was fed up with life when he had no need to be. They should be totally uprooted and thrown away for bonfire night. Then I'd get some of those new-smelling planks and laths from the woodyard and put good fences around that rosebush. He would get clean steel nails and set out those laths and offshoot wasted planks from the trunks of great trees that he got cheap because one of his mates worked there, and brush off the sawdust lovingly from each one, feeling it collect like the wooden gold-dust of life in the palm of his hands and sift between the broad flesh of his lower fingers. That half-sunk sagging fence wanted a good dose of the boot, to be followed of course by a bit of loving skill for her sake.

He had it because he was divorced. His spirit was turned upside down, the sand in his brain rifting through as in the old days to body and heart, an eggtimer letting its intoxication into the crevice of every vein and vesicle, bone and sinew. He worked and worked, walked from one step to another between elevation and misery. At work they thought him a happy and reliable mate, but every second night he forgot to wind up his watch and had to call on a neighbour to check the time in order to say hello in the morning, otherwise he'd be late getting up for work (or might never get up at all) and that would never do.

He had four brothers and two sisters, all of them married, and all divorced, except one who was killed in a car crash. It wasn't that his family was unlucky or maladjusted, simply that they were normal and wholesome, just conforming like the rest of the world and following in the family tradition with such pertinacity that at the worst of times it made him laugh, and at the best it sent him out in carpet slippers on Sunday morning to buy a newspaper and read what was happening to other families. What else could you do and think, if the razor-blade of fate isn't to cut you down and spare you even more sufferings? Sometimes he thought he'd buy a Bible and make prayer-wheels to send zipping into outer space, which seemed the only possible alternative to drinking himself to death, which he couldn't afford to do. But the world keeps going round, and it was no use asking what had happened to all the good times. The ocean was too deep and wide to escape from the island on which he found himself.

She kept her roses well, and he remarked on them when passing the backyard where her fence was ready to lie down and never get up again, though it wasn't the worst of them in that terrace by any means. She leaned on the gate smoking a cigarette, a young woman with dark short curly hair, sallow and full in the face below it. Her eyes, a sharp light-blue, gave her expression a state of being lit up and luminous, aware of everything inside her but not of the world. Why she was standing there he didn't know, because there was nothing to look at but a brick wall two yards away. He stopped, nothing else in his mind except: 'I like those roses. I could smell 'em as I went by.'

'They aren't exactly Wheatcroft specials,' she said, not smiling.

'Where'd you get 'em?'

'My brother lives in Hertfordshire, and he gen me a few cuttings from his garden. Only one took, but look how it blossomed!'

'It has, an' all,' he said. Neither of them could think of anything else to say.

'Goodbye, missis.'

'Goodbye, then.'

He didn't see her for a long time, but thought about her. He worked at a cabinet-making factory as a joiner, making doors one week and window frames the next, lines of window frames and rows of doors. The bandsaws screamed all day from the next department like the greatest banshee thousand-ton atomic bomb rearing for the spot-middle of the earth which seemed to be his brain. Planing machines went like four tank engines that set him looking at the stone wall as if to see it keel towards him for the final flattening, and then the milling machines buzzing around like scout cars searching for the answers to all questions ... It was like the Normandy battlefield all over again when he was eighteen, but without death flickering about. Not that noise bothered him, but he often complained to himself of minor irritations, and left the disasters to do their worst. It was like pinching himself to make sure he was alive.

He gave her names, but none seemed to fit. Her face was clear, but he couldn't remember what clothes she had been wearing. It was just after midday and he wrenched his memory around like wet plywood to try and remember if the smell of any cooking dinner had been drifting from her kitchen door, whether she'd been leaning there waiting for her husband to come up the street from the factory. He expected that she had, though it didn't seem important.

After heavy spring rain the Trent flowed fast at Gunthorpe, as if somebody was feeding it along the narrows with an invisible elbow and tipping it towards the weir that was almost levelled out. But after rain there was sunshine and he cycled up the hill. At Kneeton hamlet he stood at the top of the hill with his bike, looking down through the gloomy bracken, along the descending hedge-tunnel towards the ferry and over the opposite flat bank. But for a better view he turned and leaned his bike against a wall, and went into Kneeton churchyard. The river was as grey as battleship paint, none of the small white clouds of the sky visible in it. They were reflected rather on the glistening fields beyond, and the dry red-roofed houses of various farms and villages.

He walked over the soddened grass, around the small cemetery. The gravestone of Sarah Ann Gash had split in the middle and fallen. She was born on September 1st but it didn't say what year because the split of the slate had gone right through it. Where was Sarah now? he wondered, Sarah who no longer walked around these high woods and looked now and again across the Trent for signs of storm and sunshine.

He'd left his room early, hoping to get in the full brightness of Sunday before the piss of heaven belted down again. He looked across the valley as he'd done dozens of times and brooded on it as he always did, a valley fair and shallow as himself. He told himself it was different now, without being sharp enough at the moment to know why. Locked in his Nottinghamshire room he thought about the past, but seeing this blue sky and so much open land, he wondered about the future, though in such a way that he would allow no useful answer to come out of his musing. He doubted that an answer could come under any conditions, though however unsatisfied he did not want to return to his room and brood without the benefit of such good and placid scenery.

He was a man of forty who considered that nothing had happened in life so far – apart from the death of his parents, and the loss of his wife and child by a divorce which she had wanted, and been willingly given. Just as he believed that a clerk did not work because you could not see his calloused hands and blackheads dotting his face, so he believed that he hadn't suffered because he wasn't physically scarred, crippled, or blind. It seemed that a sense of realism regarding the world and what it could do to you, and you to it, hadn't yet given him the opportunity of being fully born to its wrath, and whenever he felt something near to peace – gazing for too long over the snaky Trent and slowly rising fields on the far side – his face looked more puzzled than pleased. The wind blew against his jersey shirt, and he felt it to the flesh. Anything he felt, he noticed, and this if nothing else brought a smile to his face.

The lane descending to the river went between high hedges with sharp buds scattered over them like green snow, bent slightly on its route to the narrow band of meadow bordering the river-bank. A smell of wet cloud and fields came from the bushes. He wanted to reach the river, but not to plough in his bike and boots through the mud when a paved lane behind would get him there in a little more time but far less trouble.

Four great engines were detonated against the sky, and over the trees to his right a huge plane slid off an aerodrome runway and carried its grey belly far off across the opposite flat fields, suddenly climbing and merging completely with the sky like a bird. Something in him waited for a blue-white flash along the body, a silent unobtrusive packed explosion that would make it vanish for ever from both world and sky, as if it had no right up there where only birds of flesh and feathers could travel. But when it went on its flight he was happy and relieved that nothing happened to it. There is something greater than love, he thought. Far greater. I feel it, something that makes love seem primitive. I can't say what it is, but I know that it exists, though one can only get to it through love.

He cycled over the long tarmac bridge, considered stopping on the pavement to look at the river's floodspeed over the parapet, but knew it finally could only interest a child, so turned across the line of traffic and down the lane towards field and gravel-stones sloping between the inn and the water's edge. The nearby weir was almost level yet still let out a thunderous roar of water from its depths, and in various sidepools of the river men sat fishing, oblivious to it. He lay his bike down, and set off for a walk.

A woman and two children were picnicking beyond the first clump of bushes, and not having a very good time of it. A khaki groundsheet had been fixed on two sticks as a shield against the irritating windbite gusting across the river to scatter sandwich papers and salt. They crouched under it, and he heard the grit of discontented voices. It was difficult to light a cigarette in such a cunning wind, except by opening his jacket and holding it as a buffer. So as not to intrude upon their private feast he walked behind them, but when he was closest he knew he had seen the woman before, leaning against the backyard gate of a house in Radford. A boy of seven felt under a blanket and pulled out a transitor radio the size of a two-ounce tobacco tin, and switched on a thin screech of music. Ducks flew over from the woods, and when their beaks moved during a low swerve towards the fishermen behind, he heard no sound because of the radio.

The mother switched it off: 'You can play it after you've had something to eat' – and gave him and his sister a hardboiled egg. He heard the soft crack of shell on a stone, and remembered that he had eaten no breakfast. Her thick plum-coloured coat was open to show a pale-green sweater. His stare drew her head around, and he was astounded now that he had a full view of her face, to see how much it had altered, or how much his memory had embellished it with features it had probably never possessed. The sallowness lay on thinner and smaller bones, and she was darker under her eyes. But she drew him with the same force, like a girl he'd been in love with as an adolescent and just by accident met again, suddenly bringing back to him youth and naïvety and the unforgettable depth and freshness of first love that he knew could never come twice in anybody's lifetime. It struck him that whenever he thought of something that happened a few years ago it always felt as if he were recapturing adolescence.

He stood back, but said when she looked hard at him: 'I was passing, and recognised your face. You live down Radford, don't you?'

'Who's that, mam?'

'Shurrup and get your picnic.' She was puzzled, and not pleased at this plain intrusion.

'I remember your rosebush,' he said with a smile. 'How's it getting on?'

'Not very well. I didn't know you knew me.'

'I passed your gate, and yours was the only back garden with roses in it.'

She gave each child a radish, and the girl who got the biggest held it like a doll, then grasped the green sprouts and chewed it while thoughtfully looking at the river. 'What's your name?'

'Jean,' she said, 'if you like.'

He smiled. 'That's a funny way of putting it.'

'Jean then, whether you like it or not.'

'We talked about your roses. Don't you remember?'

She pulled her coat to. 'Wipe your nose, Paul. Don't let it go all over your food. A lot's happened since.' She was not eating, handled all food respectfully and passed it to her children. A gang of boys went by, waving sticks and swinging tadpole jars at the end of string.

'That's lucky,' he said, 'no matter how bad it is.'

'I don't care, one way or the other.' Yet her face had relaxed almost into a smile in the few words bartered since he'd stopped.

'That's no way, either,' he said. 'You know what they say about Don't Care?' The boy and girl looked up at him, with more interest than their mother. The girl smiled, waiting.

'It goes like this, I think:

>'*Don't Care had golden hair*
>*Don't Care was green at the face*

> *Don't Care was tall and lame*
> *Don't Care wore a shirt of lace*
> *Don't Care took the Devil's name*
> *Don't Care was hung:*
> *Don't Care fell down through the air*
> *Into a pit of dung!'*

He felt foolish at such recitation, yet less so when he saw that all three were amused.

'Where did you learn that?'

He winked. 'Read it in a book.'

'What sort of book?' asked the boy.

'Any book. No, I tell a lie. I remember my father saying it to me as a boy.'

'A rum thing to tell a child,' she said. Wet blue clouds were coming eastwards over the summit of the woods, cold grey at the edges, but a line of sun still cut the mother from her children, moving and warming them in turn.

'I hope it doesn't think to rain,' she said.

'So do I. I biked up from Nottingham, and now I'm off for a walk. What happened to you in the last two years, then?' He saw she wouldn't want to talk about it, but asked just the same, because it was up to her to decide, not him.

'It's a long story,' she said, snubbing him by the silence that followed.

It must be a bloody bad one, he thought, from the way she looks: 'I'll tell you one thing, though: no stories have an ending. They never end. So maybe it won't turn out to be as bad as you think. Take me, for instance. I'm only really happy when I'm working.'

His way of speaking had aroused her interest, as if she was unaccustomed to hearing people speak at all. She asked if he lived alone.

'I do,' he said.

'Me too; but I've got two kids. You keep yourself looking well and clean for a man who lives alone!'

He laughed: 'It's not too difficult.'

'Some men find it so.'

'I'll be going for a stroll then.'

'What's your name, anyway?'

'Mark,' he told her. 'Maybe I'll pass your house again for another look at your roses. I've never seen such fine ones in Radford.'

He climbed a gate and made his way through wet nettles that came up to his knees and brushed his trousers above the tops of his leather boots. Across the path striated puddles barred his way, an edge of the yellow round sun reflected in them. The sky was blue and heavy, patched, rimmed, and streaked with thinning grey cloud. Whenever faced with a long walk he began to feel self-indulgent, wished he hadn't set out, and speculated on his point of no return. The fields stretched into the distance, reluctant to slope up through mist into the hills beyond Southwell. He stood by the edge of a copse that barred his way, black trunks and evergreen tops forming an impenetrable heart in his path. There was a paralysis in his legs that would not allow him to find the free flow around it so as to continue his roaming. What was the point in going on if you could not get easily to the heart? Two pigeons flew out of the field and buried themselves in it without difficulty. It looked even more of a job to get into that than one's own soul, a million times harder, in fact.

It started to rain. The soul was a moth fluttering in smoke, down on the concrete floor of his personality, sometimes touching it with the tips of its wings, flying above it, but always conscious that it was there in the smoke and darkness, and that it could never get through to the richer fields below, where connection with the universe and the clue to the real meaning of life lay. He could not burst that concrete as others presumably had, blast a way through to his soul with the dynamite of hardship and suffering. It was a mystery to him how it was done. Where does one begin? What is the secret or quality of disposition towards nature that one must have in one's marrow? Two pigeons, back out of the copse, were flying through the rain towards the river, and without thinking he headed back in that direction himself. Jean and her children had packed up and gone – which didn't surprise him because the thin consistent rain already reached through to his skin. He rubbed the beads of water from his bicycle handlebars and rode with head down along the main road back towards Nottingham.

The rose bushes had indeed withered: some organic malevolence had bitten them at the root and travelled up to every point of life. The blight had crippled it, in spite of all hope and intermittent care between bitter and useless quarrels with her husband. His departure had been the talk of the yard, but everyone had known right from the beginning that their marriage had been broken-backed and would dissolve one day. So did Jean know, now that it was all over. Even the children had stopped asking for him after a few weeks, knowing that to go on doing so would make her unendurably irritable for hours.

She tried to revive them, bought various compost powders from the ironmonger's and dug up the rock-cake soil around each one, but they seemed unwilling to risk flowering in the closed-off urban air. Their thorns stayed rusty in summer, shining under the blue complacent sky.

While cooking the children's breakfast she remembered the man who had talked to them on their last excursion to Gunthorpe. If only it had been as fine a day as this, she thought, glancing out of the window at a clean warm sky, I'd have felt more like chatting him back instead of driving him away with megrims and miseries. She could find excuses for it, but no reason, though the memory by no means depressed her as she stirred porridge and put sausages under the grill. They had a meal at school, and got their own tea till she came in at six. As for men, she did not care if she never had another one near her for the rest of her life. She'd had two bellyfuls from Ken, and got no joy out of either. Any of that, and she could manage it herself, as most self-respecting women had to do.

Janice came down, dressed already, but Paul still had his pyjama-bottoms on and his clothes bundled up like a bomb under his arm. She snapped and tugged him into a dressed creature in two minutes, and Janice was pouring cold milk into his porridge when she went out of the back door to catch the bus for work.

Mark cycled over in his dinner hour, but she wasn't in. He didn't like being seen in his overalls, but was able to look towards her back door while smoking a cigarette, careful not to lean on the sagging fence which looked as if it would stay up for ever it was so rotten. The neighbours assumed he was her boy-friend, and couldn't understand that someone who must have crept into her house now and again when it was dark – though no one had actually seen him – should be so gormless as to come here in the middle of the day merely to stand and look at the scullery window.

I ought to mend that fence, he told himself. A few good posts and a line of deep holes filled with concrete, and I'd ram in the supports to last till the slum clearance brigade comes round. Wouldn't take me a day.

He'd had the disease most of his life of asking questions before the time was ripe – if it ever was – and so destroying what pleasure he might be destined to feel if he did the impossible and kept his mind closed. But at half past eight that evening (while it was still light: The neighbours thought he had a cheek) he knocked at the back door with a definite proposition in mind.

A large white towel was swathed around her sopping head, just up from its final rinse at the scullery tap. The two top buttons of her blouse were open, and he turned red at the face. 'I was passing, so I thought I'd say hello.'

'Oh!' she said, the green-eyed twilight blank and clear at the back of his head. 'It's you! I thought it was going to be Flo Holland. What do you want?' The offputting brutality of this abrupt question was lessened by an assumption in her tone that he had a right to come there and want something, and that for some reason she by no means considered him a total stranger. Her face seemed less pale, a little more healthy with the dark hair invisible, lines slightly hard like a woman's in a bathing cap and devoid of make-up or lipstick. Through the main window he saw the white electric flash of the telly reflection. 'I've just washed my hair,' she said. 'It saves a few bob to do it at the sink. You can come in for a cup of tea in a minute.'

She closed the door, and he was sure she'd forget him, accidentally-on-purpose, as it were. He stood by the fence smoking, only this time on her side of the gate, and it was amazing how strong that gate looked in comparison to the rotten decrepit lines of paling on either side.

When he was about to walk away the door pulled open. The scarf that bundled the drying hair gave her a gipsy look, darkened her eyes and narrowed the face. 'Come on,' she said, 'I've got the kettle on.' Sometimes when cycling he would go for miles deep in thought, and suddenly realise he could not remember passing any of the familiar landmarks on the road behind. So now, filled with happiness instead of thought, he could not recollect details of getting to the table and facing her from his abstracted melancholy stance by the gate.

'What made me call,' he said, 'was the sight of that fence.'

'I thought it was me,' she said.

'Don't get sarky. I'm a chippie and can fix it for you.'

'How much do you want for it?' she asked.

'I'll do it for fun.'

She held a slice of bread at the fire with a long fork. 'I wouldn't bother. It's been like that for so long. Anyway, if we have a bad winter like the last one I'll use it for firewood to save me or the kids queuing at the coke-yard.'

'The toast's burning,' he said. She buttered it, and poured a mug of tea. 'I don't eat till the kids are upstairs. I get indigestion at their antics. When Paul broke a cup tonight I screamed as if somebody had thrown a knife at me. Frightened the poor little bogger out of his wits.'

'No use getting nervous,' he laughed.

'It's no use telling me that. I was born like it.'

'Who wasn't? Fag? Sometimes it goes.'

'In middle age,' she said, 'I'm waiting.'

'There's a long time yet,' he said.

She leaned over for a light. 'Ever go to the pubs?'

'Not as a rule. Do you?'

'Not really. It'd get me out a bit if I did, I suppose.'

'Where do you go for your holidays?' he said.

'You met me on them.'

'Up Gunthorpe?'

'I take the kids now and again. Last year it was Matlock for the day, boating on the Derwent and then into the caves. They enjoyed it, I'm glad to say. We have better times since Ken left, though there's a bit less money to throw around.'

'I expect he'll be back,' he said, as if very happy at the idea.

'When the kids asked me where he'd gone – they didn't like him all that much, but they missed him at first – I said he was off to work in London for a while. But they know he won't come back. I was down town a few weeks ago with Janice, and we was just crossing the road in Slab Square when a bus stopped at the traffic lights, and out of the window I heard this voice shout: 'How are you, Jean, my duck?' and when I looked it was him sitting there as large as life with another bloody woman! Janice asked me who it was so I said it was nothing to do with us, and pulled her round when she tried to look. No, he'll never come back to me. Not that it would do him much good if he tried. More tea?'

'Please. I'll do that fence on Saturday. I often go to work then, but I can leave off overtime for once.'

Neighbours stopped and looked into the small of his back as they passed along the yard, or from the end of it turned to see what he was on with. Clouds were low, and the heavy oppressive warmth of summer weighed over the kitchens and lines of lavatories. Once started on a job he didn't want to stop till it was over and done with. It was a change from making the eternal doors and windows at the factory. He uprooted the rotten palings and prised out rusty nails so that he could lay each piece of redundant wood under the front window for next winter's kindling. The holes were plotted with a ruler, marked by temporary sticks while he mixed the concrete. He'd pushed the new palings up on two journeys by bike the evening before, and she grumbled but gave in when he insisted on them staying overnight in the kitchen. Out in the garden, someone would be bound to pinch them, as he had done.

Janice and Paul watched, chewing caramels he'd treated them to. 'You're making a good job of it,' Jean said, bringing a mug of tea.

'I might as well, while I'm at it.'

'I'm off shopping. I shan't be long' – as if he should be embarrassed left all alone in a strange yard.

He straightened and took the tea. The first three posts were in, packed upright by bricks. 'If you're going out to do a week's shop you might need some money. Take this' – holding a few pounds.

'No,' she said, with a finality that he could neither change nor broach, 'it's all right.'

He crushed the notes back in his hand, fingers kneading till the knuckles went white, hoping they would disappear and prove he hadn't been so stupid as to offer it.

'I'm not being fussy' she smiled, 'but I just don't need it. You're doing enough as it is.'

'It's good tea,' he said, 'and I was ready for it. I thought I'd help out, that's all.' He took off his cap and rubbed the sweat back into his hair. 'Do you play draughts?'

Arms were folded under her breasts, drawing in her blouse. 'Not for years, but I can.'

'I'll give you a game tonight.'

'All right then. I'll bring some fags back.'

He couldn't refuse them, as she had rebuffed him over the money; in fact such fine tenderness on her part sent as much pleasure through him as if they had indulged in a secret and unexpected kiss.

When the fence was finally up, and the kids packed off to bed, they sat down to a peaceful supper of sliced meat and farmhouse bread, coffee and pickles, cobs and jam. 'You've worked hard,' she said, 'and I'm glad of what you've done.'

'I've worked hard,' he said, his mouth full. 'Hard or soft, it's all the same. It'll stand up a long while. I'll guarantee that.'

They went through three games of draughts, and he beat her every time, though the last one wasn't so easy. 'I don't think we'll play any more,' he laughed, standing to put on his jacket. He felt in a pocket for his clips. 'Ever thought of taking a lodger?' he said, looking close at her.

She had, but wouldn't say so. It was too soon. He came close to kiss her, but she pushed him gently away and went with him to the door. She liked him, because he seemed to think about everything and took nothing for granted. What's more, he was kind and helpful, and such a man was rare. The sky was clear, but stars weren't often in it. Only telly aerials and chimneys were between you and the sky, and they helped to keep you warm.

'I'll think about it,' she said, touching his arm.

He seemed dejected, being at the end of the best day he'd spent in years, as he walked up the yard and out by his new-made fence.

The gate clicked, so she shut the door and went back to clear the table.

He didn't come for a month, but every day she expected him. She saw her husband several times in various parts of the city, but never once did she bump into Mark. Why doesn't he come? she wondered. He builds a brand-new marvellous fence, and then thinks he can just go off like any cock-a-doodle dandy and say no more about it. I suppose he can, she thought, sitting alone one night. He must have been offended when I wouldn't take money towards my shopping, but that's just like a man, to get haughty when they can't make a kept woman out of you in the first five minutes. They either do nothing, or want to do everything too quickly.

But he was close to her, so near, so close that sometimes she could see him clearly, though if she tried to touch him he vanished. She waited for him, but it seemed he'd gone for ever, either because he was scared of her and two children, or because he'd been discouraged by her coldness. She considered herself more hot-blooded than he knew, and as proof thought of the many times she had not been able to tolerate the knowledge of her husband going to bed with other women, until all vestige of love between them had been destroyed. Even Ken lost his jauntiness, and often his desire for whoever he was running after at the time. Their continual battles were fought with such unplanned unconscious spite that a note of fate and heroism crept into them both, bent as they then became on the complete destruction of each other's emotional base. Neither won, and neither lost – unless Ken could be said to have done so because he was the one who had walked out. She used to think during such fighting that the longer two people lived together the less possible did it become for them to do so. When she didn't speak to him for three days, at least not to say anything civilised, the atmosphere seemed to be damaging her actual brain cells, as if she would never again be able to see anything clearly without the most desperate effort. And when she did nothing else except speak to him for three days it was just as much of a torment, and the damage seemed to be even worse, because neither had a civil word left to say to each other.

But these memories vanished as soon as she thought of Mark, and she felt almost happy again. Then he came back.

He felt the soft warmth of midsummer, and an agreeable wind whose noiselessness was drowned by a gentle continuous brush of incoming water. For the first time in his life he was at peace not only with the world but also with those who lived in it. The clash of the children's spades into the stones sounded somewhere beyond his closed eyes. It was impossible to brood on the misery that had brought such good fortune. The sea excluded all unnecessary reflection. Its rhythms cut him off from any past machinery that may have had control over him. The place he lay on was a bridgehead on the land, and the stones pressing under his body were all that he owned. He reached out and met Jean's thigh, lifted higher until he could take her hand and press it tenderly. You went near the sea so that it could claim you, though it never did, dared it to send up an arm to try and pluck you off the precipitous shelf of life and happiness you had just by a miracle found, and drag you back to the death of its depths where you had come from. It couldn't. Both of them were firm in that. You were dreamy, and in any case had chosen a calm summer's day to lie there when there could be no danger whatsoever.

Jean sat up to spread their lunch, and he heard the children throw down spades and pull themselves over without standing up. 'Mark,' she said, 'I can't get the tops of these flasks off.'

'Knock 'em with a stone. That'll loosen 'em.'

She threw a pebble which struck his shoe. 'If you don't move I'll kiss you, lazy good-for-nothing.'

'Kiss me.'

She bent over, the sea on her lips, hair cutting out light when he opened his eyes. 'You weren't so lazy in bed last night.'

'The mattress was hard.' He jumped up yelling from a sharp nudge in the ribs, then got on his knees to twist the caps off. He couldn't screw his eyes down to the very stones and earth they sat on, but stared vacantly while exerting his strength, towards the far-off grey breakwater that divided a pale blue sea and a pale blue sky, its nearer arm coming out from grey shingle and off-white cliffs. They had come for a fortnight on his hundred pounds saved, taken two rooms half an hour inland on the uppers of the town, but with a wide view over the sea.

At night when the kids were sleeping they went to the front, along it and back, the sky still on fire and the sea blood-black and flat, walking out to the waterline without shoes or socks, and standing under the cry of the nightbirds, holding hands.

When they lay naked in bed together, lightbulb shining directly over them, he in her and both locked in restfulness after making love, he thought he saw her eyes screwed up with pain, until he realised it was the light from above shining through the strands and lines of her hair and reflecting them on the skin surrounding her closed eyes. The nights were becoming one night, the days one day now that the holiday was ending. The children would remember the days, but they would only remember the nights. She felt the warm thickness of his shoulders and back, the relaxed flesh of his buttocks. It was all comfort, and love, and silence, and she wondered when it would break up into the violent colours of chaos, then smiled at her pessimism and drew deeply on the hope that it never would.

'Happy, love?' he said, sensing it, never daring to ask if he knew she was not.

'Oh yes. You?'

They shifted on to their sides. 'Never more happy,' he told her. 'You know that.'

'I do.'

It was raining when they climbed into the train next day, a soft warm summer letdown from low cloud that made them happier than if they'd left the seaside with sun still shining. 'I'll save up,' he said, 'and we'll come again next year.'

'How many months is that?' Paul asked, digging his spade into the carriage floor.

Mark told him.

'How many weeks, then?'

'Fifty-odd.'

'How many minutes?'

He took out a biro and wrote on the margin of his *Daily Mirror*. 'Twenty-one thousand,' he laughed.

'I'll count them,' Paul said, as the train jerked and he fell against his mother.

The fence stood up, and so did the rosebush, every branch stem lined with concealed thorns among the remnants of decaying blossoms. More than a year had passed, and the sooty frost of winter lay over factories and houses. The factory covered more acreage than the houses. Across Ilkeston Road whole streets were cleared, a ground plan of cobbled laneways revealed. Blocks of flats, thin and high up the hill towards Canning Circus, stood like strands of hair stiffening at some apparition on the horizon that no human being could see because they were not made of concrete and girders, windows and seasoned wood. Such flats had now replaced the bucket-hovels that had held down the daisies for a hundred years, he thought, riding home on his way for dinner.

Home was where Jean and the children had once lived with her husband, and now allowed him to stay, though not in the man and wife sense, for his bed was in the parlour. 'I don't see why we can't share one bedroom,' he said.

'I do,' she retorted, 'I want some privacy in my life.'

Coming back to Nottingham after their sublime fortnight by the sea had the opposite effect to what he'd expected. The bliss of it seemed to have broken the back of their tenuous need for each other. Instead of the fabulous beginning of a full rich life together he now looked on their holiday as the height of affection and intimacy from which, through some unexplained perversity in Jean, they began to descend. Though not afraid to have the neighbours think they were living together, she seemed ashamed that she and Mark should actually do so.

At times she regretted having 'taken a lodger', useful and loving though he was. He was calm and tender, nothing upset him, neither the fact that his tea was late, nor the surge of kids jumping like mad things over him after an evening consumed in the sweat of overtime. He was goodness itself. Silver spoons must have been laid out for him at some time in his life, no matter what state he was born in. His goodness increased her feeling of guilt at having driven her husband away – though knowing in her heart that she was at least no more at fault than he had been.

Mark came home in the evening with a wide smile at the sight of her, and she tried to match him in it, would stand up from the table to greet him, while feeling desperately shy if the children were there. If they were out playing she would not even stand up. Because he was happy all of her moods were a torture to him. When he asked what was wrong, and she could not reply, it only proved that he was superfluous in the house.

'I'll go, then,' he said late one night.

She jumped up. 'No, don't Mark, don't.'

'What else can I do?'

'Stay, stay. I'd die if you left me.'

He held her. 'I don't want to go. My god I don't. I couldn't. But why aren't you happy, love?'

'You're too good,' she said, her tears wetting his close face. 'You're too good to me, Mark. I don't deserve this.'

'You do,' he said, fighting back a bleak inner weeping of his own. He questioned what she called his goodness, but it seemed no time to argue about that. 'You deserve any good thing that can happen to you,' he went on, pleading with her to accept whatever he had to give. But she went on crying, as if a moss-grown moon of despair had lodged itself in her heart that she had no hope of ever prising loose. It was hard to give comfort, impossible to reach her, but he stayed close and stroked her hair, saying that he loved her, loved her, thought she was beautiful, wonderful, the only woman of his life. But he felt empty, knew he was saying all this at the wrong time, that none of it was getting through, for she was beyond all aid and sympathy, untouchable. 'Leave me,' she moaned, 'leave me.'

'I can't. I never will.'

'Leave me alone. Go away.' It wasn't the first time she'd been so upset, but now it felt so bad that he thought his heart would burst, suffering so much himself at the manifestation of her grave unhappiness that he could in no way help her. She had so much, everything when you knew there was nothing further that she could attain or reach for.

Sometimes her sister came to look after the children and they went to see a good film, or walk around the streets talking and holding hands, going later into a pub to sit alone and lost in their own common glow. Every weekend they took the children either boating to Beeston Weir or for a picnic over Catstone Hill. He not only did his best for them, but enjoyed it so that he didn't seem to be doing anything at all. She sensed this, hoping that if he did put himself out he would perform miracles and make her life worth living after all. If she could not have everything, then the world was a desert in the depths of the night that could never be walked away from.

He was inadequate before her desolation. 'Don't be so upset, Jean. What is it? What can I do for you?'

The very fact of asking meant that he could do nothing. 'I don't know,' she said, 'I feel frightened all the time. Something's wrong, and I don't know what it is. I don't even know why I'm on this earth.'

'What does it matter? What do you want to know for? It doesn't bother me, not knowing.'

'I know it doesn't. That's why you're so good!' Her cries shook against the house, as if she were being deliberately tormented by some totally unfeeling person. But it was all coming from inside her, he thought, tightening his grip. The torture of helplessness passed on to him, the fact that his selfless love could do nothing to prevent the unexplained agony of her suffering – that he could not bear to be close to. It shook his heart to the core, and his own tears fell, filled with remorse because he could not follow Jean where some anguish he was not privileged to be part of had taken her right away from him.

They held each other tightly, sat on the floor, and wept aloud.

He got up one morning and fried an egg for breakfast. Jean did not go to work any more, and he took up a cup of tea before leaving.

A black dawn drizzle was falling outside, rattling against the loose window frame. It was a shame to sally into it, yet he liked going to work, being absorbed all day among noise and sawdust, fitting together unending rows of doors and windows. As labour it was less monotonous because he was now head man in the department, an unofficial foreman whose position was not yet confirmed by the management because they wanted to delay his increase in wages. But it would come, though he was already paying for it by having less jocular talks with his friends than before. Still, it was a better life, even if he did take a stint on actual chipping to make sure the quota was rushed out at the end of each day.

The stairs creaked under him as he went up with the tray.

The children were staying for a week with her sister, and they had slept the last few nights together in her bed. 'I'm off to work,' he said, bending to her ear.

Her white shoulders and the pink straps of her nightdress shone under the bed light, dark long hair spreading back across the pillow. She opened her eyes, and saw his thin-faced smile turned on her, an expression of uncertainty because he was never sure in what sort of mood she was going to wake up. Their faces were like the two covers of a book, and when they pressed together everything was packed between them, and nothing got out. They kissed several times, rare for a morning. 'Did you sleep well?' he asked, pouring her tea.

'Right under,' she smiled.

'You'll feel better today, then.'

She thought how good his face was, how handsome and thin, full of intelligence and feeling and everything a woman might want and be happy living with. She was tranquil and happy. 'Don't go to work.'

'I can't let a drop of rain put me off,' he smiled.

'All right. Give me another kiss before you go.'

When he went home in the evening he saw from the yard-end that the blinds were down. The gate was padlocked and bolted against him. It was dusk, and a sharp fresh wind came between the houses as if to clean out the backyards. A radio played from the lit-up house next door. He stared, as if to penetrate the bricks, fixed in his own desperate musing. In a moment the lights would mushroom and he would hear the hollow voice of the television set, and when the lock dropped away from his cold fingers he would open the back door and see her sitting there in the warmth they had created for themselves.

A man and woman passed him in complete silence, and walked into a house further down the yard. He pushed at the gate as if to split its hinges. It held firm. Then his whole weight went against the fence, wanting to smash down every foot and paling of it. He grunted and moaned, pitting black strength at it till his shoulder felt cracked and shattered. It stood straight, unbendable. Looking into the garden he saw that the rosebush had rotted and withered right to the tips of its branches, but remembered it as beautiful, petals falling, a circle of leaves and pink spots on the soil.

He went to the neighbour's house and knocked at the door. 'Where's Jean, then?' he asked when the scullery light fell over him.

'I'm sorry,' Mrs Harby said. 'Her husband fetched her in a taxi this afternoon. She left your case here. Would you like a cup of tea?'

'Was there anything else?'

'I can soon make you a cup of tea if you'd like one.'

'No thanks.'

She pulled a letter from her apron pocket. 'There was this she asked me to give you. It's a shame, that's all I can say.'

He balanced the heavy case over the crossbar of his bike. Why had she gone, in such a way and without telling him? If he had talked to her she would never have done it. They could have loved each other for ever but, having gone to the threshold of a full and tolerable life, they had shied back from it. But he didn't know. You never did know, and he wondered whether you had to live without knowing all your life, and in wondering this he had some glimmer as to why she had blown up their world and left him.

He leaned his bike against a wall, and stood the case close by. Street lamps glowed up the sloping cobbled street. Nothing had ever seemed so completely finished. The hum of the factory swamped into him, a slight relief on the pain.

He went to another lamp post, and under its light tore the unopened letter into as many pieces as he had strength for, held them above his head, gripped them tight in his fist. When his arm ached, he spread all fingers. The wind snapped the scraps of paper away, up and into the darker air beyond the lamp light, as quickly as a hundred birds vanishing before snow comes. He stood there for some time, then clenched his fist again. After a while he walked on.

CHICKEN

One Sunday Dave went to visit a workmate from his foundry who lived in the country near Keyworth. On the way back he pulled up by the laneside to light a fag, wanting some warmth under the leaden and freezing sky. A hen strutted from a gap in the hedge, as proud and unconcerned as if it owned the land for miles around. Dave picked it up without getting off his bike and stuffed it in a sack-like shopping-bag already weighted by a stone of potatoes. He rode off, wobbling slightly, not even time to kill it, preferring in fact the boasting smiles of getting it home alive, in spite of its thumps and noise.

It was nearly teatime. He left his bike by the back door, and walked through the scullery into the kitchen with his struggling sack held high in sudden light. His mother laughed: 'What have you done, picked up somebody's best cat?'

He took off his clips. 'It's a live chicken.'

'Where the hell did you get that?' She was already suspicious.

'Bought it in Keyworth. A couple of quid. All meat, after you slit its gizzard and peel off the feathers. Make you a nice pillow, mam.'

'It's probably got fleas,' Bert said.

He took it from the sack, held it by both legs with one hand while he swallowed a cup of tea with the other. It was a fine

60

plump bird, a White Leghorn hen feathered from tail to topnotch. Its eyes were hooded, covered, and it clucked as if about to lay eggs.

'Well,' she said, 'we'll have it for dinner sometime next week' – and told him to kill it in the backyard so that there'd be no mess in her clean scullery, but really because she couldn't bear to see it slaughtered. Bert and Colin followed him out to see what sort of a job he'd make of it.

He set his cap on the window-sill. 'Get me a sharp knife, will you, somebody?'

'Can you manage?' Colin asked.

'Who are you talking to? Listen, I did it every day when I was in Germany – me and the lads, anyway – whenever we went through a farm. I was good at it. I once killed a pig with a sledge hammer, crept up behind it through all the muck with my boots around my neck, then let smash. It didn't even know what happened. Brained it, first go.' He was so lit up by his own story that the chicken flapped out of his grasp, heading for the gate. Bert, knife in hand, dived from the step and gripped it firm: 'Here you are, Dave. Get it out of its misery.'

Dave forced the neck on to a half-brick, and cut through neatly, ending a crescendo of noise. Blood swelled over the back of his hand, his nose twitching at the smell of it. Then he looked up, grinning at his pair of brothers: 'You thought I'd need some help, did you?' He laughed, head back, grizzled wire hair softening in the atmosphere of slowly descending mist: 'You can come out now, mam. It's all done.' But she stayed wisely by the fire.

Blood seeped between his fingers, making the whole palm sticky, the back of his hand wet and freezing in bitter air. They wanted to get back inside, to the big fruit pie and tea, and the pale blinding fire that gave you spots before the eyes if you gazed at it too long. Dave looked at the twitching rump, his mouth narrow, grey eyes considering, unable to believe it was over so quickly. A feather, minute and beautiful so that he followed it up as far as possible with his eyes, spun and settled on his nose. He didn't fancy knocking it off with the knife-handle. 'Bert, flick it away, for Christ's sake!'

The chicken humped under his sticky palm and hopped its way to a corner of the yard. 'Catch it,' Dave called, 'or it'll fly back home. It's tomorrow's dinner.'

'I can't,' Bert screamed. He'd done so a minute ago, but it was a different matter now, to catch a hen on the rampage with no head.

It tried to batter a way through the wooden door of the lavatory. Dave's well-studded boots slid along the asphalt, and his bones thumped down hard, laying him flat on his back. Full of strength, spirit and decision, it trotted up his chest and on to his face, scattering geranium petals of blood all over his best white shirt. Bert's quick hands descended, but it launched itself from Dave's forehead and off towards the footscraper near the back door. Colin fell on it, unable to avoid its wings spreading sharply into his eyes before doubling away.

Dave swayed on his feet. 'Let's get it quick.' But three did not make a circle, and it soared over its own head and the half-brick of its execution, and was off along the pock-marked yard. You never knew which way it would dive or zigzag. It avoided all hands with uncanny skill, fighting harder now for its life than when it still had a head left to fight for and think with: it was as if the head a few feet away was transmitting accurate messages of warning and direction that it never failed to pick up, an unbreakable line of communication while blood still went through its veins and heart. When it ran over a crust of bread Colin almost expected it to bend its neck and peck at it.

'It'll run down in a bit, like an alarm clock,' Dave said, blood over his trousers, coat torn at the elbow, 'then we'll get the bleeder.' As it ran along the yard the grey December day was stricken by an almost soundless clucking, only half-hearted, as if from miles away, yet tangible nevertheless, maybe a diminution of its earlier protests.

The door of the next house but one was open, and when Bert saw the hen go inside he was on his feet and after it. Dave ran too, the sudden thought striking him that maybe it would shoot

out of the front door as well and get run over by a trolley-bus
on Wilford Road. It seemed still to have a brain and mind of
its own, determined to elude them after its uncalled-for treatment at their hands. They all entered the house without
thinking to knock, hunters in a state of ecstasy at having corn-
ered their prey at last, hardly separated from the tail of the
hen.

Kitchen lights were full on, a fire in the contemporary-style
grate, with Mr Grady at that moment panning more coal on
to it. He was an upright hard-working man who lived out his
life in overtime on the building sites, except for the treat of his
Sunday tea. His wife was serving food to their three grown kids
and a couple of relations. She dropped the plate of salmon and
screamed as the headless chicken flew up on to the table, clearly
on a last bound of energy, and began to spin crazily over plates
and dishes. She stared at the three brothers in the doorway.

'What is it? Oh dear God, what are you doing? What is it?'

Mr Grady stood, a heavy poker in his hand, couldn't speak
while the animal reigned over his table, continually hopping
and taking-off, dropping blood and feathers, its webbed feet
scratching silently over butter and trifle, the soundless echo of
clucking seeming to come from its gaping and discontinued
neck.

Dave, Bert and Colin were unable to move, stared as it
stamped circle-wise over bread and jelly, custard and cress.
Colin was somehow expecting Mr Grady to bring down the
poker and end this painful and ludicrous situation – in which
the hen looked like beating them at last.

It fell dead in the salad, greenery dwarfed by snowing
feathers and flecks of blood. The table was wrecked, and the
reality of his ruined, hard-earned tea-party reached Mr Grady's
sensitive spot. His big face turned red, after the whiteness of
shock and superstitious horror. He fixed his wild eyes on Dave,
who drew back, treading into his brothers' ankles:

'You bastards,' Grady roared, poker still in hand and
watched by all. 'You bastards, you!'

'I'd like my chicken back,' Dave said, as calmly as the sight of Grady's face and shattered table allowed.

Bert and Colin said nothing. Dave's impetuous thieving had never brought them anything but trouble, as far as they could remember – now that things had gone wrong. All this trouble out of one chicken.

Grady girded himself for the just answer: 'It's *my* chicken now,' he said, trying to smile over it.

'It ain't,' Dave said, obstinate.

'You sent it in on purpose,' Grady cried, half tearful again, his great chest heaving. 'I know you lot, by God I do. Anything for devilment.'

'I'd like it back.'

Grady's eyes narrowed, the poker higher. 'Get away from my house.'

'I'm not going till I've got my chicken.'

'Get out.' He saw Dave's mouth about to open in further argument, but Grady was set on the ultimate word – or at least the last one that mattered, under the circumstances. He brought the poker down on the dead chicken, cracking the salad bowl, a gasp from everyone in the room, including the three brothers. 'You should keep your animals under control,' he raved. 'I'm having this. Now put yourselves on the right side of my doorstep or I'll split every single head of you.'

That final thump of the poker set the full stop on all of them, as if the deathblow had been Grady's and gave him the last and absolute right over it. They retreated. What else could you do in face of such barbarity? Grady had always had that sort of reputation. It would henceforth stick with him, and he deserved it more than ever. They would treat him accordingly.

Dave couldn't get over his defeat and humiliation – and his loss that was all the more bitter since the hen had come to him so easily. On their way to the back door he was crying: 'I'll get that fat bleeding navvy. What a trick to play on somebody who lives in the same yard! I'll get the bastard. He'll pay for that chicken. By God he will. He's robbed a man of his dinner. He won't get away with a thing like that.'

But they were really thinking about what they were going to say to their mother, who had stayed in the house, and who would no doubt remind them for the next few weeks that there was some justice left in the world, and that for the time being it was quite rightly on the side of Mr Grady.

THE RAGMAN'S DAUGHTER

I was walking home with an empty suitcase one night, an up-
to-date pigskin zip job I was fetching back from a pal who
thought he'd borrowed it for good, and two plain-clothed
coppers stopped me. They questioned me for twenty minutes,
then gave up and let me go. While they had been talking to
me, a smash-and-grab had taken place around the corner, and
ten thousand nicker had vanished into the wide open spaces of
somebody who needed it.

That's life. I was lucky my suitcase had nothing but air in
it. Sometimes I walk out with a box of butter and cheese from
the warehouse I work at, but for once that no-good God was
on my side – trying to make up for the times he's stabbed me
in the back maybe. But if the coppers had had a word with me
a few nights later they'd have found me loaded with high-class
provision snap.

My job is unloading cheeses as big as beer barrels off lorries
that come in twice a week from the country. They draw in at
the side door of the warehouse, and me and a couple of mates
roll our sleeves up and shoulder them slowly down the gang-
plank into the special part set aside for cheeses. We once saw,
after checking the lists, that there was one cheese extra, so
decided to share it out between a dozen of us and take it home

to our wives and families. The question came up as to which cheese we should get rid of, and the chargehand said: 'Now, all look around for the cheese that the rats have started to go for, and that's the one we'll carve between us, because you can bet your bottom dollar that that's the best.'

It was a load of choice Dalbeattie, and I'd never tasted any cheese so delicious. For a long time my wife would say: 'When are you going to get us some more of that marvellous cheese, Tony?' And whatever I did take after that never seemed to satisfy them, though every time I went out with a chunk of cheese or a fist of butter I was risking my job, such as it is. Once for a treat I actually bought a piece of Dalbeattie from another shop, but they knew it wasn't stolen so it didn't taste as good as the other that the rats had pointed out to us. It happens now and again at the warehouse that a bloke takes some butter and the police nab him. They bring him back and he gets the push. Fancy getting the push for half a pound of butter. I'd be ashamed to look my mates in the eye again, and would be glad I'd got the sack so's I wouldn't have to.

The first thing I stole was at infants school when I was five. They gave us cardboard coins to play with, pennies, shillings, half-crowns, stiff and almost hard to bend, that we were supposed to exchange for bricks and pieces of chalk. This lesson was called Buying and Selling. Even at the time I remember feeling that there was something not right about the game, yet only pouting and playing it badly because I wasn't old enough to realize what it was. But when I played well I ended up the loser, until I learned quickly that one can go beyond skill: at the end of the next afternoon I kept about a dozen of the coins (silver I noticed later) in my pocket when the teacher came round to collect them back.

'Some is missing,' she said, in that plummy voice that sent shivers down my spine and made me want to give them up. But I resisted my natural inclinations and held out. 'Someone hasn't given their money back,' she said. 'Come along, children, own up, or I'll keep you in after all the other classes have gone home.'

I was hoping she'd search me, but she kept us in for ten minutes, and I went home with my pockets full. That night I was caught by a shopkeeper trying to force the coins into his fag and chewing-gum machines. He dragged me home and the old man lammed into me. So, sobbing up to bed, I learned at an early age that money meant trouble as well.

Next time at school I helped myself to bricks, but teacher saw my bulging pockets and took them back, then threw me into the playground, saying I wasn't fit to be at school. This showed me that it was always safest to go for money.

Once, an uncle asked what I wanted to be when I grew up, and I answered: 'A thief'. He bumped me, so I decided, whenever anybody else asked that trick question to say: 'An honest man' or 'An engine driver'. I stole money from my mother's purse, or odd coppers left lying around the house for gas or electricity, and so I got batted for that as well as for saying I wanted to be a thief when I grew up. I began to see that really I was getting clobbered for the same thing, which made me keep my trap shut on the one hand, and not get caught on the other.

In spite of the fact that I nicked whatever I could lay my hands on without too much chance of getting caught, I didn't like possessing things. Suits, a car, watches – as soon as I nicked something and got clear away, I lost interest in it. I broke into an office and came out with two typewriters, and after having them at home for a day I borrowed a car and dropped them over Trent bridge one dark night. If the cops cared to dredge the river about there they'd get a few surprises. What I like most is the splash stuff makes when I drop it in: that plunge into water of something heavy – such as a TV set, a cash register and once, best of all, a motorbike – which makes a dull exploding noise and has the same effect on me as booze (which I hate) because it makes my head spin. Even a week later, riding on a bus, I'll suddenly twitch and burst out laughing at the thought of it, and some posh trot will tut-tut, saying: 'These young men! Drunk at eleven in the morning! What they want is to be in the army.'

If I lost all I have in the world I wouldn't worry much. If I was to go across the road for a packet of fags one morning and come back to see the house clapping its hands in flames with everything I owned burning inside I'd turn my back without any thought or regret and walk away, even if my jacket and last ten-bob note were in the flames as well.

What I'd like, believe it or not, is to live in a country where I didn't like thieving and where I didn't want to thieve, a place where everybody felt the same way because they all had only the same as everyone else – even if it wasn't much. Jail is a place like this, though it's not the one I'd find agreeable because you aren't free there. The place that fills my mind would be the same as in jail because everybody would have the same, but being free as well they wouldn't want to nick what bit each had got. I don't know what sort of system that would be called.

While as a youth I went out with girls, I used to like thieving more. The best of all was when I got a young girl to come thieving with me. The right sort was better than any mate I could team up with, more exciting and safe.

I met Doris outside a fish-and-chip shop on Ilkeston Road. Going in to get a supply for supper she dropped her purse, and a few obstinate shekels rolled into the road. 'Don't worry,' I said, 'I'll find them, duck.'

A couple of other youths wanted to help, but I got one by the elbow. 'Bale out. She's my girl-friend. You'll get crippled for life.'

'All right, Tony,' he laughed. 'I didn't know it was you.'

I picked her money up: 'This is the lot' – followed her into the light of the fish-and-chip shop where I could see what she was made of. 'I'm going for some chips as well,' I said, so as not to put her off.

'Thanks for getting my money. I have butterfingers some-times.' Her hair was the colour of butter, yellow and reaching for her shoulders, where my hands wanted to be. We stood in the queue. I'd just eaten a bundle of fish-and-chips downtown, so even the smell in this joint turned my guts. 'Haven't I seen you somewhere before?' I asked.

'You might, for all I know. I've been around nearly as long as you have.'

'Where do you live, then?'

'Up Churchfield Lane.'

'I'll see you home.'

'You won't.' She was so fair and goodlooking that I almost lost heart, though not enough to stop me answering: 'You might drop your purse again.' I didn't know whether I'd passed her on the street some time, dreamed about her, or seen her drifting across the television screen in a shampoo advertisement between 'Blood Gun' and 'The Kremlin Strikes Again'. Her skin was smooth, cheeks a bit meaty, eyes blue, small nose and lips also fleshy but wearing a camouflage of orange-coloured lipstick that made me want to kiss them even more than if it had been flag-red. She stood at the counter with a vacant, faraway look in her eyes, the sort that meant she had a bit more thought in her rather than the other way round. She gave a little sniff at the billowing clouds of chip steam doubled in size because of mirrors behind the sizzling bins. It was impossible to tell whether or not she liked the smell.

'You're a long way from Churchfield Lane,' I said. 'Ain't you got chip shops up that part?'

'Dad says they do good fish here,' she told me. 'So I come to get him some, as a favour.'

'It's better at Rawson's though, downtown. You ought to let me take you there some time – for a supper. You'd enjoy it.'

It was her turn at the counter. 'I'm busy these days. Two shillings worth of chips and six fish, please.'

'Where do you work, then?'

'I don't.'

I laughed: 'Neither do I.'

She took her bundle: 'Thank you very much' – turned to me: 'You won't be able to take me out then, will you?'

I edged a way back to the door, and we stood on the pavement. 'You're a torment, as well as being goodlooking. I've still got money, even if I don't go to work right now.' We walked across the road, and all the time I was waiting for her to tell me to skid, hoping she would yet not wanting her to. 'Does it fall from heaven, then?'

'No, I nick it.'

She half believed me. 'I'll bet you do. Where from?'

'It all depends. Anywhere.' I could already see myself taking her the whole way home – if I kept my trap flapping.

'I've never stolen anything in my life,' she said, 'but I've often wanted to.'

'If you stick around I'll show you a few things.'

She laughed: 'I might be scared.'

'Not with me. We'll go out one night and see what we can do.'

'Fast worker. We could do it for kicks, though.'

'It's better to do it for money,' I said, dead strict on this.

'What's the difference? It's stealing.'

I'd never thought about it this way before. 'Maybe it is. But it's still not the same.'

'If you do it for kicks,' she went on, 'you don't get caught so easily.'

'There's no point in doing something just for kicks,' I argued. 'It's a waste of time.'

'Well,' she said, 'I'll tell you what. You do it for money, and I'll do it for kicks. Then we'll both be satisfied.'

'Fine,' I said, taking her arm, 'that sounds reasonable.'

She lived in a big old house just off Churchfield Lane, and I even got a kiss out of her before she went into the garden and called me a soft good night. Doris, she had said, my name's Doris.

I thought she was joking about stealing stuff for kicks, but I met her a few days later outside a cinema, and when the show was over and we stood by a pavement where five roads met, she said: 'I suppose you just prowl around until you see something that's easy and quiet.'

'More or less' – not showing my surprise. 'It might be a bit harder than that though.' I held up a jack knife, that looked like a hedgehog with every blade splayed out: 'That one ain't

for opening pop bottles; and this one ain't for getting stones
out of horses hoofs either. A useful little machine, this is.'

'I thought you used hairgrips?' She was treating it like a
joke, but I said, deadpan: 'Sometimes. Depends on the lock.'
A copper walked across the road towards us, and with every
flat footstep I closed a blade of the knife, slipping it into my
pocket before he was half-way over. 'Come on,' I said, lighting
a fag, and heading towards Berridge Road.

The overhead lights made us look TB, as if some big government scab had made a mistake on the telephone and had too
much milk tipped into the sea. We even stopped talking at the
sight of each other's fag-ash faces, but after a while the darker
side streets brought us back to life, and every ten yards I got
what she'd not been ready to give on the back seat of the
pictures: a fully-fledged passionate kiss. Into each went all my
wondering at why a girl like this should want to come out on
nightwork with a lout called me.

'You live in a big house,' I said when we walked on. 'What
does your old man do?'

'He's a scrapdealer.'

'Scrapdealer?' It seemed funny, somehow. 'No kidding?'

'You know – rag and metal merchant. Randall's on Orston
Road.'

I laughed, because during my life as a kid that was the place
I'd taken scrap-iron and jamjars, lead and woollens to, and her
old man was the bloke who'd traded with me – a deadbeat
skinflint with a pound note sign between his eyes and breathing
LSD all over the place. Dead at the brain and crotch the fat
gett drove a maroon Jaguar in an old lounge suit. I'd seen him
one day scatter a load of kids in the street, pumping that
screaming button-hooter before he got too close, and as they
bulletted out of his way throw a fistful of change after them.
He nearly smashed into a lamp-post because such sudden and
treacherous generosity put him off his steering.

'What's funny about it?' she wanted to know.

'I'm surprised, that's all.'

'I told a girl at school once that my dad was a scrapdealer, and she laughed, just like you did. I don't see what's funny about it at all.' You stupid bastard, I called myself, laughing for nothing when before you'd been getting marvellous kisses from her. A black cat shot through the light of a lamp-post, taking my good luck with it.

'He's better off than most people, so maybe you laugh because you're jealous.'

'Not me,' I said, trying to make amends. 'Another reason I laughed, if you want to know the truth, is that I've always wanted to be a scrapdealer, but so far I've never known how to get started. It was just the coincidence.' While she was wondering whether to believe me I tried changing the subject: 'What sort of a school did you go to where they'd laugh at a thing like that?'

'I still go,' she said, 'a grammar school. I leave at the end of the year, though.' A school kid, I thought. Still, she's a posh one, so she can be nearly seventeen, though she looks at least as old as me, which is eighteen and a half. 'I'll be glad to leave school, anyway. I want to be independent. I'm always in top class though, so in a sense I like it as well. Funny.'

'You want to get a job, you mean?'

'Sure. Of course. I'll go to a secretarial college. Dad says he'd let me.'

'Sounds all right. You'll be set for life, the way you're going.' We were walking miles, pacing innumerable streets out of our system, a slow arm-in-arm zig-zag through the darkening neighbourhood. It was a night full of star holes after a day of rain, a windy sky stretching into a huge flow over the rising ground of Forest Fields and Hyson Green and Basford, through Mapperly to Redhill and carried away by some red doubledecker loaded with colliers vanishing into the black night of Sherwood. We made a solitary boat in this flood of small houses, packed together like the frozen teeth of sharp black waves and, going from one lighthouse lamp-post to another, the district seemed an even bigger stretch than the area I was born and brought up in.

An old woman stood on a doorstep saying: 'Have you got a

fag, my duck? I'd be ever so grateful if you could manage it.'
She looked about ninety, and when I handed her one she lit
up as if ready to have a nervous breakdown. 'Thanks, my love.
I hope you'll be happy, the pair of you.'

'Same to you, missis,' I said as we went off.

'Aren't old women funny?' Doris said.

We kissed at every corner, and whenever it seemed I might
not she reminded me by a tug at my linked arm. She wore
slacks and a head scarf, a three-quarter leather coat and flat-
heeled lace-ups, as if this was her idea of a break-and-entry rig.
She looked good in it, stayed serious and quiet for most of the
walking, so that all we did now and again was move into a
clinch for a good bout of tormenting kisses. She moaned softly
sometimes, and I wanted to go further than lipwork, but how
could we in a solid wide open street where someone walking
through would disturb us? With the air so sweet and long
lasting, I knew it would be a stretch past her bed time before
she finally landed home that night. Yet I didn't care, felt awake
and marvellous, full of love for all the world – meaning her first
and then myself, and it showed in our kisses as we went at a
slow rate through the streets, arms fast around each other like
Siamese twins.

Across the main road stretched a wall covering the yard of
a small car-body workshop. As soon as I saw it my left leg
began trembling and the kneecap of my right to twitch, so I
knew this was the first place we'd go into together. I always
got scared as soon as the decision was made, though it never
took long for fright to get chased off as I tried to fathom a way
into the joint.

I told Doris: 'You go to the end of the street and keep conk.
I'll try to force this gate, and whistle if I do. If you see anybody
coming walk back here, and we'll cuddle up as if we're
courting.' She did as she was told, while I got to work on the
gate lock, using first the bottle-opener and then the nail-file,
then the spike. With a bit more play it snapped back, and I
whistled. We were in the yard.

There was no word said from beginning to end. If I'd been

doing it with a mate you'd have heard scufflings and mutter-
ings, door-rattlings and shoulder-knocks and the next thing
we'd be in a cop car on our way to Guildhall. But now, our
limbs and eyes acted together, as if controlled by one person
that was neither of us, a sensation I'd never known before. A
side door opened and we went between a line of machines into
a partitioned office to begin a quiet and orderly search. I'd
been once in a similar place with a pal, and the noise as we
pulled drawers and slung typewriters about, and took pot shots
with elastic and paperclips at light bulbs was so insane that it
made me stop and silence him as well after five minutes. But
now there wasn't a scratch or click anywhere.

Still with no word I walked to the door, and Doris came after
me. In two seconds we were back on the street, leaning against
the workshop wall to fill each of our mouths with such kisses
that I knew I loved her, and that from then on I was in the
fire, floating, burning, feeling the two of us ready to explode if
we didn't get out of this to where we could lie down. Nothing
would stop us, because we already matched and fused together,
not even if we fell into a river or snow-bank.

There was no gunning of feet from the factory so that a lawful
passing pedestrian could suspect we were up to no good and
squeal for the coppers. After five minutes snogging we walked
off, as if we'd just noticed how late it was and remembered we
had to be at work in the morning. At the main road I said:
'What did you get?'

She took a bundle of pound notes from her pocket: 'This.
What about you?'

I emptied a large envelope of postage stamps and cheques:
'Useless. You got the kitty, then.'

'I guess so,' she said, not sounding too full of joy.

'Not bad for a beginner. A school kid, as well!' I gave her
half the stamps and she handed me half the money – which
came to twenty quid apiece. We homed our way the couple of
miles back, sticking one or two stamps (upside down) on each
of the corners turned. 'I don't write letters,' I laughed. It was
a loony action, but I have to do something insane on every job,

otherwise there's no chance of getting caught, and if there's no chance of getting caught, there's no chance of getting away. I explained this to Doris, who said she'd never heard such a screwy idea, but that she was nearly convinced about it because I was more experienced than she was. Luckily the stamps ran out, otherwise the trail would have gone right through our back door, up the stairs and into my bedroom, the last one on my pillow hidden by my stupid big head. I felt feather-brained and obstinate, knowing that even if the world rolled over me I wouldn't squash.

By the banks of the Leen at Bobber's Mill we got under the fence and went down where nobody could see us. It was after midnight, and quiet but for the sound of softly rolling cold water a few feet off, as black as heaven for the loving we had to do.

Doris called for me at home, turned the corner, and came down our cobbled street on a horse. My brother Paul ran in and said: 'Come and look at this woman (he was only nine) on a horse, our Tony' – and having nothing better to do while waiting for Doris but flip through the *Mirror* I strode to the yard-end. It was a warm day, dust in the wind making a lazy atmosphere around the eyes, smoke sneaking off at right angles to chimneys and telly masts. By the pavement I looked down the street and saw nothing but a man going across to the shop in shirt-sleeves and braces, then swivelling my eyes the other way I saw this girl coming down the street on a walking horse.

It was a rare sight, because she was beautiful, had blonde hair like Lady Godiva except that she was dressed in riding slacks and a white shirt that set a couple of my Ted mates whistling at her, though most stayed quiet with surprise – and envy – when the horse pulled up at our yard-end and Doris on it said hello to me. It was hard to believe that last night we'd broken into a factory, seemed even more far gone than in a dream; though what we'd done later by the river was real enough, especially when I caught that smell of scent and freshness as she bent down from the horse's neck. 'Why don't you come in for a cup of tea? Bring your horse in for a crust as well.'

It was a good filly, the colour of best bitter, with eyes like priceless damsons that were alive because of the reflector-light in them. The only horses seen on our street – pulling coal carts or bread vans – had gone to the knackers' yards years ago. I took the bridle and led it up the yard, Doris talking softly from high up and calling it Marian, guiding it over the smooth stones. A man came out of a lavatory and had a fit in his eyes when he nearly bumped into it. 'It wain't bite you, George,' I laughed.

'I'll have it for Sunday dinner if it does,' he said, stalking off.

'It wain't be the first time,' I called. My mother was washing clothes at the scullery sink, and it pushed its head to the window for a good look – until she glanced up: 'Tony! What have you got there!'

'Only a horse, mam,' I shouted back. 'It's all right: I ain't nicked it' – as she came out drying her hands.

'A friend of mine come to see me,' I told her, introducing Doris, who dropped to her proper size on the ashphalt. My mother patted the horse as if it were a stray dog, then went in for a piece of bread. She'd been brought up in the country, and liked animals.

'We had a good time last night,' I said to Doris, thinking about it.

'Not bad. What shall we do with the money?'

'Spend it.'

Our fence was rickety, looked as if it would fall down when she tethered the horse to it. 'Funny' she said. 'But what on?'

'How much does a horse cost?' I asked, tapping its nose.

'I'm not sure. Dad got me Marian. More than twenty pounds, though.' I was disappointed, had pictured us riding in the country, overland to Langley Mill and Matlock Bath without using a road once, the pair of us making a fine silhouette on some lonely skyline. Then as on the films we'd wind our way far down into the valley and get lodgings at a pub or farmhouse. Bit by bit we'd edge to Scotland and maybe at the end of all our long wanderings by horse we'd get a job as man and wife working a lighthouse. Set on a rock far out at sea, the waves would bash at it like mountains of snow, and we'd keep the lights going, still loving each other and happy even though we hadn't had a letter or lettuce in six months.

The sun shone over our backyards, and I was happy anyway: 'I'll just get rid of my dough, enjoy myself. I'm out of work, so it'll keep me for a month.'

'I hope we don't have to wait that long before doing it again,' she said, brushing her hair back.

'We'll go tonight, if you like. I'll bet the coppers don't know we went into that factory yet.' My mother came out with a bag of crusts for the horse: 'I've just made a pot of tea,' she said. 'Go and pour it, Tony.'

When we got behind the door I pulled Doris to me and kissed her. She kissed me, as well. Not having to chase and fight for it made it seem like real love.

We went on many 'expeditions', as Doris called them. I even got a makeshift job at a factory in case anybody should wonder how I was living. Doris asked if it would be O.K. to bring a school pal with us one night, and this caused our first argument. I said she was loony to think of such a thing, and did she imagine I was running a school for cowing crime, or summat? I hoped she hadn't mentioned our prowling nights to anybody else – though she hadn't, as it turned out, and all she'd wanted was to see if this particular girl at her school would be able to do this sort of job as cool as she could. 'Well, drop it,' I said, sharp. 'We do all right by oursens, so let's keep it to oursens.'

Having been brought up as the ragman's daughter and never wanting for dough, she had hardly played with the kids in the street. She hadn't much to do with those at school either, for they lived mostly in new houses and bungalows up Wollaton and would never come to Radford to call on her. So she'd been lonely in a way I never had been.

Her parents lived in a house off Churchfield Lane, a big

ancient one backing its yards (where the old man still kept some of his scrap mountains) on to the Leen. Her dad had worked like a navvy all day and every day of his life, watching each farthing even after he was rich enough to retire like a lord. I don't know what else he could have done. Sucked icecream at the seaside? Gardened his feet off? Fished himself to death? He preferred to stick by sun, moon or electric light sorting metal or picking a bone with his own strength because, being a big and satisfied man, that was all he felt like doing – and who could blame him? Doris told me he was mean with most things, though not with her. She could have what she liked.

'Get a hundred, then,' I said.

But she just smiled and thought that wouldn't be right, that she'd only have from him what he gave her because she liked it better that way.

Every week-end she came to our house, on her horse except when the weather was bad. If nobody else was in she fastened her steed to the fence and we went up to my bedroom, got undressed and had the time of our lives. She had a marvellous figure, small breasts for her age, yet wide hips as if they'd finished growing before anything else of her. I always had the idea she felt better out of her clothes, realizing maybe that no clothes, even if expensive like gold, could ever match her birthday suit for a perfect fit that was always the height of fashion. We'd put a few Acker Bilk's low on my record player and listen for a while with nothing on, getting drowsy and warmed up under the usual talk and kisses. Then after having it we'd sit and talk more, maybe have it again before mam or dad shouted up that tea was ready. When on a quiet day the horse shuffled and whinnied, it was like being in a cottage bedroom, alone with her and in the country. If it was sunny and warm as well and a sudden breeze pushed air into the room and flipped a photo of some pop singer off the shelf and fell softly at our bare skins I'd feel like a stallion, as fit and strong as a buck African and we'd have it over and over so that my legs wobbled as I walked back down the stairs.

People got used to seeing her ride down the street, and they'd say: 'Hello, duck' – adding: 'He's in' – meaning me – 'I just saw him come back from the shop with a loaf.' George Clark asked when I was going to get married, and when I shouted that I didn't know he laughed: 'I expect you've got to find a place big enough for the horse as well, first.' At which I told him to mind his own effing business.

Yet people were glad that Doris rode down our street on a horse, and I sensed that because of it they even looked up to me more – or maybe they only noticed me in a different way to being carted off by the coppers. Doris was pleased when a man coming out of the bookie's called after her: 'Hey up, Lady Luck!' – waving a five-pound note in the air.

Often we'd go down town together, ending up at the pictures, or in a pub over a bitter or babycham. But nobody dreamed what we got up to before finally parting for our different houses. If we pinched fags or food or clothes we'd push what was possible through the letterbox of the first house we came to, or if it was too big we'd leave good things in litter-bins for some poor tramp or tatter to find. We were hardly ever seen, and never caught, on these expeditions, as if love made us invisible, ghosts without sound walking hand in hand between dark streets until we came to some factory, office, lock-up shop or house that we knew was empty of people – and every time this happened I remember the few seconds of surprise, not quite fear, at both of us knowing exactly what to do. I would stand a moment at this surprise – thankful, though waiting for it to go – until she squeezed my hand, and I was moving again, to finish getting in.

I was able to buy a motorbike, a secondhand powerful speed-ster, and when Doris called she'd leave the horse in our back-yard, and we'd nip off for a machine-spin towards Stanton Ironworks, sliding into a full ton once we topped Balloon House Hill and had a few miles of straight and flat laid out for us like an airport runway. Slag heaps looked pale blue in summer, full triangles set like pyramid-targets way ahead and I'd swing towards them between leaf hedges of the country road, hoping they'd keep that far-off vacant colour, as if they weren't real.

They never did though, and I lost them at a dip and bend, and when next in sight they were grey and useless and scabby, too real to look good any more.

On my own I rode with L plates, and took a test so as to get rid of them on the law's side of the law, but I didn't pass because I never was good at examinations. Roaring along with Doris straight as goldenrod behind, and hearing noises in the wind tunnel I made whisper sweet nothings into our four ear-holes, was an experience we loved, and I'd shout: 'You can't ride this fast on a horse' – and listen to the laugh she gave, which meant she liked to do both.

She once said: 'Why don't we go on an expedition on your bike?' and I answered: 'Why don't we do one on your hoss?' adding: 'Because it'd spoil everything, wouldn't it?'

She laughed: 'You're cleverer than I think.'

'No kidding,' I said, sarky. 'If only you could see yoursen as I can see you, and if only I could see mysen as you can see me, things would be plainer for us wouldn't they?'

I couldn't help talking. We'd stopped the bike and were leaning on a bridge wall, with nothing but trees and a narrow lane roundabout, and the green-glass water of a canal below. Her arm was over my shoulder, and my arm was around her waist: 'I wonder if they would?' she said.

'I don't know. Let's go down into them trees.'

'What for?'

'Because I love you.'

She laughed again: 'Is that all?' – then took my arm: 'Come on, then.'

We played a game for a long time in our street, where a gang of us boys held fag lighters in a fair wind, flicking them on and off and seeing which light stayed on longest. It was a stupid game because everything was left to chance, and though this can be thrilling you can't help but lose by it in the end. This game was all the rage for weeks, before we got fed up, or our lighters did, I forget which. Sooner or later every lighter goes out or gives in; or a wind in jackboots jumps from around the corner and kicks it flat – and you get caught under the avalanche of the falling world.

One summer's week-end we waited in a juke-box coffee bar for enough darkness to settle over the streets before setting out. Doris wore jeans and sweatshirt, and I was without a jacket because of the warm night. Also due to the warmth we didn't walk the miles we normally did before nipping into something, which was a pity because a lot of hoof-work put our brains and bodies into tune for such quiet jobs, relaxed and warmed us so that we became like cats, alert and ready at any warning sound to duck or scram. Now and again the noise of the weather hid us – thunder, snow, drizzle, wind, or even the fact that clouds were above made enough noise for us to operate more safely than on this night of open sky with a million ears and eyes of copper stars cocked and staring. Every footstep deafened me, and occasionally on our casual stroll we'd stop to look at each other, stand a few seconds under the wall of a side-lit empty street, then walk on hand in hand. I wanted to whistle (softly) or sing a low tune to myself, for, though I felt uneasy at the open dumb night, it was also the kind of night that left me confident and full of energy, and when these things joined I was apt to get a bit reckless. But I held back, slowed my heart and took in every detail of each same street – so as to miss no opportunity, as they drummed into us at school. 'I feel as if I've had a few,' I said, in spite of my resolution.

'So do I.'

'Or as if we'd just been up in my room and had it together.'

'I don't feel like going far, though,' she said.

'Tired, duck?'

'No, but let's go home. I don't feel like it tonight.'

I wondered what was wrong with her, saying: 'I'll walk you back and we'll call it a day.'

In the next street I saw a gate leading to the rear yard of a shop, and I was too spun up to go home without doing anything at all: 'Let's just nip in here. You needn't come, duck. I wain't be five minutes.'

'O.K.' She smiled, though my face was already set at the

loot-barrier. It wasn't very high, and when I was on top she called: 'Give me a hand up.'

'Are you sure?'

'Of course I am.' It was the middle of a short street, and lamp-posts at either end didn't shed radiance this far up. I got to the back door and, in our usual quiet way, the lock was forced and we stood in a smell of leather, polish and cardboard boxes.

'It's a shoe shop,' Doris said. I felt my path across the storehouse behind the selling part of the shop, by racks and racks of shoe boxes, touching paper and balls of string on a corner table.

We went round it like blind people in the dark a couple of times just to be sure we didn't miss a silent cashbox cringing and holding its breath as our fingers went by. People on such jobs often miss thousands through hurrying or thinking the coppers are snorting down their necks. My old man insists I get the sack from one firm after another because I'm not thorough enough in my work, but if he could have seen me on this sort of task he'd have to think again.

There was nothing in the backroom. I went into the shop part and in ten seconds flat was at the till, running my fingers over them little plastic buttons as if I was going to write a letter to my old man explaining just how thorough I could be at times. To make up for the coming small clatter of noise I held my breath – hoping both would average out to make it not heard. A couple of no-good night owls walked by outside, then I turned the handle and felt the till drawer thump itself towards my guts. It's the best punch in the world, like a tabby cat boxing you with its paw, soft and loaded as it slides out on ballbearing rollers.

My hand made the lucky dip, lifted a wad of notes from under a spring-weight, and the other scooped up silver, slid it into my pocket as if it were that cardboard money they used to lend us at infants' school to teach us how to be good shoppers and happy savers – not rattling good coin ready for grown-ups to get rid of. I went to the back room and stood by the exit to make sure all was clear.

The light went on, a brilliant blue striplight flooding every corner of the room. I froze like a frog that's landed in grass instead of water. When I could speak I said to Doris: 'What did you do that for?' – too scared to be raving mad.

'Because I wanted to.' She must have sensed how much I felt like bashing her, because: 'Nobody can see it from the street' – which could have been true, but even so.

'Kicks are kicks,' I said, 'but this is a death trap.'

'Scared?' she smiled.

'Just cool' – feeling anything but. 'I've got about fifty quid in my pocket.'

She stood against a wall of shoe boxes, and even a telly ad couldn't have gone deeper into my guts than the sight of Doris now. Yellow arms of light turned full on her left me in the shade – which was fine, for I expected to see the dead mug of a copper burst in at any moment. Yet even at that I wouldn't be able to care. I felt as if music was in my head wanting to get out, as if it had come to me because I was one of those who could spin it out from me, though knowing I'd never had any say in a thing like that.

She didn't speak, stood to her full fair height and stared. I knew we were safe, that no copper would make any capture that night because the light she had switched on protected us both. We were cast-iron solid in this strong-box of shoes, and Doris knew it as well because when I couldn't help but smile she broke the spell by saying:

'I want to try some shoes on.'

'What?'

'Maybe they've got some of the latest.'

The idea was barmy, not so that I wanted to run like a shot stag out of the place, but so that I could have done a handstand against the wall of boxes. I lifted out an armful and set them on the floor like a game of dominoes. She chose one and opened it gently. I took up a box and split it down the middle: 'Try these.'

They were too small, a pair of black shiners with heels like toothpicks. 'I wish the shopkeeper was here,' she said, 'then he could tell me where the best are. This is a waste of time.'

I scoffed. 'You don't want much, do you? You'd have to pay for them, then. No, we'll go through the lot and find a few pairs of Paris fashions.'

'Not in this shop' – contemptuously slinging a pair of plain lace-ups to the other side of the room, enough noise to wake every rat under the skirting board. From the ladder I passed down a few choice boxes, selecting every other on the off chance of picking winners. 'I should have come in skirt and stockings,' she said, 'then I could have told which ones suit me.'

'Well, next time we go into a shoe shop I'll let you know; I'll wear an evening suit and we'll bring a transistor to do a hop with. Try these square toes. They'll go well with slacks.'

They fitted but, being the wrong colour, were hurled out with the other misfits. The room was scattered with shoes, looked as if one of them Yank cyclones – Mabel or Edna or whatever you call them – had been hatched there, or as if a meeting of cripples and one-legs had been suddenly broken up by news of the four-minute warning. She still hadn't found the right pair, so went on looking as if she lived there, ordering shop-assistant me about, though I didn't mind because it seemed like a game we were playing. 'Why don't you find a pair for yourself?' she said.

'No, we'll get you fixed. I'm always well shod.'

I knew that we were no longer safe in that shop and sprang to switch off the lights. 'You silly fool,' she cried.

Darkness put us into another world, the real one we were used to, or that I was anyway because it was hard to tell which sort of world Doris felt at home in. All she wanted, I sometimes thought, was a world with kicks, but I didn't fancy being for long at the mercy of a world in pitboots. Maybe it wore carpet slippers when dealing with her – though I shouldn't get like that now that it's been over for so long.

'Why did you switch off the light?' she yelled.

'Come on, let's get outside.'

We were in the yard, Doris without any pair of shoes except those she'd come out in that evening. The skyline for me ended at the top of the gate, for a copper was coming over it, a blue-black tree trunk bending towards us about twenty yards away. Doris was frozen like a rabbit. I pushed her towards some back sheds so that she was hidden between two of them before the copper, now in the yard, spotted the commotion.

He saw me, though. I dodged to another space, then ricochetted to the safe end of the yard, and when he ran at me, stinking of fags and beer, I made a nip out of his long arms and was on the gate saddle before he could reach me.

'Stop, you little bogger,' he called. 'I've got you.'

But all he had was one of my feet, and after a bit of tugging I left my shoe in the copper's hand. As I was racing clippitty-clop, hop-skip-and-a-jump up the street, I heard his boots rattling the boards of the gate as he got over – not, thank God, having twigged that Doris was in there and could now skip free.

I was a machine, legs fastened to my body like nuts and bolts, arms pulling me along as I ran down that empty street. I turned each corner like a flashing tadpole, heart in my head as I rattled the pavement so fast that I went from the eye of a lamp-post in what seemed like no seconds at all. There was no worry in my head except the need to put a mile of zig-zags between that copper and me. I'd stopped hearing him only a few yards from the shoe shop gate, but it seemed that half an hour passed before I had to give up running in case I blew to pieces from the heavy bombs now getting harder all over me.

Making noises like a crazy elephant, I walked, only realising now that one of my shoes was missing. The night had fallen apart, split me and Doris from each other, and I hoped she'd made a getaway before the copper gave me up and went back to check on what I'd nicked.

I threw my other shoe over the wall of an old chapel and went home barefoot, meaning to buy myself some more next day with the fifty quid still stuck in my pocket. The shoe landed on a heap of cinders and rusting cans, and the softness of my feet on the pavement was more than made up for by the solid ringing curses my brain and heart played ping-pong with. I kept telling myself this was the end, and though I knew it was, another voice kept urging me to hope for the best and look on the bright side – like some mad deceiving parson on the telly.

I was so sure of the end that before turning into our street I dropped the fifty pound bundle through somebody's letter box and hoped that when they found it they'd not say a word to anybody about such good luck. This in fact was what happened, and by the time I was safe for a three-year lap in borstal the old woman who lived there had had an unexpected good time on the money that was, so she said, sent to her by a grateful and everloving nephew in Sheffield.

Next morning two cops came to our door, and I knew it was no good lying because they looked at me hard, as if they'd seen me on last night's television reading the news. One of them held my shoes in his hand: 'Do these fit you?'

A short while before my capture Doris said, when we were kissing good night outside her front door: 'I've learnt a lot since meeting you. I'm not the same person any more.' Before I had time to find out what she'd learnt I was down at the cop shop and more than half-way to borstal. It was a joke, and I laughed on my way there. They never knew about Doris, so she went scot-free, riding her horse whenever she felt like it. I had that to be glad about at least. As a picture it made a stove in my guts those first black months, and as a joke I laughed over and over again, because it would never go stale on me. I'd learned a lot as well since meeting Doris, though to be honest I even now can't explain what it is. But what I learned is still in me, feeding my quieter life with energy almost without my noticing it.

I wrote to Doris from borstal but never received an answer, and even my mother couldn't tell me anything about her, or maybe wouldn't, because plenty happened to Doris that all the district knew of. Myself though, I was kept three years in the dark, suffering and going off my head at something that without this love and worry I'd have sailed through laughing. Twenty of the lads would jump on me when I raved at night, and gradually I became low and brainless and without breath like a beetle and almost stopped thinking of her, hoping that maybe she'd be waiting for me when I came out and that we'd be able to get married.

That was the hope of story books, of television and BBC; didn't belong at all to me and life and somebody like Doris. For three solid years my brain wouldn't leave me alone, came at me each night and rolled over me like a wheel of fire, so that I still sweat blood at the thought of that torture, waiting, without news, like a dwarf locked in the dark. No borstal could take the credit for such punishment as this.

On coming out I pieced everything together. Doris had been pregnant when I was sent down, and three months later married a garage mechanic who had a reputation for flying around on motorbikes like a dangerous loon. Maybe that was how she prolonged the bout of kicks that had started with me, but this time it didn't turn out so well. The baby was a boy, and she named it after me. When it was two months old she went out at Christmas Eve with her husband. They were going to a dance at Derby on the motorbike and, tonning around a frosty bend, met a petrol bowser side on. Frost, darkness, and large red letters spelling PETROL were the last things she saw, and I wondered what was in her mind at that moment. Not much, because she was dead when the bowser man found her, and so was her husband. She couldn't have been much over eighteen.

'It just about killed her dad as well,' my mother said, 'broke his heart. I talked to him once on the street, and he said he'd allus wanted to send her to the university, she was so clever. Still, the baby went back to him.'

And I went back to jail, for six months, because I opened a car door and took out a transistor radio. I don't know why I did it. The wireless was no good to me and I didn't need it. I wasn't even short of money. I just opened the car door and took out the radio and, here's what still mystifies me, I switched it on straightaway and listened to some music as I walked down the street, so that the bloke who owned the car heard it and chased after me.

But that was the last time I was in the nick – touch wood – and maybe I had to go in, because when I came out I was able to face things again, walk the streets without falling under a bus or smashing a jeweller's window for the relief of getting caught.

I got work at a sawmill, keeping the machines free of dust and wood splinters. The screaming engine noise ripping through trunks and planks was even fiercer than the battle-shindig in myself, which was a good thing during the first months I was free. I rode there each morning on a new-bought bike, to work hard before eating my dinner sandwiches under a spreading chestnut tree. The smell of fresh leaves on the one hand, and newly flying sawdust on the other, cleared my head and made me feel part of the world again. I liked it so much I thought it was the best job I'd ever had – even though the hours were long and the wages rotten.

One day I saw an elderly man walking through the wood, followed by a little boy who ran in and out of the bushes whacking flowers with his stick. The kid was about four, dressed in a cowboy suit and hat, the other hand firing off his six-shooter that made midget sharp cracks splitting like invisible twigs between the trees. He was pink-faced with grey eyes, the terror of cats and birds, a pest for the ice-cream man, the sort of kid half stunned by an avalanche of toys at Christmas, spoiled beyond recall by people with money. You could see it in his face.

I got a goz at the man, had to stare a bit before I saw it was Doris's father, the scrap merchant who'd not so long back been the menace of the street in his overdriven car. He was grey and wax in the face, well wrapped in topcoat and hat and scarf and treading carefully along the woodpath. 'Come on,' he said to the kid. 'Come on, Tony, or you'll get lost.'

I watched him run towards the old man, take his hand and say: 'Are we going home now, grandad?' I had an impulse, which makes me blush to remember it, and that was to go up to Doris's ragman father and say – 'what I've already said in most of this story, to say that in a way he was my father as well, to say: 'Hey up, dad. You don't know much, do you?' But I didn't, because I couldn't, leaned against a tree, feeling as if I'd done a week's work without stop, feeling a hundred years older than that old man who was walking off with my kid.

My last real sight of Doris was of her inside the shoe shop trying on shoes, and after that, when I switched off the light because I sensed danger, we both went into the dark, and never came out. But there's another and final picture of her that haunts me like a vision in my waking dreams. I see her coming down the street, all clean and golden-haired on that shining horse, riding it slowly towards our house to call on me, as she did for a long time. And she was known to men standing by the bookies as Lady Luck.

That's a long while ago, and I even see Doris's kid, a big lad now, running home from school. I can watch him without wanting to put my head in the gas oven, watch him and laugh to myself because I was happy to see him at all. He's in good hands and prospering. I'm going straight as well, working in the warehouse where they store butter and cheese. I eat like a fighting cock, and take home so much that my wife and two kids don't do bad on it either.

THE MATCH

Bristol City had played Notts County and won. Right from the kick-off Lennox had somehow known that Notts was going to lose, not through any prophetic knowledge of each home-player's performance, but because he himself, a spectator, hadn't been feeling in top form. One-track pessimism had made him godly enough to inform his mechanic friend Fred Iremonger who stood by his side: 'I knew they'd bleddy-well lose, all the time.'

Towards the end of the match, when Bristol scored their winning goal, the players could only just be seen, and the ball was a roll of mist being kicked about the field. Advertising boards above the stands, telling of pork-pies, ales, whisky, cigarettes and other delights of Saturday night, faded with the afternoon visibility.

They stood in the one-and-threes, Lennox trying to fix his eyes on the ball, to follow each one of its erratic well-kicked movements, but after ten minutes going from blurred player to player he gave it up and turned to look at the spectators massed in the rising stands that reached out in a wide arc on either side and joined dimly way out over the pitch. This proving equally futile he rubbed a clenched hand into his weak eyes and squeezed them tight, as if pain would give them more strength. Useless. All it produced was a mass of grey squares dancing before his open lids, so that when they cleared his sight was no better than before. Such an affliction made him appear more phlegmatic at a football match than Fred and most of the others round about, who spun rattles, waved hats and scarves, opened their throats wide to each fresh vacillation in the game.

During his temporary blindness the Notts' forwards were pecking and weaving around the Bristol goal and a bright slam from one of them gave rise to a false alarm, an indecisive rolling of cheers roofed in by a grey heavy sky. 'What's up?' Lennox asked Fred. 'Who scored? Anybody?'

Fred was a young man, recently married, done up in his Saturday afternoon best of sports coat, gaberdine trousers and rain-mac, dark hair sleeked back with oil. 'Not in a month of Sundays,' he laughed, 'but they had a bleddy good try, I'll tell you that.'

By the time Lennox had focused his eyes once more on the players the battle had moved to Notts' goal and Bristol were about to score. He saw a player running down the field, hearing in his imagination the thud of boots on damp introdden turf. A knot of adversaries dribbled out in a line and straggled behind him at a trot. Suddenly the man with the ball spurted forward, was seen to be clear of everyone as if, in a second of time that hadn't existed to any spectator or other player, he'd been catapulted into a hallowed untouchable area before the goal posts. Lennox's heart stopped beating. He peered between two oaken unmovable shoulders that, he thought with anger, had swayed in front purposely to stop him seeing. The renegade centre-forward from the opposing side was seen, like a puppet worked by someone above the low clouds, to bring his leg back, lunge out heavily with his booted foot. 'No,' Lennox had time to say. 'Get on to him you dozy sods. Don't let him get it in.'

From being an animal pacing within the prescribed area of his defended posts, the goalkeeper turned into a leaping ape, arms and legs outstretched, then became a mere stick that swung into a curve – and missed the ball as it sped to one side and lost itself in folds of net behind him.

The lull in the general noise seemed like silence for the mass of people packed about the field. Everyone had settled it in his mind that the match, as bad as it was, would be a draw, but now it was clear that Notts, the home team, had lost. A great roar of disappointment and joy, from the thirty thousand spectators who hadn't realized that the star of Bristol City was so close, or who had expected a miracle from their own stars at the last moment, ran up the packed embankments, overflowing into streets outside where groups of people, startled at the sudden noise of an erupting mob, speculated as to which team had scored.

Fred was laughing wildly, jumping up and down, bellowing something between a cheer and a shout of hilarious anger, as if out to get his money's worth on the principle that an adverse goal was better than no goal at all. 'Would you believe it?' he called at Lennox. 'Would you believe it? Ninety-five thousand quid gone up like Scotch mist!'

Hardly knowing what he was doing Lennox pulled out a cigarette, lit it. 'It's no good,' he cursed, 'they've lost. They should have walked away with the game' – adding under his breath that he must get some glasses in order to see things better. His sight was now so bad that the line of each eye crossed and converged some distance in front of him. At the cinema he was forced down to the front row, and he was never the first to recognize a pal on the street. And it spelt ruination for any football match. He could remember being able to pinpoint each player's face, and distinguish every spectator around the field, yet he still persuaded himself that he had no need of glasses and that somehow his sight would begin to improve. A more barbed occurrence connected with such eyes was that people were beginning to call him Cock-eye. At the garage where he worked the men sat down to tea-break the other day, and because he wasn't in the room one of them said: 'Where's owd Cock-eye? 'Is tea'll get cold.'

'What hard lines,' Fred shouted, as if no one yet knew about the goal. 'Would you believe it?' The cheering and booing were beginning to die down.

'That goalie's a bloody fool,' Lennox swore, cap pulled low over his forehead. 'He couldn't even catch a bleeding cold.'

'It was dead lucky,' Fred put in reluctantly, 'they deserved it, I suppose' – simmering down now, the full force of the tragedy seeping through even to his newly wedded body and soul. 'Christ, I should have stayed at home with my missis. I'd a bin warm there, I know that much. I might even have cut myself a chunk of hearthrug pie if I'd have asked her right!'

The laugh and wink were intended for Lennox, who was still in the backwater of his personal defeat. 'I suppose that's all you think on these days,' he said wryly.

''Appen I do, but I don't get all that much of it, I can tell you.' It was obvious though that he got enough to keep him in good spirits at a cold and disappointing football match.

'Well,' Lennox pronounced, 'all that'll alter in a bit. You can bet on that.'

'Not if I know it,' Fred said with a broad smile. 'And I reckon it's better after a bad match than if I didn't come to one.'

'You never said a truer word about bad,' Lennox said. He bit his lips with anger. 'Bloody team. They'd even lose at blow football.' A woman behind, swathed in a thick woollen scarf coloured white and black like the Notts players, who had been screaming herself hoarse in support of the home team all the afternoon was almost in tears at the adverse goal. 'Foul! Foul! Get the dirty lot off the field. Send 'em back to Bristol where they came from. Foul! Foul I tell yer.'

People all around were stamping feet dead from the cold, having for more than an hour staved off its encroachment into their limbs by the hope of at least one home-team win before Christmas. Lennox could hardly feel his, hadn't the will to help them back to life, especially in face of an added force to the bitter wind, and a goal that had been given away so easily. Movement on the pitch was now desultory, for there were only ten minutes of play left to go. The two teams knotted up towards one goal, then spread out around an invisible ball, and moved down the field again, back to the other with no decisive result. It seemed that both teams had accepted the present score to be the final state of the game, as though all effort had deserted their limbs and lungs.

'They're done for,' Lennox observed to Fred. People began leaving the ground, making a way between those who were determined to see the game out to its bitter end. Right up to the dull warbling blast of the final whistle the hard core of optimists hoped for a miraculous revival in the worn-out players.

'I'm ready when yo' are,' Fred said.

'Suits me.' He threw his cigarette-end to the floor and, with a grimace of disappointment and disgust, made his way up the steps. At the highest point he turned a last glance over the field, saw two players running and the rest standing around in deepening mist – nothing doing – so went on down towards the barriers. When they were on the road a great cheer rose behind, as a whistle blew the signal for a mass rush to follow.

Lamps were already lit along the road, and bus queues grew quickly in semi-darkness. Fastening up his mac Lennox hurried across the road. Fred lagged behind, dodged a trolley-bus that sloped up to the pavement edge like a man-eating monster and carried off a crowd of people to the city-centre with blue lights flickering from overhead wires. 'Well,' Lennox said when they came close, 'after that little lot I only hope the wife's got summat nice for my tea.'

'I can think of more than that to hope for,' Fred said. 'I'm not one to grumble about my grub.'

''Course,' Lennox sneered, 'you're living on love. If you had Kit-E-Kat shoved in front of you you'd say it was a good dinner.' They turned off by the recruiting centre into the heart of the Meadows, an ageing suburb of black houses and small factories. 'That's what yo' think,' Fred retorted, slightly offended yet too full of hope to really mind. 'I'm just not one to grumble a lot about my snap, that's all.'

'It wouldn't be any good if you was,' Lennox rejoined, 'but

the grub's rotten these days, that's the trouble. Either frozen, or in tins. Nowt natural. The bread's enough to choke yer.' And so was the fog: weighed down by frost it lingered and thickened, causing Fred to pull up his rain-mac collar. A man who came level with th em on the same side called out derisively: 'Did you ever see such a game?'

'Never in all my born days,' Fred replied.

'It's always the same though,' Lennox was glad to comment, 'the best players are never on the field. I don't know what they pay 'em for.'

The man laughed at this sound logic. 'They'll 'appen get 'em on nex' wik. That'll show 'em.'

'Let's hope so,' Lennox called out as the man was lost in the fog. 'It ain't a bad team,' he added to Fred. But that wasn't what he was thinking. He remembered how he had been up before the gaffer yesterday at the garage for clouting the mash-lad who had called him Cock-eye in front of the office-girl, and the manager said that if it happened again he would get his cards. And now he wasn't sure that he wouldn't ask for them anyway. He'd never lack a job, he told himself, knowing his own worth and the sureness of his instinct when dissecting piston from cylinder, camshaft and connecting-rod and searching among a thousand-and-one possible faults before setting an engine bursting once more with life. A small boy called from the doorway of a house: 'What's the score, mate?'

'They lost, two-one,' he said curtly, and heard a loud clear-sounding doorslam as the boy ran in with the news. He walked with hands in pockets, and a cigarette at the corner of his mouth so that ash occasionally fell on to his mac. The smell of fish-and-chips came from a well-lit shop, making him feel hungry.

'No pictures for me tonight,' Fred was saying. 'I know the best place in weather like this.' The Meadows were hollow with the clatter of boots behind them, the muttering of voices hot in discussion about the lost match. Groups gathered at each corner, arguing and teasing any girl that passed, lighted gas-lamps a weakening ally in the fog. Lennox turned into an entry, where the cold damp smell of backyards mingled with that of dustbins. They pushed open gates to their separate houses.

'So long. See you tomorrow at the pub maybe.'

'Not tomorrow,' Fred answered, already at his back door. 'I'll have a job on mending my bike. I'm going to gi' it a coat of enamel and fix in some new brake blocks. I nearly got flattened by a bus the other day when they didn't work.'

The gate-latch clattered. 'All right then,' Lennox said, 'see you soon' – opening the back door and going into his house.

He walked through the small living-room without speaking, took off his mac in the parlour. 'You should mek a fire in there,' he said, coming out. 'It smells musty. No wonder the clo'es go to pieces inside six months.' His wife sat by the fire knitting from two balls of electric-blue wool in her lap. She was forty, the same age as Lennox, but gone to a plainness and discontented fat, while he had stayed thin and wiry from the same reason. Three children, the eldest a girl of fourteen, were at the table finishing tea.

Mrs Lennox went on knitting. 'I was going to make one today but I didn't have time.'

'Iris can mek one,' Lennox said, sitting down at the table.

The girl looked up. 'I haven't finished my tea yet, our dad.' The wheedling tone of her voice made him angry. 'Finish it later,' he said with a threatening look. 'The fire needs making now, so come on, look sharp and get some coal from the cellar.'

She didn't move, sat there with the obstinacy of the young spoiled by a mother. Lennox stood up. 'Don't let me have to tell you again.' Tears came into her eyes. 'Go on,' he shouted. 'Do as you're told.' He ignored his wife's plea to stop picking on her and lifted his hand to settle her with a blow.

'All right, I'm going. Look' – she got up and went to the cellar door. So he sat down again, his eyes roaming over the well-set table before him, holding his hands tightly clenched beneath the cloth. 'What's for tea, then?'

His wife looked up again from her knitting. 'There's two kippers in the oven.'

He did not move, sat morosely fingering a knife and fork,

'Well?' he demanded. 'Do I have to wait all night for a bit o' summat t'eat?'

Quietly she took a plate from the oven and put it before him. Two brown kippers lay steaming across it. 'One of these days,' he said, pulling a long strip of white flesh from the bone, 'we'll have a change.'

'That's the best I can do,' she said, her deliberate patience no way to stop his grumbling – though she didn't know what else would. And the fact that he detected it made things worse.

'I'm sure it is,' he retorted. The coal bucket clattered from the parlour where the girl was making a fire. Slowly, he picked his kippers to pieces without eating any. The other two children sat on the sofa watching him, not daring to talk. On one side of his plate he laid bones; on the other, flesh. When the cat rubbed against his leg he dropped pieces of fish for it on to the lino, and when he considered that it had eaten enough he kicked it away with such force that its head knocked against the sideboard. It leapt on to a chair and began to lick itself, looking at him with green surprised eyes.

He gave one of the boys sixpence to fetch a *Football Guardian*. 'And be quick about it,' he called after him. He pushed his plate away, and nodded towards the mauled kippers. 'I don't want this. You'd better send somebody out for some pastries. And mash some fresh tea,' he added as an afterthought, 'that pot's stewed.'

He had gone too far. Why did he make Saturday afternoon such hell on earth? Anger throbbed violently in her temples. Through the furious beating of her heart she cried out: 'If you want some pastries you'll fetch 'em yourself. And you'll mash your own tea as well.'

'When a man goes to wok all week he wants some tea,' he said, glaring at her. Nodding at the boy: 'Send him out for some cakes.'

The boy had already stood up. 'Don't go. Sit down,' she said to him. 'Get 'em yourself,' she retorted to her husband. 'The tea I've already put on the table's good enough for anybody. There's nowt wrong wi' it at all, and then you carry on like this. I suppose they lost at the match, because I can't think of any other reason why you should have such a long face.'

He was shocked by such a sustained tirade, stood up to subdue her. 'You what?' he shouted. 'What do you think you're on wi'?'

Her face turned a deep pink. 'You heard,' she called back. 'A few home truths might do you a bit of good.'

He picked up the plate of fish and, with exaggerated deliberation, threw it to the floor. 'There,' he roared. 'That's what you can do with your bleeding tea.'

'You're a lunatic,' she screamed. 'You're mental.'

He hit her once, twice, three times across the head, and knocked her to the ground. The little boy wailed, and his sister came running in from the parlour. . . .

Fred and his young wife in the house next door heard a commotion through the thin walls. They caught the cadence of voices, and shifting chairs, but didn't really think anything amiss until the shriller climax was reached. 'Would you believe it?' Ruby said, slipping off Fred's knee and straightening her skirt. 'Just because Notts have lost again. I'm glad yo' aren't like that.'

Ruby was nineteen, plump like a pear not round like a pudding, already pregnant though they'd only been married a month. Fred held her back by the waist. 'I'm not so daft as to let owt like that bother me.'

She wrenched herself free. 'It's a good job you're not; because if you was I'd bosh you one.'

Fred sat by the fire with a bemused, Cheshire-cat grin on his face while Ruby was in the scullery getting them something to eat. The noise in the next house had died down. After a slamming of doors and much walking to and fro outside, Lennox's wife had taken the children, and left him for the last time.

THE FIDDLE

On the banks of the sinewy River Leen, where it flowed through Radford, stood a group of cottages called Harrison's Row. There must have been six to eight of them, all in a ruinous condition, but lived in nevertheless.

They had been put up for stockingers during the Industrial Revolution a hundred years before, so that by now the usual small red English housebricks had become weatherstained and, in some places, almost black.

Harrison's Row had a character all of its own, both because of its situation, and the people who lived there. Each house had a space of pebbly soil rising in front, and a strip of richer garden sloping away from the kitchen door down to the diminutive River Leen at the back. The front gardens had almost merged into one piece of common ground, while those behind had in most cases retained their separate plots.

As for the name of the isolated row of cottages, nobody knew who Harrison had been, and no one was ever curious about it. Neither did they know where the Leen came from, though some had a general idea as to where it finished up.

A rent man walked down cobblestoned Leen Place every week to collect what money he could. This wasn't much, even at the best of times which, in the 'thirties', were not too good –

though no one in their conversation was able to hark back to times when they had been any better.

From the slight rise on which the houses stood, the back doors and windows looked across the stream into green fields, out towards the towers and pinnacles of Wollaton Hall in one direction, and the woods of Aspley Manor in the other.

After a warm summer without much rain the children were able to wade to the fields on the other side. Sometimes they could almost paddle. But after a three-day downpour when the air was still heavy with undropped water, and coloured a menacing gun-metal blue, it was best not to go anywhere near the river, for one false slip and you would get sucked in, and be dragged by the powerful current along to the Trent some miles away. In that case there was no telling where you'd end up. The water seemed to flow into the River Amazon itself, indicated by the fact that Frankie Buller swore blind how one day he had seen a crocodile snapping left and right down-stream with a newborn baby in its mouth. You had to be careful – and that was a fact. During the persistent rain of one autumn water came up over the gardens and almost in at the back doors.

Harrison's Row was a cut-off place in that not many people knew about it unless they were familiar with the district. You went to it along St Peter's Street, and down Leen Place. But it was delightful for the kids who lived there because out of the back gardens they could go straight into the stream of the Leen. In summer an old tin hip bath would come from one of the houses. Using it for a boat, and stripped to their white skins, the children were happy while sun and weather lasted.

The youths and older kids would eschew this fun and set out in a gang, going far beyond, to a bend of the canal near Wollaton Pit where the water was warm – almost hot – due to some outlet from the mine itself. This place was known as ''otties', and they'd stay all day with a bottle of lemonade and a piece of bread, coming back late in the evening looking pink and tired as if out of a prolonged dipping in the ritual bath.

But a swim in 'otties was only for the older ones, because a boy of four had once been drowned there.

Harrison's Row was the last of Nottingham where it met the countryside. Its houses were at the very edge of the city, in the days before those numerous housing estates had been built beyond. The line of dwellings called Harrison's Row made a sort of outpost bastion before the country began.

Yet the houses in the city didn't immediately start behind, due to gardens and a piece of wasteground, which gave to Harrison's Row a feeling of isolation. It stood somewhat on its own, as if the city intended one day to leapfrog over it and obliterate the country beyond.

On the other hand, any foreign army attacking from the west, over the green fields that glistened in front, would first have to flatten Harrison's Row before getting into the innumerable streets of houses behind.

Across the Leen, horses were sometimes to be seen in the fields and, in other fields beyond, the noise of combine harvesters could be heard at work in the summer. Children living there, and adults as well, had the advantage of both town and country. On a fine evening late in August one of the unemployed husbands might be seen looking across at the noise of some machinery working in a field, his cap on but wearing no shirt, as if wondering why he was here and not over there, and why in fact he had ever left those same fields in times gone by to be forced into this bit of a suburb where he now had neither work nor purpose in life. He was not bitter, and not much puzzled perhaps, yet he couldn't help being envious of those still out there in the sunshine.

In my visions of leaving Nottingham for good – and they were frequent in those days – I never reckoned on doing so by the high road or railway. Instead I saw myself wading or swimming the Leen from Harrison's Row, and setting off west once I was on the other side.

A tale remembered with a laugh at that time told about how young Ted Griffin, who had just started work, saw two policemen one day walking down Leen Place towards Harrison's Row. Convinced they had to come to arrest him for meter-breaking, he ran through the house and garden, went over the fence, jumped into the Leen – happily not much swollen – waded across to the field, then four-legged it over the railway, and made his way to Robins Wood a mile or so beyond. A perfect escape route. He stayed two days in hiding, and then crept home at night, famished and soaked, only to find that the police had not come for him, but to question Blonk next door, who was suspected of poaching. When they did get Ted Griffin he was pulled out of bed one morning even before he'd had time to open his eyes and think about a spectacular escape across the Leen.

Jeff Bignal was a young unmarried man of twenty-four. His father had been killed in the Great War, and he lived with his mother at Number Six Harrison's Row, and worked down nearby Radford Pit. He was short in height, and plump, his white skin scarred back and front with livid blue patches where he had been knocked with coal at the mine face. When he went out on Saturday night he brilliantined his hair.

After tea in summer while it was still light and warm he would sit in his back garden playing the fiddle, and when he did everybody else came out to listen. Or they opened the doors and windows so that the sound of his music drifted in, while the woman stayed at the sink or wash-copper, or the man at his odd jobs. Anyone with a wireless would turn it down or off.

Even tall dark sallow-faced elderly Mrs Deaffy (a kid sneaked into her kitchen one day and thieved her last penny-packet of cocoa and she went crying to tell Mrs Atkin who, when her youngest came in, hit him so hard with her elbow that one of his teeth shot out and the blood washed away most of the cocoa-stains around his mouth) – old Mrs Deaffy stood by her back door as if she weren't stone deaf any more and could follow each note of Jeffrey Bignal's exquisite violin. She smiled at seeing everyone occupied, fixed or entranced, and therefore no torment to herself, which was music enough to her whether she could hear it or not.

And Blonk, in the secretive dimness of the kitchen, went on mending his poaching nets before setting out with Arthur Bede next door on that night's expedition to Gunthorpe by the banks of the Trent, where the green escarpment between there and Kneeton was riddled with warrens and where, so it was said, if you stood sufficiently still the rabbits ran over your feet, and it was only necessary to make a quick grab to get one.

Jeff sat on a chair, oblivious to everybody, fed up with his day's work at the pit and only wanting to lose himself in his own music. The kids stopped splashing and shouting in the water, because if they didn't they might get hauled in and clouted with just the right amount of viciousness to suit the crime and the occasion. It had happened before, though Jeff had always been too far off to notice.

His face was long, yet generally cheerful – contrary to what one would expect – a smile settling on it whenever he met and passed anybody on the street, or on his way to the group of shared lavatories at the end of the Row. But his face was almost down and lost to the world as he sat on his chair and brought forth his first sweet notes of a summer's evening.

It was said that a neighbour in the last place they had lived had taught him to play like that. Others maintained it was an uncle who had shown him how. But nobody knew for sure because when someone asked directly he said that if he had any gift at all it must have come from God above. It was known that on some Sundays of the year, if the sun was out, he went to the Methodist chapel on St Peter's Street.

He could play anything from 'Greensleeves' to 'Mademoiselle from Armentières'. He could do a beautiful heart-pulling version of Handel's *Largo*, and throw in bits from *The Messiah* as well. He would go from one piece to another with no rhyme or reason, from ridiculousness to sublimity, with almost shocking abruptness, but as the hour or so went by it all appeared easy and natural, part of a long piece coming from Jeff Bignal's fiddle while the ball of the sun went down behind his back.

To a child it seemed as if the songs lived in the hard collier's muscle at the top of his energetic arm, and that they queued one by one to get out. Once free, they rushed along his flesh from which the shirtsleeves had been rolled up, and split into his fingertips, where they were played out with ease into the warm evening air.

The grass in the fields across the stream was livid and lush, almost blue, and a piebald horse stood with bent head, eating oats out of a large old pram whose wheels had long since gone. The breeze wafted across from places farther out, from Robins Wood and the Cherry Orchard, Wollaton Roughs and Bramcote Hills and even, on a day that was not too hot, from the tops of the Pennines in Derbyshire.

Jeff played for himself, for the breeze against his arm, for the soft hiss of the flowing Leen at the end of the garden, and maybe also for the horse in the field, which took no notice of anything and which, having grown tired of its oats in the pram, bent its head over the actual grass and began to roam in search of succulent pastures.

In the middle of the winter Jeff's fiddling was forgotten. He went into the coal mine before it was light, and came up only after it had got dark. Walking down Leen Place, he complained to Blonk that it was hard on a man not to see daylight for weeks at a time.

'That's why I wain't go anywhere near the bleddy pit,' Blonk said vehemently, though he had worked there from time to time, and would do so again when harried by his wife and children. 'You'd do better to come out on a bit o' poaching with me and Arthur,' he suggested.

It was virtually true that Jeff saw no daylight, because even on Sunday he stayed in bed most of the day, and if it happened to be dull there was little enough sky to be seen through his front bedroom window, which looked away from the Leen and up the hill.

The upshot of his complaint was that he would do anything to change such a situation. A man was less than an animal for putting up with it.

'I'd do anything,' he repeated to his mother over his tea in the single room downstairs.

'But what, though?' she asked. 'What can you do, Jeff?'

'Well, how do I know?' he almost snapped at her. 'But I'll do summat, you can be sure of that.'

He didn't do anything till the weather got better and life turned a bit sweeter. Maybe this improvement finally got him going, because it's hard to help yourself towards better things when you're too far down in the dumps.

On a fine blowy day with both sun and cloud in the sky Jeff went out in the morning, walking up Leen Place with his fiddle under his arm. The case had been wiped and polished.

In the afternoon he came back without it.

'Where's your fiddle?' Ma Jones asked.

He put an awkward smile on to his pale face, and told her: 'I sold it.'

'Well I never! How much for?'

He was too shocked at her brazen question not to tell the truth: 'Four quid.'

'That ain't much.'

'It'll be enough,' he said roughly.

'Enough for what, Jeff?'

He didn't say, but the fact that he had sold his fiddle for four quid rattled up and down the line of cottages till everybody knew of it. Others swore he'd got ten pounds for it, because something that made such music must be worth more than a paltry four, and in any case Jeff would never say how much he'd really got for it, for fear that someone would go in and rob him.

They wondered why he'd done it, but had to wait for the answer, as one usually does. But there was nothing secretive about Jeff Bignal, and if he'd sold his music for a mess of pottage he saw no point in not letting them know why. They'd find out sooner or later, anyway.

All he'd had to do was make up his mind, and he'd done that lying on his side at the pit face while ripping coal out with his pick and shovel. Decisions made like that can't be undone, he knew. He'd brooded on it all winter, till the fact of having settled it seemed to have altered the permanent expression of his face, and given it a new look which caused people to wonder whether he would ever be able to play the fiddle again anyway – at least with his old spirit and dash.

With the four quid he paid the first week's rent on a butcher's shop on Denman Street, and bought a knife, a chopper, and a bit of sharpening stone, as well as a wooden block. Maybe he had a quid or two more knocking around, though if he had it couldn't have been much, but with four quid and a slice of bluff he got enough credit from a wholesaler at the meat market downtown to stock his shop with mutton and beef, and in a couple of days he was in trade. The people of Harrison's Row were amazed at how easy it was, though nobody had ever thought of doing it themselves.

Like a serious young man of business Mr Bignal – as he was now known – parted his hair down the middle, so that he didn't look so young any more, but everyone agreed that it was better than being at Radford Pit. They'd seen how he had got fed-up with selling the sweat of his brow.

No one could say that he prospered, but they couldn't deny that he made a living. And he didn't have to suffer the fact of not seeing daylight for almost the whole of the winter.

Six months after opening the shop he got married. The reception was held at the chapel on St Peter's Street, which seemed to be a sort of halfway house between Harrison's Row on the banks of the Leen and the butcher's shop on Denman Street farther up.

Everybody from Harrison's Row was invited for a drink and something to eat; but he knew them too well to let any have either chops or chitterlings (or even black puddings) on tick when they came into his shop.

The people of Harrison's Row missed the sound of his fiddle on long summer evenings, though the children could splash and shout with their tin bath-tub undisturbed, floundering through shallows and scrambling up to grass on the other bank, and wondering what place they'd reach if they walked without stopping till it got dark.

Two years later the Second World War began, and not long afterwards meat as well as nearly everything else was put on the ration. Apart from which, Jeff was only twenty-six, so got called up into the army. He never had much chance to make a proper start in life, though people said that he came out all right in the end.

The houses of Harrison's Row were condemned as unfit to live in, and a bus depot stands on the site.

The packed mass of houses on the hill behind – forty years after Jeff Bignal sold his violin – is also vanishing, and high rise hencoops (as the people call them) are put in their place. The demolition crew knock down ten houses a day – though the foreman told me there was still work for another two years.

Some of the houses would easily have lasted a few more decades, for the bricks were perfect, but as the foreman went on: 'You can't let them stand in the way of progress' – whatever that means.

The people have known each other for generations but, when they are moved to their new estates and blocks of flats, they will know each other for generations more, because as I listen to them talking, they speak a language which, in spite of everything and everyone, never alters.

SCENES FROM THE LIFE OF MARGARET

The budgerigar greeted her as she came in and laid her basket down. The kids ate at school but she needed a meal herself, so took off her coat and lit the gas. Rain swept over fences and clattered against the window as if spring would never cease, she thought, hoping one day for sunshine.

A year ago the bird had got out of his cage and flown into the fire, and though Michael was there to dart in a hand and pull him free, the smell of singed feathers and burned skin was everywhere, and the poor bird lay for days doctored on warm milk and coddled in clean handkerchiefs. Bit by bit it came to life, its warm breast throbbing with song after song, and half-speech imitations that she and the kids had taught him before the accident.

His feathers had grown back in places, vivid emerald and blue, with a patch of white over the left eye. She'd never expected it to live, and found it surprising what fire and grief and God knew what else such a creature could survive. It didn't seem much to do with its own will whether it got back to life or not, but something else which neither of them knew about.

Such reminiscing reminded her of her father's death the year before, and she wondered whether it had been any worse to him than the fire the bird flew into. She'd been afraid to walk into the other ground-floor room and see him, though he was beyond all help and wouldn't have known her. She was too proud of him to see him die, and didn't want to witness what he might in after-life (if there was such a thing, but you never knew) feel ashamed that she had seen.

She mashed some tea, then ate bread and cheese. It was strange how lonely you could be with three strong kids, for they went out hand in hand after breakfast, and didn't roar in again till tea-time. The budgerigar woke from its perch of sleep near the window and sent a trill of stone-chipping notes through its wire cage.

She put in a hand and held the warm soft-feathered body, now singing out its second life as if nothing terrible had ever happened to it. Michael, who was eight at the time, willed it to get through the tunnel of that suffering, while she had given it up. Only the children's tears had brought her faith that it might choose to live after all.

When she opened the cage it darted like a blue pebble over the settee and settled near the front window. For a while they hadn't let it out when the fire was lit. Not that it would have gone there anyway, but it had become too precious for such rash chances. Nowadays it was safer because the chimney was closed, and a less harmful mock-electric fire fitted in the grate.

Carefully closing the door she walked down the path to meet the baker's van. The grey house-roofs were drying, and the freshening air reminded her how some neighbours even grumbled because the estate wasn't so black and cosy as the slum they'd not long left.

One of the eight kids who lived across the road came to buy two loaves. The baker held one hand out to get the money, and the other with the bread, but the child didn't have money to give so he put the bread back.

'I suppose his dad sent him out to try it on,' Margaret laughed, collecting her own loaves.

When he was ready to drive off the kid came again, this time with coins, so that he got the bread. Then three other kids ran from the same house to buy cakes with equally ready cash.

'You'd be surprised at some of the antics people get up to,' the roundsman said, 'just to save a couple o'bob.'

Being on National Assistance and her husband's allowance, money was short for her as well, but they still weren't as bad off as in the old days because she had a council house for one thing, and for another the rest of the family helped her along. Her mother worked at a food warehouse and brought a load of purloined groceries up on the bus every weekend. Her sister was in a shoe factory, so they never had wet feet. Her brother served at a clothing shop and rigged them out when he could. Another was a radio mechanic, so she had a reject telly in the living room. A cousin who helped in a butcher's shop did his best not to forget her.

Now and then she could swap shoes and food and clothes with somebody in the next avenue who worked at a toy depot, or she'd barter with the woman next door who packed up pots and pans for a mail order firm. Her aunt was an overlooker at a tobacco factory and Margaret, not smoking herself, was able to give pilfered fags to a man who dug her garden and occasionally whitewashed the kitchen. What was life worth if you couldn't help each other? The bird flew back to the top of its cage and whistled its agreement from there.

A radio voice talked about a leper colony in Africa, so she switched it to light music. A blue stream of soap powder spun into boiling water and she stirred at the bubbles with a huge wooden spoon that Edie across the way had brought her as a present from Majorca: 'You can use it to bash the kids with when they chelp you,' she laughed.

'Not mine, duck,' Margaret said, standing by the hole in the fence that connected the two houses. 'They do as I tell 'em without that. My kids have to be good, not having any dad. Sometimes I tell myself he don't know the joy he's missing.'

Fifty bright round faces shifted among the bubbles, rainbows breaking in the steam. 'They'll see you right,' Edie said, 'when they go to work. You'll have your joy of 'em yet.'

'They'll get married then, duck,' Margaret prophesied

soberly. 'I'll find another man, maybe, when I've got 'em off my hands.'

'I shouldn't wait too long if I was you,' Edie said. 'You're still young. Get a bit of it back up you before you're too old to feel it.'

It made Margaret laugh just to look at her sallow and serious face with its glasses and long false teeth to match, every second waiting for her to say something foul and funny. She didn't know how Edie's husband put up with it yet he seemed to like her well enough.

'I can do without that for a while,' Margaret told her. 'I keep myself company in bed at night, I do' – which sent Edie cackling back to her kitchen. It was good to laugh, even if it did show a bad tooth or two. The only chance she got was when they showed old silent comedies on the telly, which she'd look at all night if they was on.

She thought maybe Edie was right, because if somebody was found it wouldn't do to turn him down. Life was too short, but the trouble with men was that they're just like women, she reflected, no better and no worse. And who'd want to take anybody on who's got three kids already? It'd be a rope around his neck right enough, though she'd heard people say there were men who didn't want the bother of a woman having babies, and would rather step into a brood of kids ready-made or half grown up.

But if that was the case where did the woman come in? Maybe he treated her as one of the kids, a pat on the head now and again for good measure. It was surprising what you might end up doing for the kids' sake, if you didn't watch yourself, though if mine don't have a father it's no more than a lot of others have to put with. Still, it does touch my heart when I ask in the tally-man or window-cleaner for a cup of tea and see them jumping all over his legs.

Men aren't the be-all and end-all of my life, she thought, taking the long prop and wedging the line high, all signals hoisted. Pants, vests, stockings, and socks straightened and flapped in the uprising wind. The less you want something the more likely it is to take place, and the more you picture it, the less chance of it becoming real. What you never imagined were the bad things that hit you, and what you always thought of were the good things that never did. She had got over her husband leaving her. She had been too shattered and upset by it not to survive.

The sallow catkins were full of yellow dust. It was good to go up the Grove for an afternoon walk, smell the spring water of the Trent flooding by down the steep bank. There was nothing else to do but laugh, except cry, she smiled.

With three kids to be fed and looked after there'd been no time to brood herself into the grave or Mapperly Asylum. There was some justice in the world, though you only thought so when it kicked you in the chops, or hoped so when it was about to. In his rough and cunning fashion he'd made certain she'd never be able to take up with anyone else, though maybe in one sense it was generous of him to leave her the kids, otherwise she might not have got over it.

He and his 'fancy woman' had prospered after opening a corner shop to sell new and second-hand bicycles. He bought old ones at scrap prices and tarted them up in his clever way, while *she* looked after the book-keeping and window-dressing. Margaret met his mother one day in Slab Square, and was told all about it.

It didn't even hurt any more to brood on it, though a man who could forget his children so absolutely must be a real blackguard. He might stop living with his wife, but if he went on loving his kids she could at least console herself that some of this contained a bit of hidden regard for her as well. He never saw them or wrote, nor sent Christmas presents, but had rubbed them out of his life. She sat on a broken elm trunk to rest, wondering how she of all people had ever met such a man.

She thought of the man who courted her before him, as if that might give some clue to it. The war had been on for a long time, though everyone knew it was coming towards its end. Margaret was sixteen, and after two years working in a food factory she joined the Women's Land Army so as to get away from home and 'see life'. All she saw were bulls' heads and pigs' arses, glowering woods and wet fields, and a poky room in a mildewed and leaking cottage which she shared with six other girls, a muddy and sweating life which paid thirty bob a week and a rough sort of keep.

She began to feel like a slave-labouring appendage to the animals, till one of the farmer's men taught her to drive a tractor. She learned quickly and got a licence, but because things were now so much better she was able to look back on how bad they had been, and in a fit of anger that she should have been so much put upon, packed her things one Saturday and walked to the village bus stop. Reaching Nottingham in two hours, she left her case at home and went down Slab Square to see which of her girl friends were in any of the pubs.

After the cold black-out night, bruised by huddled gangs of soldiers, the Eight Bells was like a secret cave cut into the hillside of the street-cliff.

She bought a shandy and, every seat being taken, stood near the bar. An American soldier put his hand on the arm of a girl near by, who shrugged it away:

'Get your hands off me, Yank!'

'Sorry, sister.'

'I'm not your sister.'

'All right, baby.'

'I'm not your bloody baby, either. If you don't lay off I'll part your hair with this pint jar.'

Margaret knew the voice, and saw the face. Smoke and beer-smells, breath and pungent boot-dust exhilarated her. The backs and faces set colourfully along each line of mirrors after two years in the rural dullness heightened the flush in her face and made her stretched limbs tingle.

She laughed at the raucous rat-crack of the protesting voice, knowing it to come from one of her cousins. 'That's right,' she called over, 'You tell him, Eileen.'

The snow-white hair of a suicide-blonde flashed around: 'Hey up, Margaret!'

'I could tell you a mile off,' she said.

'What are yo' doin' 'ere? Up to no good, like me?'

She wished she hadn't spoken, for Eileen's reputation, even in her own family, was almost as low as you could get, her back-chat to the American being only another form of come-on, so that she smiled at him before edging over to Margaret: 'I had a nobble on an hour ago,' she said, apologising for her lack of success so far, 'but the poor bogger went out to be sick and I ain't seen 'im since. When did you get back from the cow sheds?'

'An hour ago.'

'I'd pack it in, if I was yo''.

'I did do.'

'About time.' Eileen's thin face stood out from the robust puffiness of the soldiers around. 'I don't blame you. Come and do a stint at the gun factory. You'll never look back. Too much going on up front!'

Margaret's laugh attracted someone she could not see during her talk about old times with Eileen. He told her afterwards how that vital and homely sound had gone right into his heart at a time when he met so much falsity night after night – whether he stayed in camp or not, which he usually did in order to write long letters to his parents back home.

And looking towards her laugh he'd seen someone who hadn't been there before, noting her long dark hair and the pink skin of her plump face. Every young girl was pretty, he admitted, especially if you'd parachuted in with the first wave of the invasion and had the total support of your friends scythed away in a few insane minutes, but *her* face was different, had a refined trust that, after her laugh, and while she was listening to her blonde friend, had a kind of profound and gentle helplessness. It was as if she'd come into the pub, he said, to wait for him as he had been waiting for her ever since getting to England.

He pushed his fresh yet strangely troubled face between Margaret and her cousin, buying a round for them just before closing time. She could not, even now, gainsay the fact that she was the reason for the drinks. Jimmy Chadburn seemed honest and fair of feature, except for the knife-scar caught in some tussle with a German during the Normandy landings which had closed the left side of his face up a bit. But the right and best side was turned to her, and his inside soul seemed generous enough.

He treated her courteously, and always with a smile, dusted the chair before she sat down, opened the door and prevented her from being jostled as they went out. His teeth were so clean when he smiled that she might have known she couldn't trust him. And it was difficult to tell whether he was lonely or not – as one ought to be able to do with Americans who had so much money.

Large white single clouds passed swiftly through the sky, crossing the broad avenue of trees. She had sat down too long and the damp was pressing in. Tea-time would come and the kids would be home. There was no way or wish to stop the wheel turning day after day and week after week. But she dwelt a little longer on Jimmy Chadburn. He was her first love, yet she'd heard it said that whenever you start thinking of your first love you are about to meet somebody else. Well, she could wait, especially when it was a question of having to.

She kept no mementoes in life, except memory. All letters and photos were burned, and nothing of him remained. He had gone back to the wife he said he didn't have, and left her to nurse herself through the scorching deserts of betrayal and smashed love. How could anyone do such a thing to anyone else?

She supposed it was something all people had to put up with at one time or another. It was hard to think of anybody who hadn't. It was like a vaccination to stop smallpox eating you into a cancer.

The worst thing about being jilted was in the man you took up with afterwards. You acted joyfully because you thought it was all over, not knowing that this was the final bitter kick of it. She saw how true it was now, even though she kept herself free for two years, because it took that long to get over it, which seemed like no time at all when looking back.

It was good to get the ache out of her legs. She broke off a new and living bud, shredded its stickiness with a sharp fingernail, and could hardly remember where she'd met her husband, something that doesn't speak well for any man, almost proving you were never in love with him. Meeting Albert was probably the last flicker indeed of love for Jimmy Chadburn. Some people don't believe in love, which only means they'd never suffered from it. Yet if they hadn't she supposed they were lucky.

She reflected how Albert loved to make her cry, did everything to do so. It was never difficult, but he couldn't stand it when he succeeded, so jeered to make her stop. Walking down the street she slipped on a piece of rotten pavement, and he hit her, adding insult to injury in his usual way. He used to say all's fair in love and war, but she remembered that life itself was war to him, a war to get exactly what he wanted for himself. You had to be careful not to get in the way of what he wanted.

Asking herself what she'd done wrong to make him like this, it became obvious that she was only guilty of having married him – though by then it was too late. In any case he had an equal share of responsibility in having married her. No one could deny it. But to please him she'd have to go out one day and vanish, so that he wouldn't even have the bother of a funeral, though she didn't see why she should be the one to do it and make things easy for him.

After three years and three kids he left her, as she told Edie, 'without even a piece of bread between my lips'. That was the end of that, and as for mementoes, she'd burned even the memories inside herself, stamped on them whenever they threatened to come up, till they hardly ever did any more.

Roy John Callender was an exhibition diver and champion swimmer, whose name was occasionally seen in the more obscure columns of Nottingham newspapers. Though his exhibitions weren't so enthralling, nor his championships so spectacular, he was considered a man of fair showmanship and prowess in local terms, and all who had seen him dive agreed, over their sedentary drink of beer, that at thirty he was in his prime.

'When you cut into the water like a javelin,' he said to Margaret one night in the Maid of Trent, 'and go right down, you think you're dying because it don't seem possible you'll ever get up to fresh air and see daylight again. But you do. Dead right, you do. You don't want to move your arms, like they're tied up with ten balls of string, but they move by themselves and steer you level. Then they push you up, and when your head shoots out of the water you want to go up and up till you crack your noddle on the clouds.'

'Why do you do it, though?' she asked naïvely, even after this description which he had perfected over the years, and which half the people in the pub turned round to listen to.

He laughed fit to die, she thought, and told her when he could get his breath from it: 'I just like the water, I suppose!'

Several times in his career he had dived off Trent Bridge into a canvas area below. Dressed in a one-piece black costume he climbed on to the parapet and, after mock-gymnastics to loosen his limbs in the sharp summer breeze, he faced the chosen crowd with both hands clasped in the air. His stern expression, at the point of turning to begin his dive, changed to a grin of expected success.

Motorists leaned out of their car windows, and lorry drivers waved and wished him luck above the noise of their engines. The black and pink figure framed against the white sky of the distant war memorial turned a somersault above the bridge wall – then fell through the air towards the canvas area of bottle-green water.

He loved doing it, he told Margaret in the pub, because when he made that first great leap he thought he hadn't strength to do it properly, that he would smash himself against the dark stone of the bridge. But he managed it, and the feeling of dropping down so effortlessly and with such spot-on aim was the best in the world, except the sweet dreams that came after going to bed with a woman he loved – he winked.

She suspected him of piling it on a bit. But then, all men did that. He certainly looked a liar as he swaggered in and walked to the bar for his first drink of the evening. Tall and well built, he had a sharp pink face and dark hair receding in a vee back from his forehead.

He was no empty loud-mouth however, for he had done all he told her about, and spoke sincerely enough, though when Margaret questioned Edie as to whether or not she had ever heard of a champion swimmer called Johnny Callender Edie said she hadn't, but that didn't mean much because she'd never heard of anything, anyway. So Margaret let the promise of him drop, her notion being reinforced that men were bigger bragging liars when they had something to brag about than when they hadn't. It was better to expect nothing so as not to be disappointed.

One afternoon a dark green van drew to the kerb outside the front gate and Callender himself came up the path with a television set in his arms. She met him at the door, flustered and laughing. 'Did you get that from under the water on one of your dives?'

He set it on the kitchen table, loosened his white scarf and unbuttoned his dark three-quarter overcoat. 'It's for you, missis. Or can I call you Margaret?'

'If you've brought that for me, you can. Shall I mash you a cup of tea?'

'It'll tek the sweat off me.'

'Sit down, then. What sort is it?' She dropped the kettle-lid, and bent to pick it up.

'A good one, don't worry. Brand new.'

'I'll bet it is.'

'No damaged goods where I come from,' he grinned, 'except me, perhaps.'

'You don't want to say that about yourself,' she said, with such seriousness and concern for the safety of his good name that he laughed out loud.

'What's bleddy funny about it, then?' she demanded, cut to the middle. She didn't like being made fun of just because she'd thought his phrase weightier than he could ever have done. 'If that's the way it is you can take your rammel and get out.'

'You don't think I mean it when I run myself down, do you?' he said, tears almost lighting up his deep brown eyes. 'Oh dear, love, when were you born?'

Having been out of circulation for the last nine years there was no telling when she was born, she told him. 'Though it might not have been all that long after you,' she added, 'so don't think yourself so smart.'

The tea-cosy was on the pot for five minutes till it mashed into a mellow brew, but then she poured it sharply as if to get rid of him as soon as possible. The bird warbled from its cage, and he promised next time to bring a budgie because it sounded as if it wanted a mate as well – helping himself to several spoons of sugar. He takes a lot of sweetening, she thought, and maybe he needs stirring up as well, or perhaps I do, though he's not the one to do it, swimmer or not.

'Boy or girl?' he asked, looking up, smile gone.

'Male,' she said, 'and it sings like a man as well. Men allus sing better than women, especially when they want summat. All a woman need do is bide her time. Then what she gets is twice as bad, I suppose.'

He sipped his tea as if she might have put a dash of ground glass in it. 'You sound proper old-fashioned.'

'That's nowt to what I *feel*.'

'Why don't you have a cup of tea as well, duck?' he said. 'I'm feeling a bit left out.'

'I was going to,' she said, beginning to like him again.

'Thought I'd get company after what I'd brought,' he reminded her.

It looked so much better than the cronky old set her brother had palmed her off with. 'Are you leaving it?'

'On approval. Depends whether you take to it.'

'Would you like some biscuits?'

'If there's cream in 'em.'

'I can tell you've been at tea with millionaires. It's plain biscuits at this house. If I got cream biscuits they'd go in a second.'

'Kids are like that,' he said, and she wondered if he'd got any of his own.

'Are you going to plug it in for me?'

He dipped a biscuit in his tea, and held it there too long so that most of it fell off. 'If I leave it, I'll have to.'

'It looks like it, don't it?'

The scalding tea went down his throat in one long gulp. 'Let's see to it, then.' He clattered the cup back to its saucer, and they went into the living room together.

He didn't move in, which she thought he might try in his brash fashion, but came to see her once or twice a week, and slept there. He was lavish in presents for the kids, though she saw as plain as day he didn't really like them, and that his generosity didn't come natural to him. He was uneasy under the weight of the kids when in their open good nature they clambered up as if to suck him dry. When Rachel wanted a bedtime story he almost snapped at the second asking. Margaret began to suspect he was married and had kids of his own, but when she tackled him about it he told her he was divorced.

'Why did you tell me you was single, then?'

They sat in a corner of the pub on Saturday night, and in spite of the noise that encapsulated them she almost hissed her question. He looked at her openly, as if proud of what he had done. 'I thought so much of you I didn't want you to think I was secondhand.'

She felt herself blushing. 'I'm the one who's secondhand, so I don't know what you've got to worry about.'

'That's different,' he said. 'I'm the one that's in love with you. If it was the other way round I wouldn't bother so much.'

'I don't know what to think.' She was bewildered at his calculated lies because she did not know how to let on she knew he was lying. His face deepened into seriousness, as if to disarm her even more, until she began to believe in him to such an extent that she wondered whether he wasn't about to ask her to marry him. He suddenly broke this intense silence by laughing out loud and calling the waiter to bring another pint for himself and a short for her.

Her disappointment at this breakage of their closeness increased even more because she did not know which of them was the cause of it. Another opportunity might not come around for weeks, and she didn't feel sure enough of herself to get it back on her own.

His face was such as held its own with the world, so you'd do well to look out for it putting one over on you, she thought, because like all men he treated you as part of the world as well. His face was a hard one, in spite of the gloss that came on it when he wanted something, yet she felt there was a soft centre somewhere – like in the tastiest chocolates.

She prayed for this to be true, because after they'd known each other a few months it was certain beyond all truth she was pregnant.

There was nobody she could spill it to but Edie. Her instinct told her that to let him know the news would drive him away clean and clear, which she didn't want to do, for though she'd started off being wary she now liked him enough to want him with her for good, if only he'd ever grow up and set his selfish mind to it.

The last thing she expected was to bring another kid into the world, but since one was indisputably on its way and might prove impossible to stop she ought to try and get used to the idea – not doubting for a moment that he'd help her all he could, and maybe actually marry her if nothing worked.

There was no point thinking yourself into a black sweat, so she went into the kitchen and put the kettle on for coffee. If she confided her trouble to Edie she might be able to tell her how and where to get rid of it. Certainly, she knew nobody else who would. She fancied there wasn't much Edie didn't know about a thing like that, though having an abortion had never been much in Margaret's mind when she got pregnant. But this time it was different, and nobody could tell her what to do with her own life and body. Three kids were enough in one woman's life, especially now they were getting on and the worst might soon be over.

When Edie pulled the chair from under the table to sit on, and sighed as if she had all the work in the world to do in the small space of her own house, and should never have left it for a moment, it was obvious she had something to tell Margaret, who therefore thought it friendly and polite to let her get it off her chest before coming out with her own worries. In any case, she welcomed a reason to defer it as long as possible.

'How many?' she said, reaching for the bag of sugar. 'What bleddy weather, in't it?'

'Four, Meg,' said Edie. 'Enough to turn you into a fish. Have you seen owt o' that chap o' yours lately?'

'He showed his face a week ago,' said Margaret, thinking it funny that Edie should mention him when he was on the tip of her own tongue.

'Is he married?'

Margaret thought it an outlandish question, and wondered what was coming.

'I hope you don't mind me asking,' said Edie.

'That's all right, duck. He ain't as far as I know.'

'I saw him in town yesterday, as large as life, with a woman and two kids trailing out of one o' them cheap clothes shops down Hockley. I'm not sure they was his kids, though it looked like it to me. I don't want to be nosy, but I thought you might like to know. The woman looked so miserable she must a bin his wife.'

She stirred Edie's coffee and pushed it towards her, thinking yes it was his sister because he'd mentioned her a few times, till another explanation came to her and she realised she was only making excuses for him. There could be no doubt he was married, because it fitted in with his actions ever since she'd known him. 'Thanks for telling me,' she said, drinking coffee to stop her lips trembling. 'I might have known.'

'They're all the same,' Edie said. 'It don't matter that much.'

'No,' Margaret said, 'it bleddy-well don't, I suppose. It ain't that I mind about him being married. But he might have told me. I hate sly and deceitful people. I expect he was frightened I wouldn't want him if he said he was married.'

'It's no use crying over it, duck,' said Edie, trying to comfort her, and cursing herself for a big-mouth when it suddenly came to her how things stood. 'We bloody women get all the bother, and the men go scot-free.'

Margaret's face was dry and stony: 'Nobody goes scot-free in the end,' she said.

And she didn't ask Edie how to get rid of it, because she felt too much of a fool to let her know she was pregnant.

The hot and fine summer seemed to make it worse. She waited night after night, and even went to where he said he'd worked, but that was a lie too, for he wasn't there and never had been.

He didn't come for a month, so by the time she told him even her morning sickness was beginning to ease off. When he made an excuse to leave that same evening without going to bed with her, and saying he'd come back again when he'd thought what to do about it, she knew she wouldn't see him any more, but didn't want to make too much fuss in case it turned out not to be true and he came back after all. She laid the kids' things out for school and breakfast, her lips still wet from his one kiss. I shan't die, she thought, and I shan't starve, and neither will the kid I'll have.

What she would do, she thought one tea-time while seeing to the budgerigar, was wait till he next did a bit of exhibition diving at Trent Bridge, and then when he was about to jump she'd burst out of the crowd and run to him, shouting at the top of her voice that he was a rotten no good get who'd got her pregnant and then run away and left her. Yes, she would. She'd hang on to him and go down into the water and never let go till they both drowned and were out of it for good. Let them put that in the Evening Post so that his wife could read about it while waiting for him to come home after boozing with his pals or from doing another woman. But maybe he'd led his wife a worse dance than he'd led me, and I'm well off without him in spite of having another one to feed and fend for.

The bird flew around the room while she cleaned out its cage. At the sound of seed spilling into its pot it darted back and rested a moment on her hand. 'Hello, my duck,' she said, knowing she'd do nothing of the sort, and not tackle Callender at Trent Bridge, 'you got over your little accident in the fire, didn't you?' – though not sure whether *she* would this time, as tears followed the too bright smile at her eyes.

She shut the door when it began to eat.

In the cafe, an old man sitting next to her began making funny noises.

He wore a hat and scarf and overcoat, so he wasn't even poor. But he was very old, in spite of a moustache and full head of white vigorous hair. She'd never seen him before, but it seemed nobody else had either, because they weren't disturbed by the noise he was making.

It wasn't loud, and didn't frighten her. She supposed that was why other people weren't bothered. But it was funny, somehow, though she knew it wasn't funny to him because who would feel happy with a noise like that for company – especially an old man who must be pushing eighty?

It wouldn't do to interfere, whatever happened. Maybe he was warming up for a little tiddly-song to himself. Old men were like that, and harmless as long as they weren't dirty as well. But on a bus once when she was twelve an old man put his hand on her knee. There's one thing to be said for an old woman: she wouldn't do a thing like that. So she knocked it away, without causing any fuss.

But if it came back she'd shout at the top of her voice: 'Get your hands off me, you dirty old swine.' Maybe he guessed what was on her mind, since he got up and shuffled out at the next stop. Perhaps he only wanted to tell her something, or was in need of company, or he was about to say she reminded him of his own daughter he hadn't seen for thirty years, not since she was a girl like her. Still, you had to look after yourself, even though she did feel a bit sorry for him.

Her tea was getting cold, but that wasn't the old man's fault, because he couldn't help the noise he was making. It sounded less and less that sort of noise the more it went on. She was the only one with ears. Or maybe the others hadn't washed theirs out that morning.

They sat with tea and buns, set in their newspapers, or staring into the air which must have been more interesting because they didn't even need print to hold them down. If you look into the air you look at yourself, and that must be better than any newspaper.

The old man was too busy with his tiddly-song to take much in. At the sound of such noise his eyes must have stopped looking at anything. Nobody else seemed to understand that his eyes had come to a dead end, for the few who glanced at him turned away as if they had seen nothing. Some talked together, and didn't even bother to look, though they knew what was going on right enough.

It made her uneasy, being by herself. He sat up straight as a soldier against the wall, a hand on the table beside his cup. By making such a noise he was trying to get in touch with someone, but he did not know who or where they were, which she supposed was why no one could bear to look at him in case it was them. It became more insistent until, to her, it appeared to fill the whole cafe.

She didn't find the noise meaningless or dispiriting, for it set her memory racing thirty years back to being a child and fading into sleep. Then, as now, she never went from the conscious world straight into sleep like maybe a healthy person would, but into another world between her and deep sleep itself, always a different place through which she had to pass before reaching real sleep, and she only knew she'd done that when she woke up.

She remembered feeling, once in this twilight zone, the horror of being alone to die. A huge leaden sphere pressed against her brain as if to crush all five senses at once. As big as the earth, it rolled on to her, till her eyes saw only grey matter and her breath was starting not to pump. She called for her father, who came in and brought her back to full breath by some kind and trivial gesture of distraction.

Because of this outcome it was not a bad memory that the old man's noise had set off, yet now it began to annoy her, for she had come into the cafe for a cup of tea as a break from the grind of buying scarves for the children, and hadn't been in five minutes before bumping into this.

An older woman sitting on the other side had wire glasses and straw-blonde hair, and puffed a fag while looking out of the window as if to burn her way through the glass with the acetylene smoke of it. She was nearer, but Margaret couldn't imagine her being bothered by him in a hundred years – till she had the strange idea that maybe everybody else in the cafe had their heads filled with the same thoughts and words that she had.

Her laugh at this interrupted the noise coming from the man's mouth, her face turning red with shame because he must have heard her and imagined she was laughing at him. She was almost relieved when the rattle started again.

His tie-knot was slightly below the join of the collar. A hand was limp by his side, while the other jerked at the half-empty cup. She thought it a pity he'd let the tea inside get cold, then leaped up and opened his coat, trembling with embarrassment at her big belly getting in the way but acting as if it was the only thing left to do in her life: 'Are you all right? What is it then? Tell me, for God's sake?'

He wanted help, and she wanted help in order to help him, for her voice wavered at his eyes rolling, and the sound of finger nails scraping on tin coming from his clenched lips, pressed tight as if trying to stop something getting out for the last time. She was frightened at the sight of his convulsed body.

She pulled down the knot of his tie and flung it open, snapped his collar at the stud though it wasn't in any way tight at his withered neck: 'Where do you live, duck?'

Trouser-legs chafed at the supports of the table, as if they could stop him falling down to earth, because the bench he sat on was not enough. She looked from the double-white world of his pot-eyes and shouted in a panic: 'Can't somebody give me a hand, then?'

A waitress came over, more, Margaret reflected later, because she thought I might start to give birth if she didn't, than to be of much use to the old man. 'Is he badly?'

The noise stopped, and he was dead.

'You'd better call an ambulance,' Margaret said, 'and a copper. But he's still more alive though than you bleddy lot in here.'

CANALS

When Dick received the letter saying his father hadn't long to live he put a black tie in his pocket, got leave from the school where he taught, and took the first train up.

In a tunnel his face was reflected clearly, brown eyes shadowed underneath from the pressure of a cold that had been trying to break out but that his will-power still held back. He considered that there had never been a good photograph taken of him, certainly none reflecting the fine image he saw when looking in the mirror of the thin-faced, hard, sensitive man whose ancestors must all have had similar bones and features. But photographs showed him weak, a face that couldn't retain its strength at more than one angle, and that people might look at and not know whether this uncertainty was mere charm or a subtle and conscious form of deception. He had a wide mouth and the middling forehead of a practical man whose highest ambition was, once upon a time, to be a good tool-setter, until he joined the army and discovered that he was intelligent in a more worldly sense. And when he left he knew that he would never go into a factory again.

In his briefcase was a shirt, and two handkerchiefs his wife had forced on him at the last moment, as well as a razor, and some magazines scooped up in case he had nothing to think about on the journey.

Sitting in the dining-car for lunch, alone yet surrounded by many people, he remembered his mother saying, when he was leaving home ten years before: 'Well, you'll always be able to come back. If you can't come home again, where can you go?' But on a visit after four years he walked into the house and, apart from a brief hello, nobody turned from the television set to greet him, though they'd been a close-blooded family, and on and off the best of friends all their lives.

So he never really went back, didn't see himself as the sort of person who ever would. Whether he ever went forward or not was another question, but he certainly knew there was no profit in looking back. He preferred a new block of flats to a cathedral any day, a good bus-service to a Rembrandt or historic ruin, though he realised it was better to have *all* these things and not be in the position of having to choose.

He remembered his father saying: 'A good soldier never looks back. He don't even polish the backs of his boots. You can see your face in the toecaps, though.' His father had never been a soldier, yet this was his favourite saying – because he'd never been forward anywhere, either.

So the only time he did go back was when his father was dying. It wasn't a question of having to, or even thinking about it: he just went, stayed for a week while his father died and got buried, then came back, leaving his mother in charge of brothers and sisters, even though he was the eldest son.

He stayed with his father day and night for three days, except when he queued for pills at the all-night chemist's downtown. He felt there was no need to make a song-and-dance about anyone dying, even your own father, because you should have done that while they were alive. He hoped he'd get better, yet knew he wouldn't. At fifty-four a lavish and royal grip of rottenness that refused to let go had got him in the head, a giant invisible cancerous rat with the dullest yet most tenacious teeth in the world, pressing its way through that parchment skull. He sweated to death, died at a quarter to five in the afternoon, and no one had ever told him he was going to die.

His mother didn't shed a tear. She was afraid of death and of her husband, hated him with reason because he had always without intending it turned her on to the monstrous path of having no one to hate but herself. She had hardly been in to see him during the last three days, and neither had his two daughters. Dick and his brother held each other in an embrace, two grown men unable to stop themselves sobbing like children.

A young thin woman of the neighbourhood laid the father out, and Dick went to get the doctor, who filled in a death-certificate without bothering to come and see that his patient had actually died.

The undertakers took him away. The mattress was rolled up and put outside for the dustbin men. Then the bed he'd laid on was folded back into a settee, making the small room look empty – all within an hour of him dying. An aunt who'd also lost her husband hadn't shed a tear either. Maybe it runs in the family, he thought. At the funeral, walking from the house to the waiting car, his mother wept for the first and last time – in front of all the neighbours. Of his father's five brothers none came to see him off, though all knew of it. It was almost as if he'd died in the middle of a battlefield, there were so few witnesses. But at least he didn't know about it, and might not have worried much if he had. And who am I to talk? Dick wondered, much later. I never went back to his grave, and I doubt if anyone else did, either. His mother's lack of tears didn't strike him as strange at the time considering the life she and their father had led.

Between the death and burial he was nut-loose and roaming free. At first, the brothers, sisters and mother went out together in the evenings, sticking close in a single corner of a bar-room snug, not talking except to stand up and ask who wanted what. Once they went to the pictures, but afterwards drifted into their separate ways.

It was early May, and all he wanted to do was walk. The low small sky of the bedroom ceiling had turned to blue, white angels and angles of cloud shifting across between factory and house skyline. It was vast above, and made the streets look even smaller. He hated them, wished a fire-tailed rocket would spin from the sky and wash them clean with all-enduring phosphorus. He was thirty-three, and old enough to know better than wish for that, or to think it would come when he wanted it to, or that it would make any difference if ever it did.

The greatest instinct is to go home again, the unacknowledged urge of the deracinated, the exiles – even when it isn't admitted. The only true soul is the gipsy's, and he takes home and family with him wherever he drifts. The nomad pushes his roots about like the beetle his ball of dung, lives on what he scavenges from the rock and sand of the desert. It's a good man or woman who evades it and is not poisoned precisely because he has avoided it while knowing all about it. You take on the soul of the Slav, and if you can eventually find that sort of soul it falls around you like a robe and makes you feel like a king. The wandering Jew carried the secret of creation in the pocket of his long overcoat, and now he has ploughed it into the fields of Israel. The Siberian nomad has formed his collective or joined a work-gang on some giant dam that will illuminate the wilderness his ancestors were free to wander in. Is the desert then all that is left? If the houses and factories stretching for miles around are a desert for one's soul, then maybe the desert itself is the Garden of Eden, even if one dries up and dies in it.

But he knew at the same time that life had two sides, and a base-line set firmly on the earth. The good air was blowing through the fresh-leafed trees of the cemetery he was passing. There was moss between the sandstone lumps of the wall, well bedded and livid where most damp had got at it. Between spring and summer there was a conscious feeling to the year, a mellow blight of reminiscence and nostalgia blending with the softening sweet air of late afternoon. The atmosphere made buildings and people stand out clearly, as if the meadow-and-water clouds of the Trent had not dispersed and still held that magical quality of light while passing high over the hills and roof-tops of the city. It was a delight to be alive and walking, and for some reason he wanted the day to go on for ever. There was a terrible beauty in the city he belonged to that he had never found anywhere else.

He walked over Bobber's Mill bridge, far enough out to smell soil of allotment gardens, loam of fields, water of the mill-racing Leen that had streamed down from beyond Newstead. In spite of petrol, the reek of upholstery, and fag-smoke coming from a bus-door when it stopped near him, he held on to this purity of vision that made him believe life was good and worth living.

He walked by the railway bank and through the allotment gardens – still exactly there from fifteen years ago. Feeling himself too old to be indulging in such fleshly reminiscence, he enjoyed it all the more, not as a vice but as if it were food to a starving man. Every elm tree, oak tree, apple tree, lime tree represented a leaning-post for kisses, a pausing place to talk and rest at, light cigarettes, wait while Marian fastened her coat or put on more lipstick. Every wooden gateway in the tall hedges that were as blind as walls brought to mind the self-indulgent embraces and love-making of his various courting mates. Different generations of thrushes were still loud in the same tree-tops, hawthorn, and privet, except that their notes and noise were more exactly the same.

The brook was as usual stagnant, yet water came from some-where, green button-eyed weed making patterns on the surface to blot out cloud reflections and blue sky. Tadpoles had passed away, and young frogs were jumping under the unreachable part of the hedge. To observe all this, connect it to his past life and give it no part in his future, made him feel an old man, certainly far older than he was. Maybe he was merely mature, when what you saw and thought about no longer drove you on to the next action of your life no matter how small that action turned out to be.

The uterine flight of reminiscence, the warm piss of nostalgia as he stood by a hedge and relieved himself where the shaded pathway stretched emptily in both directions, was a way of filling in the void that a recent death created, especially the death of a person whose life had been utterly unfulfilled – of which there are so many, and which makes you feel it deeply because on the watershed of such sorrow you sense that your life too could turn out at the end to have been equally unfulfilled. The vital breezes of clean air shaking the hedgetops don't let such thoughts stay long. The lack of your own persistence in real life is often bad, while the lack of it in self-destroying thoughts at such times as this is occasionally good.

The canal had dried up, been dammed and drained and in places built over. In the mouldering soft colour of dusk he walked from one bank to another. The old stone bridge had been allowed to drop into the canal below and fill it in, hump and all, and a white-lined and tarmacked road had been laid straight across it.

He followed what was left, walked along its old tow-path towards the country. A large open pond lay down to the right with indistinct banks except for a scrap of wood on the western side now touched by a barleycorn dip of the sun. A smell of raw smoke and water was wafted in his direction. The headstocks of the colliery where his grandfather had worked blocked off an opposite view, and it was so close that the noise of turbines and generators made a fitting counterpoint to reawakening senses.

It was dark by the time he stepped into the Ramrod and Musket and ordered a pint of beer. A fire burned in one of the side rooms, and he sat by it, loosening his raincoat. Everyone he saw he felt pity for. The wells of it had not stopped pumping, and the light of it was too blinding for him to turn it round on himself, a beam he alone could explore the world with, prise it from the darkness it lived in. He had come here thinking he might meet someone known from years ago, though he would never acknowledge such a lapse in case its nerve-racking mixture of pride and weakness might poison all hope in him.

Going outside to the back, there was no bulb in the socket to light his way. Indigo had faded completely from the sky, and he stepped slowly across the yard with eyes shut tight, under the illusion that he could see better than if he walked with them open and arms held out for fear of colliding with something.

The liquid in his pint went down, a spiritual Nilometer latched by the river of his momentarily stilled life. He felt comfortable, hearing the homely accents of the few other men dealing out chitchat that in London he wouldn't give tuppence for. Nostalgia was sweet, and he allowed it to seep into him with a further jar of beer. The others sat back from the fire, glasses set on labelled mats, sliding them around to make a point.

He hated beer after the third pint, a senseless waterlogging of the body that adiposed it to the earth one tried to get away from. He thought of going on to another place when no one came in that he knew, but considered a pub-crawl futile – except that the ground covered between them is different and shakes the stuff to a lower level to make room for more. Otherwise stay at the first one you stumble into.

The more he drank the more his cold bothered him. Death and the funeral had held it off, but now it spread the poison and colour of infection, a slight shifting of every feature from its spot-on proportion in order to recoup the truth and clarity of things past. One's feelings were important during a cold, in showing what you are really like and what stirs your mind from one decade to the next. It was almost as if the real you was a reactionary because it rooted you so firmly to the past without calling on detail as a support, giving it the slightly sick air which all reactionaries must have as a permanent condition. In so many cases the only key to the past is sentimentality – unless one has that cold or sickness which puts it in its place. He had reviled the past, but to loathe something was the first step to understanding it, just as to love something was the first step towards abandoning it. The past is a cellar, twisting catacombs or filled-in canals, but a cellar in which you have to walk in order to put a bullet into the back of the head of whatever monarch may be ruling too autocratically there. Only you have to tread slowly, warily, to make sure you get the right one, because if by any chance you get the wrong one you might end up putting a bullet into the back of your own head.

He was married, and had three children, one of them a few weeks old, so that his wife had not been able to come up from London with him. It was years since he had been so alone, and it was like a new experience, which he did not quite know how to handle, or realise what might come of it. People so alone rarely had chance meetings, yet the day after his father had died, walking across the city centre on his way to register the death, he heard someone from the roof-tops calling his name.

He didn't think he was hearing things, or going mad, because it was not in his nature to do so. His physical build seemed absolutely to preclude it. But he stopped, looked, then felt foolish at having been mistaken. It was a fine, blustery Nottingham day, with green double-decker buses almost surrounding the market square, and a few people actually crossing the road.

'Dick!' The voice came again, but he walked away since it was obviously some workman shouting to his mate. 'Dick! Dick!' The voice was closer, so he stopped to light a cigarette in case it really wasn't meant for him.

His cousin came scurrying down a series of ladders and dropped on the pavement a few yards away. He was, as the saying goes, 'all over him' – they hadn't met for so long, and had been such close friends, born on the same fish day of March, a wild blizzarding day in which no fish had a chance of swimming.

·Bernard was thin and wiry, even through the old jacket and trousers of a builder's labourer. His grey eyes were eager with friendship, and they embraced on the street: 'I didn't know you was in Nottingham,' he said fussily. 'Why didn't you write and tell me? Fancy meeting like this.' He laughed about it, seeing himself as having climbed down from the sky like a monkey.

'I came up all of a sudden. How did you recognise me from right up there?'

'Your face. And that walk. I'd know it anywhere.'

'Dad was ill. He died last night.'

'Uncle Joe?' he took off his cap, pushed back fair and matted hair in the wind, bewildered at the enormity of the event and, Dick thought, at not being able to say anything about it.

'He had cancer.'

There was a pub near by: 'Let's go for a drink,' Bernard said.

'Won't the foreman mind?'

'I expect so. Come on. They've had enough sweat out of me. I'm sorry Joe died.'

They sat in the otherwise empty bar. 'Come up and see us all before you go back,' he said. 'We'd be glad if you would. I don't know what you live in London for, honest I don't. There's plenty of schools you could teach at in Nottingham. They're crying out for teachers, I'll bet. I suppose it's a bit of a dump, but you can't beat it. At least I don't reckon so.'

'It's all right,' Dick said, 'but London's where I belong – if I belong anywhere.' They talked as if it were on the other side of the world, which it was against the background of their common memories – even further.

'Well, you can't beat the town you were brought up in – dragged up, I mean!' Bernard said. Dick remembered, and talked about it before he could stop himself, of when they were children, and he and Bernard used to go around houses asking for old rags and scrap, which they would then sell for picture-money and food. The houses whose gardens backed on to the recreation ground were somewhat better off than the ones they lived in, and therefore good for pickings. At one a youngish woman gave them bread and jam and cups of tea, which they gladly accepted. They didn't call often, and not many others went around to spoil their pitch. And yet, good as she was, sweet as the tea and jam tasted, they couldn't keep going there. There was some slight feeling of shame about it, probably quite unjustified, yet picked up by both of them all the same. Without even saying anything to each other they stopped calling. Dick wondered what the woman had thought, and whether she had missed them.

Though he remembered this common incident clearly, it soon

became obvious that Bernard did not, and that his mind was a blank regarding it, though at first he had looked as if he did vaguely, recollect it, and then as if he wanted to but couldn't quite pull it back. 'Still,' Dick said, laughing it away, 'you can't go home again, I know that.'

'You can't?' Bernard asked, full of surprise. 'Why can't you?'

'I can't, anyway.'

'You can do what you like, can't you?'

'Some people can.'

They drank to it.

'Bring your wife and kids here to live. Get a house up Sherwood Rise. It's healthy there. They'll love it.'

'I can't, because I don't want to.'

He laughed. 'Maybe you are better off down there, at that. I can't trap yo' into owt. I'm sorry about Uncle Joe though; Mam'll be upset when I tell her.'

'It'll be in the paper today.'

'She'll see it, then. Let me get you one now.'

'Next time. I must be off.'

Dick watched him ascend the ladders, up from the pavement to the first storey, then to the second. From the roof he straddled a parapet, turned and looked down, a gargoyle for one moment, then he took off his cap and waved, a wide frantic smile on his far-off face. Dick had time to wave back before he leapt up and was hidden by a chimney-stack.

The past is like a fire – don't put your hand in it. And yet, what is to stop you walking through it upright, all of you, body and soul? It was a weekday, and the pub hadn't filled up. Near to ten o'clock he couldn't bear the thought of going home. His impulse was to flee towards London, but he'd promised to stay on a few days. It was expected of him, and for once in his life he had to obey.

He'd called here often for a drink with Marian, though she'd always insisted on having her shandy outside because she wasn't yet eighteen, as if it would have made much difference. After a summer's night on Bramcote Hills the thirst was killing, and he drank more beer in those days than he could ever stomach now. The good food of London living had peppered his gut with ulcers – or so it felt, without having been to any doctor – and the heartburn was sure to grip him next day if he put back too much.

The last bus was at half past ten, and he thought he might as well walk home. Outside, fastening his coat in the lighted doorway, the insane idea came to call on Marian, to go down to the estate and knock on her door. Why think about it, if you intended doing it? The one advantage of dwelling on the past was to act without thought if you were to get the utmost from it. In that way, of course, it would end up getting the utmost out of you, but that was nothing to be afraid of.

Fifteen years was a long time, judging by the excitement the hope of meeting her again let loose in him. It was similar to that when they had been 'going out' with each other for what seemed a decade, but which had not felt much like being in love at the time.

Having started factory work at fourteen, he was a seasoned man by the age of eighteen, and those four years had slowed down to become the longest in his life, possibly because there was an end to them which he hadn't foreseen at the time. In them, he grew up and died. His courtships had seemed eternal, even when they only lasted several months – looking back on them. The time with Marian went on longest of all, and being the last it was also the most important in that microcosmic life.

A fine drizzle powdered across the orange sodium lights of the housing estate. The roads were just as wide as he'd remembered them. If so little alters in a man's life, who but the most bigoted can believe in progress? Such a question came, he knew, of having too little faith, and of too complete immersion in a past so far away and severed that it couldn't be anything else but irrelevant fiction. Yet it didn't feel like it, and it did not disturb him that it didn't. The familiar dank smell of coal-smoke hovered even along the wide avenues and crescents, and the closeness of his cigarette tasted the same in his mouth and nostrils as it had all those years ago. Privet hedges shone with water under the street-lamps, and a well-caped railwayman rode by on a bicycle that seemed to have no light until only a yard away. He pulled up by the kerb, and the latch clattered as he went up the path and round to his own back door.

It was a good distance, yet he wished it were longer, both because he was apprehensive at meeting Marian and because it would spin out further the pleasant anticipation of her being at home. She'd been going with his friend Barry when he first met her, a carnal and passionate love similar to the one he at the time was pursuing with someone else. But Barry went into the army, driven from home by a black-haired bossy mother and a house full of sisters, lit off at seventeen into the Engineers just as the war ended. Letters and the occasional leave were no way to keep love's fires stoked between him and Marian, and one night Dick met her by chance and, on seeing her home, fell into honeyed and violent kisses by her gate. She agreed to see him again, and he didn't realise to what extent he had run his mate off until Barry clocked on with the army for twelve years and went straight off to Greece to serve two of them. They even stayed friends over it, yet the blow to Barry had been hard, as he admitted when they met, years later.

He made up his mind to turn at the next corner and go home, to leave the past in its matchwood compartment and not smash over it with the bulldozer of his useless and idiotic obsession. She would be out, or a husband would meet him at the door and tell him he'd got the wrong house. He smiled to remember how, during the war, an American soldier had called one night on the woman next door, as had been his habit for some months. But this time his opening of the door was answered by the husband, who had unexpectedly finished his stint on nights. The American stared unbelievingly at the pudgy and belligerent face. After a few seconds he backed out with the lame remark, 'Sorry, I thought it was a public house.' The husband had accepted it as a genuine mistake, but there were some snide comments going around the street for a long time on how lucky Mrs So-and-so was to have such a numb-skull for a husband. So if Marian's husband was at home, or some man she might be living with, he'd merely say: 'Is Mrs Smith in?' and make some excuse about getting the number of the house wrong.

Having decided to go home and not be such a fool, he kept on his track towards Marian's as if locked in some deep and serpentine canal, unable to scale its side and get back to sane air. He even went more quickly, without feeling or thought or sense of direction. From the public house he had forgotten the exact streets to follow, but it didn't matter, for he simply walked looking mostly towards the ground, recognising the shadows of a bush-shelter, the precise spot reached by the spreading rays of a particular street-lamp, the height of a kerb, or twitchel posts at the opening of a cul-de-sac.

He found the road and the number, opened the gate, and walked down the path with even more self-assurance than he ever had after courting her for a year. There was a light on in the living room. The fifteen years had not been a complete blank. He'd heard that her mother had died and that she had married a man who had been sent to prison and whom she had refused to see again. Barry also told him that there had been one child, a son. The first five years after they split up must have been agony for her, blow after blow, and it was as if he were going back now to see how she had borne the suffering that followed in his wake. But no, he could never admit to so much power. He stood at the back door, in darkness for some minutes, torn at last by the indecision that should have gripped him on his way there, and splintered by the remorse he might feel after he had left. The noise of a television set came from inside, music and crass speech that made it impossible to tell whether one or a dozen people were at home.

He too had gone into the army, and when her letters grew less frequent he was almost glad at the sense of freedom he felt. But her thoughts and feelings were not of the sort she could put easily in writing and transmit that way, as he found when they met on his first leave. Passion, because it was incommunicable, was her form of love. It was fully flowered and would go on forever with regard to him, incapable of development yet utterly complete. He expected letters, subtlety, variation, words,

words, words, and couldn't stand the emptiness of such fulfil-
ment. She could foresee no greater happiness than that they
get married, and would have demanded little more than the
most basic necessities of life. If he had been a man he would
have accepted this, because he also loved her; and if he were a
man now he would not have come back looking for her, unable
to say what he wanted, whether it was love or chaos he hoped
to resurrect.

It was no use standing in the dark with such thoughts, so he
knocked at the door. She opened it, set up the two steps in an
oblong of pale orange light. 'What do you want?' she said,
seeing only a stranger and at this time of night. The protective
voice of a boy called from inside:

'Who is it, Mam?'

Regret, indecision, dread had gone, for he had acted, had
the deepest instincts of his heart carried out for him, which
really meant that he had been acted upon. He smiled, telling
her who it was.

She repeated the name, and looked closer, eyes narrowing
almost to a squint, 'You! Fancy you!'

'Well,' he said, 'I was passing and thought I'd see if you still
lived here.'

She asked him in, and they stood in the small kitchen. He
saw it was painted white instead of cream, had an electric stove
in place of the old gas one, but with the same sink now patched
and stained.

'Who is it, Mam?'

'I'm surprised you still knew where I lived.'

'I don't suppose I could ever forget it. In any case it's not
that long ago.'

'No? It is, though.'

'It doesn't feel like it to me.'

But, to look at her, it was. And she was thinking the same.
She seemed taller, was more full-bodied, no longer the pale,
slim, wildlife girl of eighteen. The set lines running from her
mouth, which he remembered as being formed by that curious
smile of wanting to know something more definite and signifi-

cant about what had caused her to smile in the first place, had hardened and deepened because her curiosity hadn't been responded to, and because the questions could never be formed clearly enough in her to ask them. The smile had moved to the grey eyes, and was more forthright in its limitations, less expressive but no longer painful.

'Come in,' she said. 'I'll make you a cup of tea, if you'd like one.'

'All right. I will for a minute.' Once inside he forgot his absence and hesitancy and took off his coat. Her twelve-year-old son lay as far back as he could get in an armchair, watching television from too close by, a livid perpetual lightning flicker to Dick, who wasn't facing it. His mother made him turn it down. 'This is Peter,' she said. 'Peter, this is an old friend of your Mam's.'

Peter said nothing, an intelligent face blighted by sudden resentment of another man in the house. He looked harder into the telly in case his mother should ask him to turn it right off. Marian's hands shook as she poured the tea, put in sugar and milk. 'I can't get over it,' she said, 'you coming to see me. Of all people! Do you know anybody else around here?'

'Nobody. Only you.'

She was happy at the thought that he had come especially to see her. 'You haven't altered much in all these years.'

'Neither have you.'

Her ironic grin was the same. 'Not much I haven't! You can't lie to me any more. You did once though, didn't you, duck?'

He might have done, and the fact that he'd forgotten was made to seem unforgivable by the slight shock still on her face at his sudden reappearance. Still, she managed to laugh about the thought of him having lied to her once, though he knew better than to take such laughs at their face value. 'Did you come up by car?' she asked. 'What sort is it?'

'I don't have a car.'

'I thought you would have. Then you could have taken me and Peter for a ride in it some time. Couldn't he, Peter?'

A 'yes' broke from the back of Peter's mind. 'You know,' she said, 'when I heard you'd become a schoolteacher I had to see the funny side of it. Fancy me going out for so long with a man who was going to become a schoolteacher! No wonder you chucked somebody like me up. I don't blame you, though.'

'That wasn't why I chucked you up. If I did.'

'You might have done – anyway,' she reflected.

'I don't remember who chucked who up.'

'You loved me though, didn't you?' She said this so that Peter wouldn't hear, from within the clatter and shouting of his private gunfight.

'I did,' he answered.

'You said you wanted to stay in the army for good, and so getting married wouldn't be fair to either of us. I remember all of it clearly. But I could see that that wasn't it at all, though. You'd just lost interest. There was nowt else you could get to know about me, after all the times we had. We didn't even fall out with each other. I didn't know what to tell the girls at work when they asked me about you.'

Every word and nuance of her recollected past was accurate. It was no use saying he was only eighteen at the time, because he (as well as she) held himself totally responsible for his actions. Four years at work made him man enough already, and it wasn't so much shame he felt now as a failure of masculine responsibility. Yet some innate and ruthless sense had steered him from a life he was unfitted for. She spoke as if it were last year, whereas to him it was a whole lifetime ago, and could be considered in one way as the immature skirt-chasing of a callow youth, and in another as the throwback past of a man who, being incapable of forgetting it, had been unable to grow up. And if, beyond all this, he had stepped from one world and settled himself securely in another with a wife, three children, and an all-absorbing job, why had he made this painful and paranoid expedition to the world he had launched out from? His age didn't justify it. Maybe in his deracinated life he was forgetting where he had come from, yet wasn't a visit home enough to remind him? One had to make journeys in all directions, was the only answer that came while listening to Marian. Happy are those who don't make journeys and never need to, he thought, yet luckier are those who do.

Peter had gone to bed, more willingly than he expected. He opened a half-bottle of whisky bought in the pub, and Marian set out two glasses: 'To you and your life,' he said.

'To yourn,' she answered, 'I hardly ever drink, but this tastes good for a change. It might buck me up.' She sat on the sofa they had made love on countless times, and he stayed on a straight-backed chair at the table on which plates, cups, and sauce-bottle still rested. A clothes-horse barricaded the fire from them.

'I work at the same place still,' she said, 'at the stocking factory. I've got a better job now, though: I fault them, prick them under a glass so that they won't last more than three months. It's a good job, faulting. I can make twelve pounds a week on piecework. It's hard though in wintertime, because I go to work on my bike, riding up the hill with a January wind hitting me head-on. I went on a bus once, but halfway there the driver had a dizzy spell. He turned round, shouting for everybody to jump off, before he was able to stop it. The only time I ever went on the bus, as well! Everything happens to me!'

'What was this I heard about your husband?' he asked, noticing the regularity of her teeth. All were false, and none of his had come out yet.

'Him?' she said. 'Oh, when you left me I got married a year later. I met him at a dance, and never realised he was no good. Not long after we were married, while Mam was still alive – though on that morning she'd gone out shopping, thank God, or she'd have died at the shock I'm sure – I was in here washing up when two policemen knocked at the back door and asked if Arthur Baldwin lived here. I felt my heart going like mad, pitter-patter, and thought he'd been run over or killed in a machine at work, ready for the tears to burst out of me. But it wasn't that at all. They'd picked him up on the street because they'd found out he'd been breaking into houses, and I don't know what else he'd done. I didn't go to court, and never even read the papers about it. In fact he hadn't been at work for a long time, and I thought he had. I was such a baby I never realised what was going on. He'd been in trouble with the police before we met, but I didn't know anything about it, and nobody thought to tell me. He'd even got another woman he was keeping, in the Meadows. His mother asked me to go down to the court and plead for him, because I was pregnant already, but I didn't. I wouldn't have anything to do with it. "He's got hisself into it," I told her, "so he can get hisself out of it." She threatened me, but I still wouldn't do it, and then my mother nearly threw her out of the house. It wouldn't have helped much, anyway, I know that, because the police had really got it in for him, just as I had as well for the way he'd done it on me.

'He was sent to prison for two years, and I haven't seen him since. As I say, I was pregnant, and Peter was born while he was in prison. He don't know anything about it yet, though he'll have a right to some day. I just tell him that his father left me when he was a baby. Mam and me got a bed down from upstairs when I had Peter, and fixed it up in this corner, and I had him on it. Then a year later Mam went, and I've lived alone ever since, the last ten years. I wouldn't get married again now, though, not for a fortune. All I've got is Peter, and it's enough for me, bringing him up. He's a bit of a handful at times, being without a dad, but when he is he gets my fist. Mind you, we have some good times together as well. We go fishing now and again, and he loves it, sitting by the canal with all his tackle and bait, net and floats. He feels a proper man, and I don't mind buying him the best stuff to do it with. He's very clever though at mechanical things. All he does is build things up. He's got all sorts of radio kits and construction sets. I never have to touch a fuse: he mends them all. He fixed a transistor radio last week for Mrs Barnes next door, and she was ever so pleased. She gave him ten bob.

'I work hard, so we live well. Last year we rented a caravan at Cleethorpes with the couple next door, and stayed a fortnight. I look a sight in a bathing costume, but we went swimming every day, and had a marvellous time. Mr Barnes got a car and we went all over Lincolnshire picnicking. It won't be all that long now before Peter starts work, and then he'll be bringing in some money as well. He doesn't want to stay on at school, at least he says he don't, though I don't think he'll be able to change his mind if he decides to.

'I suppose it was hardest for me though when Mam went. It was cancer, but she wasn't badly for very long. She never went to bed, stopped going when she knew she was going to die, though nobody told her, just lay on this sofa at night and sat in that armchair during the day. I don't know how we managed with just each other. I knew she was going to die, and that when she went there'd be no one left. Then I'd hear Peter crying, and knew that there would be, but it didn't make much difference for a long time. Still, we've all got to go, though it don't do to think about it.'

'We're young yet,' Dick said. 'We're just over thirty.' He sat by her on the sofa and took her hand. Was it true then that in all the troubles people had, no one could help anyone else, be of much use to soothe and comfort? Was everyone alone in their own black caverns and never communicating by tunnel or canal?

'I had help,' she said. 'The neighbours did what they could. At a time like that only God can help you, and it's only then you realise He can't. We aren't taking a holiday this year. I can't afford it because I got Peter a pickup and tape-recorder. But the year after, if we're still here, we're hoping to go to Norfolk for ten days. Gives us summat to look forward to.'

'I expect you'll get married again one day,' he said.

'Married?' she jeered. 'Not me, mate. I've had my life. No more kids, either. The woman next door had a baby last week, and when she came in to see me with it I laughed at her for being so quick in her visiting and said: "Hey, don't come in here spreading your feathers!" And she laughed as well, as if it might not be a bad idea, but I knew it worn't. All I want to do is bring Peter up, get him a good start in life. I don't mind

working for that, and living for it. I'll work till I drop, but as
for getting married, you don't know what I've had to go
through. And don't think I'm squealing about it. I might have
done at one time, but not any more, because it's all over. I'm
not going to get married and have them all come back.'

'You can fall in love, you know.' He detected a weakness in
her that she had obviously long brooded on.

'No, I won't.'

'That's what you say now. There's no telling when it'll come.'

'I loved you,' she said, 'and you can only be in love once in
your life, the first time. There ain't any other.' Her conviction
was quiet, all jeering gone. She pressed his hand, and he leaned
over to kiss her on the cheek. 'It's like a dream,' she said,
smiling, her eyes shining as if the tears would break. 'You
coming back. I can't believe it. I can't, duck, honest I can't.'

She wasn't in love with him, no more than he was with her,
but he had lured her into the spider-trap of the past, and she
was sweetening within it. 'No,' she said, 'I'll never fall in love.'

'You don't have to be in love to get married,' he said.

'That's what I thought before,' she answered, 'and look what
happened.'

'Love is a destroyer if you wait for it too long. If you like
somebody, love can come out of it. It's no use wrecking your
life for want of being in love. Sometimes I think that as soon
as you start talking about love, it's on its way out, that really
it's nothing more than the bloody relic of a bygone age that
civilisation no longer needs. There's something wicked and
destructive about it.'

'I don't properly understand you,' she said gently, 'but you're
wrong, anyway. You're only saying it to soothe me. You don't
need to, you know, I'm all right. I'm not as sour as I sound.'

The door opened without warning and Peter appeared in his
dressing-gown, eyes blinded by the light as if he'd already been
half asleep, though Dick thought he may have been listening
to their talk for a while. 'What do you want?' Marian asked.

'I'm looking for my comic.' He found it, under a cushion of

the sofa they were sitting on. 'Don't stay up late, duck,' she said. 'You've got to go to school in the morning.'

He stood by the door, looking at them. 'Are you coming to bed then, Mam?'

'Soon. We're just having a talk about old times. I shan't be long.'

He went up the stairs, slowly, dragging the sleeve of his dressing-gown against the wall.

She made more tea, took out a box of photographs and went through them one by one, then got him to empty his wallet and show pictures of his wife and children. The past was impotent, finally, with no cleansing quality in its slow-burning fires. Yet they could never be put out because the canals that led to them were baked dry at the bottom with the rusting and tattered debris of the life you lead.

'I didn't think you'd ever go to live in London, though,' she said. 'It's a long way off.'

'Two hours by train. There and back in half a day. Nothing.'

'Not if you live there, and was born here. Shall you come and see me again?'

He stood up and put on his coat. 'I'd like to, if you won't kick me out.'

'Well, maybe I won't.'

'I don't come up too often, though.'

'It don't matter. We could go to a pub or summat, couldn't we?'

He held her close. 'We could.'

'It don't matter though, if you don't want to. But come in and see me.'

'All right, love.'

They held each other close, and kissed for a few seconds, standing near the kitchen door. 'I can't believe it,' she said. 'I still can't. Why did you come back? Why?' He couldn't say. He didn't know. The fifteen years fizzled down to nothing. It wasn't that he'd been a man at eighteen. He was a youth, and the raging sweet waves of it crushed into him, two flat heads of vice-steel closing with nothing in between.

'What did you say?' he asked.

'Nothing. I didn't say owt.' He kissed the tears out of her eyes.

After midnight he walked through fire, tattered and burned, going the same track home as on the hundreds of occasions when he had stayed late and missed his bus, blinded and blindfolded across the wide roads and by the black hedge-bound footpath of Collier's Pad. Only the train might take him out of it.

Lights crouched in the distance all around, every tree-root holy, the foliage damned. The narrow path was hedged in by uncertainty and chaos, life's way spun out of suffering and towards death. Artificially lighted air blighted your lungs, and you now and again stopped on your walk by some half-conce-aled bran-tub to dip your hands into the entrails of the past when destruction wasn't coming on you fast enough; the past is only good when what you pull up can be seen as part of the future.

But his heart was full of Marian's fate, up to her death and his death, and he felt better in knowing that at least they had this much in common whether they saw each other again or not.

THE BIKE

The Easter I was fifteen I sat at the table for supper and Mam
said to me: 'I'm glad you've left school. Now you can go to
work.'

'I don't want to go to wok,' I said in a big voice.

'Well, you've got to,' she said. 'I can't afford to keep a pit-
prop like yo' on nowt.'

I sulked, pushed my toasted cheese away as if it was the
worst kind of slop. 'I thought I could have a break before
starting.'

'Well you thought wrong. You'll be out of harm's way at
work.' She took my plate and emptied it on John's, my younger
brother's, knowing the right way to get me mad. That's the
trouble with me: I'm not clever. I could have bashed our John's
face in and snatched it back, except the little bastard had
gobbled it up, and Dad was sitting by the fire, behind his paper
with one tab lifted. 'You can't get me out to wok quick enough,
can you?' was all I could say at Mam.

Dad chipped in, put down his paper. 'Listen: no wok, no
grub. So get out and look for a job tomorrow, and don't come
back till you've got one.'

Going to the bike factory to ask for a job meant getting up
early, just as if I was back at school; there didn't seem any

point in getting older. My old man was a good worker though, and I knew in my bones and brain that I took after him. At the school garden the teacher used to say: 'Colin, you're the best worker I've got, and you'll get on when you leave' – after I'd spent a couple of hours digging spuds while all the others had been larking about trying to run each other over with the lawn-rollers. Then the teacher would sell the spuds off at threepence a pound and what did I get out of it? Bogger-all. Yet I liked the work because it wore me out; and I always feel pretty good when I'm worn out.

I knew you had to go to work though, and that rough work was best. I saw a picture once about a revolution in Russia, about the workers taking over and everything (like Dad wants to) and they lined everybody up and made them hold their hands out and the working blokes went up and down looking at them. Anybody whose hands was lily-white was taken away and shot. The others was O.K. Well, if ever that happened in this country, I'd be O.K., and that made me feel better when a few days later I was walking down the street in overalls at half-past seven in the morning with the rest of them. One side of my face felt lively and interested in what I was in for, but the other side was crooked and sorry for itself, so that a neighbour got a front view of my whole clock and called with a wide laugh, a gap I'd like to have seen a few inches lower down – in her neck: 'Never mind, Colin, it ain't all that bad.'

The man on the gate took me to the turnery. The noise hit me like a boxing-glove as I went in, but I kept on walking straight into it without flinching, feeling it reach right into my guts as if to wrench them out and use them as garters. I was handed over to the foreman; then the foreman passed me on to the toolsetter; and the toolsetter took me to another youth – so that I began to feel like a hot wallet.

The youth led me to a cupboard, opened it, and gave me a sweeping brush. 'Yo' do that gangway,' he said, 'and I'll do this one.' My gangway was wider, but I didn't bother to mention it. 'Bernard,' he said, holding out his hand, 'that's me. I go on a machine next week, a drill.'

'How long you been on this sweeping?' I wanted to know, bored with it already.

'Three months. Every lad gets put on sweeping first, just to get 'em used to the place.' Bernard was small and thin, older than me. We took to each other. He had round bright eyes and dark wavy hair, and spoke in a quick way as if he'd stayed at school longer than he had. He was idle, and I thought him sharp and clever, maybe because his mam and dad died when he was three. He'd been brought up by an asthmatic auntie who'd not only spoiled him but let him run wild as well, he told me later when we sat supping from our tea mugs. He'd quietened down now though, and butter wouldn't melt in his mouth, he said with a wink. I couldn't think why this was, after all his stories about him being a mad-head – which put me off him at first, though after a bit he was my mate, and that was that.

We was talking one day, and Bernard said the thing he wanted to buy most in the world was a gram and lots of jazz records – New Orleans style. He was saving up and had already got ten quid.

'Me,' I said, 'I want a bike, to get out at week-ends up Trent. A shop on Arkwright Street sells good 'uns second hand.'

I went back to my sweeping. It was a fact I've always wanted a bike. Speed gave me a thrill. Malcolm Campbell was my bigshot – but I'd settle for a two-wheeled pushbike. I'd once borrowed my cousin's and gone down Balloon House Hill so quick I passed a bus. I'd often thought how easy it would be to pinch a bike: look in a shop window until a bloke leaves his bike to go into the same shop, then nip in just before him and ask for something you knew they hadn't got; then walk out whistling to the bike at the kerb and ride off as if it's yours while the bloke's still in the shop. I'd brood for hours: fly home on it, enamel it, file off the numbers, turn the handlebars round, change the pedals, take lamps off or put them on . . . only, no, I thought, I'll be honest and save up for one when I get forced out to work, worse luck.

But work turned out to be a better life than school. I kept

as hard at it as I could, and got on well with the blokes because I used to spout about how rotten the wages was and how hard the bosses slaved us – which made me popular you can bet. Like my old man always says, I told them: 'At home, when you've got a headache, mash a pot of tea. At work, when you've got a headache, strike.' Which brought a few laughs.

Bernard was put on his drill, and one Friday while he was cleaning it down I stood waiting to cart his rammel off. 'Are you still saving up for that bike, then?' he asked, pushing steel dust away with a handbrush.

'Course I am. But I'm a way off getting one yet. They rush you a fiver at that shop. Guaranteed, though.'

He worked on for a minute or two, then, as if he'd got a birthday present or was trying to spring a good surprise on me, said without turning round: 'I've made up my mind to sell my bike.'

'I didn't know you'd got one.'

'Well' – a look on his face as if there was a few things I didn't know – 'I bus it to work: it's easier.' Then in a pallier voice: 'I got it last Christmas from my auntie. But I want a record player now.'

My heart was thumping. I knew I hadn't got enough, but: 'How much do you want for it?'

He smiled. 'It ain't how much I want for the bike, it's how much more dough I need to get the gram and a couple of discs.'

I saw Trent Valley spread out below me from the top of Carlton Hill – fields and villages, and the river like a white scarf dropped from a giant's neck. 'How much do you need, then?'

He took his time about it, as if still having to reckon it up. 'Fifty bob.' I'd only got two quid – so the giant snatched his scarf away and vanished. Then Bernard seemed in a hurry to finish the deal: 'Look, I don't want to mess about, I'll let it go for two pounds five. You can borrow the other five bob.'

'I'll do it then,' I said, and Bernard shook my hand like he was going away in the army. 'It's a deal. Bring the dough in the morning, and I'll bike it to wok.'

Dad was already in when I got home, filling the kettle at the scullery tap. I don't think he felt safe without there was a kettle on the gas. 'What would you do if the world suddenly ended, Dad?' I once asked when he was in a good mood. 'Mash some tea and watch it,' he said. He poured me a cup.

'Lend's five bob, Dad, till Friday.'

He slipped the cosy on. 'What do you want to borrow money for?' I told him. 'Who from?' he asked.

'My mate at wok.'

He passed me the money. 'Is it a good 'un?'

'I ain't seen it yet. He's bringing it in the morning.'

'Make sure the brakes is safe.'

Bernard came in half an hour late, so I wasn't able to see the bike till dinner-time. I kept thinking he'd took bad and wouldn't come at all, but suddenly he was stooping at the door to take his clips off – so's I'd know he'd got his – my – bike. He looked paler than usual, as if he'd been up the canal-bank all night with a piece of skirt and caught a bilious-bout. I paid him at dinner-time. 'Do you want a receipt for it?' he laughed. It was no time to lark about. I gave it a short test around the factory, then rode it home.

The next three evenings, for it was well in to summer, I rode a dozen miles out into the country, where fresh air smelt like cowshit and the land was coloured different, was wide open and windier than in streets. Marvellous. It was like a new life starting up, as if till then I'd been tied by a mile long rope round the ankle to home. Whistling along lanes I planned trips to Skegness, wondering how many miles I could make in a whole day. If I pedalled like mad, bursting my lungs for fifteen hours, I'd reach London where I'd never been. It was like sawing through the bars in clink. It was a good bike as well, a few years old, but a smart racer with lamps and saddlebag and a pump that went. I thought Bernard was a bit loony parting with it at that price, but I supposed that that's how blokes are when they get dead set on a gram and discs. They'd sell their own mother, I thought, enjoying a mad dash down from Canning Circus, weaving between the cars for kicks.

'What's it like, having a bike?' Bernard asked, stopping to slap me on the back – as jolly as I'd ever seen him, yet in a kind of way that don't happen between pals.

'You should know,' I said. 'Why? It's all right, ain't it? The wheels are good, aren't they?'

An insulted look came into his eyes. 'You can give it back if you like. I'll give you your money.'

'I don't want it,' I said. I could no more part with it than my right arm, and he knew it. 'Got the gram yet?' And he told me about it for the next half-hour. It had got so many dials for this and that he made it sound like a space ship. We was both satisfied, which was the main thing.

That same Saturday I went to the barber's for my monthly D.A. and when I came out I saw a bloke getting on my bike to ride it away. I tagged him on the shoulder, my fist flashing red for danger.

'Off,' I said sharply, ready to smash the thieving bastard. He turned to me. A funny sort of thief, I couldn't help thinking, a respectable-looking bloke of about forty wearing glasses and shiny shoes, smaller than me, with a moustache. Still, the swivel-eyed sinner was taking my bike.

'I'm boggered if I will,' he said, in a quiet way so that I thought he was a bit touched. 'It's my bike, anyway.'

'It bloody-well ain't,' I swore, 'and if you don't get off I'll crack you one.'

A few people gawked at us. The bloke didn't mess about and I can understand it now. 'Missis,' he called, 'just go down the road to that copperbox and ask a policeman to come up 'ere, will you? This is my bike, and this young bogger nicked it.'

I was strong for my age. 'You sodding fibber,' I cried, pulling him clean off the bike so's it clattered to the pavement. I picked it up to ride away, but the bloke got me round the waist, and it was more than I could do to take him off up the road as well, even if I wanted to. Which I didn't.

'Fancy robbing a working-man of his bike,' somebody called out from the crowd of idle bastards now collected. I could have mowed them down.

But I didn't get a chance. A copper came, and the man was soon flicking out his wallet, showing a bill with the number of the bike on it: proof right enough. But I still thought he'd made a mistake. 'You can tell us all about that at the Guildhall,' the copper said to me.

I don't know why – I suppose I want my brains testing – but I stuck to a story that I found the bike dumped at the end of the yard that morning and was on my way to give it in at a copshop, and had called for a haircut first. I think the magistrate half believed me, because the bloke knew to the minute when it was pinched, and at that time I had a perfect alibi – I was in work, proved by my clocking-in card. I knew some rat who hadn't been in work though when he should have been.

All the same, being found with a pinched bike, I got put on probation, and am still doing it. I hate old Bernard's guts for playing a trick like that on me, his mate. But it was lucky for him I hated the coppers more and wouldn't nark on anybody, not even a dog. Dad would have killed me if ever I had, though he didn't need to tell me. I could only thank God a story came to me as quick as it did, though in one way I still sometimes reckon I was barmy not to have told them how I got the bike.

There's one thing I do know. I'm waiting for Bernard to come out of borstal. He got picked up, the day after I was copped with the bike, for robbing his auntie's gas meter to buy more discs. She'd had about all she could stand from him, and thought a spell inside would do him good, if not cure him altogether. I've got a big bone to pick with him, because he owes me forty-five bob. I don't care where he gets it – even if he goes out and robs another meter – but I'll get it out of him, I swear blind I will. I'll pulverise him.

Another thing about him though that makes me laugh is that, if ever there's a revolution and everybody's lined-up with their hands out, Bernard's will still be lily-white, because he's a bone-idle thieving bastard – and then we'll see how he goes on; because mine won't be lily-white, I can tell you that now. And you never know, I might even be one of the blokes picking 'em out.

THE FISHING-BOAT PICTURE

I've been a postman for twenty-eight years. Take that first sentence: because it's written in a simple way may make the fact of my having been a postman for so long seem important, but I realise that such a fact has no significance whatever. After all, it's not my fault that it may seem as if it has to some people just because I wrote it down plain; I wouldn't know how to do it any other way. If I started using long and complicated words that I'd searched for in the dictionary I'd use them too many times, the same ones over and over again, with only a few sentences – if that – between each one; so I'd rather not make what I'm going to write look foolish by using dictionary words.

It's also twenty-eight years since I got married. That statement is very important no matter how you write it or in what way you look at it. It so happened that I married my wife as soon as I got a permanent job, and the first good one I landed was with the Post Office (before that I'd been errand-boy and mash-lad). I had to marry her as soon as I got a job because I'd promised her I would, and she wasn't the sort of person to let me forget it.

When my first pay night came I called for her and asked: 'What about a walk up Snakey Wood?' I was cheeky-daft and on top of the world, and because I'd forgotten about our arrangement I didn't think it strange at all when she said: 'Yes, all right.' It was late autumn I remember and the leaves were as high as snow, crisp on top but soggy underneath. In the full moon and light wind we walked over the Cherry Orchard, happy and arm-in-arm. Suddenly she stopped and turned to me, a big-boned girl yet with a good figure and a nice enough face: 'Do you want to go into the wood?'

What a thing to ask! I laughed: 'You know I do. Don't you?'

We walked on, and a minute later she said: 'Yes, I do; but you know what we're to do now you've got a steady job, don't you?'

I wondered what it was all about. Yet I knew right enough. 'Get married,' I admitted, adding on second thoughts: 'I don't have much of a wage to be wed on, you know.'

'It's enough, as far as I'm concerned,' she answered.

And that was that. She gave me the best kiss I'd ever had, and then we went into the wood.

She was never happy about our life together, right from the start. And neither was I, because it didn't take her long to begin telling me that all her friends – her family most of all – said time and time again that our marriage wouldn't last five minutes. I could never say much back to this, knowing after the first few months how right everybody would be. Not that it bothered me though, because I was always the sort of bloke that doesn't get ruffled at anything. If you want to know the truth – the sort of thing I don't suppose many blokes would be ready to admit – the bare fact of my getting married meant only that I changed one house and one mother for another house and a different mother. It was as simple as that. Even my wage-packet didn't alter its course: I handed it over every Friday night and got five shillings back for tobacco and a visit to the pictures. It was the sort of wedding where the cost of the ceremony and reception go as a down payment, and you then continue dishing-out your wages every week for life. Which is where I suppose they got this hire purchase idea from.

But our marriage lasted for more than the five minutes everybody prophesied: it went on for six years; she left me when I was thirty, and when she was thirty-four. The trouble was that when we had a row – and they were rows, swearing, hurling pots: the lot – it was too much like suffering, and in the middle of them it seemed to me as if we'd done nothing but row and suffer like this from the moment we set eyes on each other, with not a moment's break, and that it would go on like this for as long as we stayed together. The truth was, as I see it now – and even saw it sometimes then – that a lot of our time was bloody enjoyable.

I'd had an idea before she went that our time as man and wife was about up, because one day we had the worst fight of them all. We were sitting at home one evening after tea, one at each end of the table, plates empty and bellies full so that there was no excuse for what followed. My head was in a book, and Kathy just sat there.

Suddenly she said: 'I do love you, Harry.' I didn't hear the words for some time, as is often the case when you're reading a book. Then: 'Harry, look at me.'

My face came up, smiled, and went down again to my reading. Maybe I was in the wrong, and should have said something, but the book was too good.

'I'm sure all that reading's bad for your eyes,' she commented, prising me again from the hot possessive world of India.

'It ain't,' I denied, not looking up. She was young and still fair-faced, a passionate loose-limbed thirty-odd that wouldn't let me sidestep either her obstinacy or anger. 'My dad used to say that on'y fools read books, because they'd such a lot to learn.'

The words hit me and sank in, so that I couldn't resist coming back with, still not looking up: 'He on'y said that because he didn't know how to read. He was jealous, if you ask me.'

'No need to be jealous of the rammel you stuff your big head with,' she said, slowly to make sure I knew she meant every word. The print wouldn't stick any more; the storm was too close.

'Look, why don't *you* get a book, duck?' But she never would, hated them like poison.

She sneered: 'I've got more sense; and too much to do.'

Then I blew up, in a mild way because I still hoped she wouldn't take on, that I'd be able to finish my chapter. 'Well let me read, anyway, wain't you? It's an interesting book, and I'm tired.'

But such a plea only gave her another opening. 'Tired? You're allus tired.' She laughed out loud: 'Tired Tim! You ought to do some real work for a change instead of walking the streets with that daft post bag.'

I won't go on, spinning it out word for word. In any case not many more passed before she snatched the book out of my hands. 'You booky bastard,' she screamed, 'nowt but books, books, books, you bleddy dead-'ead' – and threw the book on the heaped-up coals, working it further and further into their blazing middle with the poker.

This annoyed me, so I clocked her one, not very hard, but I did. It was a good reading-book, and what's more it belonged to the library. I'd have to pay for a new one. She slammed out of the house, and I didn't see her until next day.

I didn't think to break my heart very much when she skipped off. I'd had enough. All I can say is that it was a stroke of God's luck we never had any kids. She was confined once or twice, but it never came to anything; each time it dragged more bitterness out of her than we could absorb in the few peaceful months that came between. It might have been better if she'd had kids though; you never know.

A month after burning the book she ran off with a house-painter. It was all done very nicely. There was no shouting or knocking each other about or breaking up the happy home. I just came back from work one day and found a note waiting for me. 'I am going away and not coming back' – propped on the mantelpiece in front of the clock. No tear stains on the paper, just eight words in pencil on a page of the insurance book – I've still got it in the back of my wallet, though God knows why.

The housepainter she went with had lived in a house on his own, across the terrace. He'd been on the dole for a few months and suddenly got a job at a place twenty miles away I was later told. The neighbours seemed almost eager to let me know – after they'd gone, naturally – that they'd been knocking-on together for about a year. No one knew where they'd skipped off to exactly, probably imagining that I wanted to chase after them. But the idea never occurred to me. In any case what was I to do? Knock him flat and drag Kathy back by the hair? Not likely.

Even now it's no use trying to tell myself that I wasn't disturbed by this change in my life. You miss a woman when she's been living with you in the same house for six years, no matter what sort of cat-and-dog life you led together – though we had our moments, that I will say. After her sudden departure there was something different about the house, about the walls, ceiling and every object in it. And something altered inside me as well – though I tried to tell myself that all was just the same and that Kathy's leaving me wouldn't make a blind bit of difference. Nevertheless time crawled at first, and I felt like a man just learning to pull himself along with a clubfoot; but then the endless evenings of summer came and I was happy almost against my will, too happy anyway to hang on to such torments as sadness and loneliness. The world was moving and, I felt, so was I.

In other words I succeeded in making the best of things, which as much as anything else meant eating a good meal at the canteen every midday. I boiled an egg for breakfast (fried with bacon on Sundays) and had something cold but solid for my tea every night. As things went, it wasn't a bad life. It might have been a bit lonely, but at least it was peaceful, and it got as I didn't mind it, one way or the other. I even lost the feeling of loneliness that had set me thinking a bit too much just after she'd gone. And then I didn't dwell on it any more. I saw enough people on my rounds during the day to last me through the evenings and week-ends. Sometimes I played draughts at the club, or went out for a slow half pint to the pub up the street.

Things went on like this for ten years. From what I gathered later Kathy had been living in Leicester with her housepainter. Then she came back to Nottingham. She came to see me one Friday evening, payday. From her point of view, as it turned out, she couldn't have come at a better time.

I was leaning on my gate in the backyard smoking a pipe of tobacco. I'd had a busy day on my rounds, an irritating time of it – being handed back letters all along the line, hearing that people had left and that no one had any idea where they'd moved to; and other people taking as much as ten minutes to get out of bed and sign for a registered letter – and now I felt twice as peaceful because I was at home, smoking my pipe in the backyard at the fag-end of an autumn day. The sky was a clear yellow, going green above the housetops and wireless aerials. Chimneys were just beginning to send out evening smoke, and most of the factory motors had been switched off. The noise of kids scooting around lamp-posts and the barking of dogs came from what sounded a long way off. I was about to knock my pipe out, to go back into the house and carry on reading a book about Brazil I'd left off the night before.

As soon as she came around the corner and started walking up the yard I knew her. It gave me a funny feeling, though: ten years ain't enough to change anybody so's you don't recognise them, but it's long enough to make you have to look twice before you're sure. And that split second in between is like a kick in the stomach. She didn't walk with her usual gait, as though she owned the terrace and everybody in it. She was a bit slower than when I'd seen her last, as if she'd bumped into a wall during the last ten years through walking in the cock o' the walk way she'd always had. She didn't seem so sure of herself and was fatter now, wearing a frock left over from the summer and an open winter coat, and her hair had been dyed fair whereas it used to be a nice shade of brown.

I was neither glad nor unhappy to see her, but maybe that's what shock does, because I was surprised, that I will say. Not that I never expected to see her again, but you know how it is, I'd just forgotten her somehow. The longer she was away our married life shrunk to a year, a month, a day, a split second of sparking light I'd met in the black darkness before getting-up time. The memory had drawn itself too far back, even in ten years, to remain as anything much more than a dream. For as soon as I got used to living alone I forgot her.

Even though her walk had altered I still expected her to say something sarky like: 'Didn't expect to see me back at the scene of the crime so soon, did you, Harry?' Or: 'You thought it wasn't true that a bad penny always turns up again, didn't you?'

But she just stood. 'Hello, Harry' – waited for me to lean up off the gate so's she could get in. 'It's been a long time since we saw each other, hasn't it?'

I opened the gate, slipping my empty pipe away. 'Hello, Kathy,' I said, and walked down the yard so that she could come behind me. She buttoned her coat as we went into the kitchen, as though she were leaving the house instead of just going in. 'How are you getting on then?' I asked, standing near the fireplace.

Her back was to the wireless, and it didn't seem as if she wanted to look at me. Maybe I was a bit upset after all at her sudden visit, and it's possible I showed it without knowing it at the time, because I filled my pipe up straightaway, a thing I never normally do. I always let one pipe cool down before lighting the next.

'I'm fine,' was all she'd say.

'Why don't you sit down then, Kath? I'll get you a bit of a fire soon.'

She kept her eyes to herself still, as if not daring to look at the old things around her, which were much as they'd been when she left. However she'd seen enough to remark: 'You look after yourself all right.'

'What did you expect?' I said, though not in a sarcastic way.

She wore lipstick. I noticed, which I'd never seen on her before, and rouge, maybe powder as well, making her look old in a different way, I supposed, than if she'd had nothing on her face at all. It was a thin disguise, yet sufficient to mask from me – and maybe her – the person she'd been ten years ago.

'I hear there's a war coming on,' she said, for the sake of talking.

I pulled a chair away from the table. 'Come on, sit down, Kathy. Get that weight off your legs' – an old phrase we'd used though I don't know why I brought it out at that moment. 'No, I wouldn't be a bit surprised. That bloke Hitler wants a bullet in his brain – like a good many Germans.' I looked up and caught her staring at the picture of a fishing boat on the wall: brown and rusty with sails half spread in a bleak sunrise, not far from the beach along which a woman walked bearing a basket of fish on her shoulder. It was one of a set that Kathy's brother had given us as a wedding present, the other two having been smashed up in another argument we'd had. She liked it a lot, this remaining fishing-boat picture. The last of the fleet, we used to call it, in our brighter moments. 'How are you getting on?' I wanted to know. 'Living all right?'

'All right,' she answered. I still couldn't get over the fact that she wasn't as talkative as she had been, that her voice was softer and flatter, with no more bite in it. But perhaps she felt strange at seeing me in the old house again after all this time, with everything just as she'd left it. I had a wireless now, that was the only difference.

'Got a job?' I asked. She seemed afraid to take the chair I'd offered her.

'At Hoskins,' she told me, 'on Amber Gate. The lace factory. It pays forty-two bob a week, which isn't bad.' She sat down and did up the remaining button of her coat. I saw she was looking at the fishing-boat picture again. The last of the fleet.

'It ain't good either. They never paid owt but starvation wages and never will I suppose. Where are you living, Kathy?'

Straightening her hair – a trace of grey near the roots – she said: 'I've got a house at Sneinton. Little, but it's only seven and six a week. It's noisy as well, but I like it that way. I was always one for a bit of life, you know that. "A pint of beer and a quart of noise" was what you used to say, didn't you?'

I smiled. 'Fancy you remembering that.' But she didn't look as though she had much of a life. Her eyes lacked that spark of humour that often soared up into the bonfire of a laugh. The lines around them now served only as an indication of age and passing time. 'I'm glad to hear you're taking care of yourself.'

She met my eyes for the first time. 'You was never very excitable, was you, Harry?'

'No,' I replied truthfully, 'not all that much.'

'You should have been,' she said, though in an empty sort of way, 'then we might have hit it off a bit better.'

'Too late now,' I put in, getting the full blow-through of my words. 'I was never one for rows and trouble, you know that. Peace is more my line.'

She made a joke at which we both laughed. 'Like that bloke Chamberlain!' – then moved a plate to the middle of the table and laid her elbows on the cloth. 'I've been looking after myself for the last three years.'

It may be one of my faults, but I get a bit curious sometimes. 'What's happened to that housepainter of yours then?' I asked this question quite naturally though, because I didn't feel I had anything to reproach her with. She'd gone away, and that was that. She hadn't left me in the lurch with a mountain of debts or any such thing. I'd always let her do what she liked.

'I see you've got a lot of books,' she remarked, noticing one propped against the sauce bottle, and two more on the sideboard.

'They pass the time on,' I replied, striking a match because my pipe had gone out. 'I like reading.'

She didn't say anything for a while. Three minutes I remember, because I was looking across at the clock on the dresser. The news would have been on the wireless, and I'd missed the best part of it. It was getting interesting because of the coming war. I didn't have anything else to do but think this while I was waiting for her to speak. 'He died of lead-poisoning,' she told me. 'He did suffer a lot, and he was only forty-two. They took him away to the hospital a week before he died.'

I couldn't say I was sorry, though it was impossible to hold much against him. I just didn't know the chap. 'I don't think I've got a fag in the place to offer you,' I said, looking on the mantelpiece in case I might find one, though knowing I wouldn't. She moved when I passed her on my search, scraping her chair along the floor. 'No, don't bother to shift. I can get by.'

'It's all right,' she said. 'I've got some here' – feeling in her pocket and bringing out a crumpled five-packet. 'Have one, Harry?'

'No thanks. I haven't smoked a fag in twenty years. You know that. Don't you remember how I started smoking a pipe? When we were courting. You gave me one once for my birthday and told me to start smoking it because it would make me look more distinguished! So I've smoked one ever since. I got used to it quick enough, and I like it now. I'd never be without it in fact.'

As if it were yesterday! But maybe I was talking too much, for she seemed a bit nervous while lighting her fag. I don't know why it was, because she didn't need to be in my house. 'You know, Harry,' she began, looking at the fishing-boat picture, nodding her head towards it, 'I'd like to have that' – as though she'd never wanted anything so much in her life.

'Not a bad picture, is it?' I remember saying. 'It's nice to have pictures on the wall, not to look at especially, but they're company. Even when you're not looking at them you know they're there. But you can take it if you like.'

'Do you mean that?' she asked, in such a tone that I felt sorry for her for the first time.

'Of course. Take it. I've got no use for it. In any case I can get another picture if I want one, or put a war map up.' It was the only picture on that wall, except for the wedding photo on the sideboard below. But I didn't want to remind her of the wedding picture for fear it would bring back memories she didn't like. I hadn't kept it there for sentimental reasons, so perhaps I should have dished it. 'Did you have any kids?'

'No,' she said, as if not interested. 'But I don't like taking your picture, and I'd rather not if you think all that much of it.' We sat looking over each other's shoulder for a long time. I wondered what had happened during these ten years to make her talk so sadly about the picture. It was getting dark outside. Why didn't she shut up about it, just take the bloody thing? So I offered it to her again, and to settle the issue unhooked it, dusted the back with a cloth, wrapped it up in brown paper, and tied the parcel with the best post-office string. 'There you are,' I said, brushing the pots aside, laying it on the table at her elbows.

'You're very good to me, Harry.'

'Good! I like that. What does a picture more or less in the house matter? And what does it mean to me, anyway?' I can see now that we were giving each other hard knocks in a way we'd never learned to do when living together. I switched on the electric light. As she seemed uneasy when it showed every-thing up clearly in the room, I offered to switch it off again.

'No, don't bother' – standing to pick up her parcel. 'I think I'll be going now. Happen I'll see you some other time.'

'Drop in whenever you feel like it.' Why not? We weren't enemies. She undid two buttons of her coat, as though having them loose would make her look more at her ease and happy in her clothes, then waved to me. 'So long.'

'Good night, Kathy.' It struck me that she hadn't smiled or laughed once the whole time she'd been there, so I smiled to her as she turned for the door, and what came back wasn't the bare-faced cheeky grin I once knew, but a wry parting of the lips moving more for exercise than humour. She must have been through it, I thought, and she's above forty now.

So she went. But it didn't take me long to get back to my book.

A few mornings later I was walking up St Ann's Well Road delivering letters. My round was taking a long time, for I had to stop at almost every shop. It was raining, a fair drizzle, and water rolled off my cape, soaking my trousers below the knees so that I was looking forward to a mug of tea back in the canteen and hoping they'd kept the stove going. If I hadn't been so late on my round I'd have dropped into a café for a cup.

I'd just taken a pack of letters into a grocer's and, coming out, saw the fishing-boat picture in the next-door pawnshop window, the one I'd given Kathy a few days ago. There was no mistaking it, leaning back against ancient spirit-levels, bladeless planes, rusty hammers, trowels, and a violin case with the strap broken. I recognised a chip in the gold-painted woodwork near the bottom left corner of its frame.

For half a minute I couldn't believe it, was unable to make out how it had got there, then saw the first day of my married life and a sideboard loaded with presents, prominent among them this surviving triplet of a picture looking at me from the wreckage of other lives. And here it is, I thought, come down to a bloody nothing. She must have sold it that night before going home, pawnshops always keeping open late on a Friday so that women could get their husbands' suits out of pop for the week-end. Or maybe she'd sold it this morning, and I was only half an hour behind her on my round. Must have been really hard up. Poor Kathy, I thought. Why hadn't she asked me to let her have a bob or two?

I didn't think much about what I was going to do next. I never do, but went inside and stood at the shop counter waiting for a grey-haired doddering skinflint to sort out the popped bundles of two thin-faced women hovering to make sure he knew they were pawning the best of stuff. I was impatient. The place stank of old clothes and mildewed junk after coming out of fresh rain, and besides I was later than ever now on my round. The canteen would be closed before I got back, and I'd miss my morning tea.

The old man shuffled over at last, his hand out. 'Got any letters?'

'Nowt like that, feyther. I'd just like to have a look at that

picture you've got in your window, the one with a ship on it.'
The women went out counting what few shillings he'd given
them, stuffing pawn-tickets in their purses, and the old man
came back carrying the picture as if it was worth five quid.

Shock told me she'd sold it right enough, but belief lagged a
long way behind, so I looked at it well to make sure it really
was the one. A price marked on the back wasn't plain enough
to read. 'How much do you want for it?'

'You can have it for four bob.'

Generosity itself. But I'm not one for bargaining. I could
have got it for less, but I'd rather pay an extra bob than go
through five minutes of chinning. So I handed the money over,
and said I'd call back for the picture later.

Four measly bob, I said to myself as I sloshed on through
the rain. The robbing bastard. He must have given poor Kathy
about one and six for it. Three pints of beer for the fishing-
boat picture.

I don't know why, but I was expecting her to call again the
following week. She came on Thursday, at the same time, and
was dressed in the usual way: summer frock showing through
her brown winter coat whose buttons she couldn't leave alone,
telling me how nervous she was. She'd had a drink or two on
her way, and before coming into the house stopped off at the
lavatory outside. I'd been late back from work, and hadn't
quite finished my tea, asked her if she could do with a cup. 'I
don't feel like it,' came the answer. 'I had one not long ago.'

I emptied the coal scuttle on the fire. 'Sit down nearer the
warmth. It's a bit nippy tonight.'

She agreed that it was, then looked up at the fishing-boat
picture on the wall. I'd been waiting for this, wondered what
she'd say when she did, but there was no surprise at seeing it
back in the old place, which made me feel a bit disappointed.
'I won't be staying long tonight,' was all she said. 'I've got to
see somebody at eight.'

Not a word about the picture. 'That's all right. How's your
work going?'

'Putrid,' she answered nonchalantly, as though my question had been out of place. 'I got the sack, for telling the forewoman where to get off.'

'Oh,' I said, getting always to say 'Oh' when I wanted to hide my feelings, though it was a safe bet that whenever I did say 'Oh' there wasn't much else to come out with.

I had an idea she might want to live in my house again seeing she'd lost her job. If she wanted to she could. And she wouldn't be afraid to ask, even now. But I wasn't going to mention it first. Maybe that was my mistake, though I'll never know. 'A pity you got the sack,' I put in.

Her eyes were on the picture again, until she asked: 'Can you lend me half-a-crown?'

'Of course I can' – emptied my trouser pocket, sorted out half-a-crown, and passed it across to her. Five pints. She couldn't think of anything to say, shuffled her feet to some soundless tune in her mind. 'Thanks very much.'

'Don't mention it,' I said with a smile. I remembered buying a packet of fags in case she'd want one, which shows how much I'd expected her back. 'Have a smoke?' – and she took one, struck a match on the sole of her shoe before I could get her a light myself.

'I'll give you the half-crown next week, when I get paid.' That's funny, I thought. 'I got a job as soon as I lost the other one,' she added, reading my mind before I had time to speak. 'It didn't take long. There's plenty of war work now. Better money as well.'

'I suppose all the firms'll be changing over soon.' It occurred to me that she could claim some sort of allowance from me – for we were still legally married – instead of coming to borrow half-a-crown. It was her right, and I didn't need to remind her; I wouldn't be all that much put out if she took me up on it. I'd been single – as you might say – for so many years that I hadn't been able to stop myself putting a few quid by. 'I'll be going now,' she said, standing up to fasten her coat.

'Sure you won't have a cup of tea?'

'No thanks. Want to catch the trolley back to Sneinton.' I

said I'd show her to the door. 'Don't bother. I'll be all right.'
She stood waiting for me, looking at the picture on the wall
above the sideboard. 'It's a nice picture you've got up there. I
always liked it a lot.'

I made the old joke: 'Yes, but it's the last of the fleet.'

'That's why I like it.' Not a word about having sold it for
eighteen pence.

I showed her out, mystified.

She came to see me every week, all through the war, always
on Thursday night at about the same time. We talked a bit,
about the weather, the war, her job and my job, never anything
important. Often we'd sit for a long time looking into the fire
from our different stations in the room, me by the hearth and
Kathy a bit further away at the table as if she'd just finished
a meal, both of us silent yet not uneasy in it. Sometimes I made
a cup of tea, sometimes not. I suppose now that I think of it I
could have got a pint of beer in for when she came, but it never
occurred to me. Not that I think she felt the lack of it, for it
wasn't the sort of thing she expected to see in my house anyway.

She never missed coming once, even though she often had a
cold in the winter and would have been better off in bed. The
blackout and shrapnel didn't stop her either. In a quiet off-
handed sort of way we got to enjoy ourselves and looked forward
to seeing each other again, and maybe they were the best times
we ever had together in our lives. They certainly helped us
through the long monotonous dead evenings of the war.

She was always dressed in the same brown coat, growing
shabbier and shabbier. And she wouldn't leave without
borrowing a few shillings. Stood up: 'Er . . . lend's half-a-dollar,
Harry.' Given, sometimes with a joke: 'Don't get too drunk on
it, will you?' – never responded to, as if it were bad manners
to joke about a thing like that. I didn't get anything back of
course, but then, I didn't miss such a dole either. So I wouldn't
say no when she asked me, and as the price of beer went up
she increased the amount to three bob then to three-and-six
and, finally, just before she died, to four bob. It was a pleasure

to be able to help her. Besides, I told myself, she has no one else. I never asked questions as to where she was living, though she did mention a time or two that it was still up Sneinton way. Neither did I at any time see her outside at a pub or picture house; Nottingham is a big town in many ways.

On every visit she would glance from time to time at the fishing-boat picture, the last of the fleet, hanging on the wall above the sideboard. She often mentioned how beautiful she thought it was, and how I should never part with it, how the sunrise and the ship and the woman and the sea were just right. Then a few minutes later she'd hint to me how nice it would be if she had it, but knowing it would end up in the pawnshop I didn't take her hints. I'd rather have lent her five bob instead of half-a-crown so that she wouldn't take the picture, but she never seemed to want more than half-a-crown in those first years. I once mentioned to her she could have more if she liked, but she didn't answer me. I don't think she wanted the picture especially to sell and get money, or to hang in her own house; only to have the pleasure of pawning it, to have someone else buy it so that it wouldn't belong to either of us any more.

But she finally did ask me directly, and I saw no reason to refuse when she put it like that. Just as I had done six years before, when she first came to see me, I dusted it, wrapped it up carefully in several layers of brown paper, tied it with post-office string, and gave it to her. She seemed happy with it under her arm, couldn't get out of the house quick enough, it seemed.

It was the same old story though, for a few days later I saw it again in the pawnshop window, among all the old junk that had been there for years. This time I didn't go in and try to get it back. In a way I wish I had, because then Kathy might not have had the accident that came a few days later. Though you never know. If it hadn't been that, it would have been something else.

I didn't get to her before she died. She'd been run down by a lorry at six o'clock in the evening, and by the time the police had taken me to the General Hospital she was dead. She'd been knocked all to bits, and had practically bled to death even before they'd got her to the hospital. The doctor told me she'd not been quite sober when she was knocked down. Among the things of hers they showed me was the fishing-boat picture, but it was so broken up and smeared with blood that I hardly recognised it. I burned it in the roaring flames of the firegrate late that night.

When her two brothers, their wives and children had left and taken with them the air of blame they attached to me for Kathy's accident I stood at the graveside thinking I was alone, hoping I would end up crying my eyes out. No such luck. Holding my head up suddenly I noticed a man I hadn't seen before. It was a sunny afternoon of winter, but bitter cold, and the only thing at first able to take my mind off Kathy was the thought of some poor bloke having to break the bone-hard soil and dig this hole she was now lying in. Now there was this stranger. Tears were running down his cheeks, a man in his middle fifties wearing a good suit, grey though but with a black band around his arm, who moved only when the fed-up sexton touched his shoulder – and then mine – to say it was all over.

I felt no need to ask who he was. And I was right. When I got to Kathy's house (it had also been his) he was packing his things, and left a while later in a taxi without saying a word. But the neighbours, who always know everything, told me he and Kathy had been living together for the last six years. Would you believe it? I only wished he'd made her happier than she'd been.

Time has passed now and I haven't bothered to get another picture for the wall. Maybe a war map would do it; the wall gets too blank, for I'm sure some government will oblige soon. But it doesn't really need anything at the moment, to tell you the truth. That part of the room is filled up by the sideboard, on which is still the wedding picture, that she never thought to ask for.

And looking at these few old pictures stacked in the back of my mind I began to realise that I should never have let them go, and that I shouldn't have let Kathy go either. Something told me I'd been daft and dead to do it, and as my rotten luck would have it it was the word dead more than daft that stuck in my mind, and still sticks there like the spinebone of a cod or conger eel, driving me potty sometimes when I lay of a night in bed thinking.

I began to believe there was no point in my life – became even too far gone to turn religious or go on the booze. Why had I lived? I wondered. I can't see anything for it. What was the point of it all? And yet at the worst minutes of my midnight emptiness I'd think less of myself and more of Kathy, see her as suffering in a far rottener way than ever I'd done, and it would come to me – though working only as long as an aspirin pitted against an incurable headache – that the object of my having been alive was that in some small way I'd helped Kathy through her life.

I was born dead, I keep telling myself. Everybody's dead, I answer. So they are, I maintain, but then most of them never know it like I'm beginning to do, and it's a bloody shame that this has come to me at last when I could least do with it, and when it's too bloody late to get anything but bad from it.

Then optimism rides out of the darkness like a knight in armour. If you loved her . . . (of course I bloody-well did) . . . then you both did the only thing possible if it was to be remembered as love. Now didn't you? Knight in armour goes back into blackness. Yes, I cry, but neither of us *did anything about it*, and that's the trouble.

NO NAME IN THE STREET

'Do you know, you get on my bloody nerves, you do.'

Albert's black-and-white dog ran between his feet, making him scuffle out of the way in case he should tread on it and commit an injury. 'You've got on my bleddy nerves all day.'

It was almost dark when they set out for the golf course. A cool wind carried a whiff of hay from large square bales scattered about the field like tank-traps in the war when, as a youth in the Home Guard, he used to run from one to another with a rifle in his hand. It smelled good, the air did. He hadn't noticed in those distant days whether it had smelled good or not. Or perhaps he didn't remember. But you could tell it had been a hot day today because even though the wind had a bit of an edge to it the whiff of hay was warm. 'You do, you get on my bleddy nerves.'

The dog quickened its pace, as if a bit more liveliness would mend matters. And Albert lengthened his stride, not in response to the dog but because he always did when he made that turning in the lane and saw the wood's dark shape abutting the golf course. His dog anticipated this further increase of speed. Having been pulled in off the street a couple of years ago when it was starving, it couldn't afford not to. Even a dog knew that nothing was certain in life.

They'd come this way on most nights since, so there was no reason why it shouldn't know what to do. Why it got on his nerves so much he'd no idea, but what else could you expect from a dog?

'Get away from my feet, will yer?' His voice was little more than a sharp whisper because they were so near. The 'will yer?' – which he added with a certain amount of threat and venom – caused the dog to rub against his trousers and bounce off, then continue walking, almost in step despite both sets of legs still perilously close. 'You'll drive me up the pole, yer will. My nerves are all to bits.'

It wasn't a cold evening, following a hot day at the end of June, but he wore a long dark blue overcoat, a white nylon scarf, and a bowler hat, more because he was familiar with them than to keep warm. He felt protected and alive inside his best clothes, and in any case he usually put them on when he left the house in the evening, out of some half surfaced notion that if anything happened so that he couldn't get back home then at least he would be in clothes that would last a while, or fetch a bob or two at the ragshop if he had to sell 'em.

There was no reason why he should be this way, but that didn't make it less real. Apart from which, he couldn't go to the golf course wearing his shabby stuff. The adage that if you dressed smart you *did* well was about the only useful advice his father had ever tried to tell him, though it was so obvious a truth that it would have made no difference had he kept his trap shut, especially since neither he nor his father had ever done well at anything in their lives.

'Here we are, you aggravating bogger.' He stopped at the fence, then turned to the dog which, as always at this point, and for reasons best known to itself, hung back. 'Don't forget to follow me in – or I'll put me boot in your soup-box.'

No hole was visible, but Albert knew exactly where it was. He got down on his haunches, shuffled forwards, and lifted a strand of smooth wire. The dog saw him vanish. When he stood up in the total blackness of the wood, he heard the dog whine because it was still on the wrong side of the fence.

It showed no sign of coming through to join him, even though it was a job so much easier for a dog than a man. At least you might have thought so, but the bleddy thing was as deaf as a haddock when it came to telling it what to do. It hesitated so long that, after a suitable curse, Albert's pale bony hand at the end of his clothed arm at last appeared under the fence, grabbed it by the collar (you had to give the damned thing a collar, or somebody else might take it in) and yanked it through, briars and all.

It didn't yelp. Whatever happened was no more than it expected. 'You get on my bleddy nerves,' Albert said, holding its wet nose close, and staring into its opaque apologetic eyes.

When he walked along the invisible path he knew that the dog was obediently following. They went through the same haffle-and-caffle every time, and it got on his nerves no end, but it would have chafed them even more if the dog had done as it was supposed to do, because in that case Albert might not even know it was there. And then there would be no proof that he had any nerves at all worth getting on. He often told himself that there was at least some advantage in having such a mongrel.

He could do this zig-zag walk without cracking twigs, but the dog rustled and sniffled enough for both of them, biting leaves as if there was a rat or ferret under every twig. On first bringing the tike into his house it had shivered in a corner for three days. Then one morning it got up, jumped on to the table (treading its muddy paws all over the cloth) and ate his pot of geraniums almost down to the stubs. Afterwards it was sick on the lino. Then he gave it some bread and milk, followed by a bowl of soup (oxtail) – and from that point on there was no holding it. He even had to get a key to the food cupboard.

Albert hadn't felt right since his mother died three years ago, unable to work after losing her, finding that nobody would set him on at any job because they saw in his face that the guts had been knocked out of him. That's what he thought it was, and when he told them at the Welfare that he felt he was on the scrapheap, they gave him money to keep the house and himself going.

It wasn't a bleddy sight. The dog was eating him out of house and home. Every time he had a slice of bread-and-marmalade he had to cut some for the dog as well. Same when he poured a cup of tea, he had to put a saucerful on the floor. So you had to do summat to earn a few bob extra.

There was a bit of light in the wood now they'd got used to it, and when he reached the fence he saw that the moon was coming. It wasn't much of one, but it would be a help – without being too much of a hindrance. Sandpit holes in the golf course beyond glowed like craters. The dog ran into a bush, and came out more quickly than he'd expected, nudging his leg with something hard in its jaws. Albert bent down and felt cold saliva as he took it and put it into his pocket. 'That's one, any road. Let's hope there'll be plenty more.'

Occasionally when they found one so early it ended up a bad harvest. But you never knew. Life was full of surprises, and dreams. He had visions of coming across more lost golf balls than he could carry, pyramids that would need a wheelbarrow to take away. He saw a sandy depression of the golf course levelled off with them. He even had the odd picture of emerging from the wood and spotting a dozen or so, plain and white under the moon, and watching himself dart over the greenery, pocketing each one. In his dream though, the golf balls seemed soft and warm in his fingers as he slipped them into his topcoat pocket.

The dog brought another while he smoked a fag, but then minutes went by without any more. 'All right,' he said, 'we'd better go and see what we can find. Best not get too close to the clubhouse: the boggers stay up boozing late enough in that cosy place they've got.'

His dog agreed, went through the fence this time even before Albert had finished muttering, glad to be in the open again. They said next door that his mother had to die sometime. Not much else they could say, being as she was nearly eighty. She used to talk to him about his father, who had gone to work one day twenty-five years ago complaining of pains in his stomach, and not come back alive. Something about a ruptured ulcer, or maybe it was cancer. There was no point in caring, once it had happened. The doctor had been kind, but told them nothing – a man who looked at you with the sort of glittering eyes that didn't expect you to ask questions.

Then *she* went as well. He bent down one morning to look, and saw that she'd never wake up. He sat with her a few minutes before going to get the doctor, not realising till he got out of the door that he'd been with her ten hours in that long moment, and that dusk was begining to glow up the cold street.

He was glad to be in the actual golf course because the wood was full of nettles, and brambles twisting all over the place. Stark moonlight shone on the grass so that it looked like frost. Even before he'd gone five yards the dog came leaping back, and pushed another ball into his hand, the sand still gritty on its nose. That was three already, so maybe a jackpot-night was coming up, though he didn't like to think so, in case it wasn't. Perhaps he should hope it would turn out rotten, then every find would be encouraging, though at the same time he'd feel a bit of a cheat if he ended up with loads. Yet he'd also be more glad than if he'd hoped it would finish well and it turned out lousy. He'd appear foolish sooner than lose his dream, though he'd rather lose his dream if it meant things seeming too uncomfortably real. The best thing was, like always, not to forecast anything, and see what happened.

Every golf ball meant fifteen pence in his pocket from the secondhand shop, and some weeks his finds added up to a couple of quid on top of his Social Security. He earned more by it than when he used to hang around caddying as a youth of fourteen before the war. Every little had helped in those far-off days, but there'd been too many others at it. Things had altered for the better when he'd got taken on at Gedling Pit, because as well as getting work he was exempted from the army.

After the funeral he sat in the house wearing his best suit, and wondering what would happen to him now. Going for a walk in the milk-and-water sunshine he wandered near the golf course one day and saw a ball lying at his feet when he stopped to light a cigarette. He picked it up, took it home, and put it in a cut-glass bowl on the dresser. Later he went back looking for more.

He ran his fingers over the hard indented pattern, brushing off sand grains and grass blades as they went along. It was an ordinary night, after all, because they found no more than four. 'Come on, then, you slack bogger,' he said to the dog. 'Let's be off, or you'll be getting on my nerves again!'

'It's a good dog,' he said, sitting at a table with his half pint of ale, 'but it gets on my nerves a bit too much at times.'

They wondered what nerves he had to get on, such an odd-looking well-wrapped up fifty year old whose little Jack Russell, dog had followed him in. One of the railwaymen at the bar jokingly remarked that the dog was like a walking snowball with a stump of wood up its arse.

Albert sat brushing his bowler hat with his right-hand sleeve, making an anti-clockwise motion around the crown and brim. Those who'd known him for years could see how suffering had thinned his face, lined his forehead, and deepened the vulnerable look in his eyes. Yet they wouldn't have admitted that he had anything to suffer about. Hadn't he got house, grub, clothes, half pint, and even a dog? But whatever it was, the expression and the features (by now you couldn't tell where one ended and the other began) made him seem wiser and gentler than he was, certainly a different man to the knockabout young collier he'd been up to not too long ago.

He indicated the dog: 'He's got his uses, though.'

The railwayman held up a crisp from his packet, and the animal waited for it to drop. 'As long as it's obedient. That's all you want from a dog.'

'It'll have your hand off, if you don't drop that crisp,' Albert told him. The railwayman took the hint, and let it fall under a stool. The crunch was heard, because everyone was listening for it.

'As long as it's faithful, as well,' a woman at the next table put in.

You were never alone with a dog, he thought. Everybody was bound to remark on it before long.

'A dog's got to be faithful to its owner,' she said. 'It'll be obedient all right, if it's faithful.'

'It's a help to me,' Albert admitted, 'even though it does get on my nerves.'

'Nerves!' she called out. 'What nerves? You ain't got *nerves*, have you?'

She'd tricked him squarely, by hinting that some disease like worms was gnawing at his insides.

'I'm not mental, if that's what you mean.' Since he didn't know from her voice whether she was friendly or not, he looked at her more closely, smiling that she had to scoff at his nerves before his eyes became interested in her.

The dog came back from its crisp. 'Gerrunder!' he told it harshly, to prove that his nerves were as strong as the next person's.

Her homely laugh let him know that such a thing as strong nerves might certainly be possible with him, after all. She had a short drink of gin or vodka in front of her, and a large flat white handbag. There was also an ashtray on the table at which she flicked ash from her cigarette, even when there seemed to be none on its feeble glow, as if trying to throw the large ring on her finger into that place as well. Her opened brown fur coat showed a violet blouse underneath. He'd always found it hard to tell a woman's age, but in this case thought that, with such short greying hair fluffed up over her head, she must be about fifty.

'Let him know who's boss,' she said.

He felt the golf balls in this overcoat pocket. 'I expect he wants his supper. I'll be getting him home soon.'

Her hard jaw was less noticeable when she spoke. 'Don't let him run your life.'

'He don't do that. But he's fussy.'

He observed that she had mischief in her eyes as well as in her words. '*I'll* say it is. Are you a local man?'

'Have been all my life,' he told her.

She stood up. 'I'll have another gin before I go. Keeps me warm when I get to bed.'

He watched her stop at the one-armed bandit, stare at the fruit signs as if to read her fortune there, then put a couple of shillings through the mill. Losing, she jerked her head, and ordered the drinks, then said something to the men at the bar that made them laugh.

'You needn't a done that,' Albert said, when she set a pint of best bitter down for him. 'I never have more than half a jar.'

He needed it, by the look of him, this funny-seeming bloke whom she couldn't quite fathom – which was rare for her when it came to men. She was intrigued by the reason for him being set apart from the rest of them in the pub. It was obvious a mile off that he lived alone, but he tried to keep himself smart, all the same, and that was rare.

She pushed the jar an inch closer. 'It'll do you good. Didn't you ever get away in the army?'

'No.'

'Most men did.'

The dog nudged his leg, but he ignored it. Piss on the floor if you've got to. He'd go home when he was ready. 'I was a collier, and missed all that.'

She drank her gin in one quick flush. 'No use nursing it. I only have a couple, though. I kept a boarding house in Yarmouth for twenty years. Now I'm back in Nottingham. I sometimes wonder why I came back.'

'You must like it,' he suggested.

'I do. And I don't.' She saw the dog nudge him this time. 'Has it got worms, or something?'

'Not on the hasty-pudding he gets from me. He's a bit nervous, though. I expect that's why he gets on my nerves.'

He hadn't touched his pint.

'Aren't you going to have that?'

'I can't sup all of it.'

She thought he was only joking. 'I'll bet you did at one time.'

When his face came alive it took ten years off his age, she noticed.

He laughed. 'I did, an' all!'

'I'll drink it, if you don't.'

'You're welcome.' He smiled at the way she was bossing him, and picked up the jar of ale to drink.

Sometimes, when it was too wet and dreary to go to the golf course he'd sit for hours in the dark, the dog by his side to be conveniently cursed for grating his nerves whenever it scratched or shifted. At such times he might not know whether to go across the yard for a piss or get up and make a cup of tea. But occasionally he'd put the light on for a moment and take twenty pence from under the tea-caddy on the scullery shelf, and go to the pub for a drink before closing time.

If he'd cashed his Social Security cheque that day and he saw Alice there, he'd offer to get her a drink. Once, when she accepted, she said to him afterwards: 'Why don't we live together?'

He didn't answer, not knowing whether he was more surprised at being asked by her, or at the idea of it at all. But he walked her home that night. In the autumn when she went back to his place with him she said: 'You've got to live in my house. It's bigger than yours.' You couldn't expect her to sound much different after donkeys' years landladying in Yarmouth.

'My mother died here.' He poured her another cup of tea. 'I've lived all my life at 28 Hinks Street!'

'All the more reason to get shut on it.'

That was as maybe. He loved the house, and the thought of having to leave it was real pain. He'd be even less of a man without the house. Yet he felt an urge to get out of it, all the same.

'So if you want to come,' she said, not taking sugar because it spoiled the taste of her cigarette, 'you can. I mean what I say. I'm not flighty Fanny Fernackerpan!'

He looked doubtful, and asked himself exactly who the hell she might be. 'I didn't say you was.'

She wondered when he was going to put the light on, whether or no he was saving on the electricity. He hadn't got a telly, and the old wireless on the sideboard had a hole in its face. A dead valve had dust on it. Dust on all of us. She'd picked a winner all right, but didn't she always? The place looked clean enough, except it stank of the dog a bit. 'Not me, I'm not.'

'There's not only me, though,' he said. 'There's two of us.'

She took another Craven 'A' from her handbag, and dropped the match in her saucer, since it seemed he didn't use ashtrays. 'You mean your dog?'

He nodded.

Smoke went towards the mantelshelf. 'There's two of *us*, as well.'

Here was a surprise. If she'd got a dog they'd have to call it off. He was almost glad to hear it. Or perhaps it was a cat. 'Who's that, then?'

'My son, Raymond. He's twenty-two, and not carat-gold, either. He's a rough diamond, you might say, but a good lad – at heart.'

She saw she'd frightened him, but it was better now than later. 'He's the apple of my eye,' she went on, 'but not so much that *you* can't come in and make a go of it with me. With your dog as well, if you like.'

If I like! What sort of language was that? He was glad he'd asked her to come to his house after the pub, otherwise he wouldn't know where to put his face, the way she was talking. 'The dog's only a bit o' summat I picked off the street, but I wouldn't part with him. He's been company, I suppose.'

'Bring him. There's room. But I've always wanted a man about the house, and I've never had one.' Not for long enough, anyway. She told him she might not be much to look at (though he hadn't properly considered that, yet) but that she *had* been at one time, when she'd worked as a typist at the stocking factory. It hadn't done her much good because the gaffer had got her pregnant. O yes, she'd known he was married, and that he was only playing about, and why not? It was good to get a bit of fun out of life, and was nice while it lasted.

He'd been generous, in the circumstances. A lot of men would have slived off, but not him. He'd paid for everything and bought her a house at Yarmouth (where he'd taken her the first weekend they'd slept together: she didn't hide what she meant) so that she could run it as a boarding house and support herself. The money for Raymond came separate, monthly till he was sixteen. She saved and scraped and invested for twenty years, and had a tidy bit put by, though she'd got a job again now, because she didn't have enough to be a lady of leisure, and in any case everybody should earn their keep, so worked as a receptionist at a motoring school. I like having a job, I mean, I wouldn't be very interesting without a job, would I? Raymond works at the Argus Factory on a centre lathe – not a capstan lathe, because anybody can work one of them after an hour – but a proper big centre lathe. She'd seen it when she went in one day to tell the foreman he'd be off for a while with bronchitis – and to collect his wages. He was a clever lad at mechanics and engineering, even if he had left school at sixteen. He made fag lighters and candlesticks and doorknobs on the Q.T.

He could see that she liked to talk, to say what she wanted out of life, and to tell how she'd got where she was – wherever *that* was. But he liked her, so it must have been somewhere. When she talked she seemed to be in some other world, but he knew she wouldn't be feeling so free and enjoying it so much if he hadn't been sitting in front to take most of it in. She'd had a busy life, but wanted somebody to listen to her, and to look as if what she was saying meant something to them both. He could do that right enough, because hadn't he been listening to himself all his life? Be a change hearing somebody else, instead of his own old record.

'There's a garden for your dog, as well, at my place. He won't get run over there. And a bathroom in the house, so you won't have to cross the yard when you want to piddle, like you do here.'

He'd guessed as much, looking at it from the outside when he'd walked her home but hadn't gone in. It was a bay-windowed house at Hucknall with a gate and some palings along the front.

'It's all settled then, duck?'

'I'll say yes.' It felt like jumping down a well you couldn't see the bottom of. He couldn't understand why he felt so glad at doing it.

She reached across to him. He had such rough strong hands for a man who took all night to make up his mind. Still, as long as there was somebody else to make it up for him there'd be no harm done.

'Every old sock finds an old shoe!' she laughed.

'A damned fine way of putting it!'

'It's what a friend at work said when I told her about us.'

He grunted.

'Cheer up! She was only joking. As far as I'm concerned we're as young as the next lot, and we're as old as we feel. I always feel about twenty, if you want to know the truth. I often think I've not started to live yet.'

He smiled. 'I feel that, as well. Funny, in't it?'

She liked how easy it was to cheer him up, which was something else you couldn't say for every chap.

He polished his black boots by first spreading a dab of Kiwi with finger and rag: front, back, sides and laces; then by plying the stiff-bristled brush till his arms ached, which gave them a dullish black-lead look. He put them on for a final shine, lifting each foot in turn to the chair for a five-minute energetic duffing so that he could see his face in them. You couldn't change a phase of your life without giving your boots an all-round clean; and in any case, his face looked more interesting to him reflected in the leather rather than staring back from the mirror over the fireplace.

A large van arrived at half past eight from the best removal firm in town. She knew how to do things, he'd say that for her. Your breakfast's ready, she would call, but he might not want to get up, and then where would they be? Dig the garden, she'd say, and he'd have no energy. What about getting a job? she'd ask. Me and Raymond's got one, and you're no different to be without. I'm having a bit of a rest, he'd say. I worked thirty years at the pit face before I knocked off. Let others have a turn. I've done my share – till I'm good and ready to get set on again. She was the sort who could buy him a new tie and expect him to wear it whether he liked it or not. Still, he wouldn't be pleased if he took her a bunch of flowers and she complained about the colour. You didn't have to wear flowers, though.

He stood on the doorstep and watched the van come up the street. There was no doubt that it was for him. With thinning hair well parted, and bowler hat held on his forearm, he hoped it would go by, but realised that such a thing at this moment was impossible. He didn't want it to, either, for after a night of thick dreams that he couldn't remember he'd been up since six, packing a suitcase and cardboard boxes with things he didn't want the removal men to break or rip. He'd been as active as a bluebottle that spins crazily to try and stop itself dying after the summer's gone.

When you've moved in with me we'll have a honeymoon, she'd joked. Our room's ready for us, though we'll have to be a bit discreet as far as our Raymond's concerned. They would, as well. He'd only kissed her in fun the other night, but it had knocked Raymond all of a heap for the rest of his short stay there. He'd seen that she was a well-made woman, and that she'd be a treat to sleep with. He hadn't been with anyone since before his mother died, but he felt in need of a change now. I'll have to start living again, he told himself, and the thought made him feel good.

The dog's whole body and all paws touched the slab of the pavement as if for greater security on this weird and insecure morning. 'Now don't *you* start getting on my bleddy nerves,' he said as the van pulled up and the alerted animal ran into the house, then altered its mind and came out again. 'That's the last thing I want.'

He wondered if it would rain. Trust it to rain on a day like this. It didn't look like rain, though wasn't it supposed to be a good sign if it did? What was he doing, going off to live in a woman's house at his age? He didn't know her from Adam, though he'd known people get together in less than the three months they'd known each other. Yet he had never wanted to do anything so much in his life before as what he was doing now, and couldn't stop himself even if he wanted to. It was as if he had woken up from a dream of painful storms, into a day where, whatever the weather, the sun shone and he could breathe again. He smiled at the clouds, and put his hat on.

But if that was so, why had he got a scab on his lip? He'd been running the gamut of a cold a week ago, and had expected it to be all over by now. Maybe the cold had been operating at his innards even a week before that, and had twisted his senses so much that only it and not his real self was responsible for leading him into this predicament. He was disturbed by the possibility of thinking so. Yet because he wasn't put out by the impending split-up and change he'd rather think it than worry that he'd been taken over by something outside his control. You couldn't have everything, and so had to be grateful for the bit of good to be got out of any situation, whether you'd done it all on your own, or whether it was the work of God or the Devil.

'This is it, George,' the driver called to his mate's ear only a foot away in the cab. 'I'll pull on to the pavement a bit. Less distance then to carry his bits of rammel.'

He heard that remark, but supposed they'd say it about every house unless it was some posh place up Mapperley or West Bridgford. Maybe the dog caught it as well, for it stood stiffly as the cab door banged and they came towards the house.

'Get down, you bleddy ha'porth, or you'll get on my nerves!'

The dog, with the true aerials of its ears, detected the trouble and uncertainty of Albert's soul, something which Albert couldn't acknowledge because it was too much hidden from him at this moment, and would stay so till some days had passed and the peril it represented had gone. The dog's whine, as it stood up with all sensitivities bristling, seemed to be in full contact with what might well have troubled Albert if he'd had the same equipment. Albert knew it was there, though, and realised also that the dog had ferreted it out, as usual, which lent some truth to his forceful assertion that it was already beginning to get on his bleddy nerves.

The dog went one way, then spun the other. All nerves and no breeding, Albert thought, watching the two men stow his belongings in the van. It didn't take long. They didn't even pull their jackets off when they came in for the preliminary survey. It was a vast contraption they'd brought to shift him to Hucknall, and had clearly expected more than two chairs, a table, wardrobe and bed. There'd been more when his mother was alive, but he'd sold the surplus little by little to the junk shop for a bob or two at a time. It was as if he'd broken off bits of himself like brittle toffee and got rid of it till there was only the framework of a midget left. That was it. His dream had been about that last night. He remembered being in a market place, standing on a stage before a crowd of people. He had a metal hammer with which he hit at his fingers and hand till the bits flew, and people on the edge of the crowd leapt around to grab them, stuffing them into their mouths and clamouring for more. This pleased him so much that he continued to hammer at his toes and arms and legs and – finally – his head.

Bloody fine thing to dream about. All his belongings were stowed aboard, but the terrified dog had slid to the back of the gas stove and wouldn't come out. 'You get on my *bleddy* nerves, you do,' he called. 'Come on, come away from there.'

It was dim, and in the glow of a match he saw the shivering flank of the dog pressed against the greasy skirting board. He looked for an old newspaper to lie on, and drag it out, not wanting to get his overcoat grimy. It was damned amazing, the grit that collected once you took your trappings away, not to mention nails coming through the lino that he hadn't noticed before.

'Come on, mate,' the van driver called, 'we've got to get cracking. Another job at eleven.'

There wasn't any newspaper, so he lay in his overcoat, and spoke to it gently, ignoring the hard bump of something in his pocket: 'Come on, my old duck, don't let me down. There's a garden to run in where you're going. Mutton bones as well, if I know owt. They'll be as soft as steak! Be a good lad, and don't get on my nerves at a time like this.'

The men in the van shouted again, but he took no notice, his eyes squinting at the dim shape of the dog at the back of the stove. It looked so settled, so finally fixed, so comfortable that he almost envied it. He wanted to diminish in size, and crawl in to join it, to stay there in that homely place for ever. We'd eat woodlice and blackclocks and the scrapings of stale grease till we got old together and pegged out, or till the knockdown gangs broke up the street and we got buried and killed. Make space for me and let me come in. I won't get on *your* nerves. I'll lay quiet as a mouse, and sleep most of the time.

His hand shot out to grab it, as he'd pulled it many a time through a hedge by the golf course: 'Come out, you bleddy tike. You get on my nerves!'

A sudden searing rip at his knuckles threw them back against his chest.

'Leave it, mate,' the man in the doorway laughed. 'You can come back for it. We ain't got all day.'

Standing up in case the dog leapt at his throat, he banged his head on the gas stove. He belonged in daylight, on two feet, with blood dripping from his hand, and a bruise already blotching his forehead.

'Smoke the bogger out,' the driver advised. 'That'll settle its 'ash.'

He'd thought of it, and considered it, but it would smoke *him* out as well. Whatever he did to the dog he did to himself. It seemed to be a problem no one could solve, him least of all.

'It's obstinate, in't it?' the younger one observed.

'Go on, fume it out,' urged the driver. 'I'd bleddy kill it if it was mine. I'd bleddy drown it, I would.'

Albert leaned against the opposite wall. 'It ain't yourn, though. It's got a mind of its own.' It was an effort to speak. I'll wring its neck.

'Some bleddy mind,' remarked the driver, cupping his hand to light a cigarette, as if he were still in the open air.

'I can't leave it,' Albert told them.

'What we'll do, mate,' the driver went on, 'is get your stuff to Hucknall, and unload it. You can come on later when you've got your dog out. And if I was you, I'd call in at a chemist's and get summat put on that bite while you're about it. Or else you'll get scabies.'

'Rabies,' his mate said. 'Not fucking scabies.'

'Scabies or rabies or fucking babies, I don't care. But he'd better get summat purronit, I know that fucking much!'

Albert's predicament enraged them more than it did him, and certainly more than the dog. The only consolation came at being glad the dog wasn't doing to them what it was to him. He heard the tailgate slam during their argument, the lynchpins slot in, the cab door bang, and all he owned driven away down the street. There wasn't even a chair to sit on, not a stick, nothing on the walls, nothing, only himself and the dog, and that crumbling decrepit gas stove that she'd said could be left behind because it wasn't worth a light.

He sat on the floor against the opposite wall, feeling sleepy and waiting for the dog to emerge. 'Come on, you daft bogger, show yourself. You get on my nerves, behaving like this.' But there was no hurry. It could stay till it got dark for all he cared. He'd sat out worse things with similar patience. No, it wasn't true that he had, because the ten hours by the body of his mother had passed like half a minute. That was three years ago. He felt as if he had no memory any more. He didn't need one. If everything that had happened seemed as if it had happened only yesterday you didn't need to dwell too much on the past. It didn't do you any good, and in any case it was just as well not to because as you got older, things got worse.

It was daylight, but it felt as if he were sitting in the dark. The dog hadn't stirred. Maybe it was dead, and yet what had it got to die for? He'd fed it and housed it, and now it was playing this dirty trick on him. It didn't want to leave. Well, nobody did, did they? *He* didn't want to leave, and that was a fact, but a time came when you had to. You had to leave or you had to sink into the ground and die. And he didn't want to die. He wanted to live. He knew that, now. He wanted to live with this nice woman who had taken a fancy to him. He felt young again because he wanted to leave. If he'd known earlier that wanting to change your life made you feel young he'd have wanted to leave long before now. Anybody with any sense would, but he hadn't been able to. The time hadn't come, but now it had, the chance to get out of the tunnel he'd been lost in since birth.

But the dog was having none of it. After all he'd done for it – to turn on him like this! Would you credit it? Would you just! You had to be careful what you took in off the street.

'Come on out, you daft bogger!' When it did he'd be half-minded to kick its arse for biting him like that. He wrapped his clean handkerchief around the throbbing wound, spoiling the white linen with the blood. She'd asked if it was faithful when they'd first met in the pub: 'It'll be obedient all right, as long as it's faithful,' she had said. Like the hell it was. If you don't come from under that stove I'll turn the gas on. Then we'll see who's boss.

No, I won't, so don't worry, my owd duck. He lay down again near the stove, and extended his leg underneath to try and push it sideways. He felt its ribs against the sole. What a damned fine thing! It whined, and then growled. He drew his boot away, not wanting the trousers of his suit ripped. He sat again by the opposite wall, as if to get a better view of his downfall. The world was coming to an end. It's *my* head I'll put in the gas oven, not the dog's. Be a way to get free of everything.

The idea of shutting all doors and windows, and slowly turning on each brass tap, and lying down never to wake up, enraged him with its meaningless finality. If he died who would regret that he had disappeared? Especially if, as was likely, he and the dog went together. His heart bumped with anger, as if he'd just run half a mile. He wanted to stand up and take the house apart brick by brick and beam by rotten beam, to smash his fist at doors and floors and windows, and fireplaces in which the soot stank now that the furniture had gone.

'I'll kill you!' He leapt to his feet: 'I'll kill yer! I'll spiflicate yer!' – looking for some loose object to hurl at the obstinate dog because it was set on spoiling his plans, rending his desires to shreds. He saw himself here all day, and all night, and all next week, unable to lock the door and leave the dog to starve to death as it deserved.

His hat was placed carefully on the least gritty part of the floor, and he drew his hand back from it on realising that if he put it on he would walk out and leave the dog to die. It's either him or me, he thought, baffled as to why life should be that way. But it was, and he had really pulled back the hand to wipe his wet face, his tears in tune with the insoluble problem.

He leapt to his feet, full of a wild energy, not knowing whether he would smash his toffee head to pieces at the stationary hammer of the stove or flee into the daylight. He spun, almost dancing with rage. Feeling deep into his pocket, he took out something that he hadn't known was there because it had slipped through a hole into the lining. He dropped on to his haunches and hurled it at the dog under the stove with all his strength: 'I'll kill you, you bleeder!'

It missed, and must have hit the skirting board about the dog's head. It ricocheted, shooting back at an angle to the wall near the door. He couldn't believe it, but the dog leapt for it with tremendous force, propelled like a torpedo after the golf ball that he'd unthinkingly slung at it.

Albert, his senses shattered, stood aside for a good view, to find out what was really going on on this mad day. The dog's four paws skidded on the lino as the ball clattered away from the wall and made a line under its belly. Turning nimbly, it chased it across the room in another direction, trying to corner it as if it were a live thing. Its feet again sent the ball rattling out of range.

There'd be no more visits to the golf course tatting for stray balls. The dog didn't know it, but he did, that he'd as like as not be saying goodbye to his tears and getting a job somewhere. After his few dead years without one, he'd be all the better for the continual pull at his legs and muscles. Maybe the dog knew even more than he did, and if it did, there was nothing either of them could do about it.

The dog got the ball gently in its teeth, realising from long experience that it must leave no marks there if the object was to make Albert appreciate its efforts. It came back to him, nudging his legs to show what it had got.

His boot itched to take a running kick at the lousy pest. 'That's the last time you get on my bleddy nerves, and that's straight.'

It was, he thought, the last time I get on my own. It wasn't a case any more of a man and his dog, but of a man and the woman he was going to. He bent down to take the gift of the ball from its mouth, but then stopped as if the shaft of cunning had at last gone into him. No, don't get it out, he told himself. You don't know what antics it'll spring on you if you do. Without the familiar golf ball in its trap the bleddy thing will scoot back to its hide-away. Maybe he'd learned a thing or two. He'd certainly need to be sharper in the situation he was going into than he'd been for the last few years.

He straightened up, and walked to the door. 'Let's get after that van. It's got all our stuff on board.' He raised his voice to its usual pitch: 'Come on, make your bleddy heels crack, or we'll never get anything done.'

With the golf ball still in its mouth there was no telling where it would follow him. To the ends of the earth, he didn't wonder, though the earth had suddenly got small enough for him not to be afraid of it any more, and to follow himself there as well.

MIMIC

Part One

I learned to mimic at an early age, probably at two or three when I sat in front of the fire and stared at the cat. A mimic has a long memory, fine hands, and a face he can't bear to look at in the mirror, unless he puts on somebody else's with such intensity that he cannot recognise himself there. His soul is his own, but he buries it deeply with many others because under such a mound it is finally safe. Eventually of course it is so far lost and gone that he is unable to get down to it when he wants to, but that is another matter, and finally unimportant when one knows that age and death will settle everything.

In the early days of infancy I did not know I was becoming a mimic. By all accounts I was such a handsome baby that when my mother pushed me through town in a pram men would stop to admire me and give her five shillings to buy me a new rattle. At least that was her story, though my memory is better than any story, for another line was that because she was so pretty they gave money to me as an excuse for getting off with her.

A still further version could be I was so rotten-faced and

ugly they gave her money to show sympathy at her being loaded with such a terrible burden. Anyway, that's how she met her second husband, which only proves that mimics usually have pretty and wayward mothers, while they may be fair-to-ugly themselves. You can't be a mimic with a fine-featured face, but for the first few years must stare at the world and take nothing in so that your face stays flat and putty-coloured, with a button-nose, beehive-mouth, and burdock-chin that deflects what sunlight hopes to make your features more heavenly to the world.

While father was at work and my mother in the scullery I'd romp on the rug for a while, then settle down and look at the cat, a black tabby with a white spot between its ears. I'd stare right into its splinter eyes till it opened its great mouth and yawned. Then, facing it on all fours, I'd open my mouth as well, full of small new teeth, stretching the side skin as far as it would go. The way the cat looked at me I knew I was successful, and because of this it seemed as if I felt alive for the first time in my life. I'll never forget this strong impression. When I mimicked, the light went on, as if somebody had sneaked up behind and slyly lifted off the dark glasses I didn't have. Finally the cat walked away, as if embarrassed.

I practised on animals for years, on the assumption, rightly I think, that if I could mimic animals so that they recognised themselves in me when I was doing it in front of them, then it would be quite easy to do it to human beings when I was ready for the changeover.

I remember at the age of nine that a young woman in our yard had a puppy, a small dark fat one that had been ill, that she wanted to get rid of. So she asked me to take it to the PDSA, gave me a shilling to put into their contribution box, and threepence to myself for the errand of taking it. The place was about a mile away, and going there I called in many sweet shops, buying chocolate at every stop. The puppy was wrapped in a towel in my arms, and after stocking up at a shop I would sit on a wall to eat the loot, and take another goz at the puppy who was going to be 'put to sleep' as the woman had said. I knew of course what that meant, and though the puppy squinted at me and licked my hand when I gave it chocolate it still looked as if it might welcome what was in store for it. I stared hard at those brown eyes, at that fat half-blind face that could never have any say in how the world was run, and between one snap of chocolate and the next I'd borrow its expression, take on that look, and show it to the puppy to let him feel he was not alone.

A mimic does what he is paid to do. By the time I got to the PDSA I had only threepence left for the contribution box. A shilling had gone on chocolate for me and the dog, and for the dog it was the last thing it would ever eat.

On the way home a hump-backed bridge crossed a canal. I went down through a gate on to the towpath. On the opposite side was a factory wall, but on my side was a fence and an elderberry bush. The water was bottle green, and reflected both sides in it. My eyes turned from grey to brown, and I barked as the dog had barked when the woman in the white overall had taken him from me.

This isn't a story about childhood. It is about a mimic, and mimics have no childhood. In fact it would almost be fair to say that they don't even have a life of their own. There is a certain price to pay for taking on another face, another voice, even though mimicry need bring no profit. But what mimicry does give is a continuation of one's life when for some reason that life had been forfeited even before birth. Whether one had done it oneself as a spirit from another age, or whether someone in another age had got hold of your spirit before it was born and squeezed the life out of it, who can ever be able to say? One may be born innocent, but in order to make one's mark on life, one has to get rid of that innocence.

One puts one's devilries as a mimic into other people if one is guilty of what blasted one's life before birth; one takes others' devilries upon oneself if one was innocent before birth.

To borrow a face is to show no mercy to it. In order to call it your own, you leave the owner of it with nothing. Not only do you see something of an advantage in using someone else's face, but you seek to rob them of what strength they also get from wearing it. At the same time you mimic them to hide yourself. A mimic therefore can't lose, except of course that he has lost everything before birth, more than anyone else can lose unless he is a mimic too.

The first *person* I mimicked, or tried to, was my mother, and I did this by falling in love with her. This is not so easy as it sounds, especially since she had been responsible for giving me birth, but being the person with the power of life and death over me there surely wasn't any fitter person to fall in love with. But I didn't let her see it, because my way of doing it was to mimic her one day, and I expected that since she had already given me so much she wouldn't mind this at all, would be flattered by it in fact. But all she saw was that I was taking everything.

She'd just had a blinding row with my father, and he'd stormed off to see his mates in the pub. At the heart-rending smash of the door behind him she sat by the fire waiting for the kettle to boil. When it did, she burst into tears. I thought to myself that if I did the same, her misery would be halved, so I put on the same expression (the half-closed eyes and twisted mouth, hands to my face-side with two fingers over my ear) and drew tears out with almost exactly the same noise. I'd meant to let my heart flow with hers, to be with it as a sort of comfort, but what I didn't know was that I'd only irritated her, mocked her – which is what she called mimicking for many years. This barefaced imitation made it worse, though instead of increasing her tears (it could hardly do that) it stopped them altogether. This was what I had hoped for, but only in such a way as to soften her heart, not to harden her. She smacked my face: 'Don't mock me, you little bleeder. You're almost as bad as he is.' I don't need to say who 'he' was, though in spite of our similarity he never became the mimic that I did.

So I mimicked my father, seeing how my attempt at love for mother had failed. It was quite a while before I stopped tormenting my mother by only mimicking my father in front of her, and began mimicking him to his face. When I did, he laughed, and I'd never seen him in such a good mood. Life is full of surprises for a mimic. He'd loosened his belt one Sunday dinner because he was too full of beer and food. He pulled me on to his knee and kissed me, my mother looking wryly over her shoulder now and again as she washed the pots. He was so pleased at my exact imitation of him, of seeing himself so clearly in me, that he gave me a shilling.

This momentary gain went to my head and, before he could fall into a doze by the fire, I thought I would put on the best show he'd seen by mimicking my mother for him. If he could laugh at himself in me, he'd be more touched than ever to see mother in my face.

I drew myself up on the hearthrug as if I were tall and thin, curved my arms outward from my side, tilted my head, and drew in my cheeks, completely altering the shape of my mouth and putting that fire into my eyes that expected to be swamped out any second by a tidal wave.

'You've been a long time at the pub,' I said in her voice, 'don't you know your dinner's burnt? It's a wonder you couldn't smell it right from the bar.'

His eyes grew small, and the smile capsized like a boat in a gale. Before I knew where I was I was flat on my face. Then a boot got me in the ribs and I was curled up by the stairfoot floor.

Somehow, mimicking my mother in front of my father hadn't upset *her* at all, not like when I'd done it for her alone. In fact she was amused now, so when the old man lashed out at me with the old one-two of fist and boot, she cried and railed in my defence, calling him all the cruel gets under the sun.

'You leave my son alone,' she shouted, 'you drunken bully. I'll get the police in next time you kick him like that. He's never done any harm to a living soul, and you've never treated him right, either.'

Father was baffled. He'd not liked me being disrespectful, he said, as if he'd been at church instead of a pub. I hadn't any right to mock her. As for him, he could stand it because it was only a bit of a joke, but he didn't like me doing it to her, the wife and mother of the house.

By the time I'd uncurled myself from the hedgehog position (I could imitate a hedgehog very well at times) and had seated myself at the table. I wasn't crying. A mimic soon learns to stop that sort of thing, otherwise he'd never do any mimicking at all. To get kicked was one of the risks you ran. And because I wasn't in tears, they soon made up their quarrel which, after all, had only started because of me. He put more coal on the fire, and she made him some fresh tea. When that was finished they talked and laughed, and she sat on his knee. Then they went upstairs together for a Sunday sleep, and I was left down-stairs alone on the hearthrug wondering where I'd gone wrong. I didn't even have the energy to mimic a strong man booting the cat out of the way because things hadn't gone too well for him at work.

Some people believe that simplicity can only come out of madness, but who wants to go through madness in order to achieve the dubious advantage of becoming simple? Only a mimic can straddle these two states and so avoid being himself. That is to say, he finds a way of not searching for himself in order to avoid discovering that he has no self, and therefore does not exist. To see finally that there is nothing behind all the faces of one's existence is to find real madness. And what simplicity is there in that?

At school, I was the sort of person of whom the older boys asked: 'Is it going to rain today?' even though I looked nothing like a sage or weatherman. But the clouds or empty sky seemed to be on my side, and I was often right when I told them one thing or the other. It wasn't so much that I could guess the weather as that I'd take a chance on saying what I thought was going to happen. This comes easy to a mimic, because every person or object that he decides to imitate has a vein of risk in it.

In my young days it took a long while for me to realise that whenever I decided to mimic someone, and actually went through the process of doing so, I was filled with a deep interest in life and did no harm to anybody. But in between times I was remote and restless in turn, and liable to delve into all kinds of mischief. If I was not inspired for weeks to mimic, and at the same time found no opportunity otherwise to work off my bilious spirit by getting into trouble, then I took ill with some current letdown of the body such as pneumonia or mumps. My father and mother would have liked to have blasted me for the bother I gave them but after I had mimicked them successfully so early on they went out of my life for ever in any important way, and I took so little notice of their rage against me that many people and other members of my family began to look on me as a saint – until my next rampage.

One Christmas at school there was a fancy-dress party before breaking up for the holidays. I went as a moth, with two great wings and white powder all over me. Some came as musketeers and spacemen, but most appeared as nothing at all, simply wearing a badge, or hat. It was an old school, but there was a stage at one end of a big classroom. I received first prize, somebody else got second, and another boy third. The other two were told to get on the stage and act out what they were supposed to be. They did their best, then I went up.

A teacher put a candle on a low table, and I became a moth, weaving around it so that everybody stopped talking and looked. Maybe the teachers told them to be quiet. It was raining in the street, and perhaps being out of it and in the warmth made it easier for me to mimic a moth, with two wings and dry powder all over me. I went round and round the candle, my eyes half closed, and the flame hardly moving. I took the moth into me, and later heard that they began to laugh. I must have known this, yet didn't know it, at the time. But I went on circling the candle, and nobody thought to stop me, to break my spell and their spell.

If life is one long quest to avoid deciding what you are, I suddenly knew that I was a moth when one whole wing was touched off by the candle.

The flame came up suddenly and without smoke, but it

wasn't as swift to others as it was to me, and before more than a slight scorch was done the flame was killed stone dead by two of the teachers.

Everybody thought that my days of mimicking were done for good. So did I, because on that occasion it seemed to have got out of control, and though I thought I might like such a thing to happen at some time in my life, I wasn't ready for it yet.

Before leaving that part of my life for ever (I still can't bring myself to call it childhood) I remember a photograph of me, that showed a big self-absorbed boy of thirteen. It was taken by an uncle, and then enlarged, and my mother had it framed and put on the sideboard in the parlour where nobody went and so hardly anybody, thank God, ever looked at it. I'd been out of her care and bother for a long time, but she'd taken to liking me again. It made no difference, because once a decision is taken through a failure to mimic, nothing can alter it. Maybe I reminded her of my father who had long since gone and given place to another person, and who she still in some way liked. But I'd never mimic him for her, even so, though I could have done it so that the house would have crowed around us.

This photo seemed to have no connection with me, but everybody swore that it had, and that there couldn't be a better one. In my heart I'd come to the age where I wanted to please them, so I decided I must mimic that photo so as to become like the image on it. It wasn't long before I saw that such a thing was not feasible. If you don't know what you are, how is it possible to imitate yourself? This was the issue that burned me. I could not imitate something that had no life, not even myself if I didn't have any. And certainly judging by the photo there was no life there whatever. That was what everyone liked about it, my mother most of all, who stuck it on the sideboard in what was to her the place of honour.

Nevertheless, I looked at that photo for a long time, since other people had given it so much meaning. It was there for the world to see, above all, those who close their hearts and say: Know thyself. But I say: Get me a mirror, and according to the antics performed in it you can then (if you have that sort of desire) know everybody in the world.

But a photograph is not a mirror. You do not even see yourself as others see you. For a moment I almost went into the spirit of that photograph, but pulled myself back in time. That would have been evil. I preferred not to know what I was. There was almost triumph in that decision. If I don't know what I am, nobody can know, not even God. And if God doesn't know, then there is no God.

Rather than mimic the photograph of myself and believe in God I decided that I'd sooner be a moth.

Being such a good mimic I couldn't hold down any job for long. Sooner or later the foreman was bound to turn up when I was doing an imitation of him before all my mates. I worked harder than most though because I was so self-absorbed that nothing was too difficult or arduous for me. It was always with great regret that I was sacked.

On the other hand, all women love a mimic, except the mimic's mother, who ceases to matter by the time he becomes interested in other women. If you want to get off with a woman all you have to do is talk. Let the steamroller roll, and talk, talk, talk. Flatter her if you must, but the main thing is to talk. No woman can resist a constant stream of fulsome talk, no matter how inane and irrelevant, as long as you keep it up and make her laugh. Even if she laughs at you, it doesn't matter. By that time she's softening, you can bet.

And a mimic, even if he's so much speechless putty when left alone with himself, can mimic a funny and talkative man when the need arises. Of course, when the girl falls in love she never gets what she thinks she is getting. But then, who does? There is much wisdom in the world. Certain basic rules were formulated for me by Sam England who worked in the plywood factory where I took my first job. Never, he said, marry a girl who hates her mother, because sooner or later she will start to hate you. He also added that if you want to know what your girl friend is going to look like in thirty years' time, look at her mother now. And if you want to know what your girl friend expects you to look like in *ten* years' time, look at her father.

Whenever I met a girl I had to decide, by her face and talk, and the sort of home she came from, what sort of a person she'd like me to be. There weren't many girls who could ever put up with a strong silent type for the first three dates while he weighed up the situation. But after that I fell into the slot, and the talk began, the endless jokes and self-revelations that come from anyone no matter what sort he is.

If I wanted to get rid of a girl, I made an abrupt change of character. None of them could stand this. They thought I had either gone mad, or lost my respect for them. In the soiled territory of the heart the precise configuration of the land only comes with continual and intense familarity.

One girl I could not get rid of. I changed character no less than five times, but she wouldn't go away, so there was nothing I could do except marry her.

If there's one thing I've always found it hard to mimic it's a happy man. I've often been happy, but that was no help when I was indifferent and wanted to let someone else see that I was full of the joy of life. I knew that I had to overcome this problem and prayed that on this vital issue my talent for mimicry would not let me down.

In the very act of getting married, in order to appear happy to the girl I was to live with, I had to behave like a fool. When I should have slipped the ring on her finger I put it on mine – then on to hers. When we were declared married I attempted to kiss the best man, a fellow clerk from an office I was then working at. He fought free and pleaded with me not to be bloody silly, so then I kissed the bride, and apologised to everyone later by saying I'd been too happy to know what I was doing. They believed this, and forgave me, and I loved them so much I could have mimicked them all, one after another to the end of time.

When I changed for the sixth time it was only to mimic a man getting married. That was the one character she couldn't stand, and by the time I had come to believe in the act, and had almost grown to like it, it was the one finally by which I got rid of her. When we parted six months later I did a very tolerable job of mimicking an amicable man, who had taken one step wrong in life and wanted to go two steps back. She went home to her parents, and took the television set among all her cases in the second run of the taxi. We had always made love in the most perfect way, because I'd had enough experience to mimic that like a stallion, but it had made no difference to our final feeling for each other. She'd never been able to get through to the real me, no more than I had. And after a year of trying she imagined she never would, and I couldn't help but admire her promptitude in getting out as quickly as she did.

This is not a tale of love, or the wail of a broken marriage, or a moan about impossible human relationships. I won't dwell long on any of that. I can go on for years telling you what all this is *not*. It'll be up to you to tell me what it is.

Ambition has never been strong in my veins. To be ambitious you have first to know what you are. Either that, or you do not have to be concerned with what you are. My talent for mimicry was an end in itself. If I could observe someone, I thought in the early days, and then become exactly the same, why should I go through years of work to accomplish it in the reality of society?

I had never any intention of working, but what society demands of you is in fact what life itself wants. So you must imitate it – instead of allowing your soul to be destroyed by believing in it. As soon as you accept something, and cease to play a role regarding it, you are done for. Your soul is in danger. You have even less chance then of ever getting to know the real nature of yourself.

The same must be with everything you are called upon to do in life, whatever action, whether it lasts a minute or a year. Mimic it, I told myself at times of danger when caught by a suspicious joy of life I was about to aquiesce to. The successful mimic is he who not only takes on a role completely so that everyone is deceived, but actually from a distance sees himself with his own eyes doing it so that he himself is never deceived. I only learned to do this later, probably after I broke up with my first wife.

One might imagine that if the main thing in life was the survival of the fittest, then one as a mimic would be wise to imitate and continue to imitate one of the fittest. But not only would that be boring, it would be inhuman, and above all foolish. We know that it is not the fittest who survive, but the wise. The wise die, but the fittest perish, and they perish early on from having settled on to one role in life. They have determined to keep it to the very end, and also to defend it to the death against those who would try to show them that the world is richer than they have made it.

It is the easiest thing in the world for me to recognise those who believe in the survival of the fittest, which means most people. It is, conversely, difficult for me to meet another person like myself, because there are so few of us.

But I once met a woman who was also a mimic. What I could never understand was why those qualities that I had, made people trust and love me, especially women. If to mimic is to betray (which it certainly is) then you would expect to be generally disliked, but strangely enough it was more often the opposite. She said exactly the same thing, except that it was especially men who loved and trusted her.

A friend of mine from the insurance office where I worked was getting married, and I met her at the reception for it. She was a thin green-eyed girl from the tobacco factory, and I listened to her during the meal mimicking the parson, for she had also been at the church. As a lesser friend of the bride's she was assigned to a more remote table, and I happened to be passing on my way back from the lavatory, where I had mimicked a disgusted man and thrown up what food I'd already eaten.

The people around her didn't know whether to be amused or offended. I was merely interested. Her face lost its pallor and grew weightier with the sombre voice she put on. She had great range of tone, and as she went through the service I took the part of bridegroom. Instead of saying 'I will,' at the correct moment, I said: 'I'm damned if I will,' and the two nearest tables joined in the applause.

The actual bride, as this went on, shook at the mouth and dropped tears on to her cheeks. The best man and the bridegroom demanded that we pack it in, but some devil was in us both, and our duet went on as if we were in the middle of a field with no audience at all. There was silence for a few minutes before the uproar. A pair of fine mimics had met, an accident of two stars clashing in interstellar space, and nothing could stop us getting to the end of the act.

The last word was with the best man. I suppose the bridegroom was saving himself for the first night. He only nodded in despair, knowing that it couldn't end in any other way. When the man hit me I pulled two chairs over and half dragged the tablecloth on to the floor. I sprang up and, mimicking an outraged partygoer whose best piece was being unjustly spat on, punched him right over the table, where his head spliced down through the four-tier cake.

The bride screamed as if her husband had been killed. I'd had enough. Grabbing the slender fingers of my fellow mimic I ran out of that doom-laden party for all I was worth, wondering how long the marriage would last after such an inauspicious beginning.

Our association was interesting, but disastrous from the start. We didn't live together, but shared each other's rooms. For a few months it was champagne and roses. Coming back to one of the rooms from our respective jobs we would eat a supper (imitating each others mastication all the way through), then we would dare each other to mimic certain characters, such as an airline pilot, a policewoman, an insurance man, girl shop assistant. We played with each other, tested each other, acted God and the Devil with the deepest penetrable parts of our hearts and souls. We mimicked each other mimicking each other. We mimicked each other mimicking people we both knew. We mimicked the same person to see who could do it best. When we emptied each other we made love, and it came marvellously on such occasions. We thought we had come to the end of the road, gone over the cliff hand in hand like a couple of Gadarene swine and found we had landed in paradise.

But to think such things only means that the road is about to enter a swamp. I wanted her to marry me, but it turned out she was already married. So was I. Her husband knocked on my door one Sunday afternoon, and what could I do but ask him in? He was a van driver of thirty, but with his sweater and quiff he looked seventeen. He appeared stupid and sensitive, a not uncommon combination. 'I know you're living with him,' he said, 'but I've come to ask you to come back and live with me. That's why I've come.'

I stood up and made a quiff in my hair, threw off my jacket, and pulled the sweater down. Then I repeated his speech in exactly the same voice. It's dangerous mimicking simple people, but I couldn't resist. He must have gone through all the possible situations that could arise before he knocked at my door, but this wasn't one of them. He looked horror-struck, and leaned against the outside door. At this, Jean, who'd said nothing so far, got up and stretched her spine against the door to the kitchen with exactly the same expression.

'What's going on?' he demanded.

'What's going on?' I mimicked.

He lifted his fists as if about to fly through the room and crash against me. Jean lifted her fist and prepared to spring in exactly the same way. They would have collided and died in an apotheosis of glorious mimicry.

He turned to the door and opened it. Jean pulled at the kitchen door. We heard him running downstairs, and he never came back.

I passed him a few months later as I was walking through town. A girl was with him, and he didn't notice me in my misery. But I saw him all right because I hadn't seen anyone so obviously happy for a long time.

*

I followed Jean from the factory one night, and she met another man.

She'd been seeing me less and less. I'd expected it, but because we couldn't live together, could only exist like two cripples, taking turns to hold each other up, I was struck by jealousy as if a javelin had shuddered deep between my shoulder blades.

When two vampires meet, they meet for ever, until another comes to set them free. But freedom is painful, for a while. For a mimic who doesn't believe in it, it can be catastrophic.

I rang the bell of his flat one Sunday morning. As he opened the door Jean made a good imitation of the ringing noise. I saw that I was in for a bad time. Think of what situation you want from the bottom of your soul to avoid, and when you have decided what it is, consider what you'll do when it comes about.

He was grinning by the window, and Jean actually offered me a cup of tea. While she was giving it to me I could see her imitating her actions. She had learned a lot, and I wondered where. I never knew his name. To the world he was an ordinary chap in some trade or other, but to me I saw he was trying to mimic something and I didn't know what it was. I was puzzled, but sat and drank my tea.

I asked Jean how she was, but she only smiled, and didn't seem to know. I wondered if she was happy, and could only say that she was. I knew that if I asked direct questions they would combine to defeat me in mimicry, and I had no wish to bring on to myself what Jean and I had poured on to her husband. They knew this. He stayed by the window, grinning, and I withered under the stare that went with it. Nevertheless I looked up at him from time to time. His face seemed a shade paler and thinner. I would fight on my own ground, in other words get up and go – but not before I could see what he was imitating.

But the stare grew ashen and luminous, especially after I had nothing left to say. I stood up and made for the door, but Jean blocked it. Where had she met such a person?

'I'm going,' I said calmly. A mimic cannot give up the ground he stands on, without knowing that another piece of land is waiting for him. Here, I was isolated, and the ocean was wide. It wasn't an honour to be defeated at this moment, but it was essential to me as a man. In defeat one can begin to know what one is, in victory – never. 'Get out of my way.'

Behind my back I heard: 'I'm going. Get out of my way' – in my own voice exactly.

'Guess what he's mimicking?' she said.

Without turning around I saw reflected in her eyes the sky-blue bones of his skull head, and the fixed grin of the victory I'd been forced to give him.

I mimicked her: 'Guess what he's mimicking?' and didn't give her time to answer. 'A corpse,' I said, forcing her gently aside, opening the door, and walking away. Between bouts of mimicking one person and another, my entity becomes blank. To be able to mimic someone I had to like them. That was the first rule, just as, in the reverse sense, in order to love someone you have to be able to mimic them. When I mimicked people now, they ceased to like me, if they had ever done so. But then, treachery always begins with a kiss. For these reasons I had found it impossible to imitate God, and not only because I'd never seen Him.

Later, in my isolation, I only mimicked people to myself instead of out loud or for the benefit of others. Don't force the pace. This isn't a story. Switch off if you're not with me. I'll go on as long as you can, if not longer. I've had everything: booze, pot, shock, solitary. Yet though I may be sane, and a mimic of the world, can I imitate Mr Sand or Mr Water, Mr Cloud or Mr Sky with sufficient conviction to become all of them rolled into one realistic and convincing ball?

I mimic myself trying to mimic myself when I don't know who I am or what my real self is. I sit on my own in a pub laughing inwardly because I am more king of the world than anyone else. I see faces around me both troubled and serene, and don't know which one to choose for the great grand mimic of the night. I give up trying to mimic myself, and choose a man talking earnestly to his wife. I stand in the middle of the floor. Everything is clear and steady, but no one looks at me. I talk as if the man's wife were standing two inches from my face, grinning at the jokes I'm (he's) obviously making, then looking slow-eyed and glum when she mentions the children. Somebody pushes by with an empty glass as if I don't exist. I pull him back and he knocks me down. I do exist. I live, and smile on the floor before getting up. But only he notices me, and does so no more as his glass is filled and he steps by me back to his table. It is quite a disturbance, but they don't even call the police.

Was Jean's new man mimicking himself, or was it me? I shall never know. But I would not see her again, even though she might want to take up with me. She'd been in contact with evil, and the evil had rubbed off on to her. Some of it in that short time had jumped to me, and I was already trying to fight free of it.

When I was mimicking someone I was walking parallel with the frontiers of madness. When I did it marvellously well, the greater was the drop of madness below me. But I didn't know this. I was driven to mimicry by threat and fear of madness. For some months I totally lost the skill to mimic, and that's why I got a note from my doctor and presented myself at the door of the local head-hospital. They welcomed me with open arms, and I was able to begin making notes from the seven millionth bed.

I did well there, announced to all assembled that I was now going to put on a show of mimicking Doctor So-and-so, and what to me was a brilliant act for them turned out to be perfectly still flesh and a blank stare from a person who was me in the middle of the room.

I had to start again from the beginning. In order to imitate a sneeze I was thrown on to the floor by the force of it. I turned into a dog down one side of my face, and a moth on the other.

As I came up from the pit I started to write these notes. I have written them out five times already, and on each occasion they have been snatched from me by the attendant and burned.

While I write I am quiet; when I stop, I rave. That is why they are taken from me.

Part Two

I didn't stay long: it took me two years to recover. To imitate was like learning to speak again. But my soul was filled with iron, and I went on and on. The whole world was inside of me, and on any stage I chose I performed my masterpiece of mimicry. These were merely rehearsals for when I actually figured as the same person over and over again, a calm, precise, reasonable man who bore no relation to the real me seething like a malt-vat inside. The select audience appreciated my effort. I don't think anything was lost on them, except perhaps the truth.

No one can mimic time and make it go away, as one can sometimes make friends and enemies alike disappear when you mimic them. I had to sit with time, feed it my bones in daylight and darkness.

This great creation of mine, that I dredged up so painfully from the bottom of my soul, was someone I'd sidestepped from birth. I breathed life in him, a task as hard as if he were a stone, yet I had to perfect him and make him live, because in the looney bin I realised the trap I'd walked into.

I made a successful imitation of a sane man, and then they let me out. It felt like the greatest day of my life. I do not think my performance could have been better than it was.

An insane man can vanish like a fish in water, and hide anywhere. I am not insane, and it was never my intention to become so. But one is forced to mimic to perfection a sane man so as to become free, and what greater insanity is there than that? Yet it widens the horizons of the heart, which is no bad thing for someone who was born a mimic.

Years have passed, and in my pursuit and mimicry of sanity I have become the assistant manager of a large office. I am thirty-five years of age, and never married again. I took some winter leave and went to Switzerland. Don't ask me why – that means you, the one I'm imitating, and you, who I am not. I planned the space off work and set off for London with my pocket full of traveller's cheques and a passport. In my rucksack was a hammock, nylon groundsheet, blanket, tobacco, matches, soap, toothpaste, toothbrush, compass, a book, notebook, and pencils. That's all. I don't remember where I got such a list from but I did, and stuck to it religiously. I was determined that every action from now on should have some meaning, just as in the past every time I had ever mimicked anyone had also had some important significance. One cannot live in the world of chance. If fate will not act for you, then take it by the neck.

It was so cold I thought my head would break like an old teapot, but as I walked away from the lake and along the narrow road between banks of trees I got used to it. The walls of the mountains on either side were so steep it seemed that if anybody were foolhardy enough to climb up they would fall off and down – unless they were a fly. Perhaps I could mimic a fly, since already in the cold I had conjured a burning stove into my belly. A car passed and offered me a lift. I waved it on.

It was getting dark by five, and there wasn't much snow to be seen, a large sheet of luminous basilisk blue overhead, and behind me to the south a map-patch of dying fluorescent pink. The air was pure, you could certainly say that for it. The sun must have given the valley an hour each day, then a last wink before it vanished on its way to America.

There was snow underfoot, at certain higher places off the road, good clean snow that you could eat with honey on it. I could not see such snow and fading sun without death coming into my heart, the off-white powder humps in the dusk thrown between rock and tree-boles, flecked among the grey and scattered rooftops of a village I was coming to.

Bells were sounding from the church, a leisurely mellow music coming across the snow, so welcoming that they made me think that maybe I had had a childhood after all. I walked up the steep narrow lanes, slipping on the snow hardened into beds of ice. No one was about, though lights were in the windows of dark wooden houses.

Along one lane was a larger building of plain brick, and I went inside for something to eat. A girl stood by the counter, and said good evening in Italian. I took off my pack and overcoat, and she pointed to tables set in the room behind.

They did not ask me what I wanted but brought soup, then roast meat, bread and cabbage. I gave in my passport, intending to stay the night. A woman walked in, tall, blonde, rawboned and blue-eyed. She sat at another table, and fed half her meal to the cat. After my long trek from the railway station (stopping only in the town to buy a map) I was starving, and had eyes for nothing but my food. The first part of the walk was agony. I creaked like an old man, but now, in spite of my exhaustion, I felt I could walk on through the night.

I did not sleep well. In dreams I began to feel myself leaving the world. My hand was small and made of copper, tiny (like hammers that broke toffee when I was a child), and I placed it on my head that was immense and made of concrete, solid, but that suddenly started to get smaller. This was beginning to be an actual physical state, so I opened my eyes to fight it off. If I didn't I saw myself being pressed and squeezed into extinction, out of the world. It didn't seem as if I would go mad (nothing is that simple) but that I would be killed by this attrition of total insecurity. It seemed as if the earth were about to turn into concrete and roll over my body.

I got out of bed and dressed. The air in the room, which had firmly shut double windows and radiators, was stifling. When you think you're going mad it's a sign you're getting over it. The faces of everyone I'd ever mimicked or made love to fell to pieces in turn like a breaking jigsaw puzzle.

My boots bit into the snow as I closed the door behind. It wasn't yet midnight. There was a distinct ring around the full and brilliant moon. There was snow on the mountain sides, and it seemed as if just over the line of their crests a neon light was shining. I walked along the lanes of the village, in the scorching frosty cold.

To question why one is alive means that one is only half a person, but to be a whole person is to be half dead.

Sun was shining over the snow next morning as I sat by the window drinking coffee. I was near the head of the valley, and the mountain slopes opened out. Most of it was sombre forest with occasional outcrops of rock, but to the west, at a place shone on directly by the sun, I could see green space. Then nothing but rock and snow, and blue sky. My eyes were always good. I never needed glasses or binoculars, and just above the meadow before the trees began was a small hut. No smoke came from it.

I paid my bill, collected my pack, and said goodbye. At the road a cow had been hit by a car and lay dying. The car's headlamp was shattered and the animal lay in a pool of blood, moving its hoofs slightly. A group of people stood around, and the driver was showing his papers. Another man rested a notebook on the car-top to write. It was all very orderly. I pushed through and looked into the eyes of the dying animal. It did not understand. As a last gesture it bellowed, but no one was interested in it, because the end was certain. No one even heard it, I was sure. The damson eyes were full of the non-comprehension of understanding.

The mountains were reflected in one, and the village in the other – or so it seemed as I paced back and forth. Another bellow sounded, even after it was dead, and when all the people looked at me at last to make sure that the noise was coming from me and not out of the sky I walked on alone up the road, away from the spoiled territory of the heart, and the soiled landscape of the soul.

I am wild. If I lift up my eyes to the hills a child cries. A child crying makes me sad. A baby crying puts me into a rage against it. I imagine everything. If I go into the hills and sit there, birds sing. They are made of frost, like the flowers. Insanity means freedom, nothing else. Tell me how to live and I'll be dangerous. If I find out for myself I'll die of boredom afterwards. When I look along the valley and then up it seems as if the sky is coming into land. The mountains look as tall as if they are about to walk over me. If they want to, let them. I shall not be afraid.

The wind is fresh except when it blows smoke into my face. I build a fire by the hut, boil water on it for tea. The wind is increasing, and I don't like the look of the weather.

The hut is sheltered, and when I came to it I found as if by instinct a key just under the roof. There's nothing inside, but the floor is clean, and I have my hammock as well as food. When it is dark it seems as if the wind has been moaning and prowling for days, plying its claws into every interstice of the nerves. I wanted to get out and go after it, climb the escarpment above the treeline with a knife between my teeth, and fight on the high plateau in the light of the moon, corner that diabolic wind and stab it to death, tip his carcass over the nearest cliff.

I cannot mimic either Jack Frost or a windkiller. It's too dark, pit-shadows surround me, but there's no fear because outside in the mountains the whole fresh world stretches, waiting for children like me to get up in the morning, to go out into it and be born again.

I have finished with mimicking. I always thought the time would come, but could never imagine when or where. I cannot get into anyone any more and mimic them. I am too far into myself at last, for better or worse, good or bad, till death do me part.

One man will go down into the daylight. In loneliness and darkness I am one man: a spark shot out of the blackest pitch of night and found its way to my centre.

A crowd of phantoms followed me up, and I collected them together in this black-aired hut, tamed them and tied them down, dogs, moths, mothers, and wives. Having arrived at the cliff-face of the present there's little else to say. When my store

of food is finished I'll descend the mountainside and go back
to the inn, where I'll think some more as I sit drinking coffee
by the window, watching the snow or sunshine. I'll meet again
the tall, blonde, rawboned, blue-eyed woman who fed half her
meal to the cat – before setting off on my travels. Don't ask me
where, or who with.

THE MAGIC BOX

I

Fred made his way towards the arboretum bench.

Though it was well gone eleven he hadn't yet clocked in, and wouldn't either. There were some things a man would be glad to work for, but that morning his head was full of thoughts that would have got him hung – if anything could have been gained by swinging.

He sat down, drew two porkpies from their cellophane wrappers and exposed them to daylight. Half closing his eyes (as if his palate were up there and not in his mouth) he bit into the first pie: the meat wasn't bad, but the pastry was chronic. When the crumpled bag settled in the prison of the half-filled litter basket he chewed through a prolonged stare towards the ornamental pond and park wall, hearing the breathtaking gear-change of traffic chewing its way up the hill outside.

Morning was the worse time. He hated going to bed, and he hated getting up even more, but since these two actions were necessary for life and work he preferred getting up – by himself. God alone knew why Nan had risen with him this morning, but she had, and that, as much as anything else, had been the

219

cause of the row that had burst over them – from her. In six years of marriage he'd learned that to argue at breakfast always led to a blow-up. It was better to argue in the evening (if you had any choice) because sooner or later you went to bed.

Though in many ways pleasant, half a day off work wasn't the sort of thing he could keep from Nan, since she saw his wage packet on Friday night. Not that she nosed into everything, but her skill at housekeeping demanded that each bob and tanner be accounted for. He would be laughed at by his workmates if they knew, though many of them lived by the same arrangement, and that was a fact. In any case how could they find out? Nan wouldn't drive by in a speaker van and let them know, for she often claimed: 'My place is to go shopping and clean the house, not to wait for you outside that stinking factory. When we go to the pictures on Friday you can get me a place in the queue, and I'll meet you there.'

He only hoped that one day Nan would see him as the good man from the many bad, a bloke who didn't deserve to be bossed and tormented so much. But she hated the factory, as if to punish him not only for having married her but also for stipulating soon after that she should stop going out to work. He'd only insisted on it because he loved her, thinking she wanted him to press her on this and prove even greater love than he was capable of. Not many would have loved a woman enough to see it that way. But since the gilt had worn off she became bitter about having left work at all, hinting that staying on would have made her a forewoman by now. In fact she had only offered to give in to his manly insistence because she wanted him to see that she loved him more than was considered normal, and he had been blind and selfish enough to take her up on it.

'Well' – now wanting some peace in the house – 'why don't you go and ask them to set you on again if that's the way you feel? I'm not a bleddy mind reader.'

This took the row to a higher pitch, as he'd known it would, but he hadn't the sense to sit down and say nothing, or walk out of the house whistling. 'How can I?' she called. 'I'd have to start again on a machine. I'd never get back to the old position I had when I was loony enough to take note o' you and pack my good job in.'

He didn't know how it had begun that morning. He didn't suppose she did, either. He would like to think of her as still brooding on it, but not likely. No sooner had the door closed than she'd smashed the cup he'd drunk from, though he'd bet his last dollar she was out shopping now, and laughing with other women as if there'd been no quarrel at all.

It was fine enough weather to make everyone forget their troubles. Autumn sun warmed the green banks of the park, ants and insects proliferating among juicy-looking blades of grass. Small birds fed at a piece of his cast-off porkpie beyond the diamond wirespaces of the litter basket, like a dozen thumbnail sketches that had come to life. Two pigeons joined the feast, enormous in comparison to the thrushes, but there was no bullying. Both pigeons and thrushes seemed unaware of any difference in size, and the fact that both wanted to get at the same piece of pie was, after all, a similarity.

He smoked a cigarette. A young man walked by with a back-combed suicide-blonde in a black mac, who looked as if she hadn't had a square meal for a month, and she was saying angrily: 'I'll bleddy-well nail him when I see him I bleddy-well will, an' all' – with such threat and vengeance that Fred felt sorry for whoever this was meant. The world thrives on it, he thought, but I don't, and in any case life's not always like that. Bad luck and good luck: it's like a swing on a kids playground, always one thing or the other. We've had more than our share of the bad though, by bloody Christ we have, too much to think about, and the last bit of good luck was almost more trouble than it was worth. He thought back on it, how a year ago, at the start of the football season, a cheque had come one morning for two hundred and fifty quid, and a few hours later his mug (and Nan's) was grinning all over the front of the newspaper. She enjoyed it so much that it certainly didn't occur to him to remind her of all the times she had threatened to burn the daft football coupons on which he had wasted so much time and money. No, they got in a dozen quarts of beer and a platter of black puddings, and handed manna around to anyone with the grace or avarice to drop in. The man from the *Post* had asked: 'What are you going to do with the money?' Fred was surprised at so much bother when all he felt was disappointment at not hitting the treble chance and raking in a hundred thousand. Two hundred and fifty nicker seemed so little that before Nan could spin some tale or intent to the reporter Fred butted in: 'Oh, I expect we'll just split it and use it as pocket-money.' Which was duly noted in heavy type for the day's editions (POOLS WIN: POCKET-MONEY FOR NOTTINGHAM COUPLE) so prominently displayed that though Nan had the spirit left to tell Fred he should have kept his trap shut she hadn't the nerve to make him do anything else with the money but what he'd said he would for fear of being known to defy the bold public print of a newspaper that, as far as Nan knew, everyone had read.

To spend a hundred quid in one fell bout of shopping demanded bravery, and Fred was the sort in which, if bravery existed, it was anything but spontaneous. Still, he had seen things worth buying which, so far, was more than could be said for Nan. Walking around town Fred had come across an all-wave ex-army wireless receiver staring him out from behind plate glass, the exact communications set he'd worked during his war stint with the signals in Egypt. It stayed in the same window for months, being, he surmised, too expensive for anyone to step in and say: 'I want it.' So he took his time in sparking up courage to walk by that array of valves and morse tappers, to make a purchase by pointing between heart beats towards the window.

Many afternoons he'd stood at the window fixed by the magic black box of the communications receiver, and at so many long and regular absences Nan began to wonder whether he had set himself up with a piece of fancy work met in the factory – and she said as much when he once came home looking piqued and sheepish. He still hadn't been able to walk in and buy the radio, and so felt poor enough in spirit to go straight over and kiss her: 'Hello, my angel, how are we today?'

She turned her face away. Half a dozen books were stacked on the sideboard after a visit to the library. 'What's the idea? What do you want?'

'I don't want anything.'

'You'd better not, either, until you tell me where you go and what you get up to every Saturday afternoon.'

So that was what he'd seen boiling up, something so far from his mind that he could only say: 'I've bin down town looking around the shops.'

She pulled the curtains across and set the table, while Fred dug himself in the fireside chair, watching her as she worked. Her face had altered, become sterner in the last year or two, as if it had done enough battle with the world since Ivor had been drowned. But at thirty she was still good-looking, pretty almost, with her small even features and smooth skin. Her face was round and pleasantly fleshed, her eyes cool and outgiving when she was not anguished or perturbed. He smiled as she reached into the crockery cupboard: the best might be yet to come. How can she think I'd ever look at another woman? We've been through a lot together, the worst of it being the terrible way that Ivor went. If there's anything worse than her blaming me for him having fallen into that canal while reaching for a batch of tadpoles, it's her blaming herself, which I know she does even though it was three years ago and an accident. To think we paid that batchy girl half a crown every time she took him out, and she let this happen. My first thought on hearing he'd been killed like that was: 'The daft little bogger. Wait till I get my hands on him. I'll give him what for.' I couldn't believe it then, but I can now, just about.

'Have you been looking at the shops thinking how to spend your football money?' she asked in a more amiable voice, passing a cup of tea. They'd married on his demob leave in forty-six, after a mere week of kisses five years before, and four hundred letters in which by an inexhaustable permutation every aspect of common romantic love had been exchanged between them. Distance had made both hearts grow fonder, and out of sight out of mind had been disproved, apart from the long letters, by a frequent transmission of photographic images on which were stamped the thousand proofs of far-off love that kept Fred and Nan alive for each other. It was if they were married after the first three months apart, as if they had already spent a honeymoon at Matlock and been wrenched from it by the first year, and had been long settled into an unthinking matrimonial rut by the fourth. They wrote of houses and work and children, and by the time they stood outside the church posing for their first photo together Fred anyway felt that the marriage about to begin was a plain print of black and white on positive paper, as opposed to the flimsy and transient negative of the preceding years.

Nan didn't see it like this, found it necessary to distinguish between the correspondence course and her new full status as a housewife, became more competent than Fred at tackling problems after returning from a week at Matlock. To go shopping – pale, young and full of thought – in the raw fog of a December morning and come home to see that the fire had died, brought reality closer than Fred's daily dash to his factory incarceration in which machines warmly hummed and men baited him still on his recent honeymoon. Through the war Nan had stayed in a cold and exacting climate, while Fred had picked dreamily at radio sets in his monastic army life. Fascinated by the Nile Valley, he had ventured with his pals on a trip to the Great Pyramid, and his lean young unsure face looked down from the high back of a camel in a Box Brownie snapshot sent to Nan who, though stuck with the hardships of air-raids and rationing, saw him as adventuring around wild desert with an independence boding good for when they were married.

Not that she'd had much to complain about; in fact during her pregnancy Fred was as good as gold – she told her mother. And when Ivor came along he was even better, so she was now in the position of knowing that something was wrong yet not being able to complain, a state for which she couldn't but blame him, and which led to frenzied unreasonable quarrels which he could only define as 'temper' and blame on her.

'You're always curious about how I'm going to spend my share of the football money,' he said, 'but you haven't got rid of your whack yet. What are you going to do with it?' Answers to this question lacked venom, for money was now the only discussable topic which did not disturb the unstable bed of their emotions. She looked up from the newspaper: 'I haven't thought about it much, though I daresay I shall one of these days.'

A waterhen went out from the nearest bank, going as smoothly over the water as if drawn by a piece of cotton pulled by an invisible boy on the other side. Its head with button-eye and yellow beak was perfectly proud and still, and the green and blue back-feathers were comparable to colours made by flames appearing on the surface of a fire that had acted dead and out. The sun was good, and he didn't intend going to work until after dinner-hour, even if it meant another big row with Nan. The sound of machinery would cripple all reflection, and its manufacturing teeth pulling him back like a bulldog to earning a living for himself, Nan, and a possible future kid, seemed appalling in this unexpected sunshine – just as did the idea of going home to Nan again after their awful purposeless scrap of the morning.

It was the first time such a thing had happened, and it gnawed at his peace of mind because he'd had no intention of pushing her back so hard against the sofa. His hand had left the hot side of the cup and collided with her before he could do anything about it. It frightened him. If only I'd done it deliberately, known what was in me. The gone-out stare in her face drove him from the house, and he doubted whether he'd get back into it. Then again maybe she'd have forgotten it by evening, which would only go to show how much effect these rows had on her. He wasn't even sure he wanted to get back into the house anyway. Out of it the pain was less, and sitting in the park having eaten two pork pies and a thimble of sunshine sent it right away except for occasional stabs of the memory knife.

He walked through the main gate, towards the radio shop in

the middle thoroughfare of the driving city. His football winnings took on value at last, a lump sum of over a hundred pounds to be handed in for a high-class radio set that would put him in touch with the short-wave world, give something to do and maybe stop him being such a bastard to Nan. If he ordered it now the shop van would deliver it tomorrow. After the dinner-hour he'd go back to work, otherwise, with it being Friday, he would get no wages.

II

Earphones on, he sat alone in Ivor's room, tuned-in to the Third Programme like a resistance radio operator receiving from abroad instructions that were the life blood of his cause. A fastidious voice was speaking unintelligibly on books and, as if not getting his money's worth, Fred clicked on to short wave and sent the needle rippling over hundreds of morse stations. Sounds chipped and whistled like clouds of tormented birds trying to get free, but he fixed one station and, as if from the fluttering of wings pinned firm at the middle by the hair-thin tuning needle, he deciphered its rhythm as: MEET ME TILBURY DOCK THURSDAY 24TH STOP AM DYING TO BE WITH YOU AGAIN ALL MY LOVE DARLING — MARY.

Alistair Crossbanks, 3 Hearthrug Villas, Branley was the lucky man, yet not the only one, since Fred took several more such messages. They came from sea-liners and went to waiting lovers who burned with the anguish of tormented separation — though he doubted whether any had spanned the same long time as Nan and himself before they were married. But the thought of ships steaming through a broadly striped sea at its sudden tropical darkening caused him to ignore further telegrams. He pictured a sleek liner in a thousand miles of ocean, a great circle bordering its allotted speed as, day after day, it crawled on an invisible track towards Aden or Cape-town. He felt its radio pulse beating softly in his ear, as if by listening he had some control of it, and the remoteness of this oceanic lit-up beetle set off his own feelings of isolation in this sea-like suburb spreading in terraces and streets around his room.

The room had belonged to Ivor before he had been killed. Wallpaper of rabbits and trees, trains and aeroplanes, suggested it, as well as the single bed and the cupboard of toys that, even so long afterwards, neither had the heart to empty. Ivor had dark hair and brown eyes, and up to the age of four had been sharp and intelligent, thin, voracious and bright, all running and fighting, wanting and destroying. Yet for several months before slipping into the cold pocket of the canal he had turned back from this unnatural liveliness as if, not having such life responded to, the world had failed to get through to him, to make touch with his spirit in a way he could understand. Fred couldn't even regret having ill-treated him – that anyway would have made him easier remembered. All he saw was his wild boy breaking up an alarm clock and screaming off into a corner when the bell jangled his unready ears. But the lasting image of Ivor's face was one of deprivation, and this was what Fred could not explain, for it wasn't lack of food, clothes, toys, even money that gave this peculiar look, but an expression – now he saw it clearly – bound into Ivor's soul, one that would never let him respond to them.

He threw the master switch, and sat in evening silence, overpowered by this bleak force of negative feedback. Trust me to blame an innocent dead kid for what could only have been my fault and maybe Nan's. Ships were moving over untroubled oceans, set in such emptiness and warmth that for the people on them the tree of ecstasy was still a real thing. He switched on and, by the hairsplitting mechanism of the magic box, such poems were extractable out of the atmosphere. Another tele-gram from ELIZABETH said HOPE YOU BOOKED US A ROOM STOP CAN'T WAIT, and to break such torment he turned to news agency Tass explaining some revolutionary method of oil drilling in the Caucasus – a liquid cold chute of morse that cleared all passion from his mind.

He stayed undisturbed in Ivor's room, knowing that Nan would sit feasting at the television until calling him down for supper at half-past nine. He felt strange tonight; a bad tormenting cold depressed him: at such times his senses were connected to similar bad colds in the past, and certain unwrapped scenes from them hit him with stunning vividness.

Egypt was a land of colds, brought on by a yearly inundation of the Nile widening its valley into a sea of water and mud. Triangular points of the dark brown pyramids that reared beyond appeared sordid, like old jettisoned cartons fallen somehow in such queer shape, and looking from this distance as if, should a prolonged breeze dry them of rain and floodwater, a more violent wind might uproot and lose them in the open desert like so much rubbish. In Cairo he had been a champion at morse, writing it at thirty-two words a minutes and reading it at thirty-six. His brain, perfect for reception, drew in streams of morse for hour after hour and jerked his fingers to rapid script with no thought barrier between, work from which other less dedicated operators were led glassy-eyed and muttering to some recuperation camp by the blistering bonny banks of the Suez Canal. Fred enjoyed his fame as speed king, which though pre-supposing a certain yoga-like emptiness of mind, demanded at the same time a smart brain and a dab hand. Yet in nothing did he look speedy: his sallow face made him seem always deep in slow thoughts beyond the understanding of his noisier pals – who were less efficient as radio men. Their respect for him was for his seriousness as much as for an uncommon rate of morse, which must have been so because even those in the cookhouse, to whom signalling prowess meant nothing, didn't bawl so sharply when a gap lay between Fred and the plate-filling man ahead. He was a priest of silence among blades of bed-tipping and boozing, singing and bawling and brothel-going. Some who didn't muck-in were subjected at least to apple-pie beds, but Fred was on good terms even without trying. He was somehow found congenial, and would often have tea brought back for him from the mess by someone who came off watch at a late hour. When Fred returned this favour it was even more appreciated for being unexpected.

Mostly he would sit by himself in the library writing long letters to Nan, but the one friend he made was flown up one day from Kenya in the belly of a Mosquito fighter-bomber – which dropped its extra fuel tanks like turds somewhere over the desert. The shortage of good operators was so desperate (at a time of big offensive or retreat – nobody could ever tell which, since all differences were drowned in similar confusion) that Fred was working a hundred hours a week. Not that he felt shagged by it, but the Big Battle had started and another man was needed, so in stepped Peter Nkagwe, a tall cheek-scarred black African from Nairobi – freshly changed into clean pressed khaki drill and smiling a good afternoon boys as he entered the signals office. The sergeant assigned him a set, and Fred amazed, then envious, saw his long-fingered hands trembling the key like a concert pianist at an evenness and speed never before seen.

Peter Nkagwe was no ascetic sender and receiver like Fred, but smiled and looked around as he played the key with an accurate, easy, show-off proficiency. He not only read Reuter's cricket scores from Australia but, which was where Fred failed, his fingers were nimble enough to write them down, so that his sheets of neat script went from hand to hand around the base until falling apart.

One day Fred called over, words unrehearsed, ignited from such depth that he didn't even regret them after he'd spoken: 'You beat out them messages, mate, like you was at a tom-tom.'

Peter, unflinching, finished the message at his usual speed. He then took off his earphones and stood over Fred in silence.

Fred was uncomfortable at the length of it: 'Lost owt?'

'There's a look in your eyes, MATE,' Peter said, 'as if your head's full of shit.' He went back to his radio, and from then on Fred's signalling championship was divided. They became friends.

Night after night at his communications receiver, Fred hoped to hear messages from his old HQ unit that, though long closed down, would magically send the same signals rippling between familiar stations. He might even pick up the fast melodious rhythms of Peter Nkagwe, that vanished ghost of a friend who, somewhere, still sat keying out indispensable messages whose text and meaning, put into code and cypher by someone else, was never made known to him. He turned the dial slowly, hoping to recognise both callsign and sending prowess of his old friend. It was impossible, though much time at the set was spent shamefaced in this way as if, should he try hard and stay at it long enough, those lost voices would send out tentacles and pull him back to the brilliant sun-dazzle of the Mokattam Hills.

His lean face, and expert hands moving over the writing-pad, were set before his multi-dialled altar, the whole outlined by a tassel-shaded table lamp. If I'd had this radio in Ivor's day, he laughed, the little bogger would have been at it till the light didn't shine and the valves packed in. Talk about destruction! 'Destruction, thy name is Ivor!' He remembered him, as if he were downstairs drinking tea, or being bathed in front of the fire, or gone away to his grandma's and due back next week. Anything mechanical he'd smash. He took a day on a systematic wipe-out of the gramophone, then brought the pieces to Fred, who suggested he put them together again. Ivor tried (I will say that for him) but failed, and when Fred mended it he was so overjoyed at the record spinning loud and true once more that he treated it as one thing to stay henceforth free of his hammer.

Ivor with a round, empty-eyed happiness, took huge bites of bread, and wiped jamstains down his shirt. Fred couldn't keep the sarcasm from his voice when telling him to stop, so that the bites had changed to tiny, until Fred laughed and they returned to big again, relaxing the empty desperation of his tough face. Such memories were buried deep, going down like the different seams and galleries of a coalmine. In the few months before his birth Ivor had moved inside Nan, kicking with life that had been distinct enough to wake Fred at night – and send him back to sleep smiling.

The small lamp gave one-tenth light, leaving most of the room in darkness. Fixed at the muttering radio and reaping an occasional message out of the air with his fast-moving hook of a pencil, Fred felt his mind locked in the same ratio, with that one tenth glimmer unable to burst like a bomb and explode the rest of himself into light. He composed silent questions about Ivor, like sending out telegrams that would get no answer. Why was I born? Why didn't I love him so that he stayed alive? Could I love anybody enough to make them stay alive and kicking? Would it have made any difference if I'd loved him even more than I did? He couldn't lift the dominating blackness from his brain, but struggled to free himself, ineffectually spinning the knobs and dials of his radio, fighting to keep even the one-tenth light in his consciousness.

He opened the radio lid and peered in at the valves, coloured lights of blue flame deep in bulbs as if he had cultivated in his one-tenth light a new shape of exotic onion. Thoughts passed through his mind, singly and in good order, though the one just gone was never remembered – only the sensation remained that it had been. He tried to recall the thought or picture slipping from his mind in order to lynchpin it to the one now pushing in – which might, he hoped, be seen to have some connection to the one following. It turned out to have nothing in common at all.

'Never mind, sweetheart,' I said, when Ivor was drowned. 'Never mind' – rocking her back to sense. But she turned on him, words burning now as if he had taken them down in morse: 'Always "My sweetheart",' she cried, 'You never say "My wife".' He was hurt and bitter, unable to understand, but saw now that not saying 'My wife' and never getting through to Ivor with his love, were the same thing.

The earphones blocked all sounds of children, traffic, next-door telly, and he wrote another message from the spot-middle of some ocean or other, a man-made arrowhead of peace steering from land to land: ARRIVING HOME 27TH CAN'T WAIT TO

SEE MY MUMMY AND DADDY – LOVE JANET. The big ship sailed
on: aerials sensitive, funnels powerful, people happy – sleeping,
eating, kissing or, if crew, heavy with work. He saw himself in
a smaller craft, marooned in a darkening unmapped ocean
where no one sent messages because he was the only passenger,
and no person would think to flash him a telegram anyway.
Neither could anyone wish him a good journey because he had
never announced his port of destination, and in any case no
one knew he was afloat, and there was no one to whom he
could send a marconigram stating his imminent arrival because
even if he were going somewhere he wouldn't even know where
nor when he would get there, and there was even less chance
of anyone being at that end than from where he'd started. All
he could do was fight this vision, and instead keep the big
jewel-lit liner in his mind, read what messages flashed to and
from it.

Earphones swung from the jacks-socket, and in the full overhead light he snapped open Ivor's cupboard. Horses and train-
sets, teddybear and games and forts and tricycle were piled
where the boy had last thrown them. Morse sounds no longer
hit him like snowflakes from his lit-up fabulous ship. He stared
blindly as each toy was slung across the room, towards window,
door, fireplace or ceiling, until every limbless piece had found
a new resting place. He went back to his wireless as the stairfoot
door snapped open and heavy sounds thumped their way up
at his commotion.

The ship remained. Its messages of love and arrival for some,
godspeed for others, birthday wishes and the balming oil of
common news, still sped out from it; but such words from the
black box made a picture that he couldn't break like the limbless toys all around him. His breath scraped out of his lungs
at the real and coloured vision mercilessly forming. The ship
was off centre, but he was able to watch it slowly sinking, the
calm grey water of tropical dusk lapping around it with cat-
like hunger, as if finely controlled by a brain not apparent or
visible to anyone. The ship subsided to its decks, and the
endless oil-smooth sea became more easygoing and polite,

though kept the hidden strength to force it under. As the ship flooded, people overflowed the lifeboats, until nothing remained but an undisturbed grey sheet of water – as smooth and shiny as tin that can be used for a mirror – and a voice in the earphones saying something Fred could not at first decipher. It was a gruff, homely, almost familiar tone, though one that he knew he would never be able to recognise no matter how long he concentrated.

The lock on the bedroom door burst, and several people were trying to pull him away from the radio, Nan's voice imploring above the others. Fingers of both hands – white and strong as flayed twigs – held on to the radio, which was so heavy that those pulling at him thought it was nailed to the bench and that the bench was rivetted to the floor. Fred held on with great strength, without speaking, cunning enough at the crucial moment to withdraw his hands from the radio (before superior odds could pull him clear) and clamp them with an equally steel-grip on to the bench, strange grunts sounding like trapped animals trying to jump from his mouth.

Eventually they dragged him free. Sweat glistened on him, as he waved his arms in the middle of the room: 'I heard God!' he shouted. 'Leave me be,' he roared. 'I heard God!' – then dropped.

III

Nan said not to bother with a doctor and, when they argued, stood to her full height, thanked everyone very much, and bundled them out of the house. Neighbours were a godsend, but there was an end to what goodness you could let them show. When Fred was undressed and into bed she stood by the window of Ivor's room, wondering why exactly he'd had such a fit. Hadn't he been happy? As far as she knew he lacked nothing, had all that most men had. She thought a lot of him, in spite of everything, and was quite sure he thought a lot of her, in spite of the fact that he was incapable of showing it. Neither had any reproaches to make, and apart from poor Ivor being drowned their life hadn't been so bad. Of course, she could never understand how he'd survived Ivor's death so well, though maybe it was bravery and self control that hadn't let him show what this barbaric piece of luck had done to him – which was all very well, but such dumb silence had made it ten times worse for her. She'd paid for it, by God, and it had just about done her in. It was hard to believe he'd felt it as hard as she had, in any case, when the first action of his fit had been to pulverise poor Ivor's toys. That wasn't something she could forgive and forget in a hurry, even though he may not have realized what he was doing. If he'd been full of drink it would have been a different matter, maybe, but Fred only drank much at Christmas or birthdays. Still, it wasn't like him to have such a black paralytic fit.

Next morning she phoned a doctor. He was violent and screaming all night, had ripped off great strips of wallpaper in his unreachable agony. During these long hours she was reminded of a new-born baby gripped for no reason by a blind unending temper, and there is nothing to do except draw on all the patience you have and try to soothe. Thinking of this kept her calm and able to manage. In a few bleak minutes of early morning she persuaded him to enter a mental hospital. 'I don't want you to go, love. But everybody thinks it'll be for the best. And I think so as well. They know what to do about such things there. You'll be as right as rain then in a couple of months.'

'All right,' he said, unable to care. Afloat in the ocean like his favourite unanchorable ship, he was carried away by a restful warm current beyond anyone's control.

She packed a case as if he were going again on a five-year jag to the army. She looked anxious and sorry, unable to stop her tears falling, her hand trembling as she turned out drawers for handkerchiefs and pyjamas. Fred sat in the armchair, his dressing-gown collar pulled up to his white immobile face, shaking with cold though the room was warmed by a huge, expert fire.

She travelled in the ambulance and saw him into the hospital, registered, examined, sedated, finally laid full-length in a narrow immaculate bed. Everything happened so quickly that she began to doubt that they could do any good. 'It's very nice,' she remarked, while his eyes stayed open, looking at the cream-painted blank ceiling of the ward. 'You couldn't be in a better place. I know they'll look after you, and I'll come twice a week to see you.'

'Aye,' he acknowledged, though out of it all.

'I've got to go now, love, or I'll miss the bus.'

At first there was nothing to do except keep the house clean. Polishing glass on the pictures, shining knives and forks, putting fresh paper on the kitchen shelves, she hoped his nervous breakdown wouldn't take too long to cure, though tears fell at the huge cannonball blow that had landed its weight against her: such mental things could last years. First Ivor gone, and now Fred; it was a bit bloody much. She cried to the empty house between sobs. She came in for sympathy from the neighbours: 'He was as good as gold,' a woman met shopping said, as if he'd already been buried and prayed over, 'but them's the sort that suffers first. It's a shame. Still, Mrs Hargreaves, if there's anything I can do for you, duck, just let me know.'

The novelty of living alone wore off. She began to feel young again, but it was a different sort of youth to when, every Thursday during the war, she walked across the road with her allowance book to collect Fred's fourteen shillings from the post office. It was a lonely, thrilling sort of freedom that began to dawn. She begrudged the frequent visits of both families who thought she wanted to stay in a continual state of being cheered-up, and when she told all of them in a loud voice that this wasn't so, her own parents retired hoping that she, after all, wasn't going the same way as 'that poor Fred', while Fred's mother and father went away thinking they could see at last who had made their poor son the way he was.

Dates changed on each evening paper, and months passed. Men began noticing her in the street (or she noticed them noticing her again) giving looks which meant that they would like to get in bed with her. She found this far from agreeable, but it did hold back the full misery of Fred's incarceration from turning her into an old woman. Anyway, why shouldn't she feel pleased when men smiled or winked at her in passing? she thought, seeing that it had taken misfortune to make her realise how firm her figure was at the bust and hips, how smooth-skinned and pale her face under dark hair. These sentiments descended on her with as little warning as Fred's illness had on him. To everyone else she stuck it out like a widow waiting for her husband to come back from the grave.

Twice a week she took a bus through curving lanes to the sudden tower that dominated the camplike spread of lesser buildings. Getting off the bus with her bundles and magazines, flowers and grapes, and clean handkerchiefs with the odour of ironing still on them, she felt desolate at being one of so many, as if such numbers visiting sick-minded men and women made it a shameless and guilty job that fate had hooked them into, and that they should try and hide their own stupidity and bad luck from each other.

She hurried head down to be first in the ward, going along corridors whose low ceilings sported so many reptilian pipes that it seemed as if she was deep in one of those submarine ships seen on the pictures. She then entered a light-enough ward, to find a waxen spiritual embalming of her husband that even pins would not wake up.

'Fred,' she said, still on her feet and spreading gifts over the bed, 'I've brought you these.'

'Aye,' he answered, an affirmation used by their parents, which he had taken to since his illness.

'Fred, they tell me you'll be getting better soon.'

'Aye' – again.

'Did they give you them new drugs yet?'

'Aye.'

'As long as you don't get that shock treatment. Everything's

OK at home. I'm managing all right.' She had to sit and look at him for an hour, because to leave before then, even though there was nothing left to say, was unthinkable. His mind might be a thousand miles away under his skin, but he'd remember it. She wondered what weird force had turned his life into a half sleep that she could no longer penetrate. He wasn't suffering, and that was a good job. Sometimes they saw snakes and dragons and screamed for hours, but Fred looked quiet enough, though there was no saying what he was like on days she didn't come. His brown calm eyes watched her, and she wondered if he still heard those morse codes he'd been so cranky on when they came from his expensive black radio. Of course, she nodded to her thoughts, that's what sent him, hearing those terrible squeaking messages night in night out. Once, she had switched off the television and listened by Ivor's door, and to hear the swift high-pitched dots and dashes had sounded like a monkey laughing – or trying to, which was worse. God knows what he made of such noise, and there was no way of finding out because he set fire to his papers every night, saying in his maddening know-all voice how wireless operators had to keep secret all messages they took down, otherwise it was prison for them. If she'd been the jealous sort she would have told him off about spending so much time at his wireless because, back from work, he could hardly wait to get his tea and a wash before he was up those stairs and glued to it. Still, most blokes would have been throwing their money away in a pub, and getting ulcers into the bargain. You can't have everything, and that was a fact, she supposed.

'I'll bring you a custard next week, love,' she said, wondering how else she could cheer him up.

'Aye.'

'If you want anything, drop me a postcard.' She didn't see him as helpless, treated him almost as if he had chosen to lie in that fashion and could come out of it at will – though from the way he smiled it was obvious he couldn't. In his locker were half a dozen paperback books she'd brought him, but she knew he hadn't read them. Still, they looked good in a place like this, and maybe he'd need them soon. You never knew when the steel band at the back of his eyes would snap and set him free again. She held his hand, shyly because many other visitors were in the ward, though they were too busy holding other hands to notice.

Always first into the hospital, she came out last, and so had to find a seat on the top deck of the bus, where pipe and cigarette smoke spread thickly. Surging, twisting movement was a relief – the bus eating its headlit way through winter's approaching darkness, speeding when the black canyon of trees straightened. She arched her back after the busy day, stared along the bus where other people talked out the highlights of their visit. Up to now her grief had been too new to allow for making friends, or do more than nod to a greeting, but when the man next to her asked:

'How was he today?' she replied:

'About the same,' and blushed as red as the sun which, hovering on the fields, resembled a beetroot going into the reverse of its existence, slipping back to the comfortable gloom of winter soil from which it had come. I'm a fool she thought, not daring to look. Why did I answer the cheeky devil like that? But she glanced at him, while his own eyes took in the bleak fall of night outside which, from his smile, made the bus interior feel like snug home to him. He was a young man who seemed born for nothing but work, awkward when his best clothes claimed their right to dominate him one day of the week. He was about thirty, she guessed, unmarried perhaps, since his approach was anything but furtive.

'It's a long job,' he said, 'once they get in a place like that. Longer than TB I reckon.'

'Well,' she said, thinking his face too red and healthy-looking for him to be a collier, 'they wouldn't keep 'em in longer than they had to either, would they? Cost too much.'

He took out a cigarette and, in spite of her retort, the smoke didn't increase her annoyance, for his lighting-up was debonair, matched to the feel of his dressed-up best. A cigarette suited him more than a collar and tie, and she didn't doubt that a pint of ale would suit him even more. Maybe he's nervous, she smiled, underneath it all. 'I don't suppose they would,' he said, having taken his time over it.

'It ain't the sort of thing they die from, either,' she added.

'There's that to be thankful for. I'm sorry' – out came his twenty-packet again – 'Smoke, duck?'

'No, thanks.' Who did he think he was? Who does he think I am, as well? 'Yes, I will have one.'

'I like a fag,' he said. 'Keeps me company.'

The opening was plain a mile off, but she refused it: 'Who do you see at the hospital, then?'

'A pal o' mine. He's in surgical though. Fell off some scaffolding last winter. He only broke an arm – that's what we thought, anyway – but he ain't been the same in the head since. He's an Irish bloke, a paddy, you know, and none of his family get to see him, so me and the lads tek turns at having half a day off to see he's all right. Shovel in a few fags and things. Be out in a couple o' months, according to the doctor.'

She hardly listened. 'You're a brickie, then?'

'Brickie's labourer. Who do *you* go and see? I mek good money though.'

'My husband.' At Redhill the lights of Nottingham blistered the sky in front, drew them down to its welcoming horseshoe. His naïve glance seemed too good, and she wondered if such an expression weren't the ultimate extension of his guile. 'I shan't be sorry to get home,' she told him. 'It's a long day, coming all this way.'

The frown left his face as soon as he thought she might see it: 'You can spend too much time at home. I like staying out, having a good time.'

She saw where his glance went, and began to fasten her coat. 'There is something to be said for it, I suppose.'

'There is, an' all,' he grinned.

'It's a long time since I had a drink,' she claimed, self-righteousness seeming the only defence left.

'Come and have one with me then, before you go home. You'll enjoy it.'

She flushed: he thinks I'm trying to knock on with him, and the idea made her so angry that she said, though not too loud in case she was heard and shown-up more for the flirt she might seem to be: 'What you want is a smack across the face.'

'I suppose so.' His voice verged on sadness. 'I'm sorry if I offended you, duck. But come and have a drink with me, then we can make it up.'

He was the limit. 'What do you tek me for?' – a question that puzzled him since it was too early to say. 'In any case,' she told him, 'I'm married, respectably married.'

'So am I,' he answered, 'but I'm not narrow-minded' – then kept his trap shut while the bus went slowly through bright lights and traffic, stopping and starting like possible future answers formulating in Nan's mind in case he had the nerve to speak again.

At the terminus they filed out onto the asphalt, and when he repeated his proposition in the darker shadows of the station yard both were shocked at the unequivocal 'yes' that for a few seconds kept them apart, then pulled them passionately together.

IV

Fred's brainstorm thinned-out at a predictable speed, leaving an unclouded blue-sea vision of a mind from which the large ship had slid away. He walked out of the ward, with a suitcase in one hand and a morning paper tucked under the other arm. His fervent kiss irritated Nan, but all she could say was: 'You'll be better off at home.'

'I know I shall. And I'll never want to leave it again love.' He stared with pleasure at the lush green of middle spring, the febrile smell of grass and catkins beating petrol smells through the open bus-window. Water charged under the lane, into an enormous pipe, a swollen silver arm speckling a field that cows drank from. He rubbed sun from his eyes as if after a fair spell in prison, was too absorbed in his journey to say much, enjoying his way out and back, Nan thought, as she herself had revelled in his absence once the shock of breakdown had worn off.

The first bungalows lay like tarted-up kennels over suburban fields, and he turned from them: 'I feel good, love, I feel marvellous.'

She smiled. 'I thought you did. You look as though you've had a long holiday.'

'I suppose it was, in a way.' He took her hand and squeezed it: 'Let's go down town this afternoon. Go for a stroll round, then spend a couple of hours at the pictures. We can have a real holiday between now and Monday.'

'All right' – doubting that they would.

As he walked down the yard, the neighbours thought him another of Nan's fancy men who had gone into the house via back door late at night in the last months, and slid out of the front door early next morning. She had been sly about it, but not sly enough, they grinned. Not that Fred was in danger of being informed, for it was hard to imagine him pasting her: she was beyond that by now, and in any case he would never be man enough for it. And when he did find out – as he must in time – then there'd be no point in knocking her about for what had become history.

They had to look twice before recognizing the Fred they'd known for years. His sallow face had filled out, and he had lost the lively movements of his brown eyes, that, through not being sure of themselves, had given and received sufficient warmth and sympathy to make him popular. His best suit would have shown as too tight if Nan hadn't thought to take his mac which, having always been slightly too big, hid the worst of his weight increase from curious eyes. Most obvious was his face, which had broadened. The expression of it was firmly tainted by middle age, though the neighbours were to swear how much better he looked, and what a lot of good the country air had done. 'It's fattened him,' they said, 'and it'll turn out to have fattened her as well – though it wasn't fresh air and good food as did that.' Fred caught their laughter by the back door.

The smells of the yard were familiar, tea-leaves and coal dust, car fuel and midday stew. He revelled in it, couldn't wait to get back to work next Monday and walk among those hot, oilburning machines which would make his homecoming complete. Nan hung up his mac, while he turned to the living-room. He thought they'd walked into the wrong house. 'What's this, then?'

'What's what?' She smiled at his frown, though it seemed like insult to her: 'What's what, Fred?'

'All this' – waving his arm, as if it indicated something that wasn't worth a light. He shifted his stance, uncomfortable at the change that had taken place while he was away.

'Don't you like it?'

'It's all right,' he conceded after a pause. 'It's a surprise though.'

'Aye.' He looked carefully, again. The old furniture, the old wallpaper, the old curtains and pictures – all gone, swept away by a magic wand of six dead months. The room was brighter, stippled green-contemporary and (though this didn't occur to them) resembled more the hospital he had just left than the previous homely decoration of their married life. 'You don't like it, then?'

He saw a thundercloud-quarrel looming up, and only ten minutes back from the hospital. 'It's lighter. Yes, I reckon it's OK. It's marvellous, in fact.'

'Thanks,' she said. 'I thought you'd jump for joy. I'll make you a cup of tea now.'

'It must have cost a good bit,' he called into the scullery, losing some of his strangeness at being home.

'I spent my football money on it,' she said. 'All but a few quid.'

'I suppose that's how you was able to look after me so well, bring me things every time.'

'It was,' she said.

'And I thought it was because you was such a good manager.'

'Don't be sarcastic. I often wondered what I'd do with it, you know that, and now you can see. I suppose you think I'm a dope, blowing it on the house when you spent your share on yourself, on a . . . wireless set. Well, I expect I am, but I like to keep the home nice. As long as you've got a pleasant place to live in there ain't much as can happen to you.'

'That's true.'

'Takes work and money though to keep it going, but it's worth it. Not that there's owt wrong with work.'

He stood by the fire, drinking his first cup of tea: 'You can say that again. I'll be glad to clock-in on Monday.'

'It's what makes people live,' she went on, almost happily, he thought, 'and you as well, if I know you. You've always been a lad for work. Course, after a while there gets as if there's not enough for a woman to do when she's got no kids. That's why most women in my position should be in a factory. No good moping around all day, or gossiping, or just sitting by the fire pulling a meagrim because you've read all the books at the library. You need a proper job. You can fit your housework in easy enough, and let them as say you can't come to your house and prove it.'

'What are you going on like this for, then?' he cried.

'Because I'm going to start work as well on Monday, at my old firm.'

Knowing what her game was, he became calmer. 'Maybe they don't need anybody.' They sat for a meal: cold ham, fresh salad and bread, sardines, a porkpie each in a cellophane wrapper. 'I went the other day to see 'em. They'd love to have me back, as an overlooker as well. The processing hasn't altered a bit since I was last there.'

He smiled: 'It wouldn't, not in a hundred years, no more than it would where I work.'

'I'll be like a fish back in water after an hour or two,' she exulted. 'I didn't tell 'em I'd only be there about three months, though while I am I'll put a bit of money by.'

'We don't need money,' he said, his appetite failing, 'because we'll be all right when I've pulled in a few wage-packets.'

'Not as I see it. We'll want all we can get, because I'm pregnant.'

He smiled, then the smile ran from his face before the claws of her meaning savaged it. 'Pregnant?'

'Yes,' she said. 'Can't you see it? My belly's up. We'll have a kid in the house in six months. You won't know the place.' She glared, as if hoping he'd try denying it. But the healthy bloom of fresh air had already left his cheeks. 'You've got things fixed up, then, haven't you?'

'Things often fix themselves up, whatever you do.' Her heart-beats were visible, breasts lifting and falling, making it seem to him as if her blouse were alive.

'Whose kid is it?'

'Nobody's as matters.'

He trembled the teacup back into its saucer. 'It matters to me, it bloody-well does.'

'We can have another kid between us after this, so you needn't carry on.'

He stood from his half-finished meal. 'That's what you think. You're a lunatic' – and his slow intimidating tread of disappointment on the stairs filled her more with sorrow for him than for herself.

She hadn't expected him to cave-in so deeply at the first telling, hoped he would argue, settle what had to be settled before going off to soothe his injuries in solitude. 'Maybe I am a lunatic' – and though she never imagined he lacked guts for such a vital set-to, it could be that she'd accepted too blindly the advice that things have a way of working themselves out better than you expect – given by Danny on telling him she was pregnant, and before he lit off for a new construction job at Rotherham. She remembered him saying, after their first night together, that whenever he met a woman the first thing that crossed his mind was 'If I have a kid by her, which of us will it look like?' And is that what you thought about me when you started talking to me on the bus?' 'What do you think?' he'd laughed. 'Of course it was, you juicy little piece.' But now he'd gone, and only she would be able to see how the kid turned out. Maybe that was why he wondered – because he knew he'd never be there to see. The bloody rotter – though there wasn't much else he could have done but hopped-it. Still, (her sigh was a sad one) the last few months had been heaven, a wild spree on what was left from her football money. She'd boozed and sang with Danny, in a pub tucked somewhere in the opposite end of town. It was a long while since she'd laughed so much, played darts and argued with the young men (some no older than teddy boys) all earning fair money at Gedling pit and out for a good time while they could get it. She'd never imagined her pool winnings would come in so handy, had even taken to filling coupons in again, which she and Fred had sworn never to do once they cleared a packet. Getting home at night she had felt Danny's hands and lips loving her: warm and ready for him, she came alive once more as the sweet shock of orgasm twisted her body. She hadn't bargained on getting pregnant, but couldn't feel sorry either, in spite of Fred chattering about upstairs. She'd hoped that the bliss of his absence would turn into the heaven of his coming back, but that had been too much to hope for, like most things. Tears forced a way out. Thoughts of Fred and their past life were too vivid and accurate now. 'I couldn't help it,' she said. 'I didn't want to have anything to do with Danny, but I wasn't myself.' She'd often forgot Fred's existence, her mind withdrawing to a time even before meeting him, a sense of paradise so far distant that she'd sometimes write on a postcard: VISIT HOSPITAL TOMORROW and lean it against the clock, so as not to lose him altogether.

There seemed no doubt to Fred upstairs that an end was reached but, seeing his half-filled suit-case on a chair, the end was like a sheer smooth wall blocking a tunnel in which there wasn't room enough to turn round and grope for a new beginning, though that seemed the only hope.

The fag-end nipped his fingers, fell and he let his foot slide over it. In the darkness of the cupboard he saw pictures of his London journey that afternoon, a long packed train rattling him to some strange impersonal bedroom smelling of trainsmoke and damp, and a new job, struggle, solitude, and even less reason for living than he had now. Still, there's not much for it but to get out. The moves of his departure were slow, but he smiled and told himself there was no hurry.

Ivor's toys had gone, cleared away by Nan after he'd been carted-off that morning. The jig-saw made sense, showed her returning alone from the hospital and not knowing what to do because he, Fred, was no longer part of the house. He saw himself smashing Ivor's toys by boot and hand, a lunatic flailing after a brainstorm harvest too abundant of life and energy.

Something half-concealed by a piece of clean sacking flashed into the back door of his eye before turning away from the cupboard. Pulling it clear he saw the radio set, black, deathly, and switched off, lying like some solid reproachful monster in place of the dustbinned toys. He grinned: Nan had intended hiding it where she imagined he was unlikely to see it, and he wondered why she hadn't scrapped it with the toys. He knelt towards the eyes and dials, touching and spinning in the hope that agreeable noises would lift from it.

Its size and dignity was intimidating, made him stand back and view it from a point where it disturbed him less. The vision began as half a memory striving to enter his brain. It edged a way sharply in. He laughed at it, tapped a pleasant hollow-sounding noise on the lid with his fingers, not like an army drum but something more satisfying, primitive and jungle-like. It reminded him of Peter Nkagwe, whose illuminated face was locked like stone as he battered out messages hour after hour in the signals office years ago.

The black box weighed a hundred pounds. Two hands flexed and stretched over it, pressing the sharp rim into his groin as he moved, breathless and foot by foot. His dark hair fell forward, joined beads of sweat in pricking his skin. Hospital had made him soft, but he resisted shifting the radio in two stages, found enough strength to do it the hard way, drawing on the rock-middle of himself to reach the table at one agonising go, and set it so delicately down it would have been impossible either to see or hear the soundless contact of wood and metal.

It was a minute's work to screw on aerial and power, slick

in earphones and switch a current-flow through valves and superhet. Energy went like an invisible stoat into each purple and glowing filament. The panels lit up and background static began as if, when a child, he had pressed a sea-shell to his ear and heard the far-off poise and fall of breakers at Skegness; then such subtlety went, and noise rose to the loud electric punching of a full-grown sea in continual motion. He turned the volume down and sent the fly-wheel onto morse code.

The sea calmed for its mundane messages of arrival and departure, of love and happy birthday and grandma died and I bought presents in Bombay, and from this festive liner – white, sleek and grandiose – once more seen between clear sky and otherwise desolate flat sea – signals were emitted saying that a son had been (or was it would be?) born with love from Nancy in a place where both were doing well.

He slung the pencil down and stared at the accidental words, grew a smile at the irony of the message. He frowned, as if a best friend taunted him. The calm boat flowed on and a voice spoke over his shoulder: 'What have you got there, Fred?'

'A message,' he answered, not looking round, sliding his hand over so that she wouldn't see it. 'I take them down from ships at sea.'

'I know you do.'

'All sorts of things,' he added, sociable without knowing why. The earphones fell to his neck and he needle-spun the wavelength, a noise that reminded Nancy of running by the huge Arboretum birdcages as a kid: 'What though?'

'Telegrams and things. Ordinary stuff. Listen to what this funny one says' – sliding his hand away – ' "FRED HARGREAVES LEFT HOME AT ONE O'CLOCK THURSDAY AFTERNOON." '

She turned: 'You're not going, Fred, are you? I don't believe it.'

'That's what the telegram said. Everyone I take down says the same thing. I can't get over it.'

'Talk proper,' she cried. 'It's not right to go off like this.'

He laughed, a grinding of heart and soul. 'In't it?'

'What about your job?'

'There's plenty more where that came from.'

'What about me?'

He laid his earphones down, and spoke with exaggerated awful quietness. 'You should a thought of that before you trolloped off and got a bastard in you.'

'It's all finished now. Didn't I tell you? It's about time you believed me.'

'You told me a lot of things.' It was more of a grouse than a reproach. 'All on 'em lies.'

'I thought it was better that way.'

'And going with that bloke? Was that better as well?' His shout startled her, brown eyes glittering under darkening shadows, as if his exhaustion had never been lifted by a sojourn at the hospital. Neighbours from next door and out in the yard could hear them shouting. Don't tell me he's found out already. Well, well!

She was still in the new dress worn to fetch him home, and it showed already a slight thickness at the waist. 'I couldn't help it,' she cried, able to add, in spite of tears on her face: 'Anyway, what did you expect? We'd had no life between us since Ivor died. I was fed up on it. I had to let myself go.'

'It was too bad though, worn't it?'

'I'm not saying it wasn't. But I'm not going to go on bended knees and ask you to stay. I'm not an' all.' She stiffened, looked at him with hatred: 'It's as much your fault as mine.'

'I'm leaving,' he said, 'I'm off.'

'Go on, then.' Her face turned, the tone mechanical and meant, the quiet resignation of it a hot poker burning through his eyes. It was a final torment he could not take. Dazed by the grief of her decision she didn't see his hand coming. A huge blow, like a boulder flying at top speed in a gale, hit the side of her face, threw her back, feet collapsing. Another fist caught her, and another. She crashed on to the bed, a cry of shock beating her to it there. As she was to tell her mother: 'He hadn't really hit me before then, and he wain't hit me again, either. Maybe I deserved it, though.'

He tore the message off and screwed it tight, flung it to the far corner of the room. Then he went to Nan and tried to comfort her, the iron hooves of desperate love trampling them back into the proportions of matrimonial life.

ON SATURDAY AFTERNOON

I once saw a bloke try to kill himself. I'll never forget the day because I was sitting in the house one Saturday afternoon, feeling black and fed-up because everybody in the family had gone to the pictures, except me who'd for some reason been left out of it. 'Course, I didn't know then that I would soon see something you can never see in the same way on the pictures, a real bloke stringing himself up. I was only a kid at the time, so you can imagine how much I enjoyed it.

I've never known a family to look as black as our family when they're fed-up. I've seen the old man with his face so dark and full of murder because he ain't got no fags or was having to use saccharine to sweeten his tea, or even for nothing at all, that I've backed out of the house in case he got up from his fireside chair and came for me. He just sits, almost on top of the fire, his oil-stained Sunday-joint maulers opened out in front of him and facing inwards to each other, his thick shoulders scrunched forward, and his dark brown eyes staring into the fire. Now and again he'd say a dirty word, for no reason at all, the worst word you can think of, and when he starts saying this you know it's time to clear out. If mam's in it gets worse than ever, because she says sharp to him: 'What are yo' looking so bleddy black for?' as if it might be because of something she's done, and before you know what's happening he's tipped up a tableful of pots and mam's gone out of the house crying. Dad hunches back over the fire and goes on swearing. All because of a packet of fags.

I once saw him broodier than I'd ever seen him, so that I thought he'd gone crackers in a quiet sort of way – until a fly flew to within a yard of him. Then his hand shot out, got it, and slung it crippled into the roaring fire. After that he cheered up a bit and mashed some tea.

Well, that's where the rest of us get our black looks from. It stands to reason we'd have them with a dad who carries on like that, don't it? Black looks run in the family. Some families have them and some don't. Our family has them right enough, and that's certain, so when we're fed-up we're really fed-up. Nobody knows why we get as fed-up as we do or why it gives us these black looks when we are. Some people get fed-up and don't look bad at all: they seem happy in a funny sort of way, as if they've just been set free from clink after being in there for something they didn't do, or come out of the pictures after sitting plugged for eight hours at a bad film, or just missed a bus they ran half a mile for and seen it was the wrong one just after they'd stopped running – but in our family it's murder for the others if one of us is fed-up. I've asked myself lots of times what it is, but I can never get any sort of answer even if I sit and think for hours, which I must admit I don't do, though it looks good when I say I do. But I sit and think for long enough, until mam says to me, at seeing me scrunched up over the fire like dad: 'What are yo' looking so black for?' So I've just got to stop thinking about it in case I get really black and fed-up and go the same way as dad, tipping up a tableful of pots and all.

Mostly I suppose there's nothing to look so black for: though it's nobody's fault and you can't blame anyone for looking black because I'm sure it's summat in the blood. But on this Saturday afternoon I was looking so black that when dad came in from the bookie's he said to me: 'What's up wi' yo'?'

'I feel badly,' I fibbed. He'd have had a fit if I'd said I was only black because I hadn't gone to the pictures.

'Well have a wash,' he told me.

'I don't want a wash,' I said, and that was a fact.

'Well get outside and get some fresh air then,' he shouted.

I did as I was told, double-quick, because if ever dad goes as far as to tell me to get some fresh air I know it's time to get away from him. But outside the air wasn't so fresh, what with that bloody great bike factory bashing away at the yard-end. I didn't know where to go, so I walked up the yard a bit and sat down near somebody's back gate.

Then I saw this bloke who hadn't lived long in our yard. He was tall and thin and had a face like a parson except that he wore a flat cap and had a moustache that drooped, and looked as though he hadn't had a square meal for a year. I didn't think much o' this at the time: but I remember that as he turned in by the yard-end one of the nosy gossiping women who stood there every minute of the day except when she trudged to the pawnshop with her husband's bike or best suit, shouted to him: 'What's that rope for, mate?'

He called back: 'It's to 'ang messen wi', missis,' and she cackled at his bloody good joke so loud and long you'd think she never heard such a good 'un, though the next day she cackled on the other side of her fat face.

He walked by me puffing a fag and carrying his coil of brand-new rope, and he had to step over me to get past. His boot nearly took my shoulder off, and when I told him to watch where he was going I don't think he heard me because he didn't even look round. Hardly anybody was about. All the kids were still at the pictures, and most of their mams and dads were downtown doing the shopping.

The bloke walked down the yard to his back door, and having nothing better to do because I hadn't gone to the pictures I followed him. You see, he left his back door open a bit, so I gave it a push and went in. I stood there, just watching him, sucking my thumb, the other hand in my pocket. I suppose he knew I was there, because his eyes were moving more natural now, but he didn't seem to mind. 'What are yer going to do wi' that rope, mate?' I asked him.

'I'm going ter 'ang messen, lad,' he told me as though he'd done it a time or two already, and people had usually asked him questions like this beforehand.

'What for mate?' He must have thought I was a nosy young bogger.

''Cause I want to, that's what for,' he said, clearing all the pots off the table and pulling it to the middle of the room. Then he stood on it to fasten the rope to the light-fitting. The table creaked and didn't look very safe, but it did him for what he wanted.

'It wain't hold up, mate,' I said to him, thinking how much better it was being here than sitting in the pictures and seeing the Jungle Jim serial.

But he got nettled now and turned on me. 'Mind yer own business.'

I thought he was going to tell me to scram, but he didn't. He made ever such a fancy knot with that rope, as though he'd been a sailor or summat, and as he tied it he was whistling a fancy tune to himself. Then he got down from the table and pushed it back to the wall, and put a chair in its place. He wasn't looking black at all, nowhere near as black as anybody in our family when they're feeling fed-up. If ever he'd looked only half as black as our dad looked twice a week he'd have hanged himself years ago, I couldn't help thinking. But he was making a good job of that rope all right, as though he'd thought about it a lot anyway, and as though it was going to be the last thing he'd ever do. But I knew something he didn't know, because he wasn't standing where I was. I knew the rope wouldn't hold up, and I told him so, again.

'Shut yer gob,' he said, but quiet like, 'or I'll kick yer out.'

I didn't want to miss it, so I said nothing. He took his cap off and put it on the dresser, then he took his coat off, and his scarf, and spread them out on the sofa. I wasn't a bit frightened, like I might be now at sixteen, because it was interesting. And being only ten I'd never had a chance to see a bloke hang himself before. We got pally, the two of us, before he slipped the rope around his neck.

'Shut the door,' he asked me, and I did as I was told. 'Ye're a good lad for your age,' he said to me while I sucked my thumb, and he felt in his pockets and pulled out all that was inside, throwing the handful of bits and bobs on the table: fag-packet and peppermints, a pawn-ticket, an old comb, and a few coppers. He picked out a penny and gave it to me, saying: 'Now listen ter me, young 'un. I'm going to 'ang messen, and when I'm swinging I want you to gi' this chair a bloody good kick and push it away. All right?'

I nodded.

He put the rope around his neck, and then took it off like it was a tie that didn't fit. 'What are yer going to do it for, mate?' I asked again.

'Because I'm fed-up,' he said, looking very unhappy. 'And because I want to. My missus left me, and I'm out o' work.'

I didn't want to argue, because the way he said it, I knew he couldn't do anything else except hang himself. Also there was a funny look in his face: even when he talked to me I swear he couldn't see me. It was different to the black look my old man puts on, and I suppose that's why my old man would never hang himself, worse luck, because he never gets a look into his clock like this bloke had. My old man's look stares at you, so that you have to back down and fly out of the house: this bloke's look looked through you, so that you could face it and know it wouldn't do any harm. So I saw now that dad would never hang himself because he could never get the right sort of look into his face, in spite of that fact that he'd been out of work often enough. Maybe mam would have to leave him first, and then he might do it; but no – I shook my head – there wasn't much chance of that even though he did lead her a dog's life.

'Yer wain't forget to kick that chair away?' he reminded me, and I swung my head to say I wouldn't. So my eyes were popping and I watched every move he made. He stood on the chair and put the rope around his neck so that it fitted this

to hang himself. I wasn't born yesterday, nor the day before yesterday either.

'It's a fine thing if a bloke can't tek his own life,' the bloke said, seeing he was in for it.

'Well he can't,' the copper said, as if reading out of his book and enjoying it. 'It ain't your life. And it's a crime to take your own life. It's killing yourself. It's suicide.'

The bloke looked hard, as if every one of the copper's words meant six-months cold. I felt sorry for him, and that's a fact, but if only he'd listened to what I'd said and not depended on that light-fitting. He should have done it from a tree, or something like that.

He went up the yard with the copper like a peaceful lamb, and we all thought that that was the end of that.

But a couple of days later the news was flashed through to us – even before it got to the Post because a woman in our yard worked at the hospital of an evening dishing grub out and tidying up. I heard her spilling it to somebody at the yard-end. 'I'd never 'ave thought it. I thought he'd got that daft idea out of his head when they took him away. But no. Wonders'll never cease. Chucked 'issen from the hospital window when the copper who sat near his bed went off for a pee. Would you believe it? Dead? Not much 'e ain't.'

He'd heaved himself at the glass, and fallen like a stone on to the road. In one way I was sorry he'd done it, but in another I was glad, because he'd proved to the coppers and everybody whether it was his life or not all right. It was marvellous though, the way the brainless bastards had put him in a ward six floors up, which finished him off, proper, even better than a tree.

All of which will make me think twice about how black I sometimes feel. The black coal-bag locked inside you, and the black look it puts on your face, doesn't mean you're going to string yourself up or sling yourself under a double-decker or chuck yourself out of a window or cut your throat with a sardine-tin or put your head in the gas-oven or drop your rotten sack-bag of a body on to a railway line, because when you're feeling that black you can't even move from your chair.

Anyhow, I know I'll never get so black as to hang myself, because hanging don't look very nice to me, and never will, the more I remember old what's-his-name swinging from the light-fitting.

More than anything else, I'm glad now I didn't go to the pictures that Saturday afternoon when I was feeling black and ready to do myself in. Because you know, I shan't ever kill myself. Trust me. I'll stay alive half-barmy till I'm a hundred and five, and then go out screaming blue murder because I want to stay where I am.

GUZMAN, GO HOME

Bouncing and engine-noise kept the baby soothed, as if he was snug in the belly of a purring cat. But at the minute of feeding-time he screamed out his eight-week honeyguts in a high-powered lament, which nothing but the nipple could stop. Somewhere had to be found where he could feed in peace and privacy, otherwise his cries in the narrow car threatened the straight arrow on Chris's driving.

He often had fifty miles of road to himself, except when a sudden horn signalled an overtaking fast-driven Volkswagen loaded to the gills. 'Look how marvellously they go,' Jane said. 'I told you you should have bought one. No wonder they overtake you so easily, with that left-hand drive.'

Open scrub fanned out north and west, boulders and olive trees, mountains combing the late May sky of Spain. It was sombre and handsome country, in contrast to the flat-chested fields of England. He backed into an orange grove, red earth newly watered, cool wind coming down from the fortress of Sagunto. While Jane fed the baby, he fed Jane and himself, broke off pieces of ham and cheese for a simultaneous intake to save time.

The car was so loaded that they looked like refugees leaving a city that the liberating army is coming back to. Apart from a small space for the baby the inside was jammed with cases, typewriter, baskets, flasks, coats, umbrellas, and plastic bowls. On the luggage-rack lay a trunk and two cases with, topping all, a folded pram-frame, and collapsible bath.

It was a new car, but dust, luggage, and erratic driving gave it a veteran appearance. They had crossed Paris in a hail and thunderstorm, got lost in the traffic maze of Barcelona, and skirted Valencia by a ring road so rotten that it seemed as if an earthquake had hit it half an hour before. Both wanted the dead useless tree of London lifted off their nerves, so they locked up the flat, loaded the car, and sailed to Boulogne, where the compass of their heart's desire shook its needle towards Morocco.

They wanted to get away from the political atmosphere that saturated English artistic life. Chris, being a painter, had decided that politics ought not to concern him. he would 'keep his hands clean' and get on with his work. 'I like to remember what happened in 1848 to Wagner,' he said, 'who fell in with the revolution up to his neck, helping the workers to storm the arsenal in Dresden, and organising stores for the defence. Then when the revolution collapsed he hightailed it to Italy to be "entirely an artist" again.' He laughed loud, until a particularly deep pothole cut it short in his belly.

Flying along the straight empty road before Valencia they realised the meaning of freedom from claustrophobic and dirty London, from television and Sunday newspapers, and their middle-aged mediocre friends who talked more glibly nowadays of good restaurants than they had formerly about socialism. The gallery owner advised Chris to go to Majorca, if he must get away, but Chris wanted to be near the mosques and museums of Fez, smoke *kif* at the tribal gatherings of Taroudant and Tafilalt, witness the rose-hip snake-green sunsets of Rabat and Mogador. The art dealer couldn't see why he wanted to travel at all. Wasn't England good enough for other painters and writers? 'They like it here, so why don't you? Travel broadens the mind, but it shouldn't go to the head. It's a thing of the past – old-fashioned. You're socially conscious, so you can't be away from the centre of things for long. What about the marches and sit-downs, petitions, and talks?'

For ten hours he'd driven along the hairpin coast and across the plains of Murcia and Lorca, wanting to beat the previous day's run. They hadn't stopped for the usual rich skins of sausage-protein and cheese, but ate biscuits and bitter chocolate as they went along. He hardly spoke, as if needing all his concentration to wring so many extra miles an hour from the empty and now tolerable road.

His impulse was to get out of Spain, to put that wide arid land behind them. He found it dull, its people too beaten down to be interesting or worth knowing. The country seemed a thousand years older than it had on his last visit. Then, he'd expected insurrection at any time, but now the thought of it was a big horse-laugh. The country smelt even more hopeless than England – which was saying a lot. He wanted to reach Morocco which, no matter how feudal and corrupt, was a new country that might be on the up and up.

So when the engine roared too much for good health at Benidorm, he chose to keep going in order to reach Almeria by nightfall. That extra roar seemed caused by a surcharge of rich fuel at leaving the choke out too long, that would right itself after twenty miles. But it didn't, and on hairpin bends he had difficulty controlling the car. He was careful not to mention this in case his wife persuaded him to get it repaired – which would delay them God knew how many days.

When the plains of Murcia laid a straight road in front of them, it wasn't much after midday. What did hunger matter with progress so good? The roaring of the engine sometimes created a dangerous speed, but maybe it would get them to Tangier. Nothing could be really wrong with a three-month old car – so he drove it into the remotest part of Spain, sublime indifference and sublime confidence blinding him.

He shot through Villa Oveja at five o'clock. The town stood on a hill, so gear had to be changed, causing such a bellowing of the engine that people stared as if expecting the luggage-racked car to go up any second like the Bomb, that Chris had fought so hard to get banned. The speed increased so much that he daren't take his foot from the brake even when going uphill.

The houses looked miserable and dull, a few doorways opening into cobblestoned *entradas*. By one an old woman sat cutting up vegetables; a group of children were playing by another; and a woman with folded arms looked as if waiting for some fast car full of purpose and direction to take her away. Pools of muddy water lay around, though no rain had fallen for weeks. A petrol pump stood like a one-armed veteran of the Civil War outside an open motor workshop – several men busy within at the bonnet of a Leyland lorry. 'These Spanish towns give me the creeps,' he said, hooting a child out of the way.

He waved a farewell at the last house. Between there and Almeria the earth, under its reafforestation skin of cactus and weed, was yellow with sand, desert to be traversed at high speed with eyes half-closed. The road looped the hills, to the left sheer wall and to the right precipices that fell into approaching dusk. Earth and rocks generated a silence that reminded him of mountains anywhere. He almost expected to see snow around the next bend.

In spite of the faulty engine he felt snug and safe in his sturdy car, all set to reach the coast in a couple of hours. The road ahead looked like a black lace fallen from Satan's boot in heaven. No healthy tune was played by the sandy wind, and the unguarded drop on the right was enough to scare any driver, yet kilometres were a shorter measure than miles, would soon roll him into the comfort of a big meal and a night's hotel.

On a steep deserted curve the car failed to change gear. Chris thought it a temporary flash of overheated temper from the clutch mechanism, but, trying again – before the loaded car rolled off the precipice – drew a screech of igniting steel from within the gearbox.

He was stopped from trying the gears once more by a warning yell from Jane, pulled the handbrake firmly up. The car still rolled, its two back wheels at the cliff edge, so he pressed with all his force on the footbrake as well, and held it there, sweat piling out on to the skin of his face. They sat, the engine switched off.

Wind was the only noise, a weird hooting brazen hill-wind from which the sun had already extricated itself. 'All we can do,' he said, 'is hope somebody will pass, so that we can get help.'

'Don't you know *anything* about this bloody car? We can't sit here all night.' Her face was wound up like a spring, life only in her righteous words. It was as if all day the toil of the road had been preparing them for just this.

'Only that it shouldn't have gone wrong, being two months old.'

'Well,' she said, 'British is best. You know I told you to buy a Volkswagen. What do you *think* is wrong with it?'

'I don't know. I absolutely don't bloody well know.'

'I believe you. My God! You've got the stupidity to bring me and a baby right across Europe in a car without knowing the first thing about it. I think you're mad to risk all our lives like this. You haven't even got a proper driving licence.' The wind, too, moaned its just rebuke. But the honeyed sound of another motor on the mountain road filtered into the horse-power of their bickering. Its healthy and forceful noise drew closer, a machine that knew where it was going, its four-stroke cycle fearlessly cutting through the silence. While he searched for a telling response to her tirade, Jane put her arm out, waving the car to stop.

It was a Volkswagen (of course, he thought, it bloody well had to be), a field-grey low-axled turtle with windows, so fresh-washed and polished that it might just have rolled off the conveyor line. Its driver leaned out while the engine still turned: '*Que ha pasado?*'

Chris told him: the car had stopped, and it wasn't possible to change gear, or get it going at all. The Volskwagen had a Spanish number plate, and the driver's Spanish, though grammatical, was undermined by another accent. He got out, motioned Chris to do the same. He was a tall, well-built man dressed in khaki slacks and a light-blue open-necked jersey-shirt a size too small: his chest tended to bulge through it and gave the impression of more muscle than he really had. His bare arms were tanned, and on one was a small white mark where a wristwatch had been. There was a more subtle tan to his face, as if it had done a slow change from lobster red to a parchment colour, oil-soaked and wind-worn after a lot of travel.

To Chris he seemed like a rescuing angel, yet there was a cast of sadness, of disappointment underlying his face that, with a man of his middle-age, was no passing expression. It was a mark that life had grown on him over the years, and for good reason, since there was also something of great strength in his features. As if to deny all this – yet in a weird way confirming it more – he had a broad forehead, and the eyes and mouth of an alert benign cat, and like so many short-sighted Germans who wore rimless spectacles he had that dazed and distant look that managed to combine stupidity and ruthlessness.

He sat in the driver's seat, released the brake, and signalled to Chris to push. '*Harémos la vuelta.*'

Jane stayed inside, rigid from the danger they had been in, weary in every vein after days travelling with a baby that was feeding from herself. She turned now and again to tuck the sheet under the baby. The man beside her deftly manoeuvred the car to the safe side of the road, and faced it towards the bend leading back to Villa Oveja.

He started the engine. The turnover was healthy, and the wheels moved. Chris saw the car sliding away, wife, luggage, and baby fifty yards down the road. He was too tired to be afraid they would vanish for ever and leave him utterly alone in the middle of these darkening peaks. He lit a cigarette, in a vagrant slap-happy wind that, he had time to think, would never have allowed him to do so in a more normal situation.

The car stopped, then started again, and the man tried to change gear, which brought a further roaring screech from the steel discs within. He stopped the car, leaned from the window and looked with bland objective sadness at Chris. Hand on the wheel, he spoke English for the first time, but in an unmistakable German accent. He grinned and said, a high-pitched rhythmical rise and fall, a telegraphic rendering of disaster that was to haunt Chris a long time:

'England, your car has snapped!'

II

'Lucky for you, England, I am the owner of the garage in Villa Oveja. A towing-rope in my car will drag you there in five minutes.

'My name is Guzman – allowing me to introduce myself. If I hadn't come along and seen your break-up you would perhaps have waited all night, because this is the loneliest Iberian road. I only come this way once a week, so you are double lucky. I go to the next town to see my other garage branch, confirm that the Spaniard I have set to run it doesn't trick me too much. He is my friend, as far as I can have a friend in this country where, due to unsought-for happenings, I have spent nearly the same years as my native Germany. But I find my second garage is not doing too wrong. The Spaniards are good mechanics, a very adjustable people. Even without spare parts they have the genius to get an engine living – though under such a system it can't last long before being carried back again. Still, they are clever. I taught my mechanics all I know: I myself was once able to pick tank engines into morsels, under even more trying conditions than here. I trained mechanics well, and one answered by taking his knowledge to Madrid, where I don't doubt he got an excellent job – the crooked, ungrateful. He was the most brainful, so what could he do except trick me? I would have done the same in his place. The others, they are fools for not escaping with my knowledge, and so they will never get on to the summit. Likewise they aren't much use for me. But we will fix your car good once we get right back to the town, have no fear of it.

'You say it is only three months old? Ah, England, no German car would be such a bad boy after three months. This Volkswagen I have had two years, and not a nut and bolt has slipped out of place. I never boast about myself, but the Volkswagen is a good car, that any rational human being can trust. It is made with intelligence. It is fast and hard, has a marvellous honest engine, that sounds to last a thousand years pulling through these mountains. Even on scorched days I like to drive with all my windows shut-closed, listening to the engine nuzzling swift along like a happy cat-bitch. I sweat like rivers, but the sound is beautiful. A good car, and anything goes wrong, so you take the lid off, and all its insides are there for the eye to see and the hand-spanner to work at. Whereas your English cars are difficult to treat with. A nut and bolt loose, a pipe snapped, and if you don't burn the fingers you surely sprain the wrist trying to get at the injured fix. It's as if your designers hide them on purpose. Why? It isn't rational why, in a people's car that is so common. A car should be natural to expose and easy to understand. On the other hand you can't say that because a car is new nothing should happen to it. Even an English car. That is unrealistic. You should say: This car is new, therefore I must not let anything happen to it. A car is a rational human being like myself.

'Thank you. I've always had a wanton for English cigarettes, just as I have for the language. The tobacco is more subtle than the brutal odours of the Spanish. Language is our best lanes of communication, England, and whenever I meet travellers like yourself I take advantage from it.

'You don't like the shape of the Volkswagen? Ah, England! That is the prime mistake in choosing a car. You English are so aesthetic, so biased. When I was walking through north Spain just after the war – before the ink was dry on the armistice signatures, ha, ha! – I was very poor and had no financial money – and in spite of the beautiful landscapes and marvellous towns with walls and churches, I sold my golden spectacles to a bruto farmer so that I can buy sufficing bread and sausage to feed me to Madrid. I didn't see the pleasant things so clearly, and being minus them the print in my Baedeker handbook blurred my eyes, but here I am today. So what does the shape of a car mean? That you like it? That you don't wear spectacles yet, so you'll never have to sell them, you say? Oh, I am laughing. Oh, oh, oh! But England, excuse me wagging the big finger at you, but one day you may not be so fortunate.

'Ah! So! Marvellous, as you say: clever Guzman has flipped into second gear, and maybe I do not need my towing rope to get you back to town. I don't think you were so glad in all your life to meet a German, were you, England? Stray Germans like me are not so current in Spain nowadays.'

Shadows took the place of wind. A calm dusk slunk like an idling panther from the hips and peaks of the mountains. A few yellow lamps shone from the outlying white houses of Villa Oveja. Both cars descended the looping road, then crept up to these lights like prodigal moths.

As he stopped outside Guzman's garage, Chris remembered his ironic goodbye of an hour ago. A small crowd gathered, who'd perhaps witnessed other motorists give that final contemptuous handwave, only to draggle back in this forlorn manner. God's judgement, I suppose they think, the religious bastards. Guzman finished his inspection, sunlight seeming to shine on his glasses even in semi-darkness – which also hid what might be a smile: 'England, I will take you to a hotel where you can stay all night – with your wife and child.'

'All night!' Chris had expected this, so his exclamation wasn't so sharp.

'Maybe two whole nights, England.'

Jane's words were clipped with hysteria: 'I won't spend two nights in this awful dump.' The crowd recognised the livelier inflections of a quarrel, grew livelier themselves. Guzman's smile was less hidden: 'Rationally speaking, it must be difficult travelling with a family-wife. However, you will find the Hotel Universal modest but comfortable, I'm sure.'

'Listen,' Chris said, 'can't you fix this clutch tonight?' He turned to Jane: 'We could still be in Almeria by twelve.'

'Forget it,' she said. 'This is what . . .'

' . . . comes of leaving England with a car you know nothing about? Oh for God's sake!'

Guzman's heavy accent sometimes rose to an almost feminine pitch, and now came remorselessly in: 'England, if I might suggest . . .'

The hotel room smelled of carbolic and Flit; it was scrupulously clean. Every piece of luggage was unloaded and stacked on the spacious landing of the second floor – a ramshackle heap surrounded by thriving able-bodied aspidistras. The room dosed so heavily with Flit gave Jane a headache. Rooms with bath were non-existent, but a handbasin was available, and became sufficient during their three days there.

Off the squalor of the main road were narrow, cobblestoned streets. White-faced houses with over-hanging balconies were neat and well cared for. The streets channelled you into a spacious square, where the obligatory church, the necessary town hall, and the useful *telegrafos*, emphasised the importance of the locality. While Guzman's tame mechanics worked on the car Chris and Jane sat in the cool dining room and listened to Guzman himself. On either side of the door leading to the kitchen were two bird cages, as large as prisons, with an austere primitive beauty about the handiwork of them. In each was a hook-beaked tropical bird, and while he talked Guzman now and again rolled up a ball of bread that was left over from dinner and threw it with such swift accuracy at the cage that it was caught by the scissor-beak that seemed eternally poked without.

'I come here always for an hour after lunch or dinner,' he said, lighting a small cigar, 'to partake coffee and perhaps meet interesting people, by which I signify any foreigner who happens to be moving through. As you imagine, not many stay in our little God-forgotten town – as your charming and rational wife surmised on your precipitant arrival here. My English is coming back the more I talk to you, which makes me happy. I read much, to maintain my vocabulary, but speech is rare. I haven't spoken it with anyone for fourteen months. You express motions of disbelief? It's true. Few motorists happen to break up at this particular spot in Spain. Many English who come prefer the coasts. Not that the mosquitoes are any lesser there than here. Still, I killed that one: a last midnight black-out for the little blighter. Ah, there's another. There, on your hand. Get it, England. Bravo. You are also quick. They are not usually so bad, because we Flit them to death.

'I suppose the English like Spain in this modern epoch because of its politics, which are on the right side – a little primitive, but safe and solid. Excuse me, I did not know you were speeding through to Africa, and did not care for political Spain. Not many visit the artistic qualities of Iberia, which I have always preferred. You are fed up with politics, you say, and want to leave them all behind? I don't blame you. You are wisdom himself, because politics can make peril for a man's life, especially if he is an artist. It is good to do nothing but paint, and good that you should not linger among this country. Why does an artist sit at politics? He is not used to it, tries his hand, and then all is explosioned in him. Shelley? Yes, of course, but that was a long time ago, my dear England. Excuse me again, yes, I will have a *coñac*. When I was in London, in 1932, somebody taught me a smart toast: health, wealth, and stealth! *Gesundheit!*

'Forgive my discretion, England, but I see from your luggage that you are an artist, and I must talk of it. I have a great opinion of artists, and can see why it is that your car broke down. Artists know little of mechanical things, and those that do can't ever be great artists. I myself began as a middling artist. It is a long story, which starts when I was eighteen, and I shall tell you soon.

'Your car is in good hands. Don't worry. And you, madam, I forbid you. We can relax after such a dinner. My mechanics have taken out the engine, and are already shaping off the spare necessary on the lathe. There are no spare parts for your particular name of car in this section of Spain, therefore we have to use our intelligent handicraft – to make them from nothing, from scrape, as you say. That doesn't daunt me, England, because in Russia I had to make spare parts for captured tanks. Ah! I learned a lot in Russia. But I wish I hadn't ever been there. My fighting was tragical, my bullets shooting so that I bleed to death every night for my perpetrations. But bygones are bypassed, and are a long time ago. At least I learned the language. *Chto dyelaets?*

'Well, it is a pity you don't have a Volkswagen, which I have all the spare pieces for. Yet if *you'd* had a Volkswagen we wouldn't have been talking here. You would have been in Marrakech. Like my own country-men: they overtake every traveller on the road in their fast Volkswagens, as if they departed Hamburg that morning and have to get the ferry ship for Tangier this evening, so as to be in Marrakech tomorrow. Then after a swift weekend in the Atlas Mountains they speed back to the office work for another economic miracle, little perceiving that I am one of those that made that miracle possible. What do I mean? How?

'Ah, ah, ah! You are sympathetic. When I laugh loud, so, you don't get up and walk away. You don't stare at me or flinch. Often the English do that, especially those who come to Spain. Red-faced and lonely, they stare and stare, then walk off. But you understand my laugh, England. You smile even. Maybe it is because you are an artist. You say it is because I am an artist? Oh, you are so kind, so kind. I have been an artist and a soldier both, also a mechanic. Unhappily I have done too many things, fallen between cleft stools.

'But, believe it or not, I earned a living for longer years by my drawing than I have done as a garage man. The first money I earned in my life was during my student days in Königsberg – by drawing my uncle who was a ship-captain. My father wanted me to be a lawyer but I desired to be an artist. It was difficult to shake words with my father at that time, because he had just made a return from the war and he was very dispirited about Germany and himself. Therefore he wanted me to obey him as if I had lost the war for him, and he wouldn't let me choose. I had to give up all drawing and become a lawyer, nothing less. I said no. He said yes. So I departed home. I walked twenty miles to the railway station with all the money I'd saved for years, and when I got there, the next day, it transpires that the young fortune I thought I had wouldn't even take me on a mile of my long journey. All my banknotes were useless, yet I asked myself how could that be, because houses and factories still stood up, and there were fields and gardens all around me. I was flabbergasted. But I set off for Berlin with no money, and it took me a month to get there, drawing people's faces for slices of bread and sausage. I began to see what my father meant, but by now it was too late. I had taken the jump, and went hungry for it, like all rebellious youths.

'In my native home-house I had been sheltered from the gales of economy, because I saw now how the country was. Destituted. In Frankfurt a man landed at my foot because he had dropped from a lot of floors up. England, it was terrible: the man had worked for forty years to save his money, and he had none remaining. Someone else ran down the street screaming: "I'm ruined! Ruined utterly!" But all those other shop-keepers who would be ruined tomorrow turned back to their coffee and brandy. No one was solid, England. No solidarity anywhere. Can your mind imagine it? In such a confusion I decided more than ever that the only term one could be was an artist. Coming from Königsberg to Berlin had shown me a thrill for travel. But Berlin was dirty and dangerous. It was full of people singing about socialism – not national socialism, you understand, but communist socialism. So I soon left and went to Vienna – walking. You must comprehend that all this takes months, but I am young, and I like it. I do not eat well, but I did eat, and I have many adventures, with women especially. I think that it was the best time of my life. You want to go, madam? Ah, good night. I kiss your hand, even if you do not like my prattle. Goodnight, madam, good night. A charming wife, England.

'I didn't like Vienna, because its past glories are too past, and it was full of unemployed. One of the few sorts of people I can't like are the people without work. They make my stomach ill. I am not rational when I see them, so I try not to see them as soon as I can. I went to Budapest, walking along the banks of the Danube with nothing except a knapsack and a stick, free, healthy, and young. I was not the old-fashioned artist who sits gloomily starving in his studio-garret, or talks all day in cafés, but I wanted to get out among the world of people. But in every city there was much conflict, where maybe people were finishing off what they had started in the trenches. I watched the steamers travelling by, always catching me up, then leaving me a long way back, until all I could listen was their little toots of progress from the next switch of the river. The money crashed, but the steamers went on. What else could Germany do? It was a good time though, England, because I never thought of the future, or wondered where I would be in the years to reach. I certainly didn't see that I should throw so much of my good years in this little Spanish town – in a country even more destituted than the one in Germany after I set off so easily from my birth-home. Excuse me, if I talk so much. It is the brandy, and it is also making me affectionate and sentimental. People are least intelligent when most affec-tionate, so forgive me if I do not always keep up the high standard of talk that two artists should kindle among them.

'No, I insist that it is my turn this time. Your wife had gone, no, to look after the baby? In fact I shall order a bottle of brandy. This Spanish liquid is hot, but not too intoxicating. Ah! I shall now pour. It's not that I have the courage to talk to you only when I am up to my neck in bottle-drink, as that I have the courage to talk to you while you are drunk. You can drink me under the table, England? Ah! We shall see, dear comrade. Say when. I have travelled a long way, to many places: Capri, Turkey, Stalingrad, Majorca, Lisbon, but I never foresaw that I should end up in the awkward state I am now in. It is unjust, my dear England, unjust. My heart becomes like a flitterbat when I think that the end is so close.

'Why? Ah! Where was I? Yes. In Budapest there was even more killing, so I went to Klausenburg (I don't know which country that town is in any more) and passed many of these beautiful clean Saxon towns. The peasants wore their ancient pictorial costume, and on the lonely dusty road were full of friendships and dignity. We spoke to each other, and then went on. I walked through the mountains and woods of Transylvania, over the high Carpathians. The horizons changed every day; blue, purple, white, shining like the sun; and on days when there were no horizons because of rain or mist I stayed in some cowshed, or the salon of a farmhouse if I had pleased the family with my sketching likenesses. I went on, walking, walking (I walked every mile, England, a German pilgrim), across the great plain, through Bucharest and over the Danube again, and into Bulgaria. I had left Germany far behind, and my soul was liberal. Politics didn't interest me, and I was amazed, in freedom, at my father being sad at the war.

'How the brandy goes! But I don't get drunk. If only I could get drunk. But the more brandy I drink the colder I get, cool and icy on the heart. Even good brandy is the same. Health, wealth, and stealth! I got to Constantinople, and stayed for six months. Strangely, in the poorest city of all, I made a good living. In an oriental city unemployment didn't bother me: it seemed natural. I went around the terraces of hotels along the Bosphorus making portraits of the clientèles, and of all the money I made I gave the proprietors ten per cent. If they were modern I drew them or their wives also against the background of the Straits, and sometimes I would take a commission to portray a palace or historic house.

'One day I met a man who questioned if I would draw a building for him a few kilometres along the coast. He would give me five English pounds now, and five more when we came back to the hotel. Of course I accepted, and we drove in his car. He was a middle-aged Englishman, tall and formal, but he'd offered me a good price for the hour's drawing necessary. By now I had developed the quickness of draughtsmanship, and sat on the headland easily sketching the building on the next cape. While I worked your Englishman, England, walked up and down smoking swiftly on a cigar, and looked nervous about something. I had ended, and was packing my sketches in, when two Turkish soldiers stood from behind a rock and came to us with rifles sticking out. "Walk to the car," the Englishman said to me, hissing, "as if you haven't done anything."

' "But," I said, "we've made nothing wrong, truly."

' "I should say not, my boy," he told me. "That was a Turkish fort you just sketched."

'We run, but two more soldiers stand in front of us, and the Englishman joked with them all four, patted them on the savage head, but he had to give out twenty pounds before they let us go, and then he cursed all the way back.

'It might have been worse, I realise at the hotel, and the Englishman is pleased, but said we'll have to move on for our next venture, and he asked me if I'd ever thought of hiking to the frontier of Turkey and Russia. "Beautiful, wild country," he told me. "You'll never forget it. *You* go there on your own, and make a few sketches for me, and it'll prove lucrative – while I sit back over my sherbert here. Ha, ha, ha!"

'So I questioned him: "Do you want me to sketch Turkish forts, or Soviet ones?"

' "Well," he said, "both."

'That, England, was my first piece of stealthy work, but it never made me wealthy, and I already was healthy. Ah, ah, ah, ho, ho! You are strong, England. I cannot make you flinch when I hit you on the back like a friend. So! Before then I had been too naïve to feel dishonest. Once on the Turkish border I was captured, with my sketches, and nearly hanged, but my Englishman pays money, and I go free. Charming days. I wasn't even interested in politics.

'I hear a baby crying. What a sweet sound it is! England, I think your wife calls for you.'

III

'It is fine night tonight, England, a beautiful star-dark around this town. I have travelled most of my life. Even without trouble I would have travelled, never possessing one jot of wealth, only needing food at the sunset and hot water for breakfast. During the war my voyaging was also simple.

'In my youth, after I was exported from Turkey by the soldiers. (They took all my money before letting me go. If only we had conquered them during the war, then I would have met them again and made them repay it with every drop of their blood!) I travelled in innumerous countries of the Balkans and Central East, until I was so confused by the multiple currencies that I began to lose count of the exchange. I would recite my travellers' cataclysm as I crossed country limits: "Ten Slibs equals one Flap; a hundred Clackies makes one Golden Crud; four Stuks comes out at one Drek" – but usually I went to the next nation with not Slib Flap Clackie or Golden Crud to my name, nothing except what I wear and a pair of worn sandals. I joke about the currencies, because there is no fact I cannot remember. Some borders I have crossed a dozen times, but even so far back I can memory the dates of them, and stand aside to watch myself at that particular time walking along, carefreed, towards the customs post.

'One of my adventures is that I get married, and my wife is a strong and healthy girl from Hamburg who also likes the walking life. Once we trampled from Alexandria, stepping all along the coast of Africa to Tangier, but it was hard because the Mussulmans do not like to have their faces drawn. However, there were many white people we met, and I also sketch a lot of buildings and interesting features – which were later found to be of much use to certain circles in Berlin. You understand, eh?

'We went back to Germany, and walked in that country also. We joined groups of young people on excursions to the Alps, and had many jolly times on the *hohewege* of the Schwarzwald. My wife had two children, both boys, but life was still carefreed. There were more young people like ourselves to enjoy it with. My art was attaining something, and I did hundreds of drawings, all of which made me very proud, though some were better than others, naturally. Most were burned to cinders by your aeroplanes, I am sad to say. I also lost many of my old walking friends in that war, good men . . . but that is all in the past, and to be soonest forgotten. Nowadays I have only a few comrades, in Ibiza. Life can be very sad, England.

'In that time before the war my drawings were highly prized in Germany. They hung in many galleries, because they showed the spirit of the age – of young people striving in all their purity to build the great state together, the magnificent corporation of one country. We were patriotic, England, and radical as well. Ah! It is good when all the people go forward together. I know many artists who thought that anarchism was not enough to cure the griefs of the globe as they swung into black shirts. Children do not like the dark when they go to bed, and what can blame them? Someone has to build a fire and put on lights. But you shouldn't think I liked the bad things though, about inferior races and so on. Because if you consider, how could I be living in Spain if I did? It was a proud and noble time when loneliness was forgotten. It contained sensations I often spend my nights thinking about, because I felt that after all the travels of my young days I was getting at last some look-on at my work, as well as finding the contentment of knowing a leader who pointed to me the fact that I was different from those people I had been through on my travels. He drew me together. Ah! England, at that you get more angry than if I had banged you on the shoulder like a jolly German! You think I am so rotten that when I cut myself, maggots run out. But don't, please don't, because I can't stand that from any man. I don't

believe anything now, so let me tell you. Nothing, nothing . . .
nothing. Everyone was joining something in those days, and I
couldn't stop myself, even though I was an artist. And because
I was an artist I went the whole way, to the extremes, right
beyond the nether boundaries. I was carried along like this
coñac cork, floating down a big river. I couldn't swim out of it,
and in any case the river was so strong that I liked it, I liked
being in it, a strong river, because I was as light as a cork, and
it would never carry me under. He . . . he made us as light as
a cork, England. But politics are gone from my life's vision. I
make no distinction any more between races or systems. One
of my favourite own jokes is that of Stalin, Lenin and Trotsky
playing your money game Monopoly together in the smallest
back room of the Kremlin in 1922. Ha, ha, ha! You also think
it is funny, England, no?

'No, you don't think it is funny, I can see that. I am sorry
you don't. Your face is stern and you are gazing far away. But
listen to me though, you are lucky. So far you don't know what
it is to belong to a nation that has taken the extreme lanes, but
you will, you will. So I can see it coming because I read your
newspapers. Up till now your country has been lucky, ours has
been unlucky. We had no luck, none at all. We are rational,
intelligent, strong, but unlucky. You cut off the head of your
King Karl; we didn't of our Karl. Ah, now you smile at my
wit. You laugh. You have the laugh of the superior, England,
the mild smile of those who do not know, but once on a time,
if any foreigner laughed at me like that I could kill them. And
I did! I did!

'Stop me if I shout. Forgive me. No, don't go, England. Your
baby is not crying. Your wife does not call. Listen to me more.
I don't believe anything except that I am able to repair your
car and do it good. And that is something. How many men
can set you on the road again? It is a long way from my
exhibitions of drawings, one of which, at Magdeburg, was
opened and appreciated by You-know-who, a person who also
knew about art. Yes, actually him. He shook my own hand,
this hand! I was reconciled to my father by then: I who hated

my father more than any hatred that was ever possible since the beginnings of the civilised world was brought back to respect him, to view his point with proper sympathy. To be able to again give respect to one's father in middle-age! Can you imagine it ever, England! And who did it? He is truly a great man who can make the different generations understand each other, a dictator maybe, but great, still a genius. I tell you that my father was the proudest man in all Germany because he who had done it had shaken this – this hand!

'Well, I will not ennui you any more about my adventures in those days. Let us skip a few years and talk about romantic Spain. Not that it was romantic. It can be a very dirty place, and annoying, unlike the cleaner countries, such as ours, my dear England. Just after crossing the mountains on foot in 1945, I stayed in a shepherd's hut for two weeks of hiding. Someone paid the shepherd a terrible high rent for this stenching sty, and all the while I was attacked by ants, so that I go nearly mad. I looked mad – with my long beard and poor clothes, dreamed I was the King of Steiermark with my loptilted crown. Ants came in the door, and I start to kill them with hammer and sceptre – then I spare some lives in the hope that they would scuttle back and tell their friends that they had better not come near that hut because a crazy bone-German is conducting a proficient massacre. But it made no difference, and they kept coming on into the kill-feast. I worked for days to stop them, but they came continuously I suppose to see why it was that those before them were not coming back. There were thousands, and my romantic nature won because I got tired first. Strength and intelligence finally let me down. Ants are inhuman. Nowadays, if I see ants in my house or garage I use a Flit gun – bacteriological warfare, if you like, and that is quicker. I can let science take over and so don't need to beg stupid questions. It stops them. I think of all those poor ants who get killed, and maybe the ants themselves have no option but to start this war on me. If only they were all individuals, England, like you – or me – then maybe only one or two would have been killed before the others turned and ran. But no, they have their statues to the war, the Tomb of the Unknown Ant, who dies so that every ant could have his pebble of sugar, but who died in vain, of course. I have a sense of humour? Yes, I have. But it didn't protect me from doing great wrongs.

'How did I get to Spain? My life is full of long stories, but this time I came to Spain from necessity, from dire necessity. It was a matter of life and death. To get here I set out from Russia on a journeying much longer than the one I told you about already in my youth. Name a country, and I have been in it. Say a town and I can call the main street, because I have slept on it. I can tell you about the colour of the policeman's uniform, and where you can get the cheapest food; which is the best corner to stand and ask for money. I have done many things since the end of the war that I would not naturally do, that I should be ashamed of, except that it is man's duty to survive. And man's duty to let him? you said. Of course, quite right, quite so. Humanitarian people are right next door to my heart, my dear friend. But during the war I thought men couldn't survive, and when the war started to end I taught myself that they could. How did I come to obtain my garage business? you ask. It takes much money to buy a garage, and I tell you something now that I wouldn't tell a walking soul, not even my wife, so that instead of forgiving me, you will try to understand.

'I got to Algeria. To say how would damage a few people, so I mustn't. Part of my time I was a teacher of English in Setif, and passed myself as an Englishman. I imitated in every manner that man who was a spy back on the Turkish Bosphorus until nobody in this new place spied the difference. I taught English to Moslems as well, but earned a bad living at it. To augment my inmoney I made intricate maps of farmers' land in the area. I am a good reconnaissance man, and if a farmer had only a very poor and tiny square of land the map I drew made it look like a kingdom, and he was glad to have it square-framed, see something to fight for as he gazed at it hanging on the wall of his tinroofed domicile, at night when the mosquitoes bit him mad, and he was double mad worrying about crops, money, and drought – not to mention rebellion. Then I began selling plots of land in the *bled* that weren't accurately possessed by me – to Frenchmen who came straight out of the army from the mix-in of Indo-China – by telling people it was rich with oil. Nowadays I hear that it really is, but no matter. I sold the land only cheap, but I soon had enough real finance to buy many passports and escape to Majorca. I got fine work as a travel-agent clerk in Palma, and worked good for a year, trying to save my money like an honest man. Spain was a stone country to make a living in then – things are much easier these days since the peseta is devalued. I couldn't save, because all the time I had before me the remembering of the man in Frankfurt who dropped at my feet completely dead because his life savings wouldn't buy a postal stamp. But then an Italian asks me to look after his yacht one winter, which for him was a huge mistake, because when I had sold it to a rich Englishman I took an aeroplane to Paris.

'There I thought I had done such a deal of travelling in my scattered life that I should turn such knowing into my own business. To commence, I announced in a good newspaper that ten people were desired for a trip around the world, that it would be a co-operative venture, and that only little money would be needed, comparatively. When I saw the ten people I told that two thousand dollars each would be enough, but they had to be fed-up sufficiently with modern world-living to qualify for my expedition. I explained that out of our collective money we would comprise a lorry, and a moving-camera to take documentary films of strange places, that we would sell. Everybody said it was a shining brainwave, and I soon got the lorry and camera cheap. For two weeks we had map meetings while I planned each specific of the trip. I spent as much money on maps as on the lorry, almost, and pinned them to the wall at these gatherings. I gave them labour of cartography and collecting stores. They were all good people, so trusted me, even when I said that a supplementary cost would be laid because of the high price of film. No one would be leader of the expedition, I stipulated: it would be run by committee, with myself as the chairman. But somehow, and against my will, I achieved control. Because I was more interested in getting reactions from other people than from myself I became the real leader of them. In this aspect my good heart triumphed, because they needed me to be their overboss.

'Much of the money I put in the bank, but the peril was I began to like the idea of this world-round journey so much that I couldn't make myself disappear with it. I kept on, obsessed at the plan. I wrote to many shops and factories and (even in France) they gave me equipment. I charged it all to my clients – as I called them in my secret self. Unfortunately the newspaper wrote stories about my scheme, and put my photo in the print.

'So our big lorry set out of Paris, and snapped on the road to Marseilles. I repaired it, and from Marseilles our happy gathering steamed to Casablanca on a packet-boat. I had moved battalions of men and tanks (and many prisoners) in every complication over the eye-dust and soul-mud and numb snow of Russia, but this was a happy situation with these twenty people (by this time others had been entered to our committee). It was like being young again. Everyone loved me. I was *popular*, England, by total consent of all those dear, good friends. Tears fall into my eyes when I think of it – real tears that I can't bear the taste of. The further I gave in to my sentimental journeying and went on with my dear international companions, the less was the money that I intended to go off and begin my garage with in Spain. I had never had such a skirmish in my conscience. What could I do? Tell me, England, what could I do? Would you have done any better than such? No, you wouldn't, I know. My God! I am shouting again. Why don't you stop me?

'The lorry snapped awfully, at Colomb-Bechar, just before we intend to cross the real desert. But my talents triumph again, and I repaired it, and say I am going to try it out. They are still in the tents, eating some lunch, and I drive off, round and round in big circles. Suddenly I make a straight line and they never see me again. I don't know what became of them. They were nearly penniless. I took petrol and the cameras, everything expensive, as well as funds. It is too painful for me to speculate, so ask me nothing else, even if I tell you. From Casablanca I come to here, and when I have collected all from my banks I see there is enough to get my garage, and much to spare.

'And now I am in Spain, you think I have as much as a man could want? I have a Spanish wife, two children and an interesting work. I have had several wives, and now a Spanish woman. She is dark, beautiful, and plump (yes, you have seen her) but in bed she doesn't act with me. My children go to the convent school, and kiss crosses, tremble at nuns and priests. These I cannot like at all, but what can I do? It has been a dull life, because there's not much here. Sometimes we go to a bullfight. But I don't like it. It is a good ritual, but not attractive to a rational human being like myself. All winter we see no travellers, and hug the fireplace like damp washing. Now and again I still do some drawings. Yes, that is one of them over there, that I presented to this hotel. You don't like it? You do? Ah, you make me very happy, England. Often I go down the coast road to Algeciras, a short trip in my dependable Volkswagen. It is a very pleasant port, and I make many sketches. I know some Russians who have a hotel and let me stay at cost rate. Gibraltar is a fascinating shape to make on paper, which I see from the terrace. I also go across to your famous English fort-rock to shopping, and maybe purchase one of those intellectual English Sunday newspapers there. One of them lasts me a month at least. I find them very good, exceptionally lively and interesting to a mind like mine.

'Ah, England, let us take a walk and I will tell you why my life is finished. That's better. The air smells fresh and good. Why, we have talked the whole night through. I tell lies to everyone – with no exception. But to myself – and I talk free to you and myself now – I tell the precise ice-cold truth as far as it is possible. Telling lies to everyone else makes it more possible to tell a more accurate truth to myself. Does that make me happy? For most people happiness is letting them follow the habits their fathers developed. But *he* changed all that,

that's why we loved him, drilled truths into us so that we didn't need to live by habit. That would be worse than death – because death is at least something positive.

'That green speck in the sky over there is the first dawn, a little light, a glow-worm that the sun sends in front to make sure that all is dark for it. Your wife will never forgive you. But women are not rational human beings. Oh, oh, oh – England, you think they are? I can prove to you that they are not so, quicker than you can prove to me that they are. You say that the sun is a red sun? I can see that it will be. But I have been in Spain many times. In 1934 I came here, walking all through, sketching farmhouses and touristic monuments – later published as an album in Berlin. I surveyed the land. Spain I know exceedingly well. This beautiful land we saved from Bolshevism – though I sometimes wonder why. I am afraid of a communist government here, because if it comes, I am ended. The whole world gets dark for me. Maybe Franco will make a pact with communist Germany, and send me back to it. It has happened before. I feel my bed is not so safe to lie on.

'My life has been tragic, but I am not one of those who self-pities. It will be hot today. I sweat already. I must sell my garage and leave, go to another country. I am forced to abandon my wife and children, which is not a good fate. It gives me suffering in the heart that you cannot imagine. I am slowly taking secret luggage to my other garage, and one day I shall tell her I'm going to inspect things over there, and she will never see me again. I travel lightly, England, but I am nearly sixty years. You will notice that I have not talked about the war, because it is too hurtful to me. My home was in East Prussia: but the Soviets took the family land. They enslaved and murdered my fellow countrymen. England, don't laugh. You say they should keep the Berlin Wall there forever? Ah, you don't know what you are saying. I can see that my misfortune makes you glad. I was not there, of course, but I know what the Soviets did. My wife was killed in one of their bombardments.

'England, please, do not ask me that question. I do not know who started such wicked bombings of the mass. A war begins, and many things happen. Much water flows under the bridge-road. Let me march on with my story. Please, patience. My two sons are in the communist party. As if that was why I fought, used in my body and soul the most terrible energies for one large Germany. I want to go there and beat them both, beat them without mercy, hit at them until they are dead.

'Once I had a letter from them, and they ask me to come back to my homeland – not fatherland, but homeland. How the letter gets me I don't know, but a person in Toledo sends it. They beg me to come back and work for democratic Germany. Why do you think they ask me this? That they are innocent, and only love their father as sons should? Ah! It's because they know I shall be hanged when I get there. That is why they ask. They are devils, devils.

'I am leaving Villa Oveja, quitting Spain, because someone came to this town a few weeks ago and saw me. I think from my photo in the Paris paper and other photos issued by my enemies, he recognised me. They have fastened me down, hunted me like an animal, and know where I am now. I know they are leaving me for the time being, because perhaps there is a bigger job – someone more important before they concentrate on the small fish. This Jew wasn't like the others. He was tall, young and blond. He was browned by the sun, he was handsome, as if he'd been in Spain as much as I had, and one day he came to the door of my garage and looked at me. He looked, to make sure. I could not compete his stare, and they could have used my face for the chalk of Dover. How did I know he was a Jew, you ask? Don't mock me, England; because I am no longer against them. I hardly look at his face, but I *knew* because his eyes were like sulphur, a nice young man who could have been a pleasant tourist, but I knew, I knew without knowing why I knew, that he was one of their people. They have their own country now: if only they had their own country before the war, England. His eyes burned my heart away. I could not move. The next day he went off, but at any time they will come for me. I am still young, even while sixty, yet think that perhaps I don't care, that I will let them carry me, or that I will kill myself before they come.

'It is not possible I stay here, because the people have turned. Maybe the Jew told something before he went away, but a man stopped me in one of the alley-streets and said: "Guzman, get out, go home." The man had been one of my friends, so you can imagine how it bit deep at me. And then, to hammer it harder, I have been seeing it written on walls in big letters: "Guzman, go home," – which makes my brains burst, because this *is* my home. No one understands, that I am wanting to be solitary, to have peace, to labour all right. When I make tears like this I feel I am an old man.

'I should not have killed those people. I sat down to eat. They were hungry in the snow, and I could not stop myself. I could not tolerate the way they stood and looked, people who couldn't work because they had no food to take into them. They kept looking, England, they kept looking. I thought: their life is agony. I will end it. If I feed them Christmas food for three months they will never be strong again. I wanted to help them out of their life and suffering, to get them peace, so that they would be no more cold and hungry. I fired my gun. My way went terrible after that, out of control. I was rational. My soul was black. I killed and killed, to stop the spread of the suffering that came on to me. While I killed I was warm, and not aware of the suffering, the rheumatism of my soul. How could I have done it? I wasn't like the others. I was an artist.

'Look, don't go yet. Don't stand and leave me by. The sun is making that mountain drink fire. I shall always see mountains on fire, whenever I go and wherever else my feet tread, red mountains shaking flames out of their hat top. Even before the Jew came a dream was in me one night. I was a young scholar at the high-school, and circles were painted in the concrete groundspaces, for gymnasium games and drill. I stood in one, with a book in my hand to read. Everything changed, and the perfect circle was of white steel. A thin rod it was, a hot circle that glowed metal. I wanted to get out of it but I couldn't, because the heat from it was scorching my ankles. All the force of me was pressing against it, and though I was a highgrown man I couldn't jump out. I had a gun in my hand instead of a book, and I was going to shoot myself, because I knew the idea that if I did I should get out and be able to walk off a freed man. I shot someone passing by, a silent bullet. But then I woke, and nothing had worked for me.

'In military life they say there is a marshal's rank in every soldier's kitbag. In peace-life I think there is a pair of worn sandals in every cupboard, because you don't ever know when the longest life-trudge is going to start – whether you are criminal or not. I dig blame into my heart like donkey-dung into good soil. If I was an aristocrat I could claim that all my uncles had been hung up on meat-hooks because they tried to revolt. If I was from a factory I could say I didn't know any better. Everybody who dies dies in vain, England, so I can't do that. What shall I do? Your questions are pertinent, but I am practical. I am rational. I won't give in, because I am always rational. Maybe it is the best thing of quality obtained from my father. I look at my maps, and have the big hope of a hunted man. Do you have any dollars in currency that I could exchange? You haven't? Can you pay the repair bill on your car in dollars, then? Ah, so. I have another Volkswagen I could sell you, only a year old and going like a spark, guaranteed for years on rough roads. The man I bought it from had taken it to Nyasaland – overearth, the whole return. Pay me in pound-sterling then, in Gibraltar if you like. I can get the ferry there and back in a day, make my purchasing of necessaries for a long trek . . . no, you can't?

'It is going to be a cloudy day, good for driving because it will not be too hot. Your car is now in excellent order, and will run well for long hours. It is a reasonable car, with a stout motor and strong frame. It is not too logical for repairing, and will not have such long life as you thought when you bought it. Next time, if you want some of my best caution, you will purchase a Volkswagen. You won't regret it, and will always remember me for giving you such solid advice.

'I am tired after being up all night. Mind how you drive, on those mountain curves. Don't you see what it speaks in the sky over there? You don't? Your eyes are not good. Or perhaps you are deceiving me to save my feelings. It says: GUZMAN, GO HOME. Where can I go? I own two houses and my garage here. I own property, England, property. All my life I have wanted to own property, and shall have to sell it to them in Villa Oveja for next door to nothing. Go home, they say to me, go home.

'Rational and intelligent! Everybody is being rational and intelligent. What beautiful words – but they have to be kept in a case and admired, like those two parrots that the hotel keeper brought back from a trip to South America. You look at them, and their beauty gives you heart. An unfortunate American client once wanted to touch them, put his finger too close to the bars, and then the blood flowed after the razor-beak snapped over it. Their colour gives you soul also, but when you are at last hunted down, and only the corner wall is behind you, then what use are being rational and intelligent? Use them, and slowly rolls the big destruction. Hitler made them kill each other in every man jackboot of us.

'I am light-headed when I don't sleep the dark, but I must go to work, think some more while I am working. My name is not Guzman. That is a name the Spaniards gave me, proud, sly, and envious, because of my clever business ways. It has always surprised me that I could make my commercial career so well, when I started off life only as a poor hiker drawing faces. Now I am a wanderer, when I don't want to be.'

Chris, his face the grey-green colour of a living tree branch that had had the bark stripped from it, turned away and walked quickly through the quiet town to the hotel. His wife was feeding the baby. The day after tomorrow, they would be in Africa. Six months after that, back in London.

The car broke down again in Tangier. 'That crazy Nazi,' he thought, 'can't even mend a bloody car.'